I0817844

THE MURDER OF CRICKET COOGLER

THE MURDER OF CRICKET COOGLER

UNTOLD LEGENDS VOLUME THREE

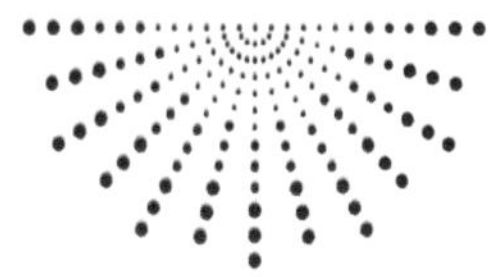

TAMSIN L. SILVER

Cover Design by Melissa McArthur

Editorial by Lucy Blue

This book is dedicated to Ovida "Cricket" Coogler and her family. She was a firecracker of a girl who was taken from this world too soon, leaving a hole in the hearts of her family, friends, and a town who has never forgotton her.

As always, this series itself is dedicated to the town of Lincoln, NM, that still honors Billy and Richard until this day, and to the amazing people who live there. You all are the reason Billy and Richard have never been forgotten. They live in your hearts so true that the town still vibrates with the love of their history...and that's what real magic looks like. Now that this trilogy has completed, I too get the chance to do as you all have done, and help people remember them forever and always.

1
WHO ARE YOU AGAIN?

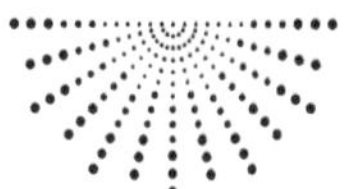

April 18, 1949

I like to speed, and I have a decent number of tickets to prove it. Best part is, it drives Brewer nuts.

"Do you have to go this fast? God, I miss travelin' by horse," my tall, broody partner complained from the passenger seat, his long legs trying to find room in my black 1950 Aston Martin DB2.

Richard M. Brewer, who now went by the name Agent Richard Baca, was six feet four in his cowboy boots with a lot of leg and wide shoulders. He looked ridiculous in my car, and he knew it. But, as it was our primary transportation for now, he was dealing with it.

"I wanted to be there yesterday, but oh no, we had to wait for proper papers and shit," I replied.

He grinned at my sarcasm. "If you want to investigate her murder, and I know you can't do anythin' but, we need to have jurisdiction there."

"The last thing I want is to be flashin' my FBI badge around. That's not gonna help matters at all," I told him.

"Better than if we showed them our SIS credentials," he pointed out.

He wasn't wrong.

If there was someone the local authorities hated more than the feds, it was law officers from another country. That's why the FBI granted the supernatural division of SIS, MI-5, special privileges. They got to carry FBI badges, and for all intents and purposes, we were FBI.

The arrangement held true as long as the SIS shared all the information with the FBI and vice versa. It got sticky from time to time, but the two branches did their best to play nice in the sandbox. If for no other reason than keeping the evidence of the supernatural community under wraps. There was no desire to panic the American people who'd only been out of World War II for four and a half years.

No one wanted to learn that their neighbor was a Nazi; let alone a witch, a werewolf, or some other creature that they would fear more than the growing polio epidemic.

Creatures like Brewer and myself, for example.

I brought the car to a stop at the last light in Albuquerque before we got on the highway to Las Cruces, and a raven landed on the passenger side mirror.

"Hey there, Gaax!" Richard said, the word sounding like, "Gawkh."

And creatures like Gaax, too, come to think of it. Most people wouldn't accept that.

The Chihuahuan Raven Skinwalker hopped through the open window and into the car with a loud QUARK before perching on my steering wheel.

"If you shift, you better have clothes. I don't want your naked ass on my leather seats."

Gaax just poked my hand hard with his beak.

"Ouch! Fine, fine...whatever," I complained and turned onto the highway as Gaax settled down in the minuscule back seat to take a nap in bird form.

If Brewer thought I was speeding before, he was in for a real treat now. From this point, there weren't any true stops between here and Las Cruces, and I planned to make up some time I'd lost waiting on official paperwork. Because Brewer was right, I could do nothing but investigate Ovida's murder. But what I hadn't shared with him yet were her parting words to me.

"If I die, will you avenge me?" she'd said playfully as she stood in the road between my car and the diner.

"To the end of my days," I'd replied.

I'd also stated firmly to her that I kept my promises, seeing as my momma taught me right. And I would keep this promise. It was the least that I could do. With that thought, I pressed down on the gas pedal a little more.

Gaax understood I'd be trying to make up time this way, hence why he rode inside the car. Flying as fast as I drove could drain him, even though he was a supernatural creature.

Likely to distract himself from my speed, Brewer did something he rarely did—he started a conversation. "Did this sheriff in Las Cruces realize what you truly are when you visited town?"

"I don't think so," I responded, flying past a sedan. "I mean, it's been what, nearly seventy years since a Spirit Warrior of Scáthach was in this part of the world? Hell, I'm probably nothin' more to the werewolves in these parts but a ghost story told to make them behave."

"So, you're the boogeyman now?" Richard said with a laugh.

"To them, I would be."

"But you have evidence Scáthach was in town," he said, pronouncing the Gaelic name SKAW-huhck. "You saw her name written by Agent Fletcher Calhoun."

"In his own blood, no less. So yeah, I'm pretty sure she was there."

"Wouldn't she have told her werewolves about you…or people like you?"

"Who knows what her twisted mind thinks is fun? That fuckin' bitch is crazy town."

"Well, she is the leader of the dark realm of the Otherworld. If that doesn't say evil, crazy bitch from hell, what really does, Billy?"

I laughed. "Good point."

"Besides, you're not the only Spirit Warrior still around. There's two of you."

"There could be more by now. I mean, come on, it's been what," I did the math in my head, "Sixty-eight years since I supposedly died and left this place."

"You came back here at least twice since then," he pointed out.

"Nope. Haven't been here."

"Uh-huh," Brewer said. "I was with you one of the times. But you came back again before this case."

"No idea what you're talkin' about."

Brewer obviously didn't believe me, and for good reason since I wasn't telling the truth, but Brewer was aware of that, so I didn't need to expound on it all. There'd be no point.

"That aside," he said, "since you were here at the end of March, she might've heard you were there and warned them."

I thought about that for a moment and chuckled. "Hell no. Scáthach likes the game. She'd not warn them in the least. Maybe she told them about Spirit Warriors ages ago, but she'd expect them to remember and wouldn't help'em out. So, no…they don't have any idea. Remember, Scáthach likes the show. She'll leave them to blunder about for a bit, and then she'll not be able to resist seeing me again…and then she'll make an entrance. It's her way."

"So, we only have until she can't take it anymore, then we're goin' to need reinforcements."

"Here's to hopin' we solve this before she returns," I said.

"I wouldn't count on it."

I exhaled. "That's what I figured. In fact, I already sent him a letter."

Brewer's eyebrows raised. "Did you now?"

"Yeah, today before we left."

"Sometimes you do a smart thing. It's promisin'," Richard teased.

"Oh, shut up," I said with a chuckle and turned up the radio as Boogie Woogie Bugle Boy by the Andrews Sisters came on.

Then, for the first time since I picked him up at the train station, Brewer laughed his big, deep laugh, and I knew things between us were good. Better than. We were back in business and about to make a lot of wicked men pay for their sins.

* * *

February 18, 1879

Jessie Evans' and Jimmy Dolan's sins are extensive and shouldn't be forgiven," I said as I lay on a blanket in Zahara's apple orchard.

Richard and I were gathered outside the new cabin and stables we and Zahara had built for us men. I had a plan and as usual, Brewer didn't like it.

"Then why did you agree to a parley with them?" Richard asked. "And on the anniversary of John's death."

I heard the tiny growl under the words of the last part and cringed internally. The fact that today was the year anniversary of John Tunstall's murder sat like a spur in my throat, but I swallowed it. "For multiple reasons. I'm tired of fightin' and runnin' from Dolan's men, who claim they have warrants for my arrest. If I'm goin' to get close enough to learn how to send Scáthach back to where she belongs, I'm gonna have to call a truce."

Brewer laughed. "And you really think Scáthach won't see this play a mile away?"

I shrugged, then tossed an apple up and caught it. "Think she's still upset I killed her Beta?"

"Kamil was a mean son of a bitch, but she cared for him. So, yeah, I think she's likely mad as a March hare," Richard said.

Watching me as I tossed the apple up again, Colonel edged a bit closer and leaned over me, making a play for the apple I was about to take a bite out of.

I glanced up at my champion of a horse. He was jet black and as sturdy as they came, except for his eyes. The military had run him blind in the war, and I had to use my power to help heal them, with touch-ups occasionally. Right now, those dark eyes were contemplating my apple with serious intent.

"Really? I can't even eat this?" I asked.

Colonel blew air out of his lips, spattering saliva all over me.

Brewer laughed deeply.

"Ugh!" I said with a chuckle as I dragged my sleeve over my face before palming the apple to Colonel. "Fine, fine…needy boy."

"He's my beautiful boy," came Zahara's voice. "And Richard is correct. She will still be angry at you and suffering from the loss. She may even have left town, to be honest. That'll cause her troops, so to speak, to be more dangerous."

Zahara, the first witch Scáthach created in North America, was a native of this land. Her light brown skin and long black hair, a trait of her people, were beautiful, as was her skin for her age. Gifted with her supernatural traits in the 1400s, she should've appeared ancient, but to anyone who didn't know her, she looked only forty-five, if you didn't look at her hands. Her fingers were riddled with arthritis, and I helped her, too, when she'd let me. She had damaged them by doing a massive bit of magic years ago that took a toll on her. Magic had a price.

"How so?" I asked her.

She smiled and sat on the blanket between Richard and me, her golden-hazel eyes playful. "When mom is away the kids will—"

"Play?" I offered with a stupid grin.

"More like burn the house down," Zahara said as she picked up some bread and cheese we had out to snack on. "They have no one telling them not to kill you. You must be extra careful. But..." She paused, looked to Brewer, then said, "I think this meet-up is a smart move."

"Really?" Brewer said, obviously astonished.

"I understand that it sounds dangerous and stupid, but if Billy can convince Dolan that all is square between the Regulators—"

"What's left of us," I murmured.

"And the Murphy-Dolan group," she continued without batting an eyelash at my interruption, "We might get more time to focus on how to get Scáthach off this plane of existence. Which is the goal, yes?"

"Yes," came a voice from behind us.

It was Tom Folliard, a good friend, Regulator, and the other living Spirit Warrior of Scáthach.

I leapt up. "Hey! You're back. Good to see you!" I gave him a hug, and it was returned. "Did you speak to them all?"

Tom nodded and removed his coat. "I sure love returnin' home to here. It feels like early fall instead of winter." He reached up, plucked an apple, and bit into it. "God, I love magic."

Zahara beamed. "I'm so happy you approve. Come, sit with us and break your fast with some bread and cheese as well."

"Don't mind if I do," Tom said and eased himself onto the portion of the blanket I'd been on. "I spoke to them all. Doc is in. So are George Bowers and José Salazar. They'll meet us in town."

"Good to hear," I said, leaning against one of the apple trees.

"I'm glad you agree with Billy and me on this," Zahara said. "I'm sure you'll also go with him to deal with Jessie, Dolan, and his lot. Dick, you'll join as well, in case they need you."

Brewer's head jerked toward her. "Uh, I can't do that. Remember, everyone in town thinks I'm dead, and I'd like to keep it that way."

"I'll give you a glamour to change your face. It won't last over twelve hours, so you must move on and hide or shift into your wolf if you don't want anyone to realize you are alive after that. I'll send Gaax with you as well. He can show you if there's danger coming around the bend."

A *QUARK-QUARK* sounded from above.

"Well then, it seems we're all set. Let's go listen to what Jessie and Dolan have to say," I said, pulling my gun and twirling it about.

"You can't kill them, Billy," Zahara said.

Oh, but I wanted to. My anger hadn't been tucked away as prettily as I made it seem. "Aw, you take all my fun away."

"I'm serious," she said.

I sighed. "Okay, fine. I won't kill them. Yet."

Zahara carved off a bit of cheese. "You promise?"

I narrowed my eyes at her and groaned. With a sigh, I said, "Yeah, I promise."

"Thank you. Now go get ready," she said and popped the cheese into her mouth.

The men and I headed toward the cabin, and I said, "I'm going to regret that promise."

"I can hear you!" she shouted.

I rolled my eyes to the heavens and headed in to prepare to do my best acting ever. Thankfully, it would be a small group gathering at the bar. If it was too many people, things could go wrong. Hell, what was I, stupid? Trouble could happen no matter the size of the party. I just prayed it didn't end with one of us six feet under.

* * *

April 1949

The gathering for Cricket's funeral was small. Just a private graveside service at the Masonic Cemetery in Las Cruces, New Mexico. Richard and I stood back near another grave, paying our respects, so we'd not draw attention to ourselves.

"How uncanny is this?" I asked. "She's bein' buried in viewing distance of his grave."

Brewer took his hat off as he stared down. When I didn't do the same, he backhanded me in the gut.

"Fine." I took off my hat.

"You aren't still holdin' a grudge against the man, are ya, Billy?" he asked.

I wanted to lie, but I didn't. Instead, I chose a safer route. "Maybe."

Brewer sighed.

"The long-legged bastard shot me. In the heart, no less."

"He did it for your own good," Richard pointed out.

"I suppose we'll have to agree to disagree about that."

Brewer looked at me. "Then why did you come back here for his funeral?"

"Who says I did?"

Brewer snorted. "Uh-huh."

Staring down at Pat Garrett's grave, I sighed. "They never could figure out who shot him. I think Miller did it, but no one could prove it."

"Wasn't he hanged a year later?"

"Yep."

Brewer took out his old tin case, the one Garrett had given him many years ago. He opened it, took out a toothpick, and offered the case to me. I plucked a toothpick out, and we both stuck them in the ground to the side of the headstone.

"Rest in peace, Regulator," Richard said.

"Amen," I replied.

I watched as the mourners sobbed over the grave of a girl I was very fond of while the pastor of some church said words aimed to console them. It didn't make me feel any better if truth be told. But that's because, simply put, I was just too mad to allow comfort regarding Garrett or Cricket. Unfinished business left me edgy and annoyed.

A large group of ravens flew overhead, squawking their fool heads off. There were easily a hundred, if not more. Then I heard the distinct QUARK of the raven I knew all too well.

"At least he blends in here well," Richard said, referring to Gaax.

I nodded, but my mind was more on those standing by Cricket's casket as they lowered it into the ground. There was a woman who was likely Cricket's mother, a young man around Cricket's age with dark hair, and a tall man with blonde hair. The latter stood with his arm wrapped around a young woman who resembled Cricket enough to give my poor heart a thump of hope for just a split second.

But I knew better, and I was, for once, without words. After they threw their roses in and watched the earth being shoveled back into the hole, the family slid away in sorrow and heartache. It was so palpable I could feel their pain in my bones, and Richard did what he does best; he stood there stoically, patiently, giving me the emotional space to decide my next move.

Once we were alone in the cemetery, I walked up to the dirt and gravel road and turned left, following it to Ovida. Richard silently followed behind me, his steps barely a whisper. Her spot was near the inside road, but not right on it.

I stepped over to the mound of dirt now above her casket and shoved my hands into the pockets of my leather jacket. I stared down in disbelief at the grave of the eighteen-year-old girl who'd had her entire life ahead of her. She'd been a beautiful young woman who I'd asked out on a date that would never be. But it was worse than that. It felt like my fault.

Emotion welled up, and I failed to swallow it back.

"Billy..."

"I'm the reason she's dead."

"What?" Brewer said, shocked by my statement.

"If I'd just stayed like she asked...or if I'd come back when your train got delayed..."

"You can't do the what if's, you know that," Richard said.

I wiped tears from my face. "No, I don't. Not this time. Hell, I could be what got her killed. What if the men we're chasin' saw me with her? I could've been the reason—"

Dick's large hand slapped down onto my shoulder. "William, look at me."

I did as he requested, finding his blue eyes more serious than usual.

He shook his head. "It doesn't matter about any of that now. What's important is that we figure out who killed her and why."

I nodded, and he took his hand back. Turning to her grave, I squatted down to face it. "You have my word, Ovida. I'll find every last one of them sons of bitches who had a hand in this, and I'll make them pay for it. I promise you that on my life."

And I always kept my promises.

* * *

February 1879

As we met up with Doc and the others in the plaza of Lincoln, I introduced Dick as Michael Brown. He had the magical charm from Zahara on him, so it altered his facial features, along with his hair color. Interestingly enough, no one questioned who he was or why he was there. In fact, after I'd introduced him, it was apparent everyone except Tom and I quickly forgot him. Likely another part of the magic, and I was thankful for it.

With Brewer on my right, Folliard on my left, and the rest filing in behind us, we approached the other group of men. Walking toward us were Jessie Evans, Jimmy Dolan, Edgar Walz, Billy Mathews, Billy Campbell, and a few men I didn't know by name.

Silence, as loud as a gunshot, settled over the town as if everyone were holding their breath. The heavy pounding of boot falls and the jangle of spurs were all we could hear in the February cold as people in town quickly disappeared into their homes. This didn't surprise me. They were likely expecting a replay of the fight in July, and if I were to be honest, I wasn't sure that wouldn't happen. But I'd made a promise, and I wanted to keep it.

Hand resting on my gun, I realized that the three men I didn't recognize in Jessie's crew were werewolves, and fight-fever heated my blood. Dick grunted, and Tom swore. So yeah, they knew too. This would not help me keep my promise.

Noticing my twitchy fingers near my gun, Jessie said, "Ya know, if you're not really here to parley, we can just kill you right here and now."

"I don't care to open negotiations with a fight, but if you'll come at me three at a time," I said, motioning to his werewolf back up, "I'll whip the whole damned bunch of you."

"Billy," Dick warned.

"If you are here to talk truce, what the hell are they doing here?" I asked.

"Muscle," Dolan replied.

"That scared of us, are ya?" Tom taunted.

Jessie stepped forward, but Dolan stopped him.

"Fair enough," Jimmy Dolan said. "You have six, we'll have six." He turned to the three werewolves and sent them away.

They argued but finally left, not going far. They headed to sit in front of what had been the Tunstall Store to watch.

"Come on, let's get a drink," Dolan said.

"Because nothin' calms temper like booze," Dick muttered so quietly under his breath that only Tom and I heard him.

We headed into a bar to talk, Jessie's werewolves staying outside. However, they were far enough away that fight-fever wasn't uncontrollable. It made me edgy, but sane. Or sane-ish.

"We need to find peace," Dolan said. "We need to find common ground to stand on. We cannot keep draggin' this town into battle. It hurts business, to be honest, and our reputation. If we're ever to become a state, we can't keep killin' each other like we have."

"Maybe you should've thought of that before you killed John Tunstall," Dick said.

"Who are you again?" Jessie asked.

"Michael Brown," Dick said. "And if you all didn't kill to get what you want, we'd not have to fight back. Ever thought of that?"

I laid a hand on Dick's shoulder. "What my friend here is tryin' to say is that we've not been fightin' with y'all for no reason. If we're gonna call a truce, it needs to be on both sides. You need to stop killin' our people, and we'll stop killin' yours."

"Seems fair enough," Dolan said.

And that started it. We agreed that neither group would kill any member of the other party without having first given notice of withdrawing from the agreement. Everyone who acted as "friends" were now included in the pact and were not to be harmed in any way. No one was to be killed for an act before the date of this parley, and neither party would appear or give evidence against the other in any civil prosecution from during the war.

Each party would give individual members of the other party every aid in their power to resist arrests on civil warrants and, if arrested, would try to secure their release. If any member of either faction failed to carry out the terms of this compact, he was to be killed on sight.

It was a solid plan and in Irish fashion, Dolan wanted to drink on it to celebrate; by ten o'clock, all were tipsy, and many were roaring drunk. Well, all but Richard, who now had been asked his name at least twenty times. I was pretty sure he was tired of the charm he wore.

Out onto the street we poured, having gained Joe Bowers and George van Sickle, and made our way down the road. Approaching Juan Patron's home, I lost vision in one eye and reached out to put a hand on Brewer for stability.

"You alright?"

"Gaax," I said, and that was all the explanation he needed.

Pretending I needed Brewer to hold myself upright, I watched through Gaax's eye as the recently elected Sheriff, George Kimbrell, and another man mounted horses.

"I might have warrants for Bonney and Salazar, but I'm not dumb enough to serve them alone. Come on!" Kimbrell shouted at the man with him, and they rode off toward Fort Stanton.

"Great," I muttered.

"What is it?" Richard asked.

I regained my sight and told him.

"We should go."

"Nah...we need to see this to the end."

"Have you noticed the town? Everyone has barred their doors and shuttered their windows. This group is louder than a drunken bachelor party."

I nodded, for he wasn't wrong. Our revels had grown increasingly raucous. "We'll head out soon. Not that I wouldn't love to see if Dolan and his boys stand in to help me with the sheriff as promised, but that's more heat than I want tonight."

"Agreed. Why don't we—"

"Juan Patron, you son of a bitch!" Billy Campbell yelled out into the night as he drew his gun on the man outside his own home. "I'll kill ya where you stand."

Brewer stepped in. "No, you won't. Leave it be."

Juan ducked to hide behind someone in the group, likely saving his own life by doing so.

"Who are you?" Campbell asked Brewer.

"Michael Brown, new to town. We don't need the attention, let's just go drink some more."

Not seeing Juan anymore, Campbell calmed down, and when Brewer urged him to lower his hand, he agreed.

Dick and I shared a glance, and I knew that it wasn't just because of Kimbrell that we'd need to be going soon. The men were out of control drunk, and that was going to lead to trouble.

"Come on, let's go over to Frank's place," Jessie shouted. "You can get him another day, Campbell."

"Yeah, yeah," Campbell replied, but he followed the rest of us, stumbling across the frozen muddy road.

"Where are we goin'?" I asked.

"Frank McCullum's Saloon and Eatin' House," Doc told me. "They recently built it adjacent to the ruins of the McSween home."

Just hearing the words "McSween home" made my heart hurt at memories of that night in July. The only good news since then was that the fifteen-year-old boy, Eugene, had survived.

Dolan's men had kicked and spit on the young man as he'd lay by the burning home, playing dead as he bled out on the ground. The boy crawled a few miles to his family's home once all of Dolan's men had passed out and had survived being shot during the firefight that had killed McSween and everyone else he'd been standing with.

I was focusing on that one good thing so I could continue to play my part when the mob of us came to an abrupt halt. A man was in our path.

He'd bundled against the wind and frigid temperatures with bandages on his face. He appeared cold, tired, and in pain.

"Who are you and where are you goin'?" Campbell said, blocking the man's path.

"Oh shit," I muttered as Dolan pulled his gun and moved to the front to stand next to Campbell.

"My name is Chapman," the man we'd stopped said with crisp enunciation, "and I am attending to my business."

"Then you dance!" Campbell shouted, pulling his six-shooter out and shoving the barrel against Chapman's chest.

Chapman appeared appalled and shook his head. "I don't dance for a drunken mob."

"You better watch how you talk, mister, or we'll make you!" Campbell slurred out.

Chapman pulled the bandages away from his face, so he could see better. But it was dark, and I was sure he saw little.

"You can't scare me, boys," Chapman said. "I know it's you and it's no use. You've tried that before. Am I talking to Mr. Dolan?"

Jessie stepped to the other side of Campbell from Dolan. "No, but you're talkin' to a damned good friend of his."

Suddenly, Dolan's gun went off and almost simultaneously, Campbell's trigger finger tightened in reflex and his gun went off as well.

"My God, I am killed!" Chapman said, and he collapsed into the street.

As he did, Chapman's clothes burst into flame by the powder flash from one of the guns.

Campbell backed away from the smell of burning flesh and cloth and led the way up the street to McCullum's, proclaiming into the night air, "I promised my God and General Dudley that I would kill Chapman, and now I've done it!

"Come on, boys, let's head up to Fort Stanton and kill Charlie Scase, Mrs. McSween's cattle detective. I promised General Dudley that I would not kill Scase on the post, but now I am going to kill him wherever I find him!"

The group moved as one up the road to McCullum's. I wanted to stay behind, but Chapman was dead. There was nothing I could do for him. We left him in the road and made our way to our next stop. Once there, everyone but Dick, Tom, and I ordered drinks and canned oysters like nothing had happened.

Dolan handed a pistol to Edgar Walz. "Go put this in Chapman's hand."

"No way," Edgar said. "I want no part of that."

I stepped forward. "I'll do it."

Dolan's dark blue eyes, glassy with drink, looked at me. "Good man," he said and placed the gun in my palm.

"No problem," I told him.

I looked over at Tom, and he tilted his head toward the door to let me know he would be sure to follow me out. I nodded and turned to leave.

"I'm goin' with him," Brewer said.

"Who are you again?" Jessie asked.

"President Lincoln, back from the dead," Brewer said, and everyone laughed before turning back to the bar to grab their drinks.

We headed out and made our way to the Ellis store.

"Let me get this straight, Campbell and Dolan just killed Chapman?" Bill Ellis, the owner's son and my good friend, asked.

"Yes, and his body is still burnin' out there," Tom said as he entered the stable.

"They see you leave?" I asked.

"Hell no. Too drunk. I might as well be Michael Brown here."

"What? Who?" Bill said.

"Nothin'," I muttered and saw Brewer roll his eyes, for we'd just introduced him to Bill a few minutes previously.

"Let's saddle up and head to San Patricio," I said. "We can get some rest there and head out in the mornin'."

"Why there?" Bill asked.

I explained about Kimbrell and his warrants.

"Oh, yeah, you best get movin'," Bill agreed.

I lifted myself up into the saddle and patted Colonel on the neck. "Let's go, buddy."

Colonel whinnied. Brewer and Folliard got on their horses as well, and we all headed out.

"If Kimbrell comes by," I said to Bill.

"You weren't here. I got it."

"Thanks! See you later."

By 11:30 p.m. we were cozied up in a guest room of a friend of ours in San Patricio, and I watched through Gaax's vision as Sheriff Kimbrell and Lieutenant Dawson, Doctor Lyon, and twenty cavalrymen entered

Lincoln from the east. They searched several houses and all the bars but didn't find me or Salazar.

They did, however, find Chapman's body. It was dark and hard to see all the detail, even with the raven's enhanced sight, but I could tell that most of the upper portion of Chapman's clothes were burnt. They then headed to the Justice of the Peace, Wilson, and with his help, moved the body to the courthouse.

At that point, Gaax flew out of Lincoln and headed toward us in San Patricio.

"Well, we just missed the cavalry," I told the boys.

"As if Lincoln isn't already stressed to the breaking point, this will put them on the edge of a knife for sure," Tom said.

"And a town on the edge is not a fun place to be," Dick pointed out.

"Stating the obvious as usual, Brewer?" I teased. "Or should I call you President Lincoln?"

"Oh, do shut up, Billy."

"Who are you again?" Tom said, pretending to slur like Dolan and his crew.

"You both suck."

With that, Tom and I burst out laughing, and Brewer joined in. But deep down I knew that Lincoln was going to be on edge for a while, and we'd be smart to steer clear of it.

2
THE MORTUARY

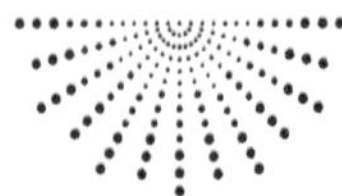

April 1949

The murder of an eighteen-year-old waitress had shaken Las Cruces to its core. Cricket's name was on the tip of everyone's tongue, both the bold and the quiet. Rumors were spreading and some gossip I heard about Cricket hurt me at my core. Of course, I didn't really know the girl well. I'd met her twice and kissed her once. She had been a vivacious, outgoing, and confident young woman with a sharp wit and an attitude that said, "I know who I am, now who are you?"

No matter what I heard, I refused to accept anything until we went to talk to the coroner. Looking it up in the phone book, there appeared to be only one: Graham's Mortuary.

"Don't you think you'll piss off the sheriff if you don't see him first?" Richard asked as we drove down Main Street.

I sighed. He was right, so I headed toward the Doña Ana County Courthouse. On my way, I noticed a sign in a store window that said, "Levi's $3.25." There was also a new Chrysler Royal four-door sedan out front of a car dealership with the price of $2,411. That got me to thinking.

"We need to get you a car," I said.

"Did we get money for that?" Dick asked.

"We did. They thought my flashy car might be a problem. Go figure.

Perfectly fine with me. Rather not put the miles on her anyway." I turned into the Chrysler dealership. "Look, these cars are totally for you, Dick. They say smaller on the outside but larger on the inside."

"That makes no sense," Dick said.

"I didn't make up the slogan, pal," I said, pointing at a sign on the window.

Two hours later, we drove out in separate vehicles. Richard had bought a 1949 Chrysler Windsor Sedan in what they called Ocean Blue. It was very practical, had a decent speed to it, but wasn't flashy. Very much a Richard Brewer car.

First, we went to the Amador Hotel and checked in, for I'd called ahead and made reservations for two rooms. We took our things upstairs and got settled. Once we locked up and set magical security measures, Richard and I headed downstairs.

"Do all the rooms have feminine Spanish names?" Brewer asked as we went down the staircase into the lobby.

"Yep. Fletcher was in the Margarita room when he was here."

"That's rather fitting, considerin' his love of tequila," Richard pointed out.

I couldn't help but chuckle. "I'd not thought of that. You are correct!"

Looking at me, Brewer opened the door for us to exit and ran right into my favorite redhead.

Kit yipped and jumped back and Brewer, all six foot four of him, turned crimson with embarrassment.

"I'm sorry, ma'am," he said, removing his cowboy hat. "I wasn't lookin' where I was..." he trailed off as he truly saw her. "...goin'," He finally finished.

"Hey there, Kit, how ya doin'?" I said, tipping my hat to her briefly. "You'll have to forgive my enormous friend here. Richard, this is Catherine Bell, also known as Kit. She works here. Kit, this is my partner I told you about, Agent Richard Baca."

Kit's eyes, a blue that appeared almost violet, widened as she took in all of the tall cowboy. "Nice to meet you. That was partly my fault, I'm in a rush...runnin' late," she said, her slight, South Carolina accent bleeding into her words.

"Well, let us not keep you," I said. "Maybe we'll see you tonight? I hear the Bow Tie Bar here is rather nice. Are you allowed to socialize in there when you're not workin'?"

"I am. But if what you told me on the phone is your focus of bein' here, we should go somewhere else. Meet me in the lobby around eight o'clock." She turned back to Richard. "It was nice to run into you…I mean, meet you. I gotta go!"

She scurried away in her maid's uniform, red hair tightly wound up in a bun on the top of her head as she jogged to wherever she needed to be.

"Don't I feel like an ass," Richard said as we walked outside.

I patted his shoulder. "Have no fear, she's a pretty hearty gal."

"She can't be more than a hundred and twenty pounds wet, Billy."

I laughed. "I mean hearty as in who she is as a person. She's the one who helped me figure out what happened, or what we *think* happened, to Fletcher. Remember?"

Richard appeared to be catching up and putting pieces together. "Okay, now I remember." He paused and was silent as we walked down the street. Finally, he said, "You didn't say how beautiful she was."

I laughed. "Why, Richard Brewer, do you fancy the girl just by runnin' into her?"

"No…I didn't say nothin' of the sort. I'm just sayin' you didn't say you'd met a lovely witch girl."

I stopped in my tracks. "Say what?"

He also came to a halt and turned to me. "You didn't smell the herbs on her?"

"Well, yeah, she's a healer like her mom…" I let that trail off. "I'll be damned. She's a witch. How'd I miss that?"

Richard grinned. "Because a wolf's nose is better."

"My ass it is," I said with a laugh.

"Ooh, do I smell a challenge?" he replied as we continued down the street.

"Ha ha, funny. You're on. We'll figure it out later. For now," I dramatically made a grand gesture to the courthouse, an enormous white building diagonally across the street from the Amador Hotel, "We need to go in there and place nicey-nice with the law."

"Should go fine, if you aren't an ass."

A one-sided grin slid up my face. "I promise nothin'."

* * *

February 1879

"Speaking of assholes," I said, "Colonel Dudley has been asked to station troops in Lincoln immediately. Seems every citizen signed a petition for this the day after Dolan—"

"Another asshole," Tom stated.

I pointed to Tom and nodded. "—killed Chapman."

"So, what you're sayin' is, it was a bad idea to go to Lincoln for a truce meeting?" Dick offered.

I glared at the big man. "No, in *theory* it was a good idea."

"Everything works in theory," Tom pointed out from where he sat at the dining table of our three-room cabin cleaning his guns.

"Too true," I concurred.

"Except this didn't," Dick replied.

My face puckered. "If Dolan wasn't such a drunk," I said, but my temper didn't hold. Brewer was right. I sighed. "It always had a fifty-fifty chance of going wrong. At least I didn't shoot anyone."

"Ah yes, the bright side," Dick said dryly.

I laughed despite myself and sat down by the fireplace on the navy-blue Biedermeier sofa Tom had procured for us. "Hell, Susan turned over the Tunstall Store to the troops for use as their barracks from what I was told today in town."

Brewer shook his head. "Maybe we ought to get out of the area for a while, Billy. Gather up some of the Regulators and go."

This wasn't a bad idea. I leaned back into the couch and stared at the flames. "Where to?"

"Hell, I don't know," Brewer said, sitting beside me. "Arizona?"

"I killed a man there," I said.

"So that's a no?" Tom joked.

"What about Colorado?" Dick offered.

Tom scratched his head. "That might work. But what if we're needed back here? I don't want to be that far away."

Then I had an idea. "What about Las Tablas, just north of the Capitan Mountain? The forest there is a safe place. Plus, Tom and I have a friend up there. We could stay with him."

"I like where your head is at," Tom said as he put bullets in his gun. "In fact, we could use the time to kill some of Scáthach's monsters. The forest between here and there is full of 'em. It would give Billy and me a chance to fill our well of souls, so we'll have the power in us to fight Scáthach when she comes back here. We've been pretty depleted since July."

I nodded in agreement and stood. "I'll send a letter and let him know we're comin'."

"No post office is secure. They read our mail," Tom pointed out.

"I will not be using the postal service," I said, crossing over to the desk that was positioned in front of one of the two front windows that looked out into the orchard.

Tom's eyebrows rose. "Then how are you going to—"

"Why send it by horse when it can be flown there?" I stated simply as I sat down and pulled out a small piece of paper to write on.

"Oh, I'm sure Gaax is going to love that," Dick said with heavy sarcasm.

"If he says no, we'll try something else, but…we ask."

Brewer shrugged.

I dipped the pen in ink and began the letter. "Edward could come with us. I think it would be a good idea. Dick?"

Brewer stood and wandered over to look out the other front window. "It might be warm here, but past the grove it's February. You honestly want to travel in this cold?"

"Says the wolf who's warm all the time," I said.

"Yeah, but you're not," he pointed out. "Either of you."

"We'll go see if Zahara wants to join us," I said. "We could use more training anyway."

"Speak for yourself," Tom chided.

"Fine, *I* could use more training. Besides, she can use some magic to help us stay warm on the journey."

"What about Roy?" Tom offered.

"He's still at the US Regulator Headquarters in New York City. Not sure when he'll be back."

"Still testifying?"

"I think so."

Silence slipped in around us. The scratching sound of pen to paper and the crackling of the fire were all that filled the room as the plan lay on the metaphorical table and each man considered it quietly in their mind.

"We could put it up for a vote," I suggested, just as the door opened.

"What are we voting on?" Edward said with a grin on his face and a bunch of dead rabbits in his hand.

"Dinner has arrived!" I shouted in glee, rolling up the tiny note to give Gaax and placing it in my Regulator tin. "Come, I'll help cook these up, and we'll fill you in. We have a plan on how to stay out of the sheriff's hair for a month or so."

* * *

April 1949

Stepping into the large white law building of Las Cruces, Dick and I made our way to the small corner sheriff's office, which also held a single desk for the state police. Sheriff Apodaca was there in all his glory. He swaggered out when he saw me looking around.

"So, you've returned," he said. "What would bring you back here? Still lookin' for that fellow agent of yours?"

"Yes and no," I said. "He's a third of the reason. Another third is who that agent was lookin' for, and no, I can't tell you, that's classified. But the last third, I can."

I handed him the papers from the SIS/FBI, and he opened them. I could see the minute he saw her name.

"Why on earth would the FBI send in anyone for a murdered girl? We can handle this ourselves. She was one of our family here. We don't need you." He slapped the folded papers on my chest as he got into my face. "You can go back to Santa Fe now."

"Is there a problem here?" Richard said, using his deepest, most authoritative voice as he stepped in and let his height loom over Apodaca.

The sheriff backed off. "And you are?"

"Oh, apologies, I'm guessin' you didn't read past the part with Cricket's name to see that I'm here with my partner. Agent Richard Baca, meet Sheriff Happy Apodaca."

"Happy?" Richard said.

"It's what they call me," he said. "First name is Alfonso."

Richard nodded and stepped over to look at a painting on the wall. "Yeah, I'd go by Happy too."

I watched as the sheriff considered a rebuttal but decided it unwise. It made me laugh.

"Okay, well, now that those pleasantries are over..." I handed the papers back to Apodaca. "This is your copy. Last time you got upset when I didn't announce my arrival in your fair city. Well, this time I'm lettin' ya know."

"We'll be stayin' at the Amador Hotel if you have any information for us," Richard said without turning around. "We'll happily come here to share what we learn as well."

"Happily come to Happy," I said and put a toothpick in my mouth. I wiggled it at the sheriff and with a quick pat on his shoulder, I added, "Let your men know we're here, would you? I'd hate to surprise them…especially the man you had follow me last time. How's his car by the way?"

"Why you son of a—"

"Language, sheriff!" I said with enough sarcasm that he would know I was just being a pain in the ass. "Come on, Richard, we have work to do."

"On your six," Brewer said as he followed behind me.

I turned before we got to the door though and looked at Happy. "Oh, and sheriff? I'd highly discourage any of your helpers breakin' into my room again. What happens to them won't be my fault. Have a good day!" I touched the brim of my hat and shoved open the door.

Richard followed behind me, quietly saying, "Have a happy day!"

I snorted out a laugh the minute the door closed. "And you told me not to be an ass."

"Well, I couldn't let you have all the fun."

"What about that thing you're always sayin'? Don't want to start off on the wrong foot?"

"You put us on the wrong foot on your first trip here…so there was no point tryin' to be pleasant. Besides, he smells of werewolf. He's not one, but he hangs out with some." Eyes narrowed, Richard finished through gritted teeth, "Which means he's dirty, and I don't play nice with dirty cops." This was a sore spot for him *and* me without question.

"It's like we're on repeat," he continued as we walked back toward the hotel. "Dirty sheriff, dirty politics, and a lot of lies."

"We're just lucky, I guess."

Richard grunted.

"Let's go see the coroner and get started. A little bit of focus will help."

"Agreed," he said. "But we're takin' my car."

"Fine by me."

* * *

February 1879

We spoke with Zahara in the morning, and by late afternoon Gaax was on his way to Las Tablas as the rest of us got on the road; a party of two soul-owning werewolves, two spirit warriors, and a witch. God help anyone who got in our way, and some did.

We killed werewolves that came across our path. At the halfway point, we stopped at an abandoned, two-room cabin that had nothing inside but two stools and a ton of dust. It was around that time in the evening when the sun began to set, and the deer came out to eat. Because of this, we unburdened our horses of our belongings, placed the bags in the small side room inside the cabin, and sent Dick and Edward to hunt while Tom and I made the fires inside and out.

Zahara stepped outside as she swept the last bit of dirt from inside the cabin. Turning toward me, she said, "Where are Richard and Edward?" But before I could reply, she held up her hand to stop me, lifting her nose to the air and inhaling. "Never mind, I hear them returning. Bring the horses close to the cabin before you finish that."

"Why?" I asked.

"Just do it," she snapped and hurried off toward the wolves and their catch.

I shrugged and did as I was told, tethering all four horses to the pole outside the cabin.

When she returned with the men and the large buck they'd caught, she instructed them on what she needed, and they settled in to skin the deer.

Though edgy throughout dinner, Zahara never mentioned why, and I didn't ask. If she wanted me to know, she'd have said something. Instead, I watched as she got out her bag of salt and put a circle around the cabin, including the area out front where the fire and our horses were.

After dinner, I tossed dirt on the fire, and we headed inside. We lay our bedrolls on the floor of the primary room near the fireplace where Zahara sat on one of the two stools. She had a pot of water over the flames and mugs set out.

"Tea?" I asked.

She hummed a yes and pointed at the second stool. "What's on your mind?"

I hated it when she did that.

I sat. "Are we safe here? I've not seen you put salt around before."

She paused, her golden-hazel eyes looking up as if she could see the sky from inside. "Yes. Just a precaution. I felt the presence of something

I've not felt in a long time and I'm…I'm just being careful." She shook it off and smiled at me. "Is there something else?"

I looked at Tom, and he nodded at me. "We was just talkin' about what ties Scáthach to this plane. Do you know? Tom here thinks it's her possession of a human body."

Tom piped up. "If we could get her into her authentic form…would she be more vulnerable?"

"Yes, yes, she would," Zahara said. "Which would not be a simple task."

"Agreed. In fact, I've only seen a partial change myself," I mentioned. "I'm not sure I want to see the whole thing."

"I've seen her real face," Edward said as he and Richard joined us from the small room where they'd used the water basin we'd filled to clean up. "When Elias was fighting the werewolf infection, we ran into her on the road as we hunted the wolf that bit him."

"You never mentioned this," I commented.

He shrugged. "I am now?"

I motioned him to continue.

"Eli killed Scáthach's man-servant. Pretty young man," Edward said. "She was livid."

"A beta?" I asked.

"No. The boy was clueless," he said sitting on his bedroll and pulling his tobacco from his pocket.

"What did she look like?" I asked.

"She was already wearing the face she goes about in now."

"Mary," I said between clenched teeth.

"Yes," he agreed. "She was on her way to make a new spirit warrior in Silver City." Edward paused, and we all took that in.

"She'd already chosen me?" I asked.

"Either that or she had a few there in mind. Your brother was probably another option. She likes to choose orphans."

Tom nodded and sat on his bedroll. "Yes, she does."

After a pause on that, I said, "What else did she say? What prompted the change in shape?"

"The killing of that boy plus her irritation with me. You see, my ties to the land helped me fight her will. She never truly had my soul, for it had flowed through the land to get to her, and I am tied to the land of my ancestors. It angered her. She showed her real face then…the pointed teeth, red eyes, and oil-black skin. She is hideous."

Zahara nodded. "She has hair of flames that float like they're on the wind, and she stands seven feet tall with limbs long and slender. You'd think she'd be weak, but you cannot let the lack of muscle on those bones fool you. She is strong enough to pick up a horse in each hand and throw them half a mile."

"Great," I said flatly.

"Then wouldn't she always want to fight that way?" Dick asked.

"She feels vulnerable in that form now that there are more people around and they tend to hunt down monsters," she explained. "Besides, do you really ever see her do the fighting?"

I let out a short laugh. "No. She doesn't fight. She pulls the strings."

"Yes. She is the puppet master of them all. One word from her and they do her bidding. To have a werewolf who does not would pique her interest." Zahara looked at Brewer. "Your pretty face paired with your own will…that will entice her greatly. So be careful, Richard."

"I figured I needed to be anyway," he said to her.

The *QUARK-QUARK* warning from Gaax suddenly filled the air, and the thump of stones hitting the front door sounded like a pounding in the utter silence. I looked to Zahara. She motioned for me to go open it and for the others to hide behind it.

I slid the bar that locked the big wooden door and opened it to find a beautiful woman laying out in front of the cabin, outside the salt circle, her face ravaged with tears. She appeared injured.

Brewer stepped forward as if he couldn't stop himself. "Ma'am, are you all right?"

"Oh, thank goodness," she wailed. "I need help, my leg, it's broken and I'm so lost and cold. I saw the light in your window and hoped you could help me."

Brewer stepped out, and I did as well. The difference was, my hand was on my gun. For me, it seemed odd that she was outside the salt circle and not at our door.

"Wait, Dick…I think—"

Before I could finish, Zahara had shoved us out of the way and stood as a shield between the woman and us.

"Do *not* invite her inside the circle," Zahara shouted, then quietly added, "She could kill us all."

The woman's face changed. An unnerving smile slowly filled her face, and she laughed. "Why hello, Zahara. It seems you *are* alive."

"I could say the same of you, *Kennedy*."

The pretty woman stood, threw her head back and laughed. That is when I saw the long canine teeth.

"Well, I'll be," I said with wonder, amazement, and zero fear, "You're a vampire."

"In the flesh," Kennedy said with a bow, her British accent now evident in her tone. "In fact, I'm *the* vampire. So, tell me, Zahara, where is she?"

"She who?" Zahara said, playing coy.

"Oh, do stop. I'm looking for Scáthach and word is, you know where she is, what body she's in."

"And why would we share that with you?" I asked, leaning back on the old wooden door of the cabin.

Kennedy's face transformed from playful beauty to the kind you know kills. "Because I want her dead even more than you do."

* * *

April 1949

We opened the wide, wooden door to the elegant and newly constructed Graham's Mortuary. Stepping inside, we saw immediately that we were on the far left of the large main room. There was a stunning fireplace in the center of the far wall with the mantle, and sides made of intricately carved oak. Inside that was a layer of black marble, but with it being a sunny day in the mid-seventies, no fire was lit.

To the left was a wall with two doorways. The first was fully open and held a large, wooden table with chairs, a couch under the front window, and bookshelves here and there with options of urns and other burial items. The second door was half-closed, but I could hear a typewriter in there and figured it was the office.

We made our way toward the couches arranged in the center of the main room, the heels of our cowboy boots easily announcing us as we walked on the large, square, white tile floor. Because of this, I wasn't surprised to hear a voice behind me.

"Can I help you?"

He'd come from the opening to a hallway, directly opposite the front door. Behind him on the wall in the hall were many types of crosses hung in a collage of sorts.

We showed him our badges.

"Yes, you can," I said. "I'm Agent William Kidwell and this is my partner, Agent Richard Baca. We're lookin' for T.J. Graham."

"You found one of them. I'm T.J. Graham, Junior."

He couldn't have been over twenty years in age, with pale skin and short dark hair that lay flat against his head because he'd brushed it forward.

"We're here to discuss Miss Ovida Coogler," Richard said.

"Ah, yes." He motioned to the comfortable furniture by the fireplace. "Please have a seat."

I looked at the furniture. None of the pieces faced a door without another one at its back. I sighed at this and sat on a couch that had its back to the office. Richard sat across from me. Behind him were double doors to a breezeway that lead to another building.

Tommy chose a cushy chair that faced the fireplace. "It's a damn shame," he said, rubbing the back of his neck. "I had to go get her, ya know."

I had not known that. I jotted it down in my small notebook that I'd pulled from the chest pocket of my short sleeve dress shirt that I wore open over my t-shirt. "How long had you known her?"

"About eight years. We went to school together until she dropped out to help the family with their finances when her dad passed away."

"When was that?" Richard asked.

"Oh, about when Cricket was fourteen."

"She started workin' that young?" I asked.

"Yeah. It's sad, but she didn't seem to mind." He coughed. "Sorry, I've got a spring cold. Would either of you like a cold Coke or a glass of water?"

I never turned down free food, drink, clothes…really anything free. "Sure would. Coke would be great."

"Same," Richard said.

"Great, be right back."

Tommy rose and left the room.

Richard looked to me. With his voice low, he said, "What happened to tea for a cold?"

"No idea," I said with a shrug. "My guess is we unsettle him, and he wants something to wet his throat." Richard raised an eyebrow at me. "Fuck if I know, Dick."

He grinned. "Think he's runnin'?"

"No," I said with a laugh. "You in the mood to chase someone?"

"Kinda."

I grinned from ear to ear. "I feel ya. I'm itchy with all this too."

Tommy came back in with three glass bottles of Coke and a bottle opener. He opened one at a time and handed them to us before sitting down to drink from his own.

"Ahh…that's better." He drank again and settled himself. When he spoke again, there was a dark sadness to his eyes. "It was horrible. I got there around 7:30 p.m. It looked as if someone had done a piss-poor job of tryin' to bury her…just thrown a few shovels' worth of sand on her."

"What shape was she in?" I asked, even though I didn't want to know.

Tommy's face contorted with his memory, and I knew he would rather sit on a fire-ant hill than relive this. "Her face was skinned," he said, the last word catching in his throat with emotion. He let out a breath and slowly inhaled to pull himself together. "In fact, her face, arms, and legs were cut up and bruised. She also appeared to have received quite a blow over her left eye." He took a sip of soda.

I figured I'd help him along. "Was she face down, up, on her side…?"

"She was face up, arms to the sides, and legs straight out." He stopped and drank again, and my heart hurt for him.

Richard stepped in this time. "Was she still dressed, Tommy?"

He nodded, then shook his head. "Her blouse was on and her skirt was down, stopping just above her knees, but her suit jacket was missin', as were her shoes and her…her panties were gone."

My chest suddenly felt like a horse sat on it, and I exhaled heavily.

"The clothes she had on, what condition were they in?" Richard asked since I was without words.

"They didn't look like they were torn…"

"Did she have her purse?" Richard said.

"No, and we've not found it, but they did find her shoes."

I made note of that. "Found? By who?"

"Sid Howard and M.O. Johnson," he replied.

I wrote that down. "So, you brought her back here straight from the scene, yes?"

"Yeah, but I had to go back and get a different ambulance because she was in such terrible shape…havin' been out in the elements for days and all. She was, forgive me for sayin' so, flattened and well, a mess."

"You came back to town?" I asked.

Tommy fidgeted and drank more Coca-Cola. "Yeah. I got a different vehicle and grabbed a waxed canvas body bag so she'd not…uh…"

"Make a mess of the vehicle," Richard said.

Tommy nodded but seemed sick to his stomach. He wasn't the only one. I too felt a bit uneasy, but not for the same reasons Tommy did.

I looked down and jotted a note about the vehicle change. Offhandedly, I asked, "Who did her autopsy?"

"She didn't have one," Tommy said.

My head snapped up. "Excuse me?"

I must've said it a little too forcefully because Richard gave me a look.

"Sorry," I said. "What I meant was, as a murder victim, why wasn't she given an autopsy?"

"We don't do 'em here. The body would've had to have been transported to El Paso."

I sat back and did my best to hold in my anger. "Then you should have sent her to El Paso."

Tommy was very uncomfortable like ants had crawled up his britches. Finally, he said, "Dr. Maddox made that decision."

I sat forward slowly. "So, you're tellin' me he what, saw she was dead and tossed her into a coffin and said that's that?"

Richard gracefully stood and came to sit beside me. "Billy," he said, laying his hand over my arm.

That's when I realized I was shaking with fury. To hold it together, I reached for my soda on the coffee table and took a sip, being careful to not set it down so hard that I broke it.

"What my partner is tryin' to say is," Richard began, "that by law she should've had an autopsy. Did the family have a religious reason for turnin' it down?"

Tommy looked ashamed as he shook his head. "No. From what I understand, they were never spoken to about it. Dr. Maddox said that since the family was too poor for one—"

I stood up at this. "Are you serious!?"

"Billy...," Richard said, his tone holding more of a warning this time.

"What kind of business are you runnin' here? Who is this Dr. Maddox? I want to see him, and I want to see him right the fuck now."

3
KENNEDY

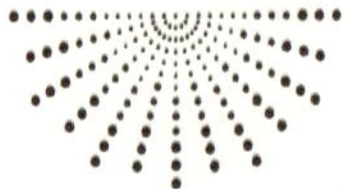

February 1879

You what?" Zahara asked, snapping her fingers so that the fire I'd dowsed not thirty minutes ago came back to life.

"I. Want. Her. Dead," Kennedy said through clenched teeth. "Come, come now, Zahara...you're not so old you can't hear me." Kennedy waved at the salt. "You don't need this. I'm not here to eat you."

"State your business," Zahara said.

With an exasperated sigh, Kennedy plopped her tiny frame onto a tree stump outside the salt line. "Fine. I want in on what you're doing."

I tossed more wood on the fire, and the light bloomed outward. "What *are* we doing?"

"You're training to fight Scáthach and her furry children. I want in," she said, her English accent now more evident.

"Why?" Richard asked, stepping into the firelight.

Kennedy stood and looked him up and down. "Well, aren't you handsome?" She sniffed, and her brow furrowed. "You smell like the wolves, but not exactly." She took at Edward. "You, on the other hand, are one of *hers*." Spitting on the ground, eyes full of disdain, she turned to Zahara. "Why in the name of the creator is there a werewolf in your circle?"

"Because he owns his soul," Zahara said. "He's the wolf that befriended and fought with Elias."

"Eli?" Kennedy's face went soft.

Edward moved forward. "Scáthach never had a full hold on my soul, but when a wolf bit Eli and we were unable to find him before the next full moon, he had me kill him to earn my full freedom."

Kennedy sat back down. "Eli is dead?"

"Yes," Zahara said.

Tom's head tilted. "You cared for him."

It wasn't a question, just a simple observation I'd thought as well, but not stated.

Kennedy glanced up, and tears plopped from her big blue eyes. "I did. He was a good man."

"I'm so confused right now." I stared at Zahara. "What the hell is going on?"

Zahara whispered a few words, and blue flames appeared in a spot close to Kennedy. "Step into the fire and be questioned."

Indignation spread across Kennedy's face. "You don't trust me?"

"Explain why I should! You've been missing for over two hundred years, and you show up here all helpful when the last thing you told me was that anyone not loyal to Scáthach was doomed to pay the price of death at your hand."

The indignation on Kennedy's face was palpable as she lifted her chin slightly. "I never said that." When Zahara merely tilted her head, Kennedy added, "My double might have."

"Get in the fire, Kennedy," Zahara said, her voice simple and soft.

The blond vampire stood and stamped her foot. "Fine. Have it your way." She moved to stand next to the blue flames. "Ugh...I hate these. Leaves such a weird taste in my mouth." Without hesitation, she stepped into the tiny circle of blue flames and let them consume her.

She didn't burn as I expected she might. Instead, she scratched her arms, as if they itched from a rash. "This magic is uncomfortable. Please do get on with it."

"Wow, it is you," Zahara said.

"Well, who the hell did you think it was?"

"Honestly? An imposter."

Kennedy grinned and motioned toward her attire. "Really now? Even a vamp with my face would never have my fashion sense."

Zahara stifled a laugh. "Why are you here?"

"To help fight Scáthach." Zahara's eyebrow raised, but Kennedy continued. "You didn't kill me that day. It was another vampire. One I'd created. She took my face, and I went on holiday." With the last word, Kennedy struck a pose and grinned.

"Went on *holiday*?" Zahara threw up her hands and turned away from her old friend, pacing about the circle.

"So, you can what, shift to look like others?" I questioned.

"Yes," Kennedy replied. "Any vampire made by Scáthach herself, or one created by that direct line, has this gift of changing his or her shape to look like another person. Once the blood dilutes further, it's not an easy gift to ascertain."

"That doesn't explain why you wish to kill Scáthach," I pointed out.

"Too true. Here, let's save you from asking questions, and I'll tell my tale. I cannot lie in here, so this will save time."

Zahara had returned to face her old friend. "Yes, tell us what happened."

Kennedy sat down in the circle of blue flame. It encapsulated her, causing her hair and skin to appear blue. "Scáthach knew I was not 100 percent happy with her choice to change me and leave me in the new land. I loved my life in England."

Looking right at me, she continued, "I was beautiful, wealthy, and had the life most would have died for. But instead of getting to enjoy that life, I fell ill with the plague and was dying. No doctor could save me. Scáthach said she could, but I had to come with her."

Kennedy laughed. "I believed I was smarter than her. My plan was to come to this land like she wanted, let her heal me, and then I'd go back to England where I belonged, and she could bugger off. Goodness, I hated this land." She shuddered and almost looked ill at remembering things. "Nothing for miles. Trees, natives, and wild animals. No parties or pretty boys...no luncheons or tea. No theatre or music. Just land and sky.

"So Scáthach promised me some fun, and I hoped that meant she and I'd go home. But no. She brought me down the coast, dropped Eli in my lap, and gave me a job to do. It was better when *you* joined us, Zahara, but I wanted more."

"Then you decided to just up and leave us," Zahara said.

"Don't you dare sound all high and mighty! From my understanding, you chopped off my head."

"Well, it wasn't *your* head now, was it?" Zahara pointed out.

Kennedy's eyes narrowed. "You thought it was. Same thing."

Zahara sighed and crossed her arms. "Maybe. But you'd gone crazy.

You were draining the sick and praising Scáthach. You wanted Eli and me to help you capture and torture humans. We refused and left."

"Well, from what I've put together, you hung out with my imposter for three months."

"And where were you?" Zahara asked.

"Oh, I didn't make it very far. Scáthach figured out my plan and quite simply foiled it. I was healing a man's wife to secure a spot on the next boat to England."

Zahara whistled low. "She'd have been livid."

Kennedy laughed without humor. "Oh, you have no idea. She showed up at the meet I'd planned, having hidden in the shadows long enough to verify what the man had told her, for he was under her spell."

"Then what?" I prodded, now sincerely invested in her tale.

"She came out, proceeded to knock me unconscious, transported me up into the mountains, and tossed me in a hole. When I awoke, she stood at the top and declared that I'd be there for three hundred years. She placed a boulder the size of a ship on top and cast magic around it. I couldn't break out. Trust me, I tried."

"It's not been three hundred years, Kennedy," Zahara stated.

"No kidding, Z," Kennedy said with a snort and an eye roll. "Look, I slept most of the time. Twenty years here, fifty years there. I survived on rats and other vermin that had the misfortune of traveling through the pocket she buried me in."

"Then how did you get out?" Tom challenged.

Kennedy waved his question away like a fly. "I'm getting to it, my, you're impatient. Fine." She resituated, fluffing her skirts. "Eventually, man, *glorious* man, set off an explosion while looking for gold and silver, and the boulder atop of my crypt cracked in half, disrupting the spell. I could see sunlight coming through. I waited until it was dark, and I jumped up, repeatedly, smashing into the stone until it eventually broke.

"I was free! I set out to find you. It was hard. I got lucky when a man from New Mexico made a comment in a hotel restaurant in New York City one night about the weird stuff going on out here. So, I got a stagecoach, and I was on my way."

"And here you are," I stated.

Dick leaned against the cabin. "How long ago was this escape?"

"Not long ago..."

Zahara laughed. "Which was?"

"Early 1840s?"

"That's way before I was born," I explained.

"I told you it took me a while to figure out where you were!" Kennedy said with a hand on her hip. "Besides, I needed to enjoy what this new land had become before I set out to find the breadcrumbs. I got derailed… okay? New York City was hopping! In fact, in the summer of 1848 I was in Seneca Falls, New York, and had the honor of attending—"

"How do you lose track of all that time?" Tom blurted out.

"Vampire time," Zahara mumbled. "What is long for us, isn't for them."

Seemingly miffed she didn't get to tell her story, she just pursed her lips and gestured toward Zahara. "Yes, that."

"When did you hear about stuff in New Mexico?" I prodded.

She contemplated the question. "Must've been in 1874 or 75, I think. A man in New York with thinning red hair and an *obnoxious* mustache was talking about unprecedented turmoil and money to gain out west."

Richard and I looked at one another and said, "McSween."

"That sounds downright familiar," Kennedy acknowledged.

"Well, I'll be damned," I said. "Of all the things." After a moment I added, "So, you're not here to kill us, or hand us over to Scáthach, but to fight her?"

"Yes," Kennedy replied, "that's exactly what I plan to do."

"And what if she were to make you an offer you couldn't refuse?" I offered.

"Excuse me?" Kennedy responded, her head tilting in a way that made me think of a bird.

"Let's say Scáthach comes to you and says, 'I just need those pesky folks killed and you can go to any city you like in the world, and I'll never bother you again.'"

Kennedy laughed. It started light but got darker and more robust. Finally, she regained control of herself. "She'd never keep that promise. Ever. I'm not dumb enough anymore to think she would."

Zahara smiled. "You're right, she'd never keep that promise. She thinks her creations are her property."

"Except me," Edward announced.

"Agreed. You played by her rules, and you won. You are your own person now," Zahara said. "But the rest of her monsters? Well, she feels like she has the right to lie to us."

"She's compelled to," Kennedy said, standing up. "She's evil. Some of my kind, and Zahara's, too, are as well. But she gave us three more free will."

This snagged my attention. "Wait…three?"

"The three original monsters of this land; a witch, a werewolf, and a vampire," Kennedy explained.

"Who's the werewolf that completes the triad?" I inquired.

Zahara turned to me. "His name is Tarack," she said, pronouncing it Tuh-rock. "I've not seen him in centuries."

"Maybe he's dead," Tom offered.

"No," Kennedy replied. "He's not. I've seen him. In my search for you, I followed energy at first. I ended up in the Appalachian Mountains. I found him there. He didn't see me, but I saw him. I left quickly. I can't have her aware that I'm alive and free…and if he knew, he'd tell her."

"I, too, do not want her to know I'm alive." Zahara snapped her fingers, and the blue flames vanished.

Kennedy stood and stepped toward Zahara. "You fooled her too, my sister?"

"I did. She doesn't know I train these warriors. We will allow you to accompany us for your help in kind. But if you double back and try to use us for your own gain, I'll have a secret weapon ready to take you out. Already do…so don't push me the wrong way, Kennedy."

The vampire was obviously attempting to work something out in her mind but nodded in agreement. Zahara opened the salt circle, and as the one who had the most souls in the chamber, I stepped out first, and Kennedy was on me in a second, standing in my way, blocking me from the safety of the cabin.

She smiled at me and I at her as I braced for impact.

* * *

April 1949

Richard walked me outside of the funeral home to calm down while we waited on Dr. Maddox to arrive. We'd gone out the double doors to a large section of grass surrounded by the U-shape of the mortuary. It reminded me of the opening inside the McSween home. One large tree grew in the space and perched in it was a singular raven. It didn't take a genius to know Gaax was monitoring us.

"Reel it in, William," Richard said.

I stopped pacing to stare up at the sky. "Ooh, he's using my full name. It must be serious."

"It is," he said. "You cannot act like you're out of control, or they'll report back on it. Mr. Earl of Gray, as you like to call him, would love nothing more than to find a reason to call you or me in to be investigated again, or to take us off this case…not because he'd want it, but because he knows it's important to you."

This got my attention. "Damn it." I squatted down and shoved my fingers into my hair. Pulling on it a bit, I added, "I hate it when you're right."

"Must be hard to be hatin' all the time," he said in jest.

This made me smile. "Thank God you're still willin' to be my partner. I need your level head."

He offered me his hand, and I took it, not because I required help up, but I needed the assistance in finding my inner steady ground again. Richard could always help me do that.

I stood and let go of his hand to pat his shoulder. "Thanks." I looked to the other building. "What do you think that is?"

He shrugged.

"Let's find out. I feel like bein' nosy."

It turned out to be a beautiful chapel with wooden pews and stained-glass windows along the sides. Not the catholic style with pictures, but a simple pattern of diamonds with color dots where the diamonds touched each other.

Up front was an open space like a stage area with curtains on the side. This was likely where the coffin would have gone, and I found myself standing in the center of the room imagining the service for Cricket that I assumed never happened but should have.

Sorrow became too heavy for me, and I silently walked out to sit on a bench in the breezeway. Richard said nothing, just sat beside me in his calming way. I appreciated him more than he knew. I was about to say so when Tommy poked his head out the door.

"Agents Kidwell and Baca? Dr. Maddox is here."

"Thank you," Richard said, "We'll be right in."

With a nod, he disappeared back inside.

I took a deep breath. "Ok, let's do this."

"You sure you're okay?" Richard asked as we walked toward the door.

"Sure," I said.

"Can you promise you won't hit the doctor?"

I opened the door and without looking back at him I said, "Nope," and walked back into the main room.

"God help us," Richard muttered, and I grinned.

Once back in the lobby, Tommy escorted us directly across to the side room with a large wooden table in the center and display cases of urns. where the large wooden table and urns were. Standing there, going through papers in a folder, was a young man in his mid to late twenties. He wore a nice suit and had slicked his hair back away from his face. He didn't acknowledge our entrance at all.

"Agent Kidwell, Agent Baca, this is Dr. Dan Maddox," Tommy said.

Maddox looked up and smiled, but it didn't touch his eyes. "And what, pray tell, have we done to be *blessed* with a visit from the FBI?" Dr. Maddox said, the sneer on his face matching the tone of voice.

"This is a good start," I muttered so quietly that only Richard's werewolf ears would hear me. He bumped my arm as he stepped up beside me as a warning. I grunted.

"It's nice to meet you, Dr. Maddox," Richard said, putting his large hand out to the well-tailored man. "We truly appreciate you takin' the time to talk to us."

This ass-kissing seemed to work, and the man's smile became more genuine. He closed the folder and shook Richard's hand. "No problem at all, but I won't be able to stay too long. Need to get back to the hospital. What can I do for you?"

"We just want to talk to you about the Coogler murder," I said. "We feel it could tie into a case we're workin' on, and so your help could be vitally important to helpin' the FBI."

The smile finally touched his eyes and now I had his number. He appeared to want us to see ourselves as lower than him. What a prick.

"I'm always happy to help the FBI."

Sure, he was.

"If your information helps us solve this case," I said, "We'll also make sure you get recognized for it."

"Well, now, gentleman, I don't need all that...but it never hurts one's reputation, right?" He took a seat at the table, set the folder down, and crossed one leg over the other. "What do you need to know?"

Smarmy bastard. I didn't want shit from him, but I knew how to play the game to get what I wanted.

Richard and I also sat at the table, and I started us off. "Where were you when you got word that Cricket had been found?"

"I was at the hospital and got a call from here and came over. Tommy told me the body had been identified as Cricket Coogler by friends before I arrived."

"And why were you called specifically?" Richard asked. "Do you work here?"

"Oh no," he said with a light laugh that if I were Tommy would have possibly offended me. "I'm the only surgeon in town. We've got no pathologist here, and autopsies are done in El Paso."

"We heard," I said, finding it hard to keep the bitterness out of my voice.

"Small town livin'," Dr. Maddox said in response.

"Did you send her for an autopsy?" Richard asked, and I looked to Tommy to let him know to keep his mouth shut.

"We discussed it, but I advised that it was unnecessary."

"Oh?" I asked.

Dr. Maddox opened the folder he'd set on the table. Flipping through as if he needed his notes, he spoke casually, saying, "An autopsy could tell us where internal organs had been moved, sure, but honestly, gentleman, her body was so thoroughly crushed that it could not be more specific than my own examination."

He stopped flipping through pages, having found what he was looking for, and continued. "She was so slim and her skin so moveable that I could easily describe fractures by simply feeling. Her chest, abdomen, shoulder, and internal organs were all crushed, and she was so torn up…it was clear she died of a massive and severe trauma." He closed the folder and handed it to Tommy. "These are my findings on Miss Coogler that my secretary typed up for me onto ditto paper. Tommy, if you'd be so kind as to go make a copy of this for these agents?"

Tommy wasn't clear on why he was being the one sent to do this, but he took the folder and with a nod, disappeared to the office. Once he left, Dr. Maddox spoke a bit more freely.

"I didn't want to say this in front of the young lad, seeing as he knew Miss Coogler personally, but if you want my flat-out opinion…"

I really didn't.

He stood and stepped to the front window to look out at the yard and road. "From what I've been told, it's not only the night of the disappearance that needs to be considered. The weekend previous she was hangin' out with politicians from Santa Fe and the law officers who work for them if you get my meanin'."

I didn't like his tone or what he appeared to be insinuating, but I kept my mouth shut.

Maddox continued, "My understandin' is that she was in the middle of that party, drinkin' with everybody for a few hours, and sittin' on the laps of all the men she was spendin' time with that evenin'. She didn't seem particular."

"What are you tryin' to say?" Richard asked as I barely held my temper in check.

With his voice at a whisper, the doctor added. "With bar flies like Miss Coogler, who are poor and in need of money and attention, it is thought that she was…soliciting herself amongst the wealthy and powerful men."

I was up on my feet. "Why you son of a bitch," I said before I could stop myself and beelined for him faster than I should have.

Richard, closer to the doctor than I was, stopped me in time.

Dr. Maddox held his ground. "The truth is the truth, even if you don't want to hear it, Agent Kidwell."

Richard stepped forward slowly, into the doctor's space. "Unless you have proof of such allegations against a woman, *any* woman, I recommend you keep your mouth shut." His voice was low, with a touch of the growl to it, which meant that his eyes likely held a bit of their silver-blue glow. Not enough to look inhuman, but enough to strike fear into the heart of the strongest of men. "Am I making myself clear?"

Now Dr. Maddox backed away. He blinked a few times as if processing what he saw. Deciding it wasn't more than was possible, he swallowed loudly and nodded. "You have, but know I'm not the only one who knows of this behavior. To stop the rumors that she was a—"

I stepped up to join Richard.

Dr. Maddox stopped speaking long enough to change his choice of words. "Available for money." Seeing the look on our faces, he added, "You'll need to stop more than me from speakin' of it."

Using this moment to press him on the autopsy, I said, "Why didn't you send her body to be examined in El Paso?"

His eyes traveled from me to Richard and back. "There was nothin' they could tell me I couldn't already see on my own. She was so small to begin with that I could feel around her flattened body and tell what I needed to know. Besides, she was indigent and thus couldn't afford it."

This time Richard couldn't stop me. I reached out and grabbed the doctor by the shirt and pulled him in. "By law, if murder is suspected, which it was, the state would cover the cost. To even ask her family would have been a dishonorable thing to do. You skipped protocol, and if I find out you did so to help cover up the murder, I swear on all I hold dear, you'll pay for it."

"Billy...," Richard warned.

I let go of the doctor and stepped away.

"I apologize for my partner's anger. But you truly screwed this one up, doctor. Did you even check to see if she was sexually assaulted?"

The doctor paused and then, as if against his own better judgment, he blurted out, "No. I did not."

"Why?" I demanded to know.

"Because with her lifestyle and missing underwear, it wasn't a hard guess to know what we'd find. That said, at her level of decomposition, we wouldn't have been able to tell, to be honest."

Eyes narrow, I glared at the man. "To be *honest*? I don't think so. No, you *assumed* and went against the procedures to save the county money, or to assist in a coverup. For that, sir, I will file a complaint. You can rest assured."

Tommy walked in with two copies of the folder, each in its own manila envelope. He handed both to Richard since he was closer and seemed less volatile. "That's everythin' from the folder Dr. Maddox gave me." The item of which he spoke he now set on the table.

The doctor moved around the table to grab it and to put the table between him and me.

I took my copy of the folder contents and waved them at the doctor. "These notes better be so goddamn clear that I can picture her down to the minutest detail. Do you hear me? Because if not, then an autopsy should've been performed, and I'll ask for her body to be exhumed to do so."

"Um...Tommy?" Richard said, a slight hesitation in his voice. "I don't see any photos here. Did anyone take pictures when Miss Coogler was found?"

Tommy swallowed, then said, "No sir, not that I know of."

Both Richard and I turned to stare at the poor young man.

"Let me get this straight," I said, laughter bubbling up, not out of humor, but by extreme anger and frustration. "You have a girl missin' for sixteen days. When she's found it's obvious someone attempted to hide her body and yet you decide that the investigation doesn't need any photographs of the scene? Why is that? Maybe one of you brilliant sons of bitches can draw it for us then. Is that it?"

Tommy opened his mouth, but nothing came out.

"Can you, Tommy? Can you draw it for me?" I demanded to know as I slowly inched toward him.

He wouldn't look at me. "No, sir."

By now I was standing in the young man's personal space. With my voice low, quiet, and controlled, I said, "Can anyone else who was there draw it for me in perfect detail?"

He looked at the floor. "No, sir."

"Then why in blazes did no one take a damn photo of the crime scene or of her afterward? Are you all idiots or are you just tryin' to cover the asses of those who killed this poor girl?"

Tommy's head snapped up, his face red with anger. "I would never! I want them caught and thrown in jail for all eternity!"

It was a genuine outburst, and I believed him. With a hand on his shoulder, I looked him in the eye and said, "Who was there when you arrived on the scene?"

"The boys who found her, Sheriff Happy Apodaca, Roy Sandman, and Max Johnson. In fact, Apodaca parked within thirty-five feet of her body. From what I saw—"

"Tommy!" Dr. Maddox said in what appeared to be an attempt to stop him.

"Her left collarbone had been broken and there seemed to be a skull fracture above her left ear." Tears came to his eyes, but he didn't let them fall. "Her face, arms, and legs were cut and bruised..."

"That could have just been decomposition—" Dr. Maddox attempted to explain.

I pointed toward the doctor but didn't look toward him. "Nobody is talkin' to you right now. Please continue, Tommy."

The young man nodded and said, "She appeared to have received quite a blow over her left eye as well."

"It was her right," the doctor said.

I rolled my eyes and turned toward him. "Great. We already have conflictin' information. Hm...I wonder why that is? Richard, care to take a guess?"

"Maybe because no one took a picture?" he offered in as smart-assy a tone as a man of his moral compass could produce.

I thumbed toward Richard. "Yeah...that right there. *That* is why you take photos, people." I placed my free hand on Tommy's shoulder. "Thank you for these and the information. You honor your friend well."

I turned toward Dr. Maddox and used the envelope like a prop in a play, shaking it toward him for emphasis. "You, on the other hand, either are on the payroll of those who killed her, or you're just an idiot. I've not decided which, but I recommend not leavin' town, 'cause we're not done talkin' to you. We'll be in touch."

Richard, attempting to soften our exit, handed a copy of our card to Tommy and set one on the table near the doctor. "We'll be here until this is solved. If you think of anything else, you can find us at the Amador Hotel. Just leave a message at the front desk."

With that, we both walked out and headed toward Richard's new vehicle.

"Well, that didn't go well."

"Hey, I didn't hit him," I offered.

"Thank God for small favors," Richard said with a tiny smile.

I chuckled. "Yes, my friend, thank God for that."

Coming around the corner of the building, a man stood on the side-walk in our way. At first, I thought nothing of the man ahead of us and was prepared to walk around when my supernatural senses picked up on him. I wasn't the only one either. Richard and I both came to a stop as we stared at one of Scáthach's cursed children in human form.

"Well, this is not what I expected," I muttered.

"Now what?" Richard muttered.

"I have no idea."

* * *

February 1879

Seeing my intent to defend myself, Kennedy stopped me with a simple grasp of both my arms, pinning them to my sides like I was caught in a vice.

"I scared you. I'm sorry," she said. "I sometimes move faster than I mean to when I'm excited. I figured something out and...well, you're a spirit warrior like Eli, aren't you?"

Her eyes glistened in the firelight, emotion high in her perfect face.

I had no idea what to think, but I made a judgment call. "Yes, ma'am, I am."

Then the vampire did something I'd never have suspected. She hugged me.

"He called me ma'am, did you hear him, Zahara?"

My eyes bulged out from both her tight squeeze and my surprise, and I gasped out one word, "Zahara?"

And now the witch, the one who I trusted and loved, laughed. "Oh, Kennedy. It's good to have you back."

The vampire let me go, and in seconds, she and Zahara were holding each other outside the circle in a strong embrace. I found myself without words for one of the few times in my life.

Tom stepped up to one side and Dick to the other.

"You said nothin' about either of us," Tom pointed out.

"No, I didn't," I whispered. "Aces in the hole, partners. Aces in the hole."

Everyone nodded. That meant Gaax wouldn't be Kennedy's only surprise if she turned out to be false. If she tried to play us, we'd need to have an upper hand. By keeping Tom, Dick, and Gaax a secret, we had multiple levels of that.

Dick placed a hand on my shoulder, one of his long fingers touching the skin of my neck. Mentally he said, "You don't trust her."

"No," I replied in kind. "She's too good to be true. We keep an eye on her and we hold our cards close to the chest."

4
THE COOGLERS

February 1879

The group went to bed. Well, Edward, Tom, and Richard did. Gaax was on watch as Zahara and Kennedy sat outside catching up. Technically I was in bed, but I, too, kept a watch on things through Gaax's eyes and ears.

"They don't trust me," Kennedy simply stated.

"Can you blame them?" Zahara said. "You are a vampire. The first they've met. Their training, some of which is from me, tells them you're more dangerous than the wolves they fight regularly."

Kennedy drank from a mug. "Thanks for thinking of me with this."

It was the blood from the deer we'd killed earlier. Zahara had drained it and put it aside, just in case.

"I had faith in you. I merely needed to know the truth."

Kennedy nodded, and when the fire roared from the wind, shooting flames her way, she backed away from it. "Where are you all headed?"

Zahara explained.

"Tell me more about the other two," Kennedy said. "Tom and Dick, yes?"

Zahara shook her head. "Yes, but their stories are their own to tell. I will say that Billy and Dick are close. Like brothers. Tom is newer to the group, but he too shares a significant bond with Billy."

"And the werewolf?"

"Edward's story overlaps with Dick, but again, not mine to tell."

"Ooh, lovers?" Kennedy said, wiggling her eyebrows.

Zahara almost spat out her warm cider. "No. But they share some history. There's magic there as well. It's a good group to work with, Kennedy. I think we'll figure out how to send her back this time."

"From your mouth to the creator's ears," Kennedy said and finished her blood. "When do we leave this place?"

"The plan was tomorrow morning, but we can head out after sundown if you wish."

"No, I have a driver. He will be here with me in my wagon in the morning. His name is Markus. If we're lucky and it's overcast, I'll be able to ride with you all."

Zahara nodded. "Tomorrow morning, then. Be ready. Make sure you've closed any connections you still have in the area. We cannot have anyone following us onward."

"Then I best get a move on. I'll see you soon."

Kennedy stood and, with a wave, disappeared in the blink of an eye.

Gaax fluttered in the tree above Zahara and she looked at him. "I know you're listening, so you might as well come out here."

Caught, I quietly left the room, stepped out the front door, and shut it silently behind me. "Do you think it's safe to have her with us? Will she try to upset our plans?"

"Safe? Not sure, but she won't get in our way if that's what you mean. We should be okay as long as she behaves."

"I was afraid you'd say that."

* * *

April 1949

The man standing in our way was over six feet, but not as tall as Richard. He wore a black hat, cowboy boots, and a matching vest with a white dress shirt and new Levi's. His dark hair fell to the top of his shoulders, and his goatee was just long enough to be trimmed to a point. He appeared familiar, but it wasn't until I saw his hooded eyes that I recognized him.

I reached out and touched Richard's shoulder, so I could speak to his mind. "That is their best tracker. He's the one they sent to sniff me out at the hotel when I came to town last month."

"Did he figure out what you were?" he mentally replied.

"No. I think he could smell the magic on me, but he couldn't place what I was."

"He'll realize what I am in a second."

I nodded. "But he'll make assumptions, and we'll let him."

Richard hummed his agreement to the plan.

I took my hand from him and hooked both thumbs in my back pockets. "We meet again," I said aloud. "How are you today, sir?"

The man's deep brown eyes flicked to Richard, and a low growl vibrated in his throat. Richard returned one in kind. The brown eyes glowed gold, and Richard's blue went silver, and that stopped the man long enough for me to stop a dog fight, for a lack of a better term.

"State your business, or I'll let my colleague eat you," I said in jest.

"Gross," Richard said, his voice lower than usual.

"Just a turn of phrase, buddy. Anyway, where was I? Oh yes, how about we all do formal introductions? My name is Agent William Kidwell, and this is my partner, Agent Richard Baca, and we are here investigatin' the disappearance of one of our own. And you are?"

"Cricket Coogler."

I laughed. "You are so profoundly not Miss Ovida Coogler."

"I mean, you're here investigating the murder of Miss Coogler, are you not?"

"We are," Richard said. "It possibly ties into our original investigation. Why does that matter to you?"

He looked to Richard and then me, the glow going out of his eyes. "My name is Duke. I work for the Sheriff's office. They instructed me to give you both my assistance. Happy wants me to keep him in the loop on what you learn."

Richard laughed briefly, ended it abruptly, and said, "No," before stepping around the man and walking away.

I shrugged. "I guess the answer is no. Catch ya later, Duke." I headed toward Richard.

Duke put his hand on me and in less than a second, I had one of my guns in his gut.

"Get your hand off me," I hissed.

He took it back. "Things will go easier for you in town if the Sheriff doesn't block you at every turn, and he will. Happy Apodaca will make sure everyone in town fears speaking with you both. You'll leave without solving either of your cases. Is that really what you want?"

"That's a dumb question," I stated, noticing an accent this time in his speech. It was hard to place, as if he'd lived all over Europe versus one country in particular.

"It was rhetorical," he explained, as if I didn't realize that. "Let me work with you and save you both a load of trouble."

I looked up into his eyes and saw something there I'd not expected: sorrow. I tilted my head like a dog would when interested in what someone has to say.

Duke understood the move and said, "She was a sweet girl. I want the person who killed her caught."

"What if that person is your boss?"

His lips pressed into a firm line, and he looked around as if he was searching his brain for how he felt about that. Finally, he focused on me and said, "Then I'll have a hard choice to make."

"Yes, you will. Meet us tomorrow at the diner Cricket worked at. We'll all have breakfast and act like civilized people…and hey, maybe you and my partner can growl at each other some more. Eight-thirty in the mornin' work okay for you?"

He nodded.

I quickly holstered my gun against my back. "Tomorrow then."

Duke grunted his agreement and walked away.

"Oh, and Duke?"

He stopped and turned to look at me. "Yeah?"

"If you double-cross us, we'll find out, and I'll send you to whatever god you worship faster than you can repent for your sins. You get me?"

He bowed his head to me. "I do."

"Good." I touched the brim of my hat. "See you at breakfast."

Duke raised his head, touched his brim as well, and with a single nod he walked off.

I calmly made my way to Richard, who was sitting in his car with the windows down. His hearing would've been good enough to know everything that went down.

"Well played," he said to me as I got into the car. "Now we have Happy not workin' extra hard to get in our way. But if Duke's gonna work with us, he's goin' to learn things we'd rather his boss didn't know."

I grunted and shut the door. "I have a plan for that. You won't like it."

Richard turned the car on and rolled his eyes. "How did I know you were going to say that?"

"Because you believe they put me on this earth to make your life Hell."

He smiled. "Truer words, Billy…truer words."

I laughed and smacked his boulder of a bicep. "Come on, let's go visit Cricket's mother. I'd like to pay my respects and let her see that someone cares about her daughter. She probably could use that right about now."

* * *

February 1879

Travel day was overcast as snow fell steadily. With no sun out, Kennedy was free to ride on her horse with us while her manservant, Markus, drove the horses that pulled her covered wagon. He was a quiet man who appeared to be of mixed race. Most I heard him say was, "Yes, Miss Kennedy."

The vampire herself? Well, she was, by my account, the funniest yet most self-involved woman I'd ever met. She spoke of parties and clothes, shoes and bags, and owned many of what she spoke of. In fact, she had a ton of all three. Enough to own a covered wagon full of them, a horse to pull it, and a man to drive it. She also owned a second horse. This one was for her to ride, which she did side-saddle. I wanted to ask where she'd gotten her money, but Zahara seemed to see the question on the tip of my tongue and shook her head at me.

This told me she likely stole from folks. Either the ones she killed when she fed or the men she seduced, for she talked of many men in her past, and Kennedy was a looker. She stood around my height at five foot seven, but she always had on a heeled boot, so she was technically shorter by an inch or two.

"You're tellin' me, men fall for this every time?" I asked.

"Damsel in distress is the best way to get a meal," she stated. Then, realizing what she'd said, she cleared her throat. "Sorry."

I waved her off. To be honest, how much weirder was she from me or the rest of us? I'd never been a prejudiced man against a person's skin color or nationality, so why the hell would I care about this? I didn't. Truth be told, she fascinated me. Such a different life to have lived. In ways, harder for sure.

We were all laying by the fire looking up at the night sky, a warm cocoon of magic around us so we'd not get cold. The night was so dark and clear that without the moon in the sky, the stars stood out like diamonds against the black.

"So...," I said. "No sunlight. Ever?"

"Ever," she said. "It'll burn me to a crisp."

"Then you came to the wrong territory," Brewer joked.

"Tell me about it," she said flatly, though I could see a tiny, lopsided grin appear on her face.

"We were told about the stake to the heart...that true too?"

"Yep." She turned her head to look at me. "You contemplating on how to kill me, Mr. Bonney?"

I smiled wide, looking into her big, baby-blue eyes. "No, ma'am. I'm just fascinated by your...species."

"Billy!" Dick said in a scolding tone.

"Oh, I'm not so easily bothered, Mr. Brewer," she said, waving off his concern. "Your species fascinates me too, Mr. Bonney."

I remembered then about Eli. "Tell me about Elias Story."

She smiled and turned to look up at the Milky Way. "He was a Puritan. Came over on the Mayflower. Eli had a very high moral code."

Edward laughed. "And he kept that until the day he died."

"Saved you while dying...that's our Eli," she said, and dabbed at her eyes. "I loved that kid. An orphan and sort of lost. He'd been working for a man and come with him from Europe. He was Dutch, actually. Tall and slender, with dark hair and green eyes. It was in those that you saw the age. They could dance with laughter one minute and then go flat with purpose the next. Such a complicated and wonderful young man."

"Scáthach has a type for her spirit warriors," Tom offered. "Orphaned young men who are lacking direction."

I wanted to say, hey, speak for yourself, but we didn't want Kennedy to know about Tom yet, so I just snickered. And seeing as he was on my other side, he smacked me playfully.

"I never understood that term," I said. "How am I a spirit warrior when I don't own my soul?"

Kennedy leaned up on an elbow to look down at me, her blonde curls dropping around to frame her pale face. "You do own your soul, Billy Bonney. Did you not know that?"

* * *

April 1949

We pulled the car up outside of a duplex on South Water Street. With badges already out to show, we approached the front door of one-hundred sixteen. I knocked, and the young woman I saw at the cemetery who resembled Cricket answered.

She kept the screen door between us and her. "Yes, can I help you?"

Badge extended for reading, I said, "Hello, my name is Agent Kidwell, and this is Agent Baca with the FBI, and we'd like to talk to you about Ovida."

"I'm her sister. Why would the FBI be interested in Cricket when the police are not?" she asked simply, the brittle cold of her anger evident in the undertone of her voice.

"Ma'am," Richard said, and the warmth of who he was, how he cared, bled through. "We don't give a damn about the law of this town or who they think they are. We care about your sister and puttin' those who killed her in a cage."

Tears touched her eyes, but she didn't let them fall.

"Ma'am," I said, "We think her death might be tied to one of our ongoing investigations, and any information you or your family could provide would be downright helpful."

A single tear fell, and she didn't bother to acknowledge it. "The sheriff himself hasn't even spoken to my mother since he took her report that Cricket was missing." She sighed. "I have no idea what is going on, but if you're here to get answers for my family, please, come in."

She opened the screen door outward, and we entered the tidy home. She shut both doors and said, "My name is Willow, but they call me Cookie. Please, have a seat. I'll fetch my mother for you."

We sat on a couch that appeared old but well taken care of. The sparsely-decorated room fit the space perfectly. Running my hand along the material of the sofa, I could imagine Cricket laying here listening to the radio or reading a book, and my heart hurt. If we found out I was the reason they killed her, I'd never forgive myself.

Likely hearing the change in my heartbeat, Richard turned to me. "You okay?"

"Just sad."

He nodded. "It's okay to be."

When Cookie returned, a woman in her early forties was with her. She may have been small in build, like her daughters, with the same dark hair, but she was stately, even in her grief. Coming up behind her was a young man with dark hair, likely Cricket's age, and a very tall man with blond hair worn swept back from his face, showing a deep widow's peak.

"Mom, these are the FBI agents I mentioned."

Brewer stood and offered her his big hand. "Thank you for takin' the time to speak with us, Mrs. Coogler. I'm Agent Richard Baca, and this is Agent William Kidwell."

I stood and took her hand after he had. "You can call me Billy if you like."

Mrs. Coolger nodded. "And you can call me Ollie." She sat in one of the two simple but pretty armchairs across from the sofa. "Cookie says you've come to talk to me about Ovida?"

"Yes, ma'am," I said, my eyes flitting up to the tall blond man who didn't look like family.

Cookie missed nothing and said, "I'm sorry, this is my husband, Carl Bamert."

Richard and I shook hands with him and then with Cricket's brother, who they introduced as Willie. Everyone found a seat in the living room, Willie choosing to sit beside Richard and Cookie sitting on the arm of the chair Carl sat in. You could tell this was a habit of theirs. He'd sit there, she'd place her tiny frame beside him, and his arm came around her lovingly. Today, however, it seemed to encircle her protectively.

"You mentioned that her death might be tied to one of your ongoing investigations. What did you mean by that?" Cookie asked.

"We have heard that Cricket was friends with the law around here, is that correct?" I replied.

Ollie spoke up. Her voice was quiet but held purpose. "Yes, she'd ridden in Sheriff Apodaca's car several times. Every now and again he'd get out of the car as well and visit with his sister-in-law; she lives in the apartment next door. She gets lonely since Santiago died. Anyway, Cricket wasn't fond of Happy. There were times when someone would mention him, and Cricket would state that she didn't like the man. If she didn't say it, she acted like it."

"I'm not his biggest fan either," I said with a small grin. "So why did she hang out with him and his group?"

Cookie shrugged. "I think she liked the attention of his friends who worked in Santa Fe. I don't know who, but she dated one of them at some point. You see, Happy is more than friendly with the political party that runs this state."

"I see," I said, writing that down. "How involved with the gamblin' in the state is he?"

Everyone looked at one another, and I waited. Finally, Cookie's husband, Carl, spoke up.

"From what I understand, he's very involved with the underground gambling that goes on here. I don't have proof, but I'd bet every dime I have that he gets kickbacks for looking the other way."

This got Richard's and my attention.

"Then it's possible he's involved in our primary case. We have been searchin' for a mobster from the east coast. He was in witness protection and ran, then promptly disappeared. The agent sent to find him has also gone missin'. Are there any other girls that hung out with her and Happy's group?"

Cookie shook her head, "Not that I know of. Mom?"

"I have no recollection of that."

Silence landed hard. I cleared my throat and said, "I understand you saw Cricket on the night she died?"

Ollie nodded. "She left here at 7 p.m. for a date, or so she said, and that was the last time I saw her."

"I'm so sorry for your loss, ma'am. I met your daughter that mornin', actually," I said. "She waited on me at the diner. She was a lovely and sweet girl with a lot of spunk. I liked her very much."

Ollie wiped tears away. "Ovida left here lookin' so pretty. She wore her new favorite gray suit. A skirt to her knees, a blouse, and a matching plaid jacket."

"And my red, open-toed pumps," Cookie said. "I'd lent them to her since she liked them so much. In fact, that's what they found first."

"T.J. from the mortuary mentioned they found her shoes," I said, "But we didn't get much more information than that."

"The day before they located Cricket, Sid Howard discovered one shoe about four feet from the west side of Highway 80," Cookie said. "Told the sheriff he'd seen it around the fourth of April but didn't think anythin' of it until he heard what Cricket had been wearin'. He brought it into town and gave it to Sheriff Apodaca. Officers came out to show us, and I identified the shoe as one of mine. Mom told them Ovida had them on that night."

"I knew right then somethin' had happened to my baby," Ollie said, her voice breaking.

"Mama," Cookie said.

Tears slid down Ollie's face, but she continued, "She'd never have let anythin' happen to your shoes. She knew you liked them very much too."

"Do you still have the heel?" Richard asked.

"No, they took it with them. I've not seen it since," Cookie said.

"And where does this Sid Howard live?" I asked.

For the first time, Willie spoke up. "He lives in Mesilla Park."

I jotted that down. "Thank you. We will go talk to him."

"Did the officers say what they were going to do with the shoe?" Richard asked.

"From what I remember," Cookie replied, "they said they'd take it to Sheriff Apodaca."

Cookie's husband, Carl, laughed. It was short and harsh, causing us all to turn toward him.

"A lot of good that did. The man has done nothin' with any of the information he was given. Absolutely nothin'," Carl spat, his accent making me think of Texas.

"Carl..." Cookie started.

"No, they should know what kind of man they're dealin' with." He stood and paced away before turning to face us. "Early on, I gave Apodaca the names of three possible suspects that they should look at. I'd asked around town and found out who she'd been hangin' with that night, and I told the sheriff."

"Who were those men you mentioned to him?" I asked.

"Jerry Nuzum, Luther Mosley, and Lauren Welch," he replied.

I'd heard the name Jerry Nuzum before but couldn't place it.

"It wasn't Lauren," Cookie said.

"Who's that?" I asked.

Ollie spoke up. "He is a bus driver that Cricket dated a while back."

"And he was cleared?" I prodded.

Cookie nodded. "He saw her outside the DeLuxe Café about 6:15 or 6:30 that evenin' in her waitress uniform on the corner of May and Main. But they confirmed he went home and out to a movie with his wife and kids when she disappeared."

"We should still talk to him," Richard said.

"My understandin' is he left on a bus on April 1st and hasn't returned."

"That's suspicious," I said.

"Word is his leavin' had to do with a failin' marriage," Cookie said, "But I'm sure you'll still wanna speak to him."

I jotted down to locate Lauren Welch for a chat.

Carl shoved his hands into his pockets. "I did find out where Mosely was and let the sheriff know. Three days after I gave him that information, he still hadn't gone to Hot Springs to see the man." Carl rubbed his chin before shoving his hands into his pockets. "Why wouldn't he go talk to the man? He'd been out with Cricket that night!"

"He didn't even follow up on the car information Carl gave him either," Willie added.

This got my attention. "Car information?"

Carl nodded, arms now crossed in front of his chest. "I located a car fittin' the description of the vehicle Cricket supposedly entered early in the mornin' on the thirty-first. One officer who saw her mentioned the type of car it was to me, you see? I gave the information about it to Apodaca as well. He did nothin'. That's why I doubt he'll do anythin' with the shoe. But you can ask and see."

"What kind of car?" I asked.

"Dark sedan with state plates," Carl said, his eyes boring into mine as if to make sure I understood what he was getting at.

"As in Santa Fe people," I said.

"Yes," Carl said. "But do you think they'll look into that? Hell no. Protect their own first, the hell with an innocent girl." He stopped and after a second said, "If you'll excuse me."

He left the room, and Cookie excused herself as well, following him.

"He's really upset," Willie said. "He worked hard to get information to help find her in time, but they did nothin'. Hell, they didn't even announce she was missin' until five days after momma talked to Sheriff Apodaca. Thought she'd run away. As if she'd do that."

"Willie, you need to watch what you say," Ollie scolded in a hushed tone.

"I don't care what him or his group of thugs threaten. I'll say it. They dropped the ball, and my twin sister is dead."

I could hear the threat of tears in his voice, but he swallowed it down, his face red with fury.

"Ollie, when did you report Cricket missing?" I asked.

Hands quietly settled in her lap, she wrung a hanky that must've been balled up in her hand before. "I rang up Sheriff Apodaca at eight in the mornin' on Friday, April first."

I jotted that down. "When did he announce that to the public?"

Willie spoke up before his mom could. "Wednesday the sixth. Title said, 'Pretty Cruces Girl Is Missing Since Tuesday.' That would've been the fifth. She'd been gone since the thirtieth, Billy. By givin' the wrong day, how could people who saw her on the actual night she disappeared know to come forward?"

"It was a deliberate late start," Carl said from the hallway.

"You don't know that," Cookie said, coming around his tall frame back into the room. She had a tray with a pitcher of iced tea and a bunch of empty glasses. She set it on the coffee table, poured us each a glass, and handed me mine first. "It wasn't until the ninth that he urged people who knew anythin' about her to contact the sheriff's office."

I thanked her for the tea and took a drink.

"The ninth?" Richard said in my stead. "She'd been gone ten days at that point!"

Cookie handed him some tea. "Yes."

I could see she was giving herself something normal to do to keep herself grounded, and I understood that. I kept running my hand over the sofa I knew Cricket would have sat on, possibly napped on, maybe cried on. It was helping me.

"By the twelfth, I'd had enough," Ollie said. "I called Sheriff Apodaca and urged him to put together a group to go look for her."

"He wouldn't have if he'd not gotten a ton of pressure from the townspeople and news headlines," Carl commented as he came back into the room with a kitchen table chair. He positioned it beside the armchair and sat in it. "He recruited thirty Boy Scouts."

I about choked on my sip of tea. "What? He thought a bunch of young boys should go lookin' for her? What if they'd found her? Can you imagine how that would affect them at that age?"

"The boys who found her weren't much older," Cookie said, placing the pitcher back on the tray. Carefully, she sat in the armchair, adding, "Why, Charles Hawkins is only fourteen."

Richard sat back in his seat and my head dropped for a moment so I could hide my anguish. When I had control again, I looked up. "Was he the only one to find her?"

"No," Willie said. "He was with both Jerrys and Glenn. They're all older."

"Both Jerrys?" Richard asked.

"Sorry. There's Jerry and Glenn Smith as well as Jerry and Charles Hawkins," Willie explained. "All but Glenn are seventeen or older."

"Thankfully they had the Boy Scouts search east of the city," Ollie said. "Cricket was found some twelve miles south. So luckily, they were nowhere near her. I'd have hated for one of them ten-year-old boys to..." She broke off, and tears slid down her face.

Touching Richard's elbow with my own as nonchalantly as I could, I mentally said to him, "Lucky or intentional?"

"Good point," he mentally replied, and I moved my arm away.

"Do you think Jerry Smith would talk to us?" I asked.

Willie nodded. "Yeah, and he don't need no parental permission. He's nineteen. I could take you over there if you'd like."

"Willie, you have no idea if he'll be wantin' to talk about it, and to strangers. No offense," Ollie said.

"None taken," Richard replied.

"Momma, he'll want to help get justice for Cricket," Willie said.

"Well then, you best be headin' over there before it gets too late," Ollie told him.

Willie got up and headed to go fetch a spring jacket and a pair of shoes.

"We'll bring him right back, Ollie," Richard said. "We won't have him out late."

"Thank you. For that and for carin' about my girl. No one else is doin' anythin' and I just...I don't know what to do. I have friends tellin' me I had better be quiet and not push the investigation if I know what's good for me."

I stood and stepped over to squat in front of Ollie Coogler. I took her hands and looked up into her dark eyes. I let a bit of energy seep through my fingers into hers and said, "You can't tell anyone we were here either. You understand that, right? The more they think we're closing in, the more they'll run, and we need them to believe they're safe. You understand?"

She nodded, and I knew she did.

Richard turned to Ollie and asked, "Did your daughter have a purse with her?"

"Yes, a red leather bag. They say it wasn't ever located."

"Did she have a lot of money in it or anything?" I asked.

She shook her head. "Strangest thing...she left her wallet here. I thought she'd put it in her bag, but I found it after she left."

As we left, Richard and I used our powers on them all, except Willie since he was going with us, and made sure they would remember us, but when asked who we were or if they'd spoken to anyone else about the case, they had no specific recollection.

I hated doing it, but after what she'd said about how others were telling her she had to be careful, I wanted to verify she was as safe as I could make her. It was bad enough I might've been what got her daughter killed. I sure as hell wanted no more of the Coogler family in danger because of me.

Willie came out dressed for the chilly night air, since the sun might set before we got back. "I'm ready."

"Then let's go," I said.

The three of us said our goodbyes and left for the Smith home, and I honestly had more questions now than when we'd arrived.

5
MY SOUL IS A CHICKEN

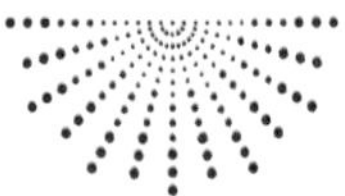

February 1879

I'm sorry, what?" I said, sitting up now. "I was told Scáthach owned my soul."

Kennedy sat up as well. "Your soul is in your body now. That's why you have free will when her werewolves do not."

"*Most* of her werewolves," Edward corrected.

"Present company excluded," Kennedy clarified, waving her other hand but not looking away from me. "Your gifts—"

"My curse, you mean," I corrected.

"No, I mean your *gifts*, and before you correct me again, young man, listen to what I have to tell you."

Her tone caught my attention, and I focused intently on her angelic face. "All right, I'm listenin'."

"Scáthach isn't evil."

Everyone around her snorted in disagreement.

"If you want to learn something," she said, her British accent heavier, "Then all of you need to hush."

We all shut our traps, and I motioned for her to continue.

With a nod of pleasure, she went on. "Scáthach is not evil. She loves chaos and her joy comes from seeing if the good guy wins or loses, and what that causes. Sure, she's the queen of the Dark Realm of the Otherworld, but mostly, she gets bored. She doesn't want you to die...nor does she wish for you to live. Scáthach wants to see how the story plays out and watch what you do with the talents she gave you."

Kennedy resituated herself and added, "That said, she doesn't wish the best for you either. She wants you to play the game. If you win, then she will applaud you like she likely does Edward. But she doesn't hold your soul, Billy Bonney. You do. It's just not free to escape this plane when you die while she is here, or you've earned it back...done enough good to fight back her dark, basically."

"That sounds to me like she owns it," I pointed out.

Kennedy shook her head. "No. She's trapped it in the game. Think of it like chickens. You don't own them. Sure, you can put them in a pen, but in the grand scheme of things, they're not yours, not really. Your soul is like that."

"My soul is a chicken?" I said with a laugh.

She lightly smacked my arm. "Yes...and it's in her cage. To be more specific, your soul is attached to this plane, not to her. The more spirits you set free, the lower those cage walls get and the stronger your wings become. All you must do is lower the fence and get your wings powerful enough to fly over, and your soul will be as free as your body. It's important to remember that."

She lay her hand gently on my arm. "Don't forget that, Billy. Stay the course, and you'll free your soul from the game."

* * *

April 1949

Richard, Willie, and I pulled up outside the Smith home to find two young men working on the yard out front.

"The taller one, that's Jerry," Willie pointed out.

We parked and got out of the vehicle just as both boys came over to see the new car and who drove it up to their home.

"Willie, what's goin' on?" Jerry asked.

"These here men need to talk to you about my sister. I know you two don't enjoy relivin' it, but they want to help find who killed her. Can ya help 'em?"

Jerry nodded. "She'd have wanted us to." He looked back at where they lived before pointing a ways down the road. "Mom and Dad don't probably want to hear us, though. Let's go out by the creek."

Everyone agreed, and we made our way down the street a bit. Finding a spot with some fresh grass growth, the young men sat down, and we joined them.

"I understand you boys were out huntin' rabbits," I said, to help start them off. "Where were you at?"

Glenn, the younger of the two, said, "That's right. We'd driven out to open desert land close to the Mesquite cemetery to hunt. In fact, we was runnin' toward a rabbit when Jerry here first saw her."

Jerry picked up the thread. "I wasn't even sure at first who it was. What it was."

"Why's that?" I asked.

Jerry looked toward Willie and then back to me.

Cricket's twin brother didn't miss a thing. "I can handle it, Jer. Just tell the truth."

Jerry took a deep breath and exhaled. "All right, if you say so, Will."

Willie urged him on with a hand motion.

Jerry picked a blade of grass and ran it between his fingers as he continued. "She'd been flattened, that's the best way I can put it. Her toes and fingers were blackened, curled, and tipped with red nail polish."

This image hurt my memory of her, but I jotted it down on my pad of paper. "What did y'all do next?"

"Well, I called the others over, and we decided we best get the sheriff. But, honestly, sir, we found her by accident. I was sure if we left, we'd never find that spot again. Plus, I didn't want to leave her alone." He paused and wet his lips. "She'd been alone long enough, I figured, so I stayed with her and sent the boys to call the sheriff."

Willie reached out and patted his friend's shoulder to show what Jerry had said and done mattered to him. Me personally, I had to fight not to reach out and hug the kid, seeing as it choked me up a bit myself.

Richard stepped in, looking at Glenn. "You and the other two boys went where?"

"We drove back to their house to call the cops. Then we went over to the Carpenter's store to wait for 'em."

"They then followed you all to where Jerry waited," I said.

"Yes, sir," Glenn replied.

"Who all came out?" Richard asked.

"Just Officer Roy Sandman," Glenn said.

Jerry tossed some grass. "They lead Sandman to where I was, and we showed him the body. When Apodaca arrived, he…well, he did somethin' weird."

This got Willie's attention. "Like what?"

"He lifted her skirt to look and then confirmed for us it was her."

Everyone shared looks, but Willie laughed. "It's not what you think. She had a scar from a burn on her left leg. Easy to see in a bathing suit, and we've been swimmin' with his family before."

I breathed a sigh of relief, but it prompted me to ask the next thing that came to mind. "We spoke to Tommy Graham. He said her skirt was down when he got there to pick her up. Is that how you found her?"

The boys shared a glance, and I knew.

"Ya covered her up, didn't you?" I asked.

The boys looked down and nodded.

"I know we're not supposed to bother evidence, but Willie, I couldn't let her be found with her skirt up around her neck or nothin'."

Willie patted Jerry again. "I appreciate it, man. She would've too."

"Tell me," Richard said, "How did Apodaca react when he got there?"

"He paced around the site, swingin' his arms…you know, like folks do when they are upset and stuff."

"Understandable," I muttered as I jotted it down.

"There is one thing I heard a border patrolman say the other day, though," Jerry mentioned. "He said that the killer must know the area where they dumped her really well."

This got my attention, and I looked up. "How so?"

"To get to where her body was by car, you'd have to turn off a canal-bank road and curve on down it about half a mile or so before turnin' west to take you to where we found her," Jerry said. "We only know the area ourselves because we like to rabbit hunt out there. It's miles of desert with a ton of mesquite bushes that grow three to five feet tall, all around the arroyos. Perfect places for rabbits to live."

Glenn and Willie nodded at this as if I didn't know where to hunt rabbits, but I didn't correct them and merely returned the gesture before writing stuff down.

"Did they try to bury her?" Richard asked.

"Yes, sir," Glenn said. "They'd thrown a bit of sand over her. Maybe it had originally been more, but you know how the winds out here get this time of year."

Richard and I both hummed in agreement at that in unison.

"To be honest," Jerry said, "the image of her like that is burned into my brain, and I wish it wasn't. But I'm glad we found her when we did."

I shut my small notebook. "So am I, Jerry. So am I."

* * *

With the memories of all three boys tampered with, we dropped Willie off at home and headed back to the Amador Hotel. We stopped in my room first to go over all the things we'd learned that day before separating so we could spruce up for an evening out with Kit.

Wanting to look nice, I pulled on my tailored black suit over a white button-down and a black vest buttoned up snug. Tying up my two-tone wingtips, black and white, I put on my belt with my guns which hid well under my dress jacket. Tie in place, I headed out to get Brewer.

When he came to the door, I gave him a low whistle. "Well, the old farmhand cleans up well."

Brewer shut his door and locked it, "Do shut up, Billy," he said, but there was a smile on his face.

Richard had opted for a navy blue pin-striped suit and white button-down which he paired with a brown pair of Moc Toe shoes.

Straightening his tie with one hand he placed his brown fedora on his head with the other. "We shouldn't keep the lady waiting."

I spun my black Homburg hat on my finger before setting it on my head. "No, we should not."

As we descended the stairs into the lobby, we saw Kit waiting on us. It was the first time I'd seen her without her maid uniform. She'd let down her curly red hair and used a wide headband to hold it back from her face. She wore a simple green dress with a matching jacket that she'd paired with stockings and a low heel.

She smiled when she saw us and gave a light wave.

We made our way down to her.

"Good evenin', Miss Bell," I said, "You look lovely."

"Why, thank you. I refuse to wear that uniform when I don't have to. And I must say, you two look ready for a night out."

"Shall we head up to the bars on Main?" I suggested. "It's a nice evenin' out for this time of year."

Kit grabbed her dark gray dress coat from where she'd draped it. "Of course."

Richard, without missing a beat, gently took it from her and held the coat out for her to slip into. She hesitated, then with a smile, she allowed him to help her into it.

Heading out of the hotel onto Amador Avenue, we walked up to Main Street, turned left, and headed north toward the bars and diners, where the town's nightlife was found.

"I take it you were worried of big ears in there," I said.

"Yes," Kit replied. "The louder the better, so we can talk freely about Cricket and Fletcher. Besides, a lot of those who work at the courthouse kitty-corner from the hotel come over there to drink and blow off steam. I want nothin' to do with 'em."

"Is Happy Apodaca one of those people?" Richard prodded.

Her violet eyes slid to the side to look at him. "Yes. Is he a person of interest?"

"No idea, but he certainly is an asshole," I replied.

"William!" Richard scolded me.

Kit laughed. "You don't need to be watchin' your language around me. I grew up with a father who'd been in the military and a bunch of brothers. If I've not heard it, it doesn't exist, boys."

Richard shoved his hands into his pant pockets. "Still."

With a laugh, she hooked her arm through the crux of his elbow before placing her other hand on my shoulder. "I'm not in the least surprised that he'd be of interest after what he said to Mrs. Eloise Ellis."

"Do tell!" I said as we made our way down the road.

"Well, I was around the corner of the hotel, comin' in for the second half of my shift as she was leavin'. Ran right into Happy, she did, and he threatened her. Told her to be careful what she said, he didn't want to bring back any more dead girls."

"Are you serious?" Brewer said.

"Very. I asked about and seems she was talkin' about the Cricket case in the bar while havin' lunch with her friends. He got wind and shut it down."

"So there's no question he's involved somehow," Richard said.

"No, sir," she said as we became more surrounded by people in town for nightlife. "The real question is though, do you two play shuffleboard?"

I raised an eyebrow at her. "Richard is actually pretty good at the game."

The corners of Richard's mouth ticked up a bit, and I saw his ruddy German cheeks go a darker red.

"I take it there is a place to play here?" I asked.

"Yep. Couple places. But I'm thinkin' we should visit the Del Rio bar; it's next to the Deluxe Café."

"Sounds good to me," I told her.

"It's also one of the places Cricket spent time the night she disappeared," she told us.

"It's sounding better and better," I replied.

"I thought you'd say so," she said with a wink.

We walked past the Deluxe Café to the Del Rio bar. It was still early enough that we found a spot at the bar itself and took a seat. We ordered drinks and toasted to Ovida.

A few moments later, the bartender stepped back over to us. "Did I hear you toast to Miss Cricket?"

"Yes, sir, you did. They buried her today," I told him.

Hearing the emotion in my voice, the man soberly nodded. "She was in here that night, ya know."

They taught me that when a door opens, you walk through it, and so I did. Looking up into his eyes, I tapped his hand, sending a sliver of energy into him. "Tell us more."

I saw the flash of my power travel across his eyes. "She walked in here around 9:30 in the evenin'. Sat here at the bar and talked to me. Ordered a drink."

"Anyone join her?" I asked, pulling out my notebook.

"Yeah, Mr. Green Eyes," the bartender said, absentmindedly cleaning a glass.

"Pardon me?" Richard said. "Is that his actual name?"

"Oh no, it's just what people call him...bein' that he always wears these glasses with green-tinted lenses in them. Proper name is Luther Mosley."

It was one of the names Carl had given us. "How long did they stay here?"

"Until she got so drunk that she knocked over her drink. Then he took her to go sober up somewhere from what I understand."

"Do you know where?" Kit asked.

"Nope, but they came back around 11:30 p.m. She seemed better, but Mosley still bought them each a drink."

"Wait, what?" Richard said. "That seems counterproductive."

Bartender shrugged. "She was drunk but not as bad as before and everythin' seemed okay until..." The bartender looked around, dropped his voice, and said, "Until Jerry Nuzum came in."

There was that name again, the one that sounded so familiar. I was about to ask, but Richard beat me to it.

"Wait, *the* Jerry Nuzum? The one who plays for the Pittsburgh Steelers?"

Kit piped up. "Yeah, he lives here. Played ball at A&M. In the off-season he lives here to finish up credits."

"That's really cool," Richard said, hitting my arm.

I knew nothing about football, so I left that alone. "What time did he come in?"

"Maybe midnight?" the bartender offered. "I'm not sure. I do know that Cricket left with him while Mr. Green Eyes was hangin' out with some of his pals. But then he sees somethin' outside and scurries out. From what I heard later, he and Jerry got into a fight out there over Cricket."

"Like, it came to blows, or they argued?" Kit said, digging for clarification.

"Just some shoutin' and shovin', nothin' more. Word is, Jerry grabbed Cricket and tried to force her into his car. That's all I know. Must not have been too big of a deal though, 'cause the three of 'em were back in here playin' shuffleboard until closing. People are weird."

"That they are," I said.

"Do you know where I could find Mr. Green Eyes?" Kit said, giving the bartender a flirty look.

He fell for it. "He hangs around here most nights. You may even see him tonight."

"Thanks so much," I said, tapping his hand again, slipping a small amount of power into him. "If anyone asks what you told us, it was just that she was in here that night, nothin' more."

He nodded, and I knew he'd be safer for my interfering.

Kit, Richard, and I took our drinks to a booth to talk about what we'd learned and then saw if Richard could hold on to his winning streak at shuffleboard. He did, and we didn't leave until around 11:30 p.m. Then, because I wanted to walk past the Coogler residence and make sure everything seemed to be all right, we followed Griggs Street west to South Water Street and took a left.

As we passed the Coogler home, everything was dark, save for a candle burning in the window of the front bedroom. I knew it was lit for Cricket, and my chest felt tight. Likely hearing the hitch in my breath when I saw it, Richard placed one of his enormous hands on my shoulder.

"I'm okay."

He nodded and took his hand back as we continued to wander down the middle of the empty street, talking and laughing about how Richard had kicked our butts in shuffleboard. We had just hit the intersection of Bowman and South Water when a small pack of large animals trotted onto the road. For a moment I thought they were dogs, but then the five of them formed a line to block our way, their golden eyes locking on us as low growls filled the air.

"Well, shit." I looked up at the moon. "Richard, get her out of here."

"What?" she asked.

Kit got nothing else out of her mouth though, except the shout that escaped her lips when Richard scooped her up and they disappeared in a flash, using his abnormal speed to whisk her back to May Street.

"Guess it's just us now, fellas. Look, I have no beef with you at this moment. So why don't y'all go on home or go hunt a deer or somethin'. I have no desire to kill you right now. I have other issues on my mind. Call it your lucky night."

I turned left on Bowman only to find another five of them stopping me from going in this direction as well. I sighed.

"You can't take them all on," I heard a man say and looked around for who it could be, but he stayed in the shadows.

"You wanna make a bet," I muttered under my breath.

The wolves growled and appeared to be on the verge of lunging.

"Show yourself!" I shouted. When he didn't, I opted for another tactic. Arms spread wide, I spun about in a circle. "What do you want?"

"For you and your partner to leave town. Go tonight. Hell, go tomorrow morning if you must, but leave and don't come back."

"And if we don't?"

All ten wolves stepped closer.

"You die," the man said.

I clasped my hands behind my back, close to my guns. "You sure about that?"

He laughed. "Like I said, you can't take all of them on."

"There's what, ten of them and one of me? You're right, it's not a fair fight."

"Exactly. So, leave."

A lopsided grin slid up my face. "Oh, I wasn't sayin' it wasn't fair in their favor, but mine. You'll need more than ten to…"

Five more showed up, blocking me from taking Bowman further west.

"Ask and you shall receive," the voice said.

I heard the pounding of four very large paws heading my way and grinned. "So, you got fifteen…so that leaves, what…eight for me and seven for you or do you want eight of them? I really hate uneven numbers."

"What are you talking about?" the voice said.

"Oh, sorry, I'm not talkin' to you."

Richard, now in wolf form, came into view as he ran under the lamp-light at the intersection of Bowman and South Water to stand beside me, his head at my elbow. Examining the other werewolves more carefully, I saw that Richard was bigger, and not merely in height or length, but in muscle mass as well. His coat was even more beautiful than I remembered, and I thought that time in Oregon had been good for him.

Richard bared his teeth and growled, the silver light seeping into his eyes.

"I was talkin' to him," I finally clarified. "Not you…whoever you are."

"A man too chickenshit to step out and fight, that's who," Kit said, stepping into the light as she came up behind Richard.

"What in the name of all that is holy are you doin' here, Miss Bell?" I looked at Richard. "Really?"

Since he was in wolf form, he couldn't shrug, so she shook.

"Uh-huh. I see how it is."

She smiled, and it wasn't one that screamed of fun jokes and flirting. It was cold and calculated.

I stepped in close to Kit, my nose merely an inch above hers, looked her in the eye, and whispered intently, "I know you're a witch, but I want nothin' happenin' to you. So, please go somewhere safe."

"If you know what I am, you know I can take these sons of bitches on," she said.

"No, I don't."

"Then maybe you need a demonstration," she replied, her grin wicked.

Before I could say anything else, Kit murmured a few words in Gaelic that had her eyes flashing to a brighter version of her already unique lavender blue. "There are fifteen, I say that's nice and fair. You boys take five and I got the rest."

I laughed. "Oh, darlin', it's not nice to take my fun away. Five each."

She lifted one shoulder, nodded in agreement, and the three of us gathered together back-to-back, each facing five wolves a piece.

"Race ya!" I said with a chuckle.

"You're on," she muttered, squatting to place her hand on the ground.

Before I could grab my guns, I felt a rumble like a minor earthquake vibrate under our feet, and the first five wolves that had stepped into the game leapt into the air with a yelp. They landed and writhed in pain, screaming horribly…until they didn't.

"Dear God," I said. "What in the hell?"

She stood and threw a blade she'd pulled from God only knew where. It flew with deadly accuracy, embedding itself into the throat of one of my wolves that had started for me when I'd faced her.

He dropped and in death, shifted to his naked, human form. This caused the other nine to run at us at the same time. I pulled my Walther PPK/S with silencers and shot my other four, taking their lives. Souls of the wolves hit me at once and I had to steady myself to accept them or go dizzy with soul-drunk brain.

I swayed a bit and stumbled. Which is why I didn't see one of Richard's wolves get up from the ground and run at us. By the time I turned, I was too late.

* * *

February 1879

It was getting late, and all but Kennedy were calling it a night. That's when I found a moment to speak with Zahara alone.

"Why didn't you tell me Scáthach didn't own my soul?"

Zahara's face told me nothing, but she said, "I didn't know."

I found that hard to believe. "You're one of her first creations on this land; how is that possible?"

"I wasn't her favorite. I also was close with Eli, and I'm sure that fact kept her from sharing things with me. Kennedy was Scáthach's pride and joy."

I snorted and looked toward the covered wagon that Kennedy had just gotten into. "And ya see where that got her."

Zahara walked past me, bent to pick up some more wood, and tossed it on the fire. "Yes. Though I think you and I both knew you still had your soul. You'd make different decisions if she'd split it between you and her."

"Like the wolves do," I stated, shoving my hands in my pockets.

"Yes." Zahara picked up more wood and added it to the fire.

"I know there's not much difference between her owning it and it being attached to this plane. It's still a curse. But I feel better about it now. Can't explain why. Just do. Night." I kissed her on the cheek and went over to my bedding.

Climbing under my blanket, which I barely needed with the warm bubble of magic around us, I placed my hands behind my head and let my mind drift. There was something staring me in the face with all the new knowledge that would help me, but I didn't know what it was.

"Billy?"

"Yeah, Dick?"

"Think we'll reach his place tomorrow?"

"Yeah. We must leave earlier than usual so Kennedy will have to stay in the wagon for a bit, but we should reach his place not long after nightfall."

"Think the Sheriff of Lincoln is still lookin' for us?" Tom asked.

"Oh, I would bet all the ammunition I own on it. I have a plan on figurin' that out. We'll talk in the mornin'. Get some sleep. It's goin' to be a long last leg of the journey."

Laying there, I let my mind wander a bit. If truth be told, I enjoyed Kennedy. That vivacious female energy was a nice addition to the group. Her smile though…it reminded me of Paulita Maxwell. They were very different women by far, but there was this light in them that was the same and it made me smile to think on it.

I touched the pocket where I carried that hanky she'd given me at the horse race. It didn't smell like her anymore, but it made my heart sing to have it. I was soft on that girl but I sure as hell wasn't going to tell anyone else.

Shaking my head at the notion, I rolled over and closed my eyes. Doing my best to let my mind clear, I tried to follow my own advice and get some rest.

6
THE TRUTH ABOUT MISS BELL

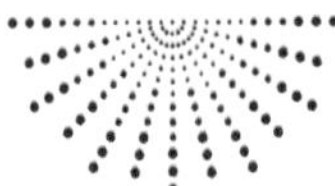

April 1949

I dropped to the ground and rolled, but the wolf was over me in a second. That's when hands, sparkling with electricity, gripped the wolf's head and electrocuted him to death. He shifted to his human form, leaving a dead, naked man on top of me. I swore, shoved him off, and rolled out from under him.

Kit grinned. "So that's seven for me and four for you."

Richard trotted over on all fours, and I saw four dead men in the road behind him, bloody and broken.

"And four for you," she said to him. "I won the bet."

Damn it if she hadn't.

Standing, I only had one thing to say. "Who the hell are you?"

Before Kit could answer my question, Richard bumped my hand, and I heard him mentally say, "Call it in."

I put my gun back in its holster at my back. "Shit, you're right. Let's go. Now."

"But the man—" Kit said.

"Not this time, darlin'," I said. Grabbing her by the arm, we headed to the Amador Hotel, where I accessed the phone in the lobby and made a coded call to headquarters for cleanup.

"Sir?" The young man at the desk said.

"Yes?"

The desk clerk handed me a folded piece of paper. "This telegram came for you."

"Telegram?" Kit asked.

"Some people are old-fashioned," I said, knowing exactly who it would be from.

We turned toward the stairs as Richard walked back in, dressed in his suit and tie again, and the three of us headed silently up to my room.

With the door shut, I turned to Kit. "Okay…spill it, missy…spill it all."

Kit shook her head and pulled a small rock out of her purse. Starting at the door, she dragged it along the walls as she whispered words of a spell until she made her way back to where she began.

Placing the rock at the door itself, she calmly turned to face us. "Okay, now we can talk."

"I thought you were an earth witch," I mused, "Or that's what Richard smelled. You know, plants, herbs, healing…"

"You…smelled me?" she asked Richard.

He shrugged. "It sounds worse than it is."

"It's who he is. A wolf with a talented nose that saves my ass regularly, so let it go."

"Smelled me?"

I rolled my eyes to the ceiling. "Patience, Billy…patience."

Kit pulled the headband out of her hair and shook the wide curls free. "I am a child of the earth, you are correct."

"Yeah, but what you did wasn't plant based," I pointed out.

"I work with plants some, and I'm good, but I'm better with stone, the living rock of the ground, and the power they hold…I harness the energy of ley lines."

"But…there are none going through Las Cruces," I said, and she looked impressed. "I checked on that before we left Santa Fe."

She sat in one of the pretty and dainty chairs that decorated the room. Crossing her legs, she elegantly did the same with her wrists atop her knee. "No. But we are in the center of a triangle of them, and I can pull on the energy they exude toward each other as they speak to one another."

"I've never heard of that," Richard said, sitting up.

"I'm sure you haven't. Las Cruces is in a special position for this. The largest line of the triangle is the bottom, and it's one of the primary lines. It runs through El Paso."

"Which is why your mother lives there," I offered.

She clucked her tongue and scratched the back of her head. "About that..."

I sat on the edge of the bed. "Out with all of it."

She sighed. "My *trainer* lives there. My mother lives elsewhere, and no, I won't tell you where. I've not seen her much since I began to train to fight Scáthach's demons."

"And why would you *choose* to do that?" I asked since if I'd had the choice, I wasn't sure I would have chosen this life.

"My family has fought Scáthach's children for centuries. In fact, some of my family fought with Elias Story."

I stopped breathing for a moment. "Who?"

She leaned forward and wagged a finger at me. "Don't play stupid with me, Spirit Warrior. You damn well know who Elias was." She turned her gaze to Richard. "I've heard of you too. There's been talk of a Spirit Warrior who has a wolf familiar. I take it that's you?"

"I am not a familiar!" Richard spat as I laughed. "I'm his Beta, thank you very much."

Her eyes grew wide. "What? How is that even possible?"

"Long story," I replied blandly. "We're not here to talk about our past. All you need to know is that Scáthach doesn't have control or pull over his soul. He is his own man."

She rolled her eyes. "That's evident. Look, I'll tell you about me, but once you feel you can trust me, I want to know more about you."

I considered, looked to Richard, who nodded, and replied, "Deal."

"Good." She sat back and relaxed. "My proper name isn't Catherine Bell. But that name keeps me safe. My family name throughout history is Stow. My great-great-great-grandfather was John Stow."

Richard and I looked at one another and just shrugged.

"Yeah, I have no idea who that was," I told her.

She blew a strand of hair out of her face. "John Stow and John Pass?"

I shook my head.

"How old are you both again?" she asked.

Richard opened his mouth, and I stopped him. "That's not the point. I wish you'd get to yours."

She sighed. "The men who made the Liberty Bell?"

"I've heard of the Liberty Bell," I said, pointing at her.

"Well gee, I'm proud of you," she said flatly. "Look, if you go back in history, you'll see how my grandfathers died young. That had to do with their life of fighting Scáthach's demons."

Richard flinched at the term "demon," but she didn't seem to notice.

"Not everyone in the family line has made this choice. But I had the aptitude at a young age, and the interest, so they sent me to live with a woman who trained me. We eventually moved to the east coast, then out to Texas when activity grew there. We followed them here. Or rather, I did.

"That said, they removed my name from the family history so that Scáthach cannot find me. But I'm done hidin'. The minute I saw her name on the bedside table in Fletcher's blood, I figured my time to fight had arrived. Then you called to say you were comin' back, and I knew for sure.

"I was always told that I'd know when it was time to come out of the shadows to fight to save this world from her, and I do. That time is now."

* * *

February 1879

The minutes ticked by slowly as we waited for the sun to set that next day. We'd reached our destination that afternoon but wanted Kennedy to ride into town with us on her horse versus in her coffin. I sent Gaax out to alert our friend with a note that we'd be there by dinner.

Once the sun was down, we went into her wagon and opened the coffin. It was large, with enough room for two, and filled with the softest of cushions and sheets. Richard had killed a deer, and as she sat up with a yawn, he handed her a mug of warm blood.

She downed it and smiled. "I really could get used to this kind of treatment, gentlemen."

I laughed. "Don't count on it. We did this today, so you'd be ready to leave sooner. We're about a mile from the home. Find your best human-looking outfit, Kennedy. It's time to go pretend you are one."

She nodded. "Understood. You boys scoot now, and I'll be ready in a few minutes."

I eyed her suspiciously. She was never ready in minutes. "I'll believe it when I see it."

She winked at me, and we left her alone to get ready. We'd only been back at the fire for two or three minutes when she joined us.

"Well, I'll be," Tom said. "That's the fastest I've ever seen you be ready. What magic happened in there?"

Kennedy skipped to Tom and kissed him on the cheek. "And good morning to you, too, darlin'." She bounced over to sit on the stump by Zahara. "I rarely use vampire speed to get ready. I like to take my time... enjoy the feminine process of preparing for the day. But you said quick, so I use the vamp speed. Tell me, Billy Bonney, do I look human enough for you?"

She looked the part. Hair pulled back from her heart-shaped face with a simple fall of blond hair behind her head with no elaborate curls. She'd chosen a road-worthy dress in dusty blue that made her eyes stand out more than usual, and she'd not over-layered her petticoats.

"I have to admit, I'm impressed," I told her as I let some energy seep from me into Colonel to help his eyes and the weariness he felt from such a long ride.

"I have clothes for all occasions in there. Sometimes my meal ticket is of the working man variety, and it helps if I appear to be the same class."

"Like the theatre," I decided, easing up into the saddle. "I enjoyed doing plays in school."

"Why, Mr. Bonney, you surprise me daily," Kennedy said.

Zahara rolled her eyes and handed Richard the spelled coins for him to use. "Yes, yes, he's a surprise to all. Now get on your horse. I want to be there in time for dinner. Unlike *some* people here, I have not had food yet, and I'm starving."

"When your diet is one thing and one thing only, it makes it easier in some ways," Kennedy stated.

"Harder in others, I would imagine," I offered.

Kennedy headed over to her horse and mounted. "That is horribly true."

We made good time and arrived in Las Tablas about fifteen minutes later. Richard activated one of Zahara's spelled coins to change his facial appearance, and we approached the cabin.

As I leapt down from Colonel, the door opened, and a young man stepped out. He was now sixteen and appeared to have healed completely of his wounds from that horrible night in July.

"Eugene!" I shouted.

"Billy," he returned in kind and gave me a hug the moment I dismounted.

I let go of the young man, and Tom moved in to embrace him next.

"It sure is good to see you up and around," Tom told him, ruffling Eugene's hair. "You gave us quite a scare."

After Tom and I had escaped the burning McSween home that night in July, we'd believe Yginio Salazar, who went by Eugene, to be dead at fifteen, and it had broken our hearts. Truth be told, they had shot him multiple times, and he lay there as the McSween home burned, playing dead as Dolan's men danced around the fire. One drunken man had even threatened to shoot Eugene in the head, but the gunman's friend had convinced him not to, saying it wasn't worth wasting his bullets on a Hispanic boy.

Once all the men had passed out and the fire died down, Eugene dragged himself a mile to a family member's home. They had nursed him back to health, along with treatment from Dr. Appel. His family brought him up here to get away from town, but now, we were bringing that drama to his door.

I cringed. "I'm so sorry to dump the usual town trouble on you, Eugene. But we need someplace to lie low for a bit."

Eugene took me by the shoulders. "You are my friend, Billy. You are always welcome."

I nodded at the sentiment. "And you are mine. Whenever I can pay this back, all you need to do is ask."

There was a clearing of a throat behind me. I turned and laughed. "Sorry, my manners got lost in sentiment. Eugene, these are Tom's and my travelin' companions. Zena, Rose, and Michael."

Eugene's smile was wide, and he shook their hands. "It's lovely to meet you. Please, come in and make yourself at home."

I looked at Kennedy, who'd I'd introduced as Rose since she said it was her middle name, and she smiled.

"You behave," I mouthed when her eyes locked on my face.

"Don't I always?" she whispered so quietly only the supernaturals could hear her.

"No," I said.

Kennedy winked, but as she walked past me, I grabbed her by the arm and quietly said, "If anything happens to Eugene, I'll kill you. If you believe I can't, think again."

Her blue eyes stared into mine, and her playful air became sullen. "I don't shit where I sleep, Billy. I know better."

"Good." I let her go, and she wandered into the house.

Zahara, who I'd named Zena, stopped and looked at me. "She'll behave."

"I'm holdin' ya to that," I replied, and waited on Brewer.

"Here's to hopin' the tweak on the spell works and I'm not givin' my name ever five minutes," he said to me.

I laughed and walked in with him. "But it's so humorous."

"For you maybe."

I would've said something else, but we both stopped when we smelled it.

Food.

"Hot damn, Eugene, I'll muck all the stalls for you tomorrow for a servin' of whatever smells so damn good."

"My aunt's stew. Made enough for y'all since I knew you'd be here by dinnertime."

Ten points for Gaax.

Eugene pulled me aside. "Do any of them know the truth about you?"

I nodded. "They all do, but I'd like to keep it to just them, okay?"

"They know you helped heal me?" he prodded.

I shook my head. "And we'll keep that between us."

Eugene smiled. "As you wish."

I followed him into the dining area and took a seat. It really was good to see him. Even if I didn't know how long we'd be able to stay.

"You not hungry, miss?" the woman spooning up stew asked of Kennedy.

"I already ate, actually," she said. "How about I go take care of the horses, and I'll catch you all later?"

Eugene stood. "Ma'am, there's no need to—"

"No, no, enjoy your time together. I'll be back." Kennedy nodded at me, and I watched her leave to go search the premises. I might trust Eugene, but I didn't trust his neighbors, at least not yet.

* * *

April 1949

That next morning, Richard and I walked up to the Deluxe Café for much-desired food and to meet with Duke.

"You trust this guy?" Richard asked me.

"Do I trust anyone other than you?"

"No," he said.

"Exactly. But we'll do the dance, get the story, and work from there," I added.

Richard grunted in understanding. "We havin' him take us to where her body was found?"

"That's the plan," I said, then pulled the telegram from the night before out and handed it to Brewer. "Read."

He plucked it from my hand, read it, and hummed. "So, he's on his way."

"Yes. The band will be back together again."

"Can we give him Duke?" Richard offered with hope on his face.

"No. Not until the cat's outta the bag."

Brewer sighed heavily and handed the telegram back to me. I shoved it into my inside jacket pocket as we stepped into the diner. The bell ringing above caused me to react just like a Pavlovian dog; the sound triggered my mind to hear Cricket say, "Sit wherever you like, cowboy."

I turned toward where I'd heard her for the first time, but she wasn't there, of course. Sorrow hit me again, and I sighed.

Everything else was the same, though. The fifty by twenty-foot diner smelled like breakfast heaven. Maple syrup, bacon, sausage, fresh bread, and real butter. To the right of the front door was a glass case with a cash register on it. Past that, on the north wall to my right was a long counter with stools, while on the left were booths, each with their own jukebox. In the center of the space were four tables that sat four people at each.

The door shut behind us, and I could suddenly hear Vaughn Monroe singing *Riders in The Sky* on full blast from one booth, and cheers went up from a table of college-age kids, causing the table who'd chosen the song to sing along.

"It's like they knew you were goin' to be walkin' in," a voice said from our left.

Turning about, I saw Katie. The waitress who'd waited on me along with Cricket that day back in March. She looked tired; her eyes were red-rimmed, and though she was usually pale, it was now more than her normal skin tone; it was grief. I hurt for her.

"Pardon me?" Richard asked her.

Katie's hands were full of dishes she was taking to the back, so she merely nodded toward the booth playing the song. "The music," was all she said.

I stepped toward her and gently touched her elbow. "How are you doin', Katie?"

Tears swam in her eyes. "How do you think I'm doin'? Have you heard?"

I nodded. "I'm devastated."

She blinked, and a tear fell. "Damn it. I promised I wasn't goin' to cry out front like this."

I wiped the tear from her cheek. "I saw nothin', and no one else did either. Return those to the kitchen and then take a minute for yourself. I'm sorry I asked."

She shook her head. "No need to be sorry, Agent Kidwell. It's not your fault. I've been like this for days. I wanted to go to her funeral yesterday, but her momma wanted it private. I'll go see her later."

"Please, call me Billy," I said kindly.

She nodded and opened her mouth, but before she could say anything, the bell in the back rang.

"Order up for table four!"

"That's me," Katie said, forcing a smile on her face. "Please, take that open booth, and I'll come back to wipe it down and get your orders."

"Thanks, Katie," I said, but she was already moving toward the back.

Richard took a seat on one side of the booth, and I sat beside him, both seats facing the door. This way we saved the other side for our new partner.

Duke walked in before Katie could come back, and we waved him over. He sat opposite us and removed his hat. Placing it beside him, he said, "Good mornin', fellas. How'd you sleep?"

I smiled at him, but I made damn sure it didn't touch my eyes. "Did you have anythin' to do with last night's show?"

He looked from me to Richard and back. "What are you talkin' about?"

I glanced at Richard. "What am I talkin' about, Richard?"

"Well, Billy, you'd be talkin' about fifteen canines with golden eyes, if you get my meanin', comin' to greet us on our way back to the hotel. Givin' us an ultimatum."

"I know nothin' about that," Duke said in his defense.

I stared him down to see if I could tell if he was lying. During this awkward silence, Katie came by.

"Good mornin', y'all," she said, and with a wet cloth in her hand, she wiped the table down. "Do you know what you want, or do you need a menu?"

I turned to look up at Katie. "Darlin', I'll have the same thing I had last time if I could."

She jotted that down on her pad of paper. "With extra bacon?"

I forced a smile. "Yes, ma'am."

"And you?" she said to Richard.

"Coffee, black. Six eggs scrambled with cheese. Two sausage patties, six pieces of bacon, toast, and a stack of pancakes."

Katie's eyebrows raised. "That just for you?"

"Yes, ma'am," he said, a bit sheepishly.

Brewer burned a lot of calories because of his condition, so I was used to this type of order.

"I'll have exactly what he's havin'," Duke said, pointing at Brewer.

Katie laughed. "All right, then. Breakfast feast for five comin' at ya in a few."

She disappeared and I said, "Now where were we? Oh yes, your pack ambushed us."

"I don't have a pack. I'm like you, Agent Baca, I'm on my own. Prefer it that way. Always have. Sure, I work for Happy Apodaca, but it's for the money. I'm not like that pack. I'm a lot older than them, and I'm not tainted."

This got my attention. "Tainted?"

"A lot of 'em started as feral, and a man named Petrov trained them to work for the law here. Before you ask, he's not here anymore. Moved on to the next job."

Things connected for me now. That explained why they were smaller than Brewer and why I had the honor of fighting a feral when I was here before. "They use 'em a lot?"

"Yeah. But don't underestimate them. They are ruthless and like the taste of blood more than those like Agent Baca and myself."

"Please, if we're going to work together, call me Richard."

Duke nodded. "Can do. So, tell me, what all did you find out yesterday?"

We filled him in on with some of what we'd learned, leaving out Kit and what she'd shared with us. We also left out what we were told by the Coogler family. I wanted nothing coming back on them. They had enough to deal with. We paused when Katie brought the coffee and picked up after she left. By the time she brought the mountain of food, we'd caught him up on what we wanted him to know.

"Thank you, Katie," I said.

With a nod, she left, and I wished I could help her feel better.

"So, what is on our plate today?" he asked.

I put salt and pepper on my eggs. "Where Cricket was found and shoes."

Duke raised an eyebrow. Then he must've remembered. "Ah yes, the red, open-toed pumps."

"Yes," Richard said, taking the salt and pepper from me. Using it, he continued, "We'll split up after the dumpsite. You and I will go talk to Max Johnson while Billy takes a crack at Sid Howard."

Duke took the shakers from Richard. "Sounds good to me. Anythin' else?"

I bit into my crispy bacon and hummed in happiness. "I think we should also see if we can find this Mr. Green Eyes."

"Also known as Luther Mosley," Richard added as he poured maple syrup on his pancakes.

"Problem is, he's a truck driver. Not even sure he lives here. We'll look into that too," I said.

"Then I suppose we need to look into that, too, before we split up. I should be able to get that information for you…I have access to state records at the sheriff's office."

"Well then, Duke, maybe havin' you along for the ride isn't such a bad thing after all," I said, and I nearly meant it.

7
KENNEDY'S THEORY

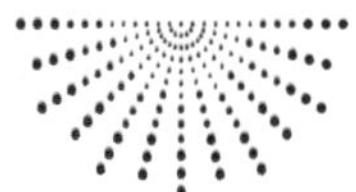

February 1879

Not five minutes after sunset, Kennedy came riding up to the house and leapt down from her horse. I was sitting out front enjoying some quiet when she strode up. I was looking down at the piece of wood I'd been carving when she stepped close enough that her laced-up boots over tailored riding pants that showed off the shape of her legs came into view.

Glancing up, I saw she'd paired those pants with a dress shirt and fitted vest. "Why, Miss Kennedy, aren't you a pretty picture in men's clothing."

"Let's go for a ride."

I raised an eyebrow. "Um…okay?"

"Colonel must need to run for a spell. Let's take him and my mare hunting."

"I never hate the sound of shootin' things," I said, standing up. "I'll be right back."

I went inside for my second six-shooter and rifle, snagged a warmer coat and my hat, and headed out.

"New look?" she said.

I stared down and noticed I'd grabbed Tom's black jacket. I had on dark pants to go with it. "Seems I snagged the wrong coat in my haste."

"It suits you, let's go."

"He can wear mine, I suppose," I said with a shrug, and we made our way to the stable.

Once I saddled Colonel, we were off, heading into the woods that filled the area at the base of the mountain. First, we took the horses for a good run, but when we slowed them down, I said, "What is it you wanted to talk to me about with no one else around?"

She laughed lightly, her head tilting back enough that it exposed her canine teeth better. "Nothing gets past you, does it, Billy Bonney?"

"Not usually," I said, and let us plod along in silence for a moment.

"I have a theory about what ties Scáthach to Mary's body, but I'm not sure yet. I've been reading over those notes I wrote in the journal I'd had with me that day Scáthach tossed me in the hole. You see, over the years we were together, she liked to over-share…especially in the beginning. For she was so proud of her accomplishments."

"Yeah, sounds like her," I muttered as we lazily rode along enjoying the night.

"In those notes, I have something that sparked my interest. I'd asked her once if she was so upset with Zahara why she didn't kill her.

"'I can't,' is what she said."

This got my attention. "Can't or won't?"

"Can't," Kennedy repeated. "Said that it would hurt her too much. Unbalance things." Then she ran her hands down the curves of the body she was in and added, "I like this body."

"You think if Zahara dies we can get her out of Mary? Um…I'm not killin' Zahara."

"I don't believe she meant Zahara specifically. I think she meant one of the three."

"Three?"

"The power of three. Remember, it wasn't just Zahara and me, there's one more. The first werewolf, Tarack, is out there too. I believe one of us three can force her out. We have the ability to disrupt her magic I think."

"So, do we or do we not need to track her first werewolf?" I asked.

"Eventually we do. Tarack is difficult to find, as Scáthach doesn't travel with him often. Only if she's up against a serious foe."

"The group of us might be serious enough for her to call him, now that I killed her Beta," I offered.

"Maybe. But if not, we will need to find him," Kennedy said.

There was quiet, the only sound was the horses' hooves in the snow.

Finally, I said, "Then that'll be what we'll do once we know what's going on further. Any idea where we'd even start?"

Kennedy laughed. "Hell no! But if we can, we could use his death."

"I'm sorry, I'm not following," I said.

"I think it would have to be something major to create a crack in her magic to release Mary. Natural disaster, maybe. Who knows? But there'd have to be death for life. That's my guess. The death of something magical would be best if my theory is correct. We should use Tarack."

"Have you told Zahara this plan?"

"Yes. We argued about it the other night. I thought she'd tell you or talk to me more about it, but she hasn't." Her blue eyes slid toward me. "So, *I'm* telling you."

Her words held two possible underlying messages, but I wasn't sure which one it was. Did she want me to talk to Zahara about it or just to back her in a group conversation?

Before I could say anything, Kennedy muttered, "She just isn't willing yet to make the hard decisions."

"And you are?" I pressed.

She looked me in the eyes, her gaze unwavering. "I am. Aren't you?"

"You know I am."

She turned away and stared out into the darkness of the wood. "I do."

When she didn't expound on that, I said, "And what do you want me to do with this information?"

"Nothing. At the moment," she said coyly. "I just want you aware…just in case."

I turned to her now. "In case of what?"

Kennedy shrugged. "No idea. I just wanted Scáthach's Spirit Warrior to know."

I nearly said I'd let Tom know, too, then swallowed it. Barely.

"You were about to say something?" she prodded.

No hiding anything from a vamp in the dark.

I inhaled deeply to settle myself before I lied. But instead, I caught the scent of wolf. My eyes grew wide, and I pointed at my nose.

She inhaled deeply and shook her head. "Nothing." She put her finger to her lips, so I'd be quiet, and she listened. Their existence registered on her face, and she thumbed to the west of us.

I nodded.

Kennedy touched her ear and showed me four fingers.

I mouthed the words, "Scouting party."

She nodded and then, with her fingers, she showed the option of running away or staying to fight.

I pulled both my six-shooters and grinned. Colonel moved beneath me in warning. I touched his neck and told him I knew.

Kennedy seemed happy as a pig in muck as she pulled her gun out.

Quietly we moved the horses behind the thickest pine trees, the mountain directly at our back, and waited. As the four came into view, she rode out behind them, and I charged out in front. Shooting first, I killed two before they even knew what had hit them.

My head swimming with their soul energy, I held onto Colonel and watched as Kennedy shot one, then the other.

"That seemed too easy," she said to me.

"Because it was. The others will be nearby and come toward the shots. These four were new and offered up as bait is my guess. Look at them."

They were young men with baby faces like me. It made my blood boil.

"From the east!" she shouted as she spun her horse about and lifted the rifle.

Ten wolves were upon us in a heartbeat. I shot and killed two and held onto Colonel, trying to breathe through the acceptance of those souls like Tom had been teaching me to do. This process helped me not to feel as dizzy, so I was able to shoot two more. However, I'd only wounded them, and they shook it off before charging toward us again.

Steadying my head, I shot and killed them. That meant I had six shots left. I saw Kennedy fire, killing another by blowing its head clean off with her rifle. When she went to shoot the next one, she got a 'click' and nothing. It was either jammed or empty, and I would've bet on the first.

Instead of panic, her face lit with excitement. Tossing the rifle to me, she said. "Use it if you can."

I caught it in one hand while shooting my six-gun with the other, taking another wolf down.

Trying to keep it all in focus, I watched as Kennedy pulled two long knives from somewhere and leapt from her horse with such grace that I was intrigued. Landing, she faced off with three wolves that had her pinned against a large pine. I was about to shoot the other two when she hissed at them, showing her teeth.

The wolves froze. They either didn't know what she was, or they did and were scared to death.

"My turn," she said, and with a speed I'd never seen, she sliced all three to pieces as the remaining two ran for their lives.

Covered in blood and loving it, or so it appeared, Kennedy grinned at me. "You really *do* know how to show a lady a good time."

I had no words. All I could do was laugh. "Why, Miss Kennedy, that was truly an education. Care to teach me how you use those long knives?"

"Sure thing. Now?"

I was going to say no, but why not? If there was ever a time, it was now.

I hopped down from Colonel. "Why not! Maybe we clean up some first?"

She laughed, pulled a handkerchief from her pocket, and wiped her face and hands clean. Looking down at her clothes, she cursed. "I liked this outfit. Here's to hoping Markus can get the blood out. He's usually pretty good at it."

"He's more than your driver," I offered.

She handed me one of her knives, now clean, and said, "Yes. He's my drudge. He protects me during the day, runs errands for me that can only be done in the daytime, and helps me any other way he can."

I felt the weight of the knife and appreciated its balance. "What does he get out of it?"

"He gets a bit of my blood from time to time. This way he doesn't get ill or age."

"And he's okay with living forever?"

She paused and tilted her head like a bird. "You don't understand that, do you? You're not happy with that part of your gift."

"I just hate the idea of livin' long after those I care about die."

She hummed in understanding. "Yes, that is a hard thing to deal with, especially for those who have already lost so many." When I didn't reply she continued, "Markus was alone in a hospital, dying of smallpox. He felt so angry that he'd seen nothing and been nowhere. I asked him if he wanted a longer life, even if it was in servitude. He agreed. I saved him. That was only a short time after I resurfaced.

"I'd actually gone there to drain someone dry. I had and was leaving when he saw me. He knew what I was. Must've been watching me. We chatted and made a deal. I gave him some of my blood to fight the disease, and the next night, he was where I told him to be. He's not disobeyed me once. He wouldn't."

"Huh…tonight has been very instructional."

"Shall we continue it?" she said, waving her knife at me.

"By all means…lead the way."

* * *

April 1949

Never thought I'd be back here," I mumbled as we drove into the town of Mesilla.

"When were you here?" Kit asked.

A small smile touched my lips. "Oh, ages ago. I was here on trial. Long story."

She raised an eyebrow. "How old are you again, Spirit Warrior?"

"Old enough to be your grandfather. Are you sure you know where we're going?"

She looked down at the address Duke had retrieved for us. "I've lived here longer than you, so yes. Turn here."

I didn't argue. I went where she instructed and in a few minutes we pulled up to a pretty little house in the Mesilla Park area. The last name, Howard, was on the mailbox, and I knew we were in the right place.

Stepping out of the car, it was too warm for my coat, so I wore a black t-shirt and cowboy boots with blue Levi's, using some of my witch powder to hide my guns from being seen.

Shutting the door, I shoved my sunglasses up and wiped the sweat from my nose. Looking around at the land with my hands on my hips, I said, "I've missed the beauty of this state, I will say that."

Kit, who'd worn a sundress the same color as the New Mexico sky, shut her door and hooked her purse over her arm. "Where have you been recently?"

"Come to think of it…seein' as it's April now…four years ago exactly I was in Berlin."

"And Richard?" she asked.

"He was with me. Prior to that…closest I got to here was Texas in 1885. But our most recent work together was in New Orleans," I looked at her and quietly said, "Vampire issue." When all she did was nod, I continued. "Then we took a break. I went off to England, then Ireland, while Richard headed to Oregon. If I'd had my way, I'd still be in Ireland, seein' as big things are goin' on there right now. But this took precedence, so I came back to the states."

Kit came close to me. "You're sayin' you weren't in New Mexico in June of 1947?"

I pulled my sunglasses down to look her in the eyes. "I have nothin' to say about that."

"Mmm-hmm…I bet you don't," she said accusingly.

I slid my glasses back up but gave her a toothy grin as the sound of a screen door shutting drew our attention to the house.

A man came down from his porch toward us wearing the simple attire of a plaid, short-sleeve, button-up shirt and a loose-fitting, pleated dress pants belted at the high waist. "Good afternoon. Can I help you folks?"

"Are you Sid Howard?" I asked.

"Sure am. Who's askin'?"

I smiled and reached out to shake his hand. "Agent William Kidwell, FBI. This is my assistant, Catherine. We're lookin' to get some information from you about the shoe of Cricket's you found."

Sadness filled his face. "That poor girl." Shaking it off, he motioned to the shade in his front yard. "Come, have a seat. We'll talk."

We followed him over to a set of white, wrought iron outdoor furniture. We took seats in three of the four chairs positioned about the round table.

"Darn shame what happened to that girl," Sid said. "If I'd known how important that shoe was when I first saw it…"

"When was that?" Kit asked.

"I saw the red pump about four feet off the side of the west side of Highway 80 on April 4th. I remember because I was drivin' south toward Mesquite. That's a village about eight miles south of Las Cruces."

I nodded as if I hadn't already known that. "Did you pick it up then?"

"Nah, no reason to. I mean, I thought it odd, but I didn't stop to get it. Why would I?"

"Not like you could wear it," Kit pointed out with humor in her voice.

He laughed. "Not my color."

I chuckled. "So, when *did* you pick it up?"

"After I heard Cricket was missin' and what she'd been wearin'. I thought of that shoe, so I went to go get it."

"I take it you called the sheriff?" I prompted.

"Yes, I did." Sid crossed one leg over the other. "I called Sheriff Apodaca and told him what I'd found. He said he'd be in touch. When he finally rang me back, he just said to bring it to town next time I was out that way."

"And did you?" I pressed.

"Yes, sir. Gave it to Happy myself. From what I understand, he took it to the Electric Shoe Shop. The workmen there identified it as Cookie's shoe. That's Cricket's sister."

"How did they do that?" I asked.

"A brace they'd fitted on the heel for Cookie."

I nodded again. We weren't learning anything I'd not heard from the Coogler family. But having confirmation of facts was just as important as new ones. However, seeing as it appeared we wouldn't get anything new, I was about to thank him for his time when he lightly slapped his hand on the table.

"There was one interestin' thing about that shoe, though," he said. "There was this paint on the bottom of the sole. Blue or green, not sure really."

This was new information that could help us move forward. We might've just caught a break. I could've done the jitterbug.

* * *

February 1879

A dance?" Zahara said.

"Yes!" I replied, then pointed at Eugene.

My sixteen-year-old pal explained. "The few who live in this area are gatherin' for a party. Music, drink, dancin'. You all should come."

"We do not want the entire area to know we are here," Zahara reminded us.

"She has a point," Dick said.

I rolled my eyes. "You're not a fan of large groups of people. Me? I am dyin' for somethin' to do that's not trainin' and sleepin'."

"I think it would be fantastic!" Kennedy said.

"I could die from that surprise," Zahara said dryly.

"Besides, if any of the wolves come to cause trouble, we could use it as a chance to take them out," Kennedy offered.

"I like how you think!" I said.

"No. We are not going to this party," Zahara said. "Eugene, if you would like to go, please feel free. But the rest of us are here to hide out. Remember, Billy?"

I sat down at the dining table. "Yeah, yeah…but it's been two weeks and I'm dyin'."

"No, you're not, you're bored," she said. "I'm sure we'll be movin' on soon. You'll stay put, and we'll start lookin' at when we need to leave."

"Fine," I grumped out.

"Kennedy?" Zahara said.

"But of course," the vampire replied.

I heard it. Just a tiny lilt in her voice that told me to look up. When no one else was paying attention, Kennedy winked at me. I bit back a laugh and went to find my dancing boots so I could shine them up proper. For if I read that vamp right, she was going no matter what, and if she was going, I was going.

Come round on eight o'clock, there was a tap at the window of the room I was sleeping in with Eugene. He'd already left for the party, so it was just me. I opened the window to find Kennedy all dolled up in a beautiful light blue gown with accents of black lace and, of course, her one-inch-wide black ribbon tied around her neck. The dress appeared slightly short for her, but with how beautiful she was, no one was going to notice.

"Why, you wouldn't be goin' to that party now, would you?" I said to her.

"Nope. You?"

I stepped through the window, dressed in my best-fitting clothes and shined shoes. "Nope."

"Uh-huh," she said with a laugh.

I put my arm out to her. "Shall we?"

"We shall," she replied, slipping her arm through mine. "We'll take my carriage."

"You have a carriage?" I asked.

With a wicked grin, she said, "It's a recent addition. Markus found one for us. Come, it's around the bend."

We made our way to the carriage, and I opened the door for her before Markus could. Once we were settled inside, he cracked his whip, and we were off.

"You sure will make an impression lookin' like that," I said.

"Stand out in a crowd around here, that's for sure," she said. "We'll fix that."

"Oh?"

She opened her handbag and pulled out a tiny glass vial. Inside was a red liquid.

"Blood is the answer?" I asked.

"Yes, for everything. Trust me."

"I am starting to, surprisingly," I said, looking outside as we rode along the dirt road. "But that's not enough blood for a meal."

"No, it's not. I ate before I came to get you."

"Did I know them?" I asked.

"Yes…but they're not dead. We don't have to kill our prey, William."

"Then what is the tiny vial for?"

"Remember how when we met, I told you vampires made by Scáthach, or a vampire not far removed from her, can shape shift? We do it with blood. A little on my tongue every hour or two, and I can hold the look of someone else."

"Fascinating," I said, and I meant it. "Show me."

Kennedy removed her cape, then opened the cork and daintily dipped her pinky into the blood. Seductively, she wiped it on her tongue and closed her mouth. Placing the stopper back on the bottle, she closed her eyes and focused on whatever she was going to do.

It started slowly. First her nose, then the shape of her eyes, and finally the edges of her face. Soon, her bosom filled out more, and she shrank in height a bit, mostly in her legs. Hair went from golden blonde to a deep brown and with a last gasp, she opened her eyes, and they were brown.

She looked like a young woman from town I only knew as Maria.

"Ooh…she's a little thicker in the waist than I thought," Kennedy said, touching the corset piece. "I'll need to let this out a smidge, but other than that, not bad." She turned her back to me. "Could you loosen it for me?"

"Uh…"

She looked over her shoulder at me. "Why Billy Bonney, you're not nervous about seeing my bare back, are you?" The realization of something hit her. "Oh dear, do you not know how?"

I sat straighter in my seat. "Please. Seein' as I know how to get a woman out of one, I'm sure I can merely loosen it."

Her playful smile made me see how attractive Maria could be, and I was glad it was too dark in the carriage for her to see me blush…or was it? Who knew with vampires.

I undid the back of her dress and untied the corset underneath. Loosening the ties, I pulled on it to make more room.

"Thank goodness!" she said.

"Did I let it out enough or do you need more?"

"My ego will not let you loosen it any further. Please tie it off and fasten me up."

I chuckled. "Yes, ma'am."

Once she'd put herself back together, Kennedy slid her cape on, sat, and stared at me with a grin. "You seem to know a corset well enough, you got a woman?"

I about choked on my tongue.

"Come come now, it's just us in here and a long drive." When I said nothing, her eyes narrowed, and she said, "You do have a lady friend, don't you? Why have you not said anything?"

"I do not. We are not a thing. She's a friend."

Kennedy's eyes grew a little wider with excitement as a wicked grin slid up her face. Leaning forward, she purred, "And what is this friend's name?"

I hesitated but finally said, "Paulita Maxwell. But she's my friend's sister so..."

"So what?" Kennedy barked with a laugh, sitting back in her seat. "If you like the girl, you ask her brother to court her. It's totally proper and acceptable."

"There's a lot goin' on in my life, in case you haven't noticed, Miss Kennedy. Now's not the time for havin' a woman."

"Bullshit," she said.

I laughed at her brashness. I liked it, and her. There was something about her that made me feel I could talk. Maybe that was a vampire trick, maybe it was just Kennedy. Either way, before I knew it, I said, "Between you and me, I'm not sure yet how I feel. I have this hanky she gave me and—"

"You saved it...keep it with you?"

"Maybe."

She laughed deeply. "Oh, Billy." She shook her head, this time obviously not saying something that was on her mind. Instead, she tapped her chin in thought. Finally, she said, "Next time you see Paulita. You pay attention to how you feel. And if you find you wouldn't want her with another man, then you let her know how you feel. If she reciprocates those feelings, you grab that joy and run with it. You hear me? Love is precious."

I was exceedingly uncomfortable talkin' about my feelings with a woman...and a vampire at that, but she had a point. "I suppose."

"I suppose?" She said, another laugh escaping her. "Goodness, I enjoy you. Oh, how I wish you'd been with me in New York City back in the day. We'd have had some fun, you and I."

"Hunting demons?"

"Yes, of course, but also killers."

"Wait, what?"

She waved it off but said, "That time between being freed and heading out to find you? I helped catch killers in old New York…and England too. I had me some fun and adventure, William. High society, parties, murder…dear me, I miss it. But this was more important. Besides, I can't live somewhere for more than twenty years without people noticing how I'm not aging. I'll tell them I'm twenty when I arrive…and by forty I need to go tend to a sick family member somewhere, and I leave, start over."

"Yep…that will be the story of my life, too, I'm sure."

"You could take a few years off from killing the wolves and let yourself age a bit if you wanted. I cannot do anything like that."

Curiosity hit me. "How old were you when she changed you?"

"Twenty-two and engaged to a wonderfully rich man."

"Then why would she—"

"A man that Scáthach wanted to use. He was friends with Jacques Cartier. She put my relationship in jeopardy unless I helped her. So, I did. But by then she's already transferred a deadly disease to me. Ever heard of the Black Death?"

The carriage went over a big bump, and I fought to hold my seat. "Yeah, my mom used to say, at least I don't have the Black Death. But consumption killed her anyway."

Kennedy touched my knee. "I'm sorry for that."

I nodded and tried not to think about it. Instead, I shoved my mind back to her and what she'd said the night we'd met. "So, she promised you the cure…I'm guessin' only if you got her on the boat with Cartier."

"Exactly. She fed me enough of her blood to hold the plague back just enough that I felt horrible but didn't die. We told others I had motion sickness, and she kept me in her room. She let no one in, bringing me meals herself. When we landed in what is now Canada, and my feet were on the land, she drained me of all my blood and fed me hers.

"And thus, I was reborn. She told me I couldn't leave this continent, or I'd die of the sickness."

"You believed her."

"I had no reason not to."

"But it wasn't true," I said.

"No. I could have gone back to England, married my fiancé, and—"

"And what? Left him in twenty years?" I offered.

She sighed. "I know. It wasn't a real option. Instead, I took a new last name, and we left. Then, one night, she was gone. Left me a note. She'd sailed back to Europe and would return for me. I wasn't to leave."

"What a bitch," I stated matter-of-factly.

"And until now she was a fluffy puppy?" Kennedy asked sarcastically.

"No…but still…"

"I did okay. I made do. She found a way to go back and forth a couple of times. Once, while she was away, I got a letter from her. She was with a group of Dutchmen and was coming back to Canada. Like I mentioned before, they were aiming for Virginia, and I was to make my way down the coast. Interestingly enough, I was running behind due to lack of food and a lot of sun that summer, and by September I was not far past what is now Massachusetts. When they landed, I felt her call me. I backtracked and found them."

"And that's when she brought Elias Story to you," I offered.

Kennedy now smiled. "Yes…plus Zahara and Tarack joined. They, too, had been called when Scáthach landed. We five traveled together for years. Then she and Tarack split off on a separate mission and I, well, I became restless…the rest you know."

Markus brought the carriage to a halt, climbed down, and opened the door for us. I exited and offered my hand to her. She took it and let me guide her down the steps to the ground. Not that she needed the help, but she was making sure she passed for human tonight.

"Tell me," I said, "If you'd not heard McSween that day in New York, would you still be there at more lavish parties than this one?"

"Without question."

"Regret it?"

"Not so far. Come, let's dance and forget her for an evening."

I couldn't lie. I liked that idea so much that I let her convince me to let down my guard for the night.

I shouldn't have. It had consequences.

8
JERRY NUZUM

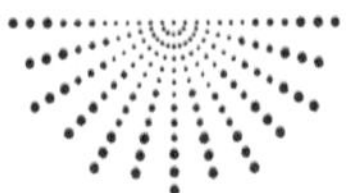

April 1949

By the time Kit and I met back up with Richard and Duke, they had information on shoe number two to give us. We all sat around the kitchen table in Kit's apartment eating sandwiches she made for us and updated the other teams. I had already spoken about Sid Howard, so it was Brewer's turn to talk about Max Johnston.

Still chewing a bite of his third sandwich, Richard pulled a map of Las Cruces from his back pocket and set it on the table. Swallowing, he said, "From what we understand, Max found the other shoe about five hundred feet south of the first one."

With his sandwich now in one hand and his plate in the other, Richard stood and took the plate to the counter. The rest of us, understanding his idea, cleared the table. The big man finished his sandwich as we spread the map out.

Washing his hands, Richard said, "Max told us that when he first found the shoe, he didn't know who it belonged to. He picked it up and placed a brick where he'd found it...then just took it home...and get this, he hung it in his tree."

I about choked on my sip of Coca-Cola. "Excuse me?"

"Wait, if he didn't think it was important, why the hell would he put a brick to mark where he found it?" Duke asked.

I pointed at Duke. "What he said."

"Hell if I know," Richard said, drying his hands off. "Kit, do you have a pencil?"

"Sure," she said and opened what appeared to be the junk drawer everyone I knew had in their kitchen. She pulled out one and handed it to him.

Sitting back down at the table so he'd not lean his large frame over the map and block it for the rest of us, Richard put an X on the spot on the map along U.S. Route 80 about a few hundred yards north of the Mesquite Cemetery where Cricket had been found. He then placed circles on the map where shoes were located. One circle had a 1 in it while the other had a 2 inside.

"If we take the word of those we've spoken to, she appears to have lost her shoes on the way to where they left her," Richard pointed out.

"Who threw them is the question," I said, getting up to get another Coke. "I'd bet she used them as a weapon, and the men tossed them."

"Or she threw them to lead to where they were taking her," Duke offered.

"Mmm...maybe," I said. "But she didn't know they wouldn't double back."

"They were too close to the edge of the road for someone to have thrown them out to get rid of them," Richard stated. "In fact, Sid's shoe was four feet off the road but not hidden by brush if he saw it that easily. Max's shoe was on the edge of the road. For goodness sake, if he'd left it there, the search party on the 16th would've seen it. But no, he hung it in the tree in his front yard."

"It wouldn't have mattered if they'd seen it that night," I said solemnly. "She was already dead, and it wouldn't have led them to her."

The silence of grief settled around us.

"Why wouldn't they have gone back to get them?" Kit said, and we all looked back at her. She had hoisted herself to sit up on the counter with a mug of tea held between both hands. "They aren't close to the body, but they are on the way to her from Las Cruces. They lead you toward the body dump site, so why leave them?"

She made a fantastic point, and I couldn't answer the question. Instead, I offered, "They were in a hurry to get out of the area? Shit, I don't know. You have a good point."

"Maybe that's why the sheriff was so uninterested in them," Richard said.

"Hold on now," Duke said. "Happy requested the shoes be brought in each time."

"Not really," Kit said. "These were definitely clues, and when people called him about them, he was like, bring it into town when you come next. No rush there at all."

Richard pointed at Kit. "Exactly. With Max, he called Happy, told him he thought he had Cricket's other shoe, and all the sheriff did was say okay and hung up."

Duke shook his head. "But remember, he said he called Happy really early on Easter Sunday morning. Probably woke the man up. Once he was more coherent, the sheriff called back and asked what Max had said to him. Then he drove out to Max Johnson's to fetch the shoe."

"That's true," Richard said with a sigh.

"If he wanted to keep that find hidden, why would he go get it?" Duke asked.

"Better if he had it and could either hide it or lose it than Max talking to a reporter about it," I pointed out.

"He still could have talked to the papers," Kit said. "I honestly don't think he thought the shoes would help or hinder, depending on where he stands in this investigation."

There was silence as we all chewed that over in our minds.

"So, we're no further along than we were this mornin'. Fuckin' great," I said and walked out of the room. I needed some time to think alone.

* * *

March 1879

About a week after the dance, I learned what our night out had caused. I'd heard a rumor that someone had recognized me. To make sure all was well, I sent Gaax on a mission to find out what was going on in Lincoln County. He sent me news faster than I expected.

It was early in the morning. I was tending to Colonel when a splitting headache engulfed me, and I sat on the ground. Whenever Gaax sent visions from a great distance, it caused this problem. He knew this and only did it in dire situations. This was no different.

I recognized the trail as the one we'd taken up here. In fact, it was the cabin we'd stayed at the night Kennedy found us. There were men there. From what I could see, it was a cavalry detail of ten men. Gaax flew closer and perched on a saddle, turning about so I could see military uniforms better. If I was right, the party consisted of a first sergeant, two officers, and seven enlisted. But why was he showing me this?

"They were likely here, Sergeant Murphy," an officer said. "It's a good place to stay. Not sure how long ago though."

Murphy nodded. "We aren't more than a two-day ride from Las Tablas. Let's get movin'. I don't want to miss bringin' in Bonney or Folliard this time."

"Yes, Sergeant," the officer said, then shouted, "Let's move on out!"

The vision ended, and I cursed. Blinking my eyes so I could see my real surroundings better, Colonel bumped my shoulder with his nose.

"I'm okay, buddy," I said, patting his leg. "But it looks like we're leaving here today." I stood, found my balance, and rushed off to tell the others.

Thankfully it was an overcast day and Kennedy could join, so the whole gang was there. I broke the news over the afternoon meal. It unsurprisingly didn't go over well, and Zahara stared holes through me as if she knew it was my fault. That was probably my guilt talking but since Kennedy didn't offer up what we'd done, neither did I. We just let it all unfold.

"We'll have to head back by a different way," Tom said.

Edward nodded. "We can ride east along the base of the mountain and go around it and south to Agua Azul."

That brought back memories. Dick and I shared a glance but didn't say a word about Morton or Baker. Instead, we just agreed, and everyone packed to leave at nightfall.

"I'm sorry to have put you in this position, Eugene," I told him as we were saddling up to leave.

He hugged me and said, "You come here whenever you need. They won't give me or my family trouble. It's all right. You be careful."

"We will." I looked at Kennedy. "Markus all set?"

"Yes," she said. "He'll meet us en route."

I nodded. "Then we are on our way. Good luck, Eugene." I hoisted myself up onto Colonel. "You can send me messages at the Ellis Store. Address them to Roy. You remember him, right? My Regulator Network Liaison?"

"I do."

"Good. The Ellis's will know to put all mail aside for me if Roy's name is on it. If I don't come for it, they'll give it to the real Roy next time they see him."

"You got it. Travel safe."

"Thank you for all your hospitality, Eugene," Zahara said and kissed him on the cheek before she pulled herself up into the saddle.

My friend blushed, and we all rode out of town, hoping to outrun the cavalry who were on our tails.

* * *

We traveled south as planned. When we got closer to the Rio Hondo, we came across news that caught our attention.

"Billy," Tom said, "Seems Governor Lew Wallace has listed you, me, Jim French, Charlie Bowdre, Henry Brown, John Middleton, Fred Waite, and a lot of others to be brought in."

"What for?" I asked as I fed an apple to Colonel.

"Murder. Has one Captain Henry Carroll in charge of it. Seems there is a one-thousand-dollar reward for you in particular."

I sighed. "Guess it's time to break the pact with Dolan."

"Oh?" Tom said.

"You'll see. I need to go talk to Zahara."

My plan wasn't foolproof, but I was hoping it would work. Ever since I heard Wallace was trying to clean up New Mexico so it could become a state, I had thought of this plan. It would take out my enemy, and it would clear me up to hunt Scáthach instead of dealing with Lincoln County stuff.

"Let me get this straight," Dick said. "You're going to use your knowledge of who killed Chapman to save yourself from being hunted."

"Yes. I'll offer a trade. I'll testify against Dolan if it'll set me free of these murder charges."

Zahara shook her head. "I'm not sure that'll work in your favor, Billy."

"I at least need to give it a try."

I wrote a letter to Governor Lew Wallace and waited to see what he thought.

* * *

April 1949

I was sitting on the steps outside Kit's apartment when Richard came to find me like he always did. I wasn't sure, but I thought that being my Beta possibly made him too much in tune with my feelings, and he would try to help to save himself the pain of my emotions. But I never wanted to ask. I suppose I preferred thinking he just gave a damn. This was Brewer, so that was likely the case.

"What do you want to do next?" he simply said as he sat on the steps next to me.

I grunted as I chewed on the toothpick I'd put between my teeth. "I don't know."

"I say we poke around town more and see what we can learn, and if we get nothin', we head up to Hot Springs."

This got my attention. "Huh? Why? You feelin' like soaking in the hot water?"

Brewer smiled. "I never turn down soaking in hot springs, but that's not my point." He bumped his arm against mine and spoke mentally. "Ran into Cookie's husband today. He told me that Mr. Green Eyes's family is in Hot Springs. I say we go pay him a visit…without Duke."

I nodded. "Good plan. We'll make a day trip up there and come back so we're not missed. I mean, it's only an hour or two north, so shouldn't be hard to do that. But I want to poke around here for a while first. I also want to convince the powers that be to exhume her body. They need to do an autopsy."

"Agreed," Richard said. "Think we could see the shoes? I want to see that paint you mentioned."

"That would be for Duke to help us with. We'll ask him."

"Well then, let's try to get the wheels movin' on those things and start talkin' to her friends. Maybe go bother Jerry Nuzum."

I chuckled. "You just want to meet him."

Richard shrugged. "Maybe. But hey, we have to interview him, so why can't it be both things?"

I patted my best friend's shoulder. "Good point. Let's work on questions for Jerry and go visit the football star."

Richard broke the bond for mental discussions and stood. "Come on back in when you want. We'll start that."

Before he could leave, I asked, "Have you seen Gaax?"

"No. Last I knew he was spending time in the Masonic Cemetery talking to the other ravens. Was hopin' to learn information."

"Okay," I said and paused. "I miss Zahara. We could use her right now."

Richard stopped. "It was a lovely ceremony you held for her."

I stood and spit the toothpick out. "Felt weird without a body to bury, but yeah, it was nice."

"On your way through Lincoln, did you stop in her orchard?" he asked as we headed back toward Kit's apartment.

I shook my head. "Couldn't. It still hurts too much, I suppose. It's not been long enough. Maybe once we close this up, we could both go by."

"It's a plan," Richard said and stepped into Kit's apartment.

I looked up to the heavens. "Zahara, I know you're lookin' down on us now and shakin' your head. Have pity on the stupid men in your life and send us help. I don't think we have long until Scáthach realizes we're here and comes to see us herself. We sure could use you."

I heard a raven cry and looked around but didn't see Gaax anywhere.

"Damn it, Zahara, I miss you."

A shimmer of energy swam around me, and I shivered. Hand on my weapon, I looked around better this time, but still, nothing.

"This town is weird…crazy weird."

With that, I went into Kit's place and shut the door. It was time to discuss the football hero, how we'd question him, and for the first time in my life, I wished I liked sports.

* * *

March 1879

We'd made our way around Capitan Mountain, and I headed into Lincoln on a night without the moon and put a note in the Regulator Network Liaisons box for Roy. I slipped out of town without being seen, having burned some soul energy to move that quickly. Easing up onto Colonel's back, I considered a visit.

"You wanna go to your stall and eat?"

Colonel whinnied.

I patted him on the neck. "You got it, pal."

With a tap on his sides, I urged him to the secret stall. Once Colonel settled, I snuck out and made my way to find Ben.

Benjamin Ellis was Ike Ellis's son and one of the few people in town who knew the truth about me. I knew what room he slept in and knocked on the door twice before sliding into the shadows. A sleepy Ben opened the door and looked about.

"It's clear," he said.

I stepped out onto the wooden plank walkway. "Hey."

"Hey yourself, get in here before some Dolan idiot sees you."

I smiled at him and hurried into his room.

Ben shut the door. "What are you doin'?"

"Good to see you too," I said and sat next to the wood-burning stove.

Ben snagged a thick robe and pulled it on. "Ya let all the cold air in here." He joined me by the stove. Picking up a kettle, he said, "I have some water left in this. Want some tea?"

"That would be great, thanks," I said.

Ben set the kettle on top of the stove and sat in the other chair. "Not that it's not good to see ya, Billy, but what are you doin' here?"

"I had to get a note to Roy. Dropped it off in the RNL box. Then realized I didn't want to ride back yet. It's cold. Besides, I've been away and don't know what's been goin' on. Figured you could bring me up to speed. I could share that with Tom and the others."

Ben sat back in the chair and got a small smile on his face. "Then you've not heard."

I allowed him the satisfaction and said, "Heard what?"

He leaned forward, "Lew Wallace finally got Dudley suspended."

"Well, I'll be damned…about time!" I said in jubilant glee.

"Yep! Captain Henry Carroll has taken command pending the return of Purington."

"Carroll is the one that came lookin' for me and Tom up in Las Tablas," I said.

"Didn't catch you, I see."

"Hell, no. I got eyes and ears in the air, Ben. But it was close. If I'd not sent Gaax out to look…"

"But you did!"

"Yeah, but what if I'd not? We'd have been caught with our pants down, and I'd have been the reason things fell apart. I've gotta try to make things right, or I'll never be free to hunt Scáthach the way I need to."

Ben nodded. "I can see that."

"Thank you!" I said, standing up and walking about. "My friends don't see it that way."

"That's because they don't trust anyone."

"And they shouldn't, but damn it, Ben, I need to put this all to bed. I wrote to Lew Wallace."

Now Ben stood. "You what?"

"You heard me." I sat back down. "He wants to close the Chapman murder, and I can help with that."

Ben narrowed his eyes at me. "Did you kill him?"

"No! Good God, Ben. You know me better than that."

"Well, if he was a werewolf, you'd have killed him."

I pressed my lips together and nodded. "You got me there. But he wasn't. He was just a lawyer who appeared to be cold and in a lot of pain."

"Who killed him then, and why do you know about it?"

I told him the story.

"Dolan and Campbell? Well damn," he said scratching his head. Feeling how his hair was all mussed up, he smoothed it down. "But whose bullet killed him? Campbell or Dolan?"

"I don't know. Did they do an autopsy on him?"

Ben shrugged. "Hell if I know. If they did, it was at Fort Stanton. You might corner Lieutenant Appel and ask him. He'd know. Dolan had his men leave Chapman out there to die and burn in the cold. That's pretty horrible."

"Yes, it was, and I'm willing to testify. Told Wallace that I knew there were indictments against me for things that happened in the Lincoln County War, and because of those I'd not come forward sooner. I told him that if it was in his power to nullify those indictments, I would testify."

Ben tapped the kettle and pulled his hand away quickly. Standing up, he grabbed two mugs from a shelf he'd put above the stove. "Do you think he can do that?"

I shrugged. "He's the damn governor. I'd guess he can do as he pleases."

Ben handed me a mug and set his own on his chair. Pulling down a five-by-eight tin, he opened it to reveal a brick of pressed black tea.

"Where did you get that?" I said with some serious interest.

"They just came in last week. I sold one of my guns and used the money to get it."

"You sold a gun?" I said in disbelief. "With all that's been goin' on, you sold a gun. Have I taught you nothin'?"

Ben smiled and used the edge of his robe to touch the lid of the kettle, removed it, and set it aside. With a knife, he shaved off some black tea leaves into the kettle. "I have four others, plus two rifles. I'm fine." He put the tea block back in its tin and placed it up on the shelf. Grabbing the metal strainer, he picked up his mug and sat back in his chair.

I put the lid back on the kettle since the heat wouldn't burn me. "Well then, okay. But still seems odd."

"It'll only seem that way until you taste this," Ben said. "Do you think Wallace will write you back?"

"I do."

"And what then?"

"Well," I said, "I suppose I'll ask to meet with him all secret like. We'll chat and see what he's willin' to do."

"I can tell you Wallace isn't a Murphy supporter, that's for sure. He's had about enough of Captain Purington. That man does everythin' he can to undermine Wallace's efforts. In fact, Wallace is formin' a militia company called the Lincoln County Rifles."

"Oh, really? You involved in this?"

Ben handed me the strainer, and I held it over my mug. He poured the tea through it, so it would catch any of the leaves that were floating, and said, "I am. Juan Patron will command it and I'm his First Lieutenant."

"Well congratulations, Ben!" I took the strainer, held it over his mug, and he poured tea for himself.

"Thanks!" he said and put the kettle on the ground to cool. Taking the strainer from me, he set it on the tiny table beside him and said, "Second Lieutenant is Martin Sanches."

He rattled off the rest of the names, and I realized that the organization was strongly pro-McSween in its sympathies. This was in our favor, and I told him so before blowing on my tea and cautiously taking a sip.

"This is definitely worth what you spent on it," I said, and I meant it.

"Told ya," Ben replied with a grin. "So, tell me, who all are you ridin' with?"

"Just Tom and a few people you don't know."

"No, Charlie or Doc?" he asked.

"Nah, Charlie is layin' low, and Doc Scurlock is probably home with his family, but then again, he could be up in the mountains too. I'm not sure. I've not seen much of the remainin' Regulators since that night in July. Been busy chasin' the real evil."

"She still in town?" Ben asked, obviously leery of my answer.

I shook my head. "Hell if I know. If so, she's bidin' her time to come at me. I'm expectin' to see her anytime now...any freakin' time..."

We talked for a little longer, but I needed to get on my way. After leaving Ben to go back to sleep, I fetched Colonel, bundled up, and headed out of town. I wasn't more than a mile from it when a figure in black rode into my path. I thought for sure it was Scáthach and pulled my weapon.

* * *

April 1949

Jerry Nuzum lived with his wife, Mary, and two children, so when we knocked on the door early that evening, we heard the kids first, followed by a woman shouting, "Be right there!"

It was a pleasant home, and it was apparent that though he was still a student, his pay from playing pro ball was substantial enough. The well-groomed front yard held no grass, but the pattern of stone and succulents was pretty and held a pathway that led to a shaded bench swing.

A pleasant and pretty-faced woman with short hair opened the door. She had a baby on her hip and a toddler hiding behind the skirts of her dress. "Hello? Can I help you?"

Richard and I showed our badges and said who we were. Mary's eyes grew before her brow furrowed.

"Okay…what can I do for you?"

"We need to speak with your husband," I said. "Is he home?"

"Yes, he's grillin' some burgers in the backyard. What's this about?"

"Your husband is one of the last people to see Ovida Coogler alive," I stated. "We need to hear what he knows."

She nodded. "Well, come on in. I'll show you to the backyard."

We stepped in, removed our hats, and headed through the tidy home to a sliding glass door that led out onto a cement patio. There we found Jerry Nuzum at the grill with the radio on, listening to music.

"Honey, these two gentlemen are from the FBI and would like to talk to you about Cricket."

Jerry turned his tall, well-built frame around, and his singing stopped. His face became stoic and sad before he sighed. "Of course." He put a hand out. "Nice to meet you."

I shook his hand. "I'm Agent Kidwell."

He reached for Richard's hand, and when my Beta shook Jerry's hand, his face was all grins. "I'm Agent Baca. It's an honor to meet you, sir. You play a good game."

Now Jerry's face softened, and the smile spread from ear to ear. "Thanks so much! Please, have a seat."

He motioned us toward a picnic table and said, "Mary, would you be so kind as to get some lemonade for our guests?"

She looked at the kid on her hip and paused.

"I can take her for you," Richard offered.

I grinned. "He's surprisingly great with kids."

Mary hemmed and hawed, but when her littlest on her hip looked at Richard, she reached for him, an obvious shock to her mother.

"This is Jan," she said and handed the baby over to Richard, who took her carefully.

"Woof," Jan said to Richard and touched his nose.

I laughed. "See?"

With how many kids loved dogs, they tended to adore Brewer. It was a strange thing that never stopped amazing me.

Mary Nuzum left, Brewer eased Jan onto his hip, bouncing her around, and we talked about Ovida.

I sat at the picnic table. "We understand you saw Cricket her last night in town."

"I did," Jerry said, turning back to the grill to check his burgers. "Left home around seven-thirty to catch a picture show...saw that new movie, El Paso. Pretty good Western."

He paused too long, so I asked, "Then where did you go?"

"Just some bar hoppin'...nothin' was planned. If what I read in the paper is right, I was home before Cricket went missin'. Got home close to three in the mornin'. My wife can vouch for that. I was too drunk, and she had to help me into the house. Honked to wake her up. Poor gal."

"You drove yourself home in that condition?" I asked.

Nuzum brushed it off. "It's not far."

That in no way meant it was safe, but I left it alone. Instead, I jotted his information down and asked, "When you were with Cricket, what was her state of mind?"

"You mean, other than lookin' for a good time?" he said with a laugh. "She was drunk as a skunk, Agent Kidwell."

"Whee!" I heard Brewer say as he spun Jan around, the little girl giggling.

"He really is good with kids. Jan can be sort of picky." He paused, flipped his burgers, and said, "First time I saw her was at the Del Rio bar.

She and some guy I've never met before hung out and played shuffleboard with me until the bar closed."

"That's it?" Brewer asked. "No scuffle out in front of the bar?"

Jerry sighed and turned toward the tall man holding his tiny daughter. "That was nothin'. Just a misunderstandin'. She asked me for a ride home, I tried to help her into the car, she told me she didn't need help and then stomped off back into the diner."

"From a passerby, it seemed to be more than all that," I said.

Mary Nuzum opened the sliding glass door and stepped out onto the patio. She reached back in for a tray with three glasses of lemonade and delivered them to us with a smile.

"Thank you, ma'am," I said.

"Jan seems right happy there with you," Mary said. "I'll just set your lemonade here on the table for when she decides she wants down." She handed one to Jerry and with another smile at us, she snatched up the oldest, who was toddling about and said, "Just give me a holler when Jan wants in. I'm going to go finish makin' dinner."

Mary headed in, shutting the door behind her, and I looked to Jerry, hoping he'd pick up the conversation. He didn't. Instead, he turned to his burgers. I rolled my eyes at Brewer.

"Where were we?" I asked, staring at Brewer to say he should pick up the thread.

Jan giggled, and Brewer bounced her around as he said, "We were askin' why others thought it was some big deal out in front of the bar with Cricket."

Jerry sighed. "She's not a quiet girl."

I noticed he still spoke in present tense with her sometimes, but I said nothing. Instead, I laughed. "No, she was not." And that's one thing I loved about her, but I didn't add that tidbit of information.

"She was drunk. Hell, we'd all been drinkin'. I got no idea, but when she sat in my car, she jumped right out. I then got out of the car, and when I came around, I might've taken her arm." He made a face like it wasn't some big deal. "She shouted at me, the guy in the green glasses came out to yell at me, and I went in after her."

"You did?" I asked, then tried my lemonade. It was wonderful.

"Yeah, but she wouldn't even turn to look at me. I said to hell with you, and was about to leave when the man who runs the joint accused me of tryin' to kidnap the girl. Can you imagine that shit? Please. I got me a lovely wife, kids, and life. Why the hell would I be tryin' to kidnap some drunk chick?"

I could think of all kinds of reasons people did horrible things, but I didn't reply since I understood the question was rhetorical. Besides, staying quiet would encourage him to continue, and he did.

"I left. Went on over to the Penguin Bar, poured myself a stiff drink, got drunk, and left there close to three in the mornin'. Look fellas, I barely knew the girl. I offered her a lift, but she didn't take it. I got drunk. End of story."

He drank deeply of his lemonade and then set it down on a small table next to the grill. He turned his focus back on the burgers, and the air hung silent, save for the babbling of Jan in Brewer's arms.

"Dogs go woof!" she said.

"That's right, Jan, dogs go woof," I said with a laugh. Brewer would be lucky if that little girl let him leave the house at all.

"You said you made yourself a drink at the Penguin Bar?" Richard asked as he settled Jan on his hip securely and used his free hand to get a drink of the lemonade.

"Yeah, I used to bartend there, so they let me do that when I come by."

I nodded and jotted this bit of information down before flipping to the notes I'd taken when I talked to the Del Rio bartender. I drank some more of the lemonade that made me think of the kind my mother used to make and said, "According to a few we spoke to who were at the Del Rio, there appeared to be two altercations out by your car. Is that true?"

Jerry turned back around with this 'lightbulb moment' look on his face. "That's right...that all happened before the bar closed." He paused, and his eyes got that faraway look in them they do when someone is reliving something they must think hard about.

"Luther came out yellin' at me to get my hands off her then went into the café. I joined them and apologized. Eventually, we went back to the Del Rio for the shuffleboard until close. I again tried to help give her a ride home, she got lippy, ran into the café, and the rest I already said happened. I drank a good amount that night, gentleman. A lot of it is a blur."

He stepped over to the sliding glass door, opened it, and stepped in. "Mary, the burgers are almost done."

"Okay, here," she said.

Jerry stepped back out with an empty plate in hand and shut the door.

He went to the grill and eased one at a time onto the plate. "Is there anythin' else I can help you two with?"

"Not at this time," I said. "We might have some follow-up questions for you, but it all seems pretty cut and dried for now."

The conversation turned to football between Richard and Jerry as I helped Mary set her table and finished my lemonade between activities.

The doorbell rang, and Mary pulled her apron off. "The Smiths are here."

Realizing they had company for dinner and that the four place settings were for adults only, I glanced up at Brewer and gave him a nod. He handed Jan to her mother and turned to Jerry.

"We don't want them askin' you why the FBI were here," I said, taking Mary's hand. "We'll leave out the back and walk around." I sent a bit of energy into her. "We were just some friends of Cricket's who came over to chat about her. That's all. My name is Bob and his is John."

I could hear Brewer behind me using his abilities to do the same to Jerry, then we left quickly out the back and around the house. Not until they'd let the couple in and headed back did we get into our car and leave.

"Back to the Amador to fill Duke in," I said.

"Not much to tell him," Richard said, putting the car in drive and heading back into town.

"No, but every piece of the puzzle makes a difference. Soon we'll have enough to build a complete picture of her last night, and that, my friend, is where we'll find answers." Or so I hoped.

9
MR. GREEN EYES

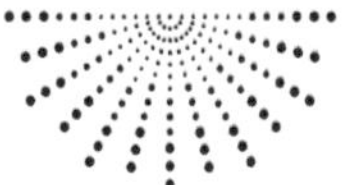

March 1879

Pulling Colonel to a full stop, I used my elevated sight to see who was in my path. "Pat Garrett, what on earth are you doin' here and in my way at this hour?"

"I needed to talk to you, and Roy informed me you were in the area."

"Damn snitch. What do you want? It's cold, and I need to be gettin' outta town."

His horse danced about before he rode up alongside me. "You need to do more than leave town. It's time you left the state."

"Why? Is Scáthach gone?"

"No. She's still here. But the Regulator Network wants you in England for formal training. You can come back afterward."

"Bullshit. No fuckin' way, Pat. I have a job to do here, and I'm gonna do it."

Garrett sighed. "The law is comin' for you, and it's not some idiot this time. Lew Wallace is not a person to mess with, Billy."

"I'm workin' on that."

Garrett's brow furrowed. "What does that mean?"

"I'll explain further when I have more information. Just know I'm workin' to nullify my charges. If I do that, can I stay?"

Garrett pondered the question. "I'm not sure it'll matter. They want you out of the states. Things are heatin' up, and it needs to calm down. We cannot take the chance that more people learn about the supernatural community. We need this territory to become a state."

I sighed. "Then you do what ya gotta do, and I'll do the same."

"Billy, the leaders of the Regulator Network do not handle the word 'no' very well."

"Well, I suppose it's time they learned how to. I'm not leavin' New Mexico while Scáthach is here, and I sure as hell am not goin' to England. If you don't wanna tell 'em that, I will."

Garrett sighed. "I can buy you some more time, but I cannot promise how long it'll last. Find a way to either pull her from Mary or send her back to Hell and soon, or they will force you to leave without finishin' the mission."

"The hell they will! I'll finish this before I go anywhere!"

I didn't let him reply. Instead, I hit my heels into Colonel's sides, and we tore off into the night.

* * *

May 1949

Having not been able to run into Luther Mosely at P.R. Burn Construction in Las Cruces, we finally took a trip up to Hot Springs to the address Duke found us for his parents. We took Richard's vehicle and arrived at ten-thirty in the morning on May 5th.

Parking the car on the road outside the house, we headed up to the door and knocked. An older gentleman came to the door, and we showed our badges, asking if Luther was there. He invited us in, and we took a seat in the living room to wait. When the young man in his early twenties came into the room, he was still in his pajamas with a robe thrown on over them.

I stood and offered him my hand. "Sorry to wake you, Mr. Mosely. I'm Agent Kidwell; this is Agent Baca, and we're here to talk about Cricket."

He tentatively shook my hand as his brow furrowed over his blue-green eyes. "Why is the FBI involved in this? I thought this was a state matter."

"Maybe, maybe not. That's what we're here to find out," I said. "Las Cruces isn't far from the border of Mexico, Mr. Mosely, or from Texas. Thus, we need to cover all the bases."

Luther squinted from the light. "Would either of you like coffee? My father said he was makin' some."

"Sure, that would be nice," Richard replied.

"Dad!" Luther shouted, "make it three!" Feeling around in the pockets of his robe, he didn't find what he was looking for and excused himself. When he returned, he had on the green lensed glasses we'd heard so much about. They made his blue-green eyes a vivid green. "That's better," he said. "My eyes are light-sensitive," he explained as he sat on a chair to the right of the couch. "How can I help you, gentlemen?"

"Richard and I need your help to reconstruct Cricket's movements the night of March thirtieth," I said. "There's a lot we already have, but not all of it. We also need to know what you two argued about that mornin'."

Surprise showed across his face for an instant, then it was gone. "Small town means everyone sees things and talks. Yeah, Cricket and I had an argument that mornin'. I voiced some concern for the people I'd seen her hangin' around with. Told her they were trouble, and she needed to stop spendin' her time with them."

"People like who?" I asked, my notebook now out.

Luther's dad carried out two mugs of coffee and brought them to Richard and me.

"Two?" Luther asked.

"You aren't a guest; you can get it yourself," Luther's father said with a wink at me.

With a huff, the young man got up, fetched a mug of his own, and came back to the living room. His father left, and Luther sat, taking a sip or two. He hummed with pleasure. "Caffeine is my savior."

"Up late last night, Luther?" I asked.

He nodded. "My mother isn't feelin' well, so I've been drivin' between here and Las Cruces, where I live and work, to help 'em out. I got in late last night and had a hard time gettin' to sleep. Now, what was your question? Oh yes, who was she hangin' around with? Just guys I didn't like the look of."

I smelled evasion. "You got in a fight over random guys you just didn't like the look of?"

"Yeah," he said, drinking more coffee.

"Okay," I said, drawing it out. "What can you tell us about your time with Cricket on the thirtieth?"

"We went to some bars…hung out, it was nothin' major. Just a typical night. Nothin' unusual."

"So, you always get in fights with pro football players over a girl?" Brewer asked.

I watched his face. Luther was at war within himself. The question was, why did he hesitate and overthink? He was going to tell us or just brush it off. Richard and I stayed silent and stared at him until he was visibly uneasy.

"Look, fellas, I'd love to help ya out…but they've ordered me to keep my mouth shut."

Richard and I looked at each other and then turned to face Luther. I simply raised an eyebrow at him. He resituated himself in his chair and glanced about the room at anywhere but us.

"Who?" I asked.

"Doesn't matter," he said, putting his mug on the side table. "It's helpin' them catch the son of a bitch who killed her. I'll talk when I can." He leaned back in the chair, hands resting on his stomach.

"Mmm-hmm," I said, and with a nod at Brewer that told him what I was up to, I stood and crossed over to Luther. Putting out my hand, I added, "Well, thank you for your time."

He took my hand, and I moved a full soul's worth of energy from my well of souls into him, jolting him hard. It caused him to pause all movement and just sit there. Using my pocketknife, I nicked my finger and squeezed a few drops of my blood into his coffee before the wound closed. Knife back in my pocket, I tapped his shoulder.

"You all right, Luther?"

He snapped out of it, blinked, and looked from me to Richard and back. "Did I fall asleep?"

I wanted to say, "For a little while," but that'd be mean, and I wasn't that person anymore. Or rather, I tried not to be. Instead, I said, "You just kind of spaced out," I said. "You might need more caffeine."

Luther blinked rapidly a few times. "You're right, sorry about that." He took up his coffee mug and sipped. "Where were we?"

"You said you were told you couldn't talk to anyone," Richard stated.

Luther drank more. "That's right."

"Who told you that?"

"An attorney," he said, and finished the rest of his cup.

I grinned. With a tiny tap of energy transference to talk to my blood in his system, I said, "You can tell us. We're safe. In fact, it'll be like you didn't tell us at all."

"I can tell you?" Luther said.

"Yes, we're safe," I said again.

"In fact," Richard said, pausing in order to pull Luther's gaze toward him. Once he did, Brewer let some silver swirl into his eyes. "Our mutual friend, the attorney, sent us to get your story for him."

Luther laughed and slapped his leg. "Well, why didn't you say so? T.K. Campbell should've said you were comin'…but our phone line has been on the fritz, so maybe he tried."

Richard jotted down the attorney's name, and I sat back down on the couch.

"Tell me, Luther, who was Cricket hangin' out with that you didn't like?" I asked.

"Well, one of 'em was New Mexico's corporation commissioner, Dan Sedillo. From my understandin', she was hangin' out with him and some of his boys one weekend, at a hotel."

My head snapped up. "What was she doing with them?"

"I don't like to speculate, but many in town do…and I didn't like what they were sayin'."

I didn't have to ask what he meant. We'd heard similar things in Las Cruces.

The heavy silence hurt Richard enough that he said, "What can you tell us about your time with her on the night of the thirtieth?"

He paused.

"Remember, it's safe to talk to us…it's like you're not talking to us at all," I said.

His head bobbed up and down, eyes going out of focus, as he pictured the night in question in his head. "I saw her at the Del Rio bar…not sure of the time. She was drunk. Practically fallin' off her stool. In fact, she'd knocked over her glass of whiskey. I turned it upright for her, and then the strangest thing happened.

"Someone warned her it was going to drip onto and ruin her new suit. Ya know what she said? It was weird. What was the exact wording again? Oh yes, it was, 'I'll never live to wear it again, anyway.' Who says that kind of thing?"

Neither Richard nor I had replied when he continued. "She then ended up going to the back of the bar and calling someone. When she came back, she lay her head on the bar and cried. All I got out of her was that she was in love with someone who didn't love her back. She asked me what I'd do in her situation."

"What did you say?" Richard said.

"I told her to forget about him. He wasn't worth it if he didn't care about her. Then she went over to the jukebox and played the song, 'There's No Tomorrow' by Tony Martin."

"Interesting choice of tune," I said.

"She said it was her favorite song," Luther said.

We all let that set in for a moment, then I asked, "Did she seem to take your advice?"

Luther shrugged. "Sorta. I mean, she let me take her down to the Tortugas Café."

I crossed an ankle over my knee. "What for?"

"Just wanted to get some coffee in her, ya know? But those assholes wouldn't serve her. Said she was too drunk. So, we went to the Union Bus Depot for doughnuts and coffee. After that, we tried to go to the café again. They let us in that time. Gave Cricket some coffee and toast. She even told the waitress she would head straight home after that."

"But she didn't, did she?" I asked.

Luther shook his head. "She had no intention of goin' home. Told me she wanted to go back to the bar…so I took her."

"Where you bought her more drinks?" I asked.

"Sure, but that was like…an hour after we left the bar. She'd had food and coffee, so I thought one drink wouldn't be such a bad thing now. Plus, she asked me to."

I rolled my eyes. "Were you tryin' to take advantage of her, Luther?"

His eyes grew wide. "No, sir! I would never!"

"So, you weren't interested in her?" Richard asked.

Luther messed with the belt of the robe he wore. "No. Yes. Look, she's a pretty girl, and I like…liked her. But I'd never have tried to take advantage of her like that. Not like—" He cut himself off.

"Like who?" I prodded. "Like Jerry Nuzum?"

This caused Luther to come out of his chair. "He tried to force her into his car. Twice!"

"But you stopped him," I offered.

"Yes, I did!"

"Is that what you had words about?" Richard asked.

"It sure is! He claimed he was just goin' to take her home, but I knew better. He'd been flirtin' with her hard. I didn't trust him to take her home. Besides, she only lived around the block. If he wanted to make sure she got home safely, he'd have walked her there."

Eyebrows furrowed, Richard said, "Jerry Nuzum is married."

"Yes, he is." Luther's face transitioned into a nasty sneer. "But let's be honest, gentleman, not all men let that stop them from tryin' to get some on the side."

Jerry hadn't struck me as a cheatin' man, but if Luther liked her, and Jerry talked to her, he likely was oversensitive and thought it was flirting. Either way, I didn't urge him to continue with that line of conversation. Instead, I said, "What time did you last see Cricket?"

He thought on it. "Shortly after three in the morning. I think. Um... she was drunk, and I was worried Nuzum might try to put her in his car again."

"But hadn't he left the Deluxe Café a bit before this?" I asked, remembering what Jerry had told us about going to the Penguin Bar.

"Not that much before. Anyway, she headed north on Main Street to the cross street there and turned right, headin' east on Griggs. A car was headin' straight for her. I shouted for her to watch out, but she kept walkin'. I don't think she even saw it."

"Did it stop?" Richard asked.

"Yeah...but it was damn close."

"What color was the car?" I asked.

"Dark gray...maybe dark brown. I'm not sure."

"Did you see the people inside?" Brewer pressed.

"Yeah," Luther said, "Two men. They said somethin' to Cricket, but I couldn't hear it. I can't remember if she replied. I don't think so. She just kept headin' east on Griggs past the post office."

"Did you follow her?" I asked.

He looked sheepish. "Yeah, but it's not what you think! I was worried about her. She was wobbly drunk and walkin' in the wrong direction. She lives to the west of Main Street, ya see?"

"That she does," I said.

"Did you continue to follow her?" Richard prodded.

"Yeah...and just as she turned right on Church, she saw somethin' that spooked her and ran."

"Was she runnin' from you, Mr. Mosely?" I questioned. "I'm sorry, but I have to ask."

"I thought so at first, and I shouted to her that it was just me. But she was screamin' and cryin'. I must've shouted out at her two or three times that it was just me, askin' her if she was hurt. She pointed north and told me to run. Then she hurried south down Church Street."

"Did you run north, Mr. Mosely?" Richard asked.

He shook his head. "No, sir. I figured I might be the one scarin' her, so I headed back up Griggs to Main and turned left...headin' toward May Street. That's when I saw her talkin' to someone in a car."

I sat forward, my head buzzing now with the piece of the puzzle that made a fuller picture. "You saw what?"

"Some guy, some car. It was a light gray, maybe blue...hell, maybe a blue-green car. I don't remember. It was almost at the midway point of the block and had pulled over, and she was leanin' in to talk to him. I think he had a hat on. But that's all I saw of him."

"Did you see the car again?" Richard asked.

"Not really. I noticed it turned off May onto Main headin' south."

"Did you see if she got in the car?" I pushed.

"I didn't..." he said, his voice fading as he blinked his eyes a few times. "I actually never saw her again..."

I could feel the connection to him sliding away as the little blood that was in him burned out of his system. He shook his head as if coming out of a trance and sat down. He looked at us and scowled. "So you see, I can't tell you nothin' at this time."

I grinned. "That's just fine, Mr. Mosely. We fully understand. You have a nice day and I hope your mother feels better."

"Thanks," he said, and walked us out.

Once we were in the car and on our way down the road, Richard said, "Well, that was the weirdest interview we've done in a while."

"No shit," I said. "Looks like we need to stop by the Tortugas Café, the bus depot, and get ourselves introduced to T.K. Campbell."

"Why is it always crooked attorneys, Billy?"

"Hell if I know..."

After a second or two I added, "Hey, we got time for a soak in the hot springs?"

This made Richard smile. "We sure do!"

"Then let's do that first. Seems a shame to come all the way up here and not take the time."

Richard turned toward the hot springs, and with joy on his face, picked up speed. We could do all the things I'd mentioned previously after we got back. No reason not to take advantage of the hot springs. Besides, when Richard soaked in them, he had better control of his powers. It was a win from all sides.

* * *

March 1879

On March 15, Lew Wallace wrote me back, and I received it the next day. I handed it to Dick. After he read it, he passed it to Edward, who read it while Tom did the same over his shoulder.

"It's a trap," Richard said.

"I'll set the rules and then it won't be," I told him.

Lew Wallace was asking me to come alone to the home of Squire Wilson at nine o'clock Monday night.

"Says right there he has the authority to exempt me from prosecution if I testify to what I told him I knew," I said, pointing at the letter.

"I don't trust him," Edward said.

"You don't trust anyone," Tom stated.

"That's true," Edward said with a nod, pointing at Tom who was still looming over his shoulder.

Placing a finger on the last sentence, Tom said, "What in the hell is that supposed to mean?"

"What line?" I prompted him.

Reading it, Tom said, "If you could trust Jessie Evans, you can trust me." He looked up at me. "Shit, no one, including you, has ever trusted Jessie Evans."

I snatched the letter out of Edward's hands. "Maybe he thinks I do. What the hell do I know?" I folded it up and put it in my pocket. "Look, I don't have a choice. If I don't take the heat off me, I'm out."

"Out of what?" Richard asked.

I breathed out a sigh, sat down at the table, and finally told them what Garrett had said to me. By the time I finished, they were all seated and silent.

"England? You?" Tom asked. "Why?"

"Do I look like a fortune-teller? I have no idea. I bet you money I don't have yet that he asks you to go, too, Tom."

"I'm not goin' to England," Tom said.

"Well then, we all better get Scáthach out of Mary's body and send her back to the Otherworld and soon, or I have a feelin' we won't have a choice in the matter."

"You're not plannin' to go alone though, are ya?" Richard said.

"To England?" I asked.

Richard rolled his eyes. "To meet Wallace."

"Oh, hell, no. I want you and Edward behind the Wilsons' place up on the mountain. Moon ain't up until three in the mornin' so you'll be good to be there with a gun. Tom, I want you on a roof nearby with a rifle. They try to take me, you all need to stop that from happenin'."

Tom nodded. "Okay then…let's put the plan together and see if we can make your gamble worth somethin'."

* * *

May 1949

Richard and I were laughing at a bet I'd lost as we entered the Amador Hotel. We went to the front desk, and I inquired if we had any messages. The young man searched under the counter and came up with a small box.

"Here you go. It was delivered today. Says Agent William Kidwell. Doesn't have your room number, but I recognized your name."

I took the six-by-nine parcel and looked at the handwriting. It was feminine, and it confused me. "Thanks."

Unsure if I should open it down here, I tucked it under my arm, and with a nod at Brewer, we headed up the stairs.

"Who's that from?" he asked.

"I don't know…but let's not act like it's a big deal," I whispered.

Once in my room I carefully opened the brown bag wrapping of the box, and opening it, I had to sit down.

"It's from her."

"Her who?" Richard asked.

"Cricket," I said, my eyes staring at the package.

Richard sat next to me and looked inside. There was an envelope that said, "Hey there, cowboy." Under it was a pretty, red and blue dress scarf and a few precious stones in a small bag.

"Why do you think that?"

"It's what she called me…and this scarf smells like her." With shaking hands, I picked up the envelope.

Brewer, recognizing I needed a moment, excused himself to his room with an, "I'll be right back."

I opened the envelope. Pulling out the tri-folded paper, I saw the date in the upper right corner and my heart sunk.

She'd dated it March 30.

Hey there, cowboy...Happy Cinco de Mayo!

If you're receiving this, then I'm dead and we're not going out dancing in El Paso tonight. I'm sorry for that. I was hoping I'd be wrong. But I know too much, and things are getting tense in the Santa Fe Ring. I'm sure that there is talk around town, now that I'm gone, that I was a whore... sleeping around with the political officials. Hell, they said it before I died, too, but that's fine. It means I did my job well...until I didn't.

Recently, I saw something I shouldn't have when I visited my family in Florida. The man who saved me there learned I lived in Las Cruces, New Mexico, and to give me some purpose to go with my new knowledge, he gave me a task...to get close to those in the Santa Fe Ring and the mobsters they hung out with.

I was to pretend to be a party girl and be too drunk half the time to remember what the men were saying. But I was never as drunk as I appeared. Ever. The problem is I think they have realized that and know that I overheard information about a dead FBI Agent and there's now a target on my back. I'm going to try and make a deal but I'm guessing that will not go as planned. Since you are holding this, it did not.

My diary is in this box, and I hope it will help you find those who killed me and make them pay for it. However, I give information in my diary that cannot get out into the world. Because of this, you cannot turn this over to the sheriff's office, especially to Happy Apodaca (he's dirty, by the way, but I'm sure you've figured that out by now) or anyone else who works with him.

You're going to read things that will make you think I'm insane...but I hope you research and see the truth. Tom will tell you I'm not lying. Find him and he'll show you that the supernatural realm is real.

I don't have much time...I'm hiding in my secret spot to write this for you. I'll drop this off at my friend's house before I head back downtown. She will have orders to deliver this to you at the Amador on the 5th of May if I cannot.

Sadly, my life choices came back to bite me, and I'll never get more than our one kiss. For that, I am truly sad. I was looking forward to dancing in your arms.

Make them pay for their dirty deeds, cowboy...I'm putting my faith in you to find Tom and take that bitch and her monsters down.

I'll save you a dance on the other side.

Love always, Ovida xoxo

I placed the letter to my right on the bed and snatched up the small diary. When I did, my business card dropped out. On the back of it was an imprint of her kissing lips with the lipstick she'd had on the day I met her. I placed it on her letter and opened the diary.

It began the day she'd seen her first werewolf…her first child of Scáthach…and I swallowed hard when I saw who had saved her.

Cursing, I shouted for Brewer. I knew his wolfy ears would hear me, and he didn't disappoint. He walked into my room ten seconds later and I showed him the part in the diary.

"Well, I'll be damned. Folliard is going to have a lot to answer for when he gets here."

"That he will," I growled.

And with that, Brewer took a seat, and we read Ovida's diary. It lay out in detail how she learned of the supernatural world, what Tom had taught her, and how she'd applied that in Las Cruces. It also named the names of those at the hotel party she'd been at that Mr. Green Eyes had spoken of.

The political world of the state was woven in with the Santa Fe Ring, the sheriff, and his men. It was as if we were back in 1878 all over again. It all had to do with money. The Santa Fe Ring had begun a partnership with the mob and gambling was bringing in a lot of money for the state, even though it was illegal. People were turning a blind eye.

We knew this state was becoming a hub for illegal gambling. Why else would Blue Jaw have been heading here? The diary talked of plans for a casino in Santa Fe and Las Cruces in particular. It also spoke of Fletcher, of the fact that Ovida heard they'd gotten rid of him, permanently, and as we read, there was one name that appeared often.

I pointed at two names in particular. "These two show up a lot in here."

"Agreed."

"Guess we need to look into Joseph Montoya and Dan Sedillo."

Brewer pointed at a page. "Victor Salazar is mentioned too, but not as much as Little Joe and Dan. We'll have to take a look at all three."

"Yes, we will."

10
ONE OF THREE

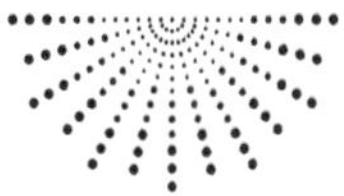

March 1879

Using my elevated eyesight, I reread the note from the governor and glanced at the time. It was eight-thirty, and we were all in position. I wanted to wait and make sure he came alone.

Keeping his word, Lew Wallace arrived just before nine o'clock, and he was by himself. At nine sharp, I left Edward and Richard hiding in the mountain's brush and knocked on the door to Wilson's jacal. With a Winchester in one hand and a six-gun in the other, I was ready for whatever awaited me inside.

However, all I found was Wilson himself at the door and the lantern inside illuminating the Governor sitting at the table, wearing a dark broadcloth suit. I could see he was tense, and that made sense since I was too.

Stepping inside, it was easy to tell I wasn't in any danger. The jacal was one room, and small at that. It consisted of a fireplace, a table with two chairs, a flat-topped trunk, and a single bed with a tiny table beside it.

Seeing as there was no one else in the room, I slid my gun into its holster and handed my rifle to Wilson to show I meant no harm.

"How's your bum doin', Wilson? It heal up okay?"

Wilson rubbed his butt cheek, obviously remembering the day the Regulators accidentally hit him with a bullet when we were firing at the

Sheriff and his deputies. "It's been ten months, so it's fine. But it hurt like hell, Billy."

"I am sorry about that. Not sure we ever got the chance to apologize, but we never meant to hurt you and for that, I'm sorry."

"You the one who left me a basket of food and medical supplies?" Wilson asked.

I grinned like a kid caught with his hand in the candy jar. "Yeah, that was me and Charlie."

Old man Wilson patted my arm. "That was thoughtful of you. Thank you."

I nodded and looked at the patient man sitting at the table. Lew Wallace sat as straight as a board, legs crossed, one hand on his knee and the other on the table. His dark hair was full but thin and flattened down to his head with a side part. However, you barely noticed any of that with such a prominent and long goatee. I had a bit of beard envy, as I couldn't grow one at all.

To say he was regal-looking would be too much, but he held an air of power and grace around him, and yet, I felt at ease. Probably more than I should have. Maybe it was the calm he was doing his best to project that helped. Who knew?

"Good evening, Governor Wallace," I finally said, and made my way to the table. I sat across from him. "Thanks for agreein' to meet with me." I stuck out my hand. "William H. Bonney, at your service."

He shook my hand. "I found your letter interesting and wanted to hear more of what you had to say. Tell me what happened to Chapman. They found two bullets in him."

Taking my hand back, I let them both stay on the table, so he would feel safe, and I told him the story of what had happened.

He nodded throughout. When I finished, he said, "Dolan and Campbell, with Evans as an accessory. Makes sense. I can see that." He sat forward and continued. "Here's my idea. We'll have you surrender, in all honesty, to a fake arrest. You'll stay in jail until the grand jury meets, and then you'll identify the murderers of Chapman."

I leaned toward him as well. "If I do that, I put my life on the line. What do I get in return?"

His intelligent-looking eyes narrowed at me. "I will let you go scot-free, with a pardon in your pocket for all your misdeeds during the Lincoln County War."

I nodded and sat back. In no way did I want to be out of the game sitting in jail for that long, but if it bought me my freedom, I could trust Tom, Dick, and Edward to hold down things while I cleared the road for our more important work.

"You have yourself a deal. Let me put my affairs in order. I'll have an associate of mine deliver a letter when I'm ready. We'll do this soon. But you must keep this between us three. Evans, Dolan, and Campbell cannot hear of this. I shook on a pact with them boys. They hear I'm goin' against that, and my life is forfeit. You hear me? And then you'll never get justice for Chapman."

"Understood," Wallace said.

I stood. "Good. I'll be in touch soon. I'll deliver to Wilson here, and he'll get that letter to you. That okay with you, Wilson?" I asked, reaching for my rifle.

He put the Winchester in my hand. "Fine by me."

"Good." I put my hand out to Wallace. "We have a deal?"

He shook my hand. "We do."

"Excellent." I let go of his hand, and with a nod, I slipped out of the jacal as quietly as I'd come in and disappeared into the dark. As I moved east along the base of the mountain, I knew Richard and Edward had me in their sights and would follow me. When I got to the Ellis Store, Tom was waiting.

"How did you beat me back here?" I asked.

He shrugged. "Better than you?"

I rolled my eyes and laughed.

"How'd it go?" he asked.

"Good. I'll tell ya more once we—"

"Billy? Is that you?" Ben Ellis said as he stepped around to the back of the stable.

"Hey, thought you'd traveled outta town," I said, surprised to see him.

"Weather kept us here," Ben explained. Then, seein' who I was with, he added, "Good to see ya, Tom!" Ben approached us with his hand out, and Tom appeared to feel awkward with the hello but shook his hand, anyway. I could've focused on that but chalked it up to Tom just being his weird self and worried about where Dick and Edward were.

"Come on in and have a bite to eat," Ben said. "We cooked us up a freshly-caught buck."

I looked at Tom, and I could see in his eyes it wasn't a wise call, but leaving would've looked weird too.

"Sure, we can come in for a bit," I said.

"Dad's got some ammunition for you too," Ben said, and he headed toward the main L-shaped building.

I was about to ask Tom to go look for Dick and Edward when they rode up with the one person I'd not expected.

"Roy!" Ben shouted out. "Well, hell, it's good to see ya!"

No longer dressed as a soldier, but in black clothing and a hat to match. Roy removed the latter briefly in a hello, exposing all his blond hair.

"Good to see you, too, Ben. How's your dad?"

"He's doin' fine! I was just invitin' Tom and Billy in for dinner. But we got us a whole deer, y'all should join."

I about heard Dick and Edward's stomachs growl from where I stood.

"We'd love to!" Roy said as he dismounted, which surprised me.

Dick and Edward whooped and dismounted.

"I'll take care of the horses," Tom said. "Then I'll stay guard. I'm not that hungry. Upset stomach a lot of the day."

"Why didn't you say so before?" I asked.

He shrugged.

"You seemed fine at lunch," I pondered aloud.

"Maybe that set me off," he said with a shrug and took the reins of Edward's and Dick's horses. "I'll do a perimeter check while I'm out here."

I nodded. "Okay."

Walking off, I wondered what was wrong with Tom but decided if he wanted me to know, he'd tell me himself. For now, I was getting some food and hopefully something to drink.

Ben looked at Brewer, who was using one of Zahara's spells, and stared. "Do I know you?"

Richard stopped walking. "Michael. I ride with Billy. This here is Edward."

Ben's eyes narrowed. "It's strange, you remind me of...never mind. Let's go on in and eat."

No one disagreed, and we headed in. Brewer and I shared a glance of worry and brought up the rear of the party.

"Ya might wanna do somethin' different with your voice," I whispered to Dick.

He nodded. "Agreed. Ben is observant."

I slapped a hand on the big man's shoulder. "At least we're gettin' a good meal before we go."

* * *

Dinner became dessert and drinks with a good cigar, and it was late. All but Roy stayed to catch a few hours down in the extra room Ben had available. I was, however, woken up around four in the morning. It was Tom.

"Wake up," he said. "We need to be back to the orchard before Zahara is awake. She'll worry."

"I'm sure she'll be fine."

"She will be up with the sun...we need to leave," he said. "Besides, there's some activity down at *The House*. Men with guns and in uniform. We need to move out."

"Damn it, yeah, we need to go. Wake up Brewer and—"

"Already did. They're gettin' ready."

I sat up and rubbed the sleep out of my eyes. He sounded off, but again, I chucked it aside. "Okay." I pulled my boots on and then my belt. Putting both guns in their holsters, I snagged my jacket and headed out to pee. Once I had, I woke Ben.

"Hey, we need to ride. We weren't here though, okay? Tell your dad."

"Figured as much. Is there trouble?"

"Maybe, Tom spotted some soldiers at the other end of town gatherin' up. We don't want to bring anythin' down on your family. Go back to sleep. Thanks again for the dinner. Good to see you."

"Same. Be safe, Billy!"

"I'll do my best," I replied, and left his room.

Brewer and Edward were already on horseback, and Tom had brought Colonel out for me. His saddle was on, and he appeared ready to go.

"Damn, you're fast," I told him.

"It's a curse," he replied.

With a smile at each other, we both mounted and the four of us headed out. We weren't more than a mile out of town when a wolf howled.

"I got a bad feeling about this," Dick said, and then a bullet hit him in the side, and he fell to the ground.

* * *

May 1949

I awoke with the fear of danger and had my gun in my hand before I knew what I was doing. Then I realized it had merely been a knock on my door that woke me up. It came again.

"Housekeeping," the voice said, and I knew it was Kit.

I was in nothing more than my underwear. "One minute!"

I put the gun under my pillow, snagged my Levi's, and pulled them on. Once fastened, I yanked a white t-shirt on and opened the door. Kit stood there in her usual uniform, her hair up in a bun. The cart was beside my door, and she held a few towels. Without a word, she walked on in, and I shut the door.

"Do come in," I said sarcastically.

She held up a finger to her lips, pulled out a rock, and sealed the room. Once finished, she set the rock by the door and turned to me. "They arrested Jerry Nuzum for the murder of Cricket."

"What? When?"

"Yesterday. I just heard this morning, so I headed straight up to tell you."

"Shit. We better wake up Richard. It's all about to get sticky."

"I agree."

* * *

March 1879

Richard!" I shouted in fear as my Beta fell from his horse. Pulling my gun, I waited for the showering of more bullets. But they didn't come.

Edward leapt down from his horse to tend to Brewer.

"Oh my god, it burns!" Richard screamed, curling himself into a fetal position.

"Silver will do that to a wolf," came a voice out in the darkness.

I didn't need to see the face to know who it was.

"You fuckin' bitch!" I screamed at Scáthach, still in Mary's body, as she rode out into the moonlight.

"Now we'll see how you like it when your Beta dies!" Scáthach screamed at me.

How had she learned about Dick? I didn't have time to think on that as

I leapt down from Colonel. Blood poured from the wound in his side, and I knew because I could smell it.

"Better get it out of there soon," she said coyly. "Before his flesh heals around it; then you'll never find it. It won't work itself out like lead; it'll just slowly poison him to death."

Brewer curled in on himself in pain, screaming out.

Tom rode toward her. "That's low, even for you, Scáthach."

"My, my…Tom Folliard, as I live and breathe," she said to him. "You two have paired up…how nice."

"Doesn't sound like you mean it," Tom said, his tone playfully sarcastic as he fearlessly got down from his horse, his motion fluid in a way I'd never seen him move. "It's not nice to lie…isn't that what you always used to say?"

Tom was acting weird, but I couldn't focus on him; I had to help Brewer. The pain in his side now echoed in mine, and I was finding it hard to take a full breath.

"I'll dig it out," I told him.

Brewer shook his head. "You can't reach it with your fingers; I can feel exactly where it is, and it's too deep. We need to get me to…Zena."

"No one can help you!" Scáthach said with a laugh as she dismounted from her pretty bay mare.

"You could," Tom said as he continued toward her. "I have to say, I don't like this body as much as the previous one you had."

"This was a means to an end," she told him. "She's attractive, but not too eye-catching. Besides, it got me close to Billy."

"You could've had anyone in Silver City. Tons of orphans like me and him there…why him?"

Scáthach sneered. "If you really must know, it's because he has a good heart. He was smart, inventive, and unlike the other boys, he was a good kid. I wanted to see if I could twist that."

"And me?" Tom asked.

"You were all those things Billy was, but you were happy. In love and starting out in life. I wanted to see what you'd do, so I pulled strings around you until I had you. It was such a shame that you left her behind to hide what you are. Why not tell her like Billy has done with some of his friends?"

"It was no life for her, you miserable bitch," he said and spat in her face.

Quick as lightning, she shot him, but he didn't react. In fact, it was as if the bullet didn't even touch him.

Brewer groaned, and I looked down to watch his skin heal.

"It's in there now," I hissed. "You hang in there, I'll get you to Zena in time."

Brewer nodded and ground out, "Go kill that bitch."

"I'm damn well gonna try." Standing, I moved toward Tom and her.

"What kind of magic is this?" Scáthach said and shot Tom another time.

Again, nothing happened.

Tom laughed, and it didn't sound right, but I couldn't figure out what was going on. "How does it feel to be fucked with, you hideous hag!?"

Without waiting for a response, he grabbed her by the throat and lifted her into the air with one hand, squeezing her neck so hard the eyes bulged.

"Don't hurt Mary's body!" I shouted as I ran toward them.

"She needs to vacate it," Tom said, squeezing harder.

"Please," I begged softly from behind him.

With a yell of irritation at the truth, Tom threw Scáthach into a tree. She dropped to the ground and flew at us. Before I could stop her, she lashed out with a blade and slit Tom's throat. But the steel blade did nothing.

He simply laughed. "Now you go over there and remove that bullet from our friend, or I'm going to kill you here and now. And with the body you stole dyin', you'll have to leave it, or face the chance of the ground swallowin' you up and takin' you home." Tom's chin jutted up and out with a bit of defiance.

That's when I thought I knew what was going on, but I wasn't sure, and Scáthach didn't either.

Tom smacked her, and Scáthach hit back, and before I knew it, they were on the ground beating the hell out of each other. It didn't take long for Tom to pin her to the ground and begin to choke her to death.

"Tom! No!" I pulled him off of her and in a move I didn't see coming, Scáthach rammed a silver stake into Tom's heart.

"Survive that, you bastard!" she screamed into his face.

Suddenly my theory proved correct, and I was now holding Kennedy and not Tom.

"Now look what you've done, you stupid bitch," Kennedy said and slumped to the ground.

"No!" Scáthach wailed, stepping back, horror on her face as she stood stock-still.

Kennedy leaned into my ear, "One of three. This is your shot, take Mary back. Use all the soul energy you can spare." She kissed me on the cheek, and with a grin at Scáthach, she said, "I'm the first pin in taking you down."

And Kennedy died…disintegrated into dust at my feet, leaving the silver stake lying where she'd been.

I didn't wait. Throwing myself onto Scáthach, with my hands on her face, I shoved as much power as I could spare into her. I imagined the energy sliding through the flesh and separating the monster from the woman. "You have no hold over her anymore!"

A tingling sensation like when I'd transfer energy to heal slid from me and under Scáthach's skin. It bubbled up and then she simply disappeared. I stepped away in horror. It was as if Mary's body had never been there. However, in its place stood Scáthach in all her horrific glory; seven feet tall with slender black limbs that were gangly like a newborn colt. She stretched and tried to find balance as glowing red eyes stared at me. Her wide mouth opened, exposing her sharp pointy teeth as she screamed, sounding like a coyote dying in excruciating pain.

I pulled my gun with silver bullets and fired, but she ran, disappearing into the night so fast, that it was a blur. The bay mare Scáthach had ridden huffed out of her nostrils like a bull and ran at me. I was planning to grab her reins and leap onto her back when out of nowhere Colonel's front hooves with his silver-infused shoes came down and hit the mare before she could reach me. Blood gushed from the shoulder wound, which threw the mare off balance, and she stumbled, missing me.

Colonel whinnied loud and came to stand by me. He shook his black mane and grunted as his front right leg pawed at the ground in challenge. The mare squared off and stared at him. I pulled my guns and waited. That's when I saw how her eyes moved. They tracked from me to Colonel, like a human would take in a scene. That's when I understood how Scáthach knew about Brewer.

"Ianna," I said. "You chose the wrong side. I don't want to hurt you, but I will."

Dark eyes glared, and before I could say anything else, she ran in the direction Scáthach had gone, and I stared into the darkness in shock. How could I have forgotten about her?

I patted Colonel's neck. "Good boy. You knew, and you made sure I did too. Extra apples for you when we get back."

Colonel playfully nibbled at my hair and then pranced away, proud of himself.

Brewer cried out in agony, and I ran to him. I would not let her take him from me too. It was going to be bad enough that I'd have to tell Zahara that Scáthach had killed Kennedy. She might never forgive me, and I needed to be prepared for that.

* * *

May 1949

Jerry Nuzum was in jail, by choice it seemed now, proving he had nothing to hide, and I wondered if his wife would forgive him for leaving her alone with the kids for so long. He was even letting them tear apart his car up in Santa Fe. We got in to see him briefly and tried to talk him into a lawyer and going home, but he refused.

On our way out, Duke motioned us to a room. We stepped in, and he handed us a bag. Inside it were two red pumps.

"See anything wrong with these?" Duke said quietly.

I turned them over. "Where's the paint our guy told us was on the bottom? There's nothing there."

"Look closer," Duke said.

I angled them to catch the light.

"Well, I'll be damned," Richard said. "You can see it's been removed. Look at the sole. It's thinner than the other one."

I looked at Richard, then Duke. "Someone tampered with evidence."

"Yes, they did," Duke said. "And that means we have a lot of dirty in this department."

"You say that like you're surprised," I said.

Duke shrugged. "Yes and no. I didn't think they'd go this far. Doing something like this shows guilt or a cover-up."

"It sure does," I said. "Get a picture of that and get that film to me. We'll get it to the home office for evidence."

Duke nodded. "There's more."

"Oh?" I replied.

"I found this while snooping about," Duke said. "So, there's been talk that a state car was seen that night…the one that Cricket leaned into to talk to the driver."

"Okay…and?" Brewer said.

"Five days after she disappeared, a burned car was found near 'A' Mountain, it's a Las Cruces landmark, anyway…it is the same make and model of the state vehicles."

"Let me guess," I said, "they did nothing with it, no connection was made and the car is in a scrap pile somewhere."

Duke nodded. "You are correct."

I ran my hands through my hair. "Fuckin' hell…this is a mess."

"It has been from the beginnin', Billy," Richard said.

I sighed. "Yeah…let's get out of here."

Duke returned the shoes and we all headed out to follow up on the other things we'd learned from Mr. Green Eyes. By that night, I was worn out and aggravated, so I went looking for trouble by taking a walk in a graveyard.

Darkness settled as I sat on the cool ground, the shadows moving as the sun rapidly descended. Ravens cawed and flew about me in large groups. One flew down and landed by me.

I wondered if Gaax was with them, but I could feel he wasn't. I couldn't feel his presence like I usually could. He likely was far away, looking into something he thought we needed to know. He'd tell me when it was time, so there was no need to worry about it.

"Ovida…" I said, laying my hand on the fresh dirt above her. "I'm sorry I wasn't here. Maybe by sitting out here like—"

"Bait," a voice said.

I looked up and sighed.

"I thought I might find you here," Brewer said, his long legs eating up the ground between us in a deliberately lazy and languid fashion. If you didn't know him well enough, you'd not see the tension under each deliberate move, but I did. This told me all I needed to know.

Not reacting to what I now understood, I looked up at him. "I felt I needed to talk it all out…so I came to tell her what we've put together so far."

Brewer squatted but looked up at the sky. Quietly, he said, "Moon's out, Billy."

"I'm packin'," I said, tapping my belt of tricks.

"If there are too many of 'em, it won't matter how much you've packed into Lilith," he said.

"Well, now *you're* here, so I'm good." I checked to see if his guns were with him, though. "I see you came prepared too. Don't feel like using your claws?"

Richard shook his head. "The trip to the hot springs has me feelin' settled. I won't need to change tonight unless I want to fight that way. You know they're in the graveyard, right?"

I grinned, and I made sure it wasn't a friendly smile. "I thought they might be, but then I saw how you came in, and I knew."

"I see," Brewer said with some irritation. "You headed here lookin' for a fight. It's why you came alone…to draw them out."

"Yep."

"That was mighty ass reckless," he snapped at me as he stood up.

"But it worked," I whispered as I got to my feet.

"Garrett is over there turnin' in his grave at your stupidity."

"More like spinning like a top," I said with a toothy smile.

"Never forgave him, did ya?"

"For what?" I said innocently enough, then I touched his arm and mentally said, "They're moving in. I count ten. You?"

"Yeah, but there's somethin' else here…it has a lot of power."

As if on cue, the man's voice we'd heard the first time we faced down the pack of Las Cruces, bellowed out. "We meet again."

It was deep, with an accent that spoke of the old tribes of the territory.

I rolled my eyes. "Well, technically, we never met last time…you hid in the shadows then like you do now, so I feel the word *meet* is incorrect," I said flippantly.

A tall man of mixed heritage stepped out onto the pathway, into the moon's light and the artificial lights of the cemetery. He appeared to be a mixture of Cherokee and Mexican. It gave him high cheekbones with dark hair to his shoulders and light grey eyes that shone in the moonlight. He wore all black, a suit minus the jacket, that fit him perfectly.

He puffed on a slender, hand-rolled cigar. "Now we have. My name is Tarack," he said, pronouncing it, Tuh-rock.

A memory stirred. I pictured beautiful Kennedy dying in my arms.

One of three, she'd said. Meaning her, Zahara, and the first werewolf. This was him.

"Well, well, well…what can I do for you, Tarack?" I asked, moving to hook my thumbs in my back pockets near my weapons.

He didn't miss the movement or step away. Instead, he raised an eyebrow and said, "I asked you to leave last time. You refused."

"Obviously," I said. "Look, Tarack, I have a job to do. Originally, I thought it had nothin' to do with you or your pack. But it's startin' to look like I was wrong. That happens from time to time."

"More often than he'll admit," Richard joked to lighten the mood.

"Agreed," I said. "Now, we can either shed blood on this ground, or we can talk. Once I have the information I need to catch a killer, I'll be out of your hair. What do you say we help each other, huh?"

"Always a sweet talker," came the purr of a woman's voice, and my blood went cold.

It wasn't Mary's voice. We'd freed Mary from *her,* but it was Scáthach's voice nonetheless. She stepped out into the light, and I had to step back. I'd seen this pretty face before. She had been in the lobby and at the bar of the Amador Hotel.

She was easily five foot ten with long, golden blonde hair and emerald-green eyes. The skin of the woman she inhabited was alabaster white and flawless. Her full lips were painted with a dark red lipstick, and the make-up she wore was just enough to be noticed but not enough to draw lingering attention from those passing by.

"I see you went for the blond version like you thought," I said. "You look good, or rather, the poor woman whose skin you're walkin' around in looks good."

She pretended to fluff her wide, blonde curls that fell past her shoulders. "Why thanks; nice of you to notice."

"So, you've known we were here the whole time," Richard said.

"Why yes, I have. I wanted to watch you in action," she said and followed it with a hideously high-pitched laugh. "It's been fun, but you're getting too close to my toys…you know I don't like to share."

"Only child syndrome isn't attractive, Scáthach," I said. "Oh wait, what name are you going by this century?"

She narrowed her eyes at me. "The humans call me Elizabeth, Liz for short. I like it. I may not give her up for a while. She's young, and this body is curved in all the right places to get me what I want."

I rolled my eyes and faked a yawn. "You're gross. You forget I've seen your actual face."

She hissed, revealing her pointy teeth.

I slowly blinked at her, my face bland and bored. Only allowing the heat to touch my eyes, I asked what I'd come here to know. "Did you kill her?"

"Her who?" Scáthach said.

It was my turn to raise an eyebrow. "Really? You're not that stupid as a blonde, are you?"

She flipped me the bird, then turned it to point downward at Cricket's grave. "You mean little Ovida? Why would you care about a girl like her, anyway?"

"Did. You. Kill. Her?" I asked through clenched teeth.

"No," she spat out. "I wanted her around, so the mysterious FBI man would come back to see her again. With the right persuasion, Katie told me the possible lawman who'd taken a shine to Ovida would be coming back. However, she didn't remember your name for me. Your doing, yes?"

I wiggled my fingers. "I'm better than I was."

She walked over to stand beside Tarack. "Ooh, a challenge. You know I like a challenge."

I sighed heavily. "Then who killed her?"

"Tsk tsk…you don't really think I'm going to tell you that, do you? Why, it would take all the fun away. I'd rather see you figure it out. It's been boring since the big war ended. I look forward to seeing if you live."

"Excuse me?" I asked.

She turned and walked away into the dark. "I'll even give you a fifteen-second head start so you don't have to die over her grave."

"Ah, fuck!" I said.

And we ran.

11
DRAMATIC ENTRANCE

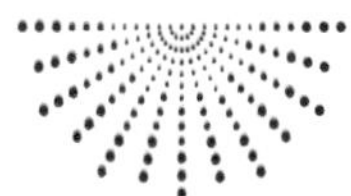

March 1879

Brewer wailed in pain, and I ran over to him. Dropping to my knees beside him. "How is he?"

"Not good, Billy," Edward said from Dick's other side. "I don't know what's going on. It should've killed him by now. But he's in tremendous pain."

"It's moving!" Dick shouted.

Edward and I shared a glance, and we both had no answers.

"We need to get him to Zahara," I stated.

He nodded. "What happened over there?"

"Mary is free of Scáthach."

"What? How?!"

"I'll explain as we go. Dick, can you ride?"

"It's moving!" he said again.

"Okay, buddy. Hang on for a sec, this is gonna hurt."

I motioned with my head that we were going to move Brewer, and Edward nodded. As quick as we could, we lifted him onto his horse and used some of his own rope to loop around him, holding him in place on Mattie as his body lay forward along the mare's neck.

I whistled, and Colonel came over. I pulled myself into the saddle, and

Edward handed me the reins to Richard's horse. Grabbing hold of the reins to Tom's horse, Edward mounted his stallion.

"We have another hour until sunrise. Let's try to get to her by then."

Edward nodded. "Wait, where is Tom again?"

I explained, and we hurried as fast as we could toward the orchard.

* * *

May 1949

Pulling on our inhuman speed, we ran through the cemetery toward West Brown Road. Many of the grave markers were flat, but some were not, and we were leaping over those as we dodged through the cemetery firing our guns with little aiming at the nearly twenty wolves on our heels.

Maybe I'd made a bad call here, but I'd be damned if I'd admit that to Brewer. Even as a wolf broadsided me, and I went tumbling about, hitting my head on a tombstone, I didn't complain. I'd brought this on myself. Go me.

Enormous jaws of the same beast who'd bowled me over snapped toward my face. I rammed my pistol under his jaw and fired. His head exploded, blood and brains spraying me and the headstone I'd hit. Wiping my face off, I apologized to the person buried below me and was on my feet running again. I breathed in the soul I'd taken in and wavered enough to trip on a dead wolf that was changing back to its original human male form.

"Damn it!" I grunted. Getting back up, I ran, picking up speed.

Brewer was now next to me, and we were firing behind us again.

"Go to the cemetery, you said, it'll be a good idea, you said...," Brewer yelled at me.

"Oh, do shut up!"

Two wolves bounded out in front of us. We both kept running, firing at them as we did. They went down, and then two more were there like magic. I jumped over mine, rolled, came up, and fired at it, killing the bastard. Brewer was losing patience, and I watched as he holstered his weapon, and with a guttural yell, leapt onto the poor beast, and with one hand on each part of the beast's jaw, he ripped it open.

"That's a choice," I said, getting up.

"Be quiet, or I'm doin' the same to you. Fuckin' idiot. Goes to the cemetery on a moon-filled night. My car is this way; we should...hold on." He pulled a handgun from each hip and shot two wolves dead as they charged. "We should get my car and roll."

"I'm down with that," I agreed.

"This way."

We ran like Hell was on our heels, because it was, and soon were running down the center of a road with no real protection. Behind us about twenty feet were another ten wolves, and they were gaining.

"How much further?" I shouted.

"I thought it smart not to park close, so they'd not know I was comin'."

"Brilliant," I said sarcastically.

"Looking back, maybe that wasn't the best call," Brewer offered as he pulled keys from his pocket.

We were within ten feet when a large van came out from a side street, cutting us off. The doors opened, and more wolves poured out.

"Are you shittin' me?" I said with a sigh. "If I only had my rifle."

I heard a boom like a good old-fashioned Winchester behind me. Spinning about, I saw the strangest thing. It was a pink truck flying down the street toward us, with a man in the bed of it holding two rifles. He wore goggles and a thin trench coat that billowed behind him as the driver hit every wolf they could.

He fired again, killing or wounding wolf after wolf, and just before the truck would've hit us, it came to an abrupt stop. The man in the goggles tossed one rifle to me and one to Brewer. He shook off the dizziness of the ride, or the killing of so many wolves, and jumped down as the remaining beasts circled around us.

"Well, you always were one for dramatic entrances," I said.

"I do like them," the man with short dark hair and a wide grin replied.

Brewer chuckled. "Good to see you, Tom."

"Likewise," Tom Folliard replied. "Now let's kill the rest of these bastards and go get some food."

"I think I can help with that," said Kit, who'd stepped out of the truck.

"Yours?" I said, pointing at the pink monstrosity.

She shut the door. "Yep. Had it painted last year for fun. Now stand back boys and let me help a little."

Tom looked at me.

I nodded. "Trust me, you wanna see this."

Showing me her hands, which wore what looked like biker gloves with the fingertips cut off, she wiggled her fingers at us. "This time I have my toys."

She didn't hesitate, and with a flat palm out toward a wolf, blue lightning streamed from her hand to the chest of the beast, killing it.

That triggered the wolves to all leap toward us at once. The four of us turned our backs to each other and in a tight diamond formation, fired on the beasts. When one noticed I'd run out of ammunition, it ran toward me. Using the rifle like a bat, I hit it in the head, sending him flying. Kit then lit him up with the energy of the earth, and he died.

Realizing they were outmatched, they ran to the van, loaded up, and the driver floored the gas pedal, leaving nothing but exhaust in their wake.

"Do we follow?" Kit asked.

"No, we've made a lot of noise out here and..." Breathing heavily, I stared at the area. "There's a lot of dead wolves now in human form that need to be scooped up before the townsfolk come investigatin'."

"I got a radio...you know, like the truckers use," Kit said. "Can we call for help from it?"

"Not without drawin' the law to us. I need a payphone."

Kit moved toward her truck. "There should be one two blocks away. I'll take ya."

"Brewer, go with her and call it in, will ya?"

"Can do," he tossed me his keys. "Not a scratch."

"Yeah, yeah...come on, Tom. We have shit to discuss."

"Okay, then ya both need a shower." Tom pointed at me, then Richard, and repeated it. "Both of ya are covered in grossness."

I rolled my eyes.

Kit and Brewer got in the pink truck and rode off. Once gone, I walked up to Tom and gave him a hug. Backing away, I decked him.

Hand to face, Tom shouted. "What the hell was that for? I just saved your ass."

"For Ovida. Get in the vehicle."

"Ovida?" Tom said, rubbing his jaw. "How do you know..." He stopped and shook his head. "How is she?"

"She's dead, Tom...that's how she is, and your meddlin' or mine possibly made her that way."

* * *

March 1879

How'd she die?" Zahara asked quietly as Edward and I lay Brewer on a table under an apple tree as the sun rose.

"Scáthach," I simply said.

Zahara nodded, and tears fell down her cheeks. "Tell me more after we take care of Richard."

"I'm so sorry," I said.

Zahara wiped the tears. "Kennedy was her own person with her own choices. She did this intentionally. I worried she might."

Richard whimpered.

Zahara placed a cold cloth on his forehead. "Shh...you're going to be all right, my lion. Focus on the pain."

"Like I'm not?" he squeezed out between his teeth.

"Not the way you need to," she said. "I have a theory. Treat it like you would a lead bullet. Focus on it leaving your body."

"But it's silver," Edward said.

"And if we get it out soon enough, he can heal internally and be back to new. Richard, do you hear me? Focus on that movement you feel. Pull it toward the closest side. It's going to hurt like hell."

"It already does," he said, breathing like a woman in labor.

"Push it out; make it leave. You've done it with lead; you can do it with silver," she encouraged.

Richard slowed his breathing down and took a deep inhale before screaming out.

"Take his shirt off," she said. "I want to see where it is."

Not caring if I was going to have to sew buttons back on his shirt, I tore it open. "It entered here," I said, pointing to his left side just under his ribcage.

Walking around to his other side, she took my hand. "Place your palm here. Use your energy to help," she said.

Brewer screamed out again.

"Now, William!" she ordered me. "Richard, focus on Billy's hand. Aim there."

Brewer bore down, and I let energy slide into him and watched as his right side turned red and purple. The skin ripped open as if being torn from within, and before my eyes, the silver bullet exited him and plopped into my hands.

Blood poured out and pooled on the ground, but to my surprise, his wound healed.

Richard turned away from us and vomited.

"His insides are likely torn to shreds, and they need time and quiet to heal. Help me get him inside, Edward. William, clean this up and wait for me. I'll be back."

I did as I was told and then sat on a stump to rest, a few apples in my lap. Colonel came over and nudged me.

"I didn't forget what I told you," I said, palming him an apple.

He crunched happily, and I bit into one myself. I was feeding him his third apple when Zahara joined us.

"Will he be okay?" I asked.

"Time will tell, but I think so."

"Why didn't the silver kill him?"

"It's not the silver alone. Sure, if we'd left it in there, it would poison him to death. But like the wolves you shoot, you must cause damage in the right spot to kill them. If she'd shot him in the head or the heart, that would've been different. Your connection to him is likely also what saved his life. Tell me about Kennedy."

I explained what had happened. and then backed up and told her of my chat with Kennedy in the woods that night up in the Capitan Mountains and about her theory.

"Was she right? Were you able to free Mary?"

"Yes. The disruption of her magical hold on this plane opened the opportunity…but where is Mary's body?" I asked, pulling out a toothpick to dislodge some apple stuck between my teeth. "I thought Scáthach had Mary's physical body. That when she left, Mary's body would be…I don't know, layin' there."

Zahara hummed in agreement. "It's magic, Billy. I'm not sure how it works. My guess? Mary has been living her life in Silver City, or wherever she ended up, unaware she was only living half a life. You don't see Scáthach all day every day. Chances are, she held the woman's soul hostage like she does yours. Along with it, she held her likeness."

"So, wait…we could have killed her and not hurt Mary ages ago?"

"I don't think so. I believe they were connected. A shared existence. No one in Mary's life will have thought her gone, but at no point that you saw Mary would she have been awake there. In fact, I would assume she'd have appeared dead or asleep when Scáthach was running about with her likeness."

When I said nothing, she continued, "It's a deep and old Otherworldly magic, Billy. I'm sorry I don't know more. I fear I need to research, learn more, because we must find a way. If Kennedy was right about the three of Scáthach's original creatures being who can send her back, I need to read her papers."

"I'll help you."

"No…this will be for me to do alone. Besides, are you not going to surrender to Lew Wallace?"

"Oh shit!" I ran a hand through my hair. "Forgot all about that. I can postpone it."

"Don't. Make things right with the law. Richard will either stay here or go with Edward to heal at his place. Gaax and I will leave to study what we can. I think I need to return to where she created me. I'll begin there."

"But—"

"I know it's hard, but Scáthach has been removed from your friend. She will have to find another person to trick into taking her on. She may look for a willing donor this time."

"What about Ianna?" I asked, reminding Zahara of the shape-shifting horse.

Zahara sighed. "She has chosen a path, and we cannot save her."

"You don't know that."

She stood and nodded. "You are correct. We must wait and see. I'll pack and return as soon as I can. I'll leave you potions and such. Please continue to use the cabin and this orchard as your base of operations while I'm gone. There will be extra magic protecting it. Only you, Edward, Richard, and Tom will find the grove."

I stood. "Speaking of Tom, where is he?"

* * *

May 1949

I swallowed the anger that wanted to erupt and sat on my bed with a loud sigh. I was exhausted. Since Richard had gone off to find a payphone to call the cleanup crew for the graveyard, it was just Tom and me in my hotel room, and I was having trouble managing my anger.

Trying to keep things conversational, I said, "So, you're tellin' me you've been stationed in New York City since we finished Triple H?" I asked Tom as I sat on the bed and pulled my boots off.

"Save for a trip here and there," Tom replied. "Some trips were longer, like the work we did in 1945, but I've made NYC my home. Strange, right?"

"For a boy from Texas in the 1800s? Yeah." I yanked my brain-matter-spattered shirt off, tossing it aside. "Trips, you say. Like maybe…Florida?"

Tom's eyes found mine and stared. Silence and stillness snagged us both, and we stood there for just a moment. I saw on his face that he knew what I was referring to. "It's a long story," he said, sitting in the ornate chair against the wall.

I went to the safe. Opening it, I pulled Cricket's diary out. Showing it to him, I said, "I know. She wrote the whole thing down and left it for me. There's information in here that might help us determine who killed her. From what I've read, I'd bet money a member of the Santa Fe Ring ordered her death…I just don't know which one, though my money is on Montoya or Sedillo." I slapped the diary into his hand. "We read it already. You can start reading while I grab a shower. Maybe you'll understand what she says better than Brewer or me. She gets excitable and some things are a bit out of order."

"Billy, I'm sorry she—"

"Don't!" I breathed, not looking at him. "I can't hear you say how sorry you are right now, Tom. You sent her in undercover, a girl with no trainin', and she's dead."

"What was I supposed to do, Billy?" he said, standing up. "She saw them with her own eyes! Plus, considerin' where she lived and who she knew, she was in the perfect place to help us. I reported it, and they gave me orders."

I turned toward him and stepped into his face. "And you followed orders instead of considerin' the life of a young girl. How typical!" I turned to walk away.

"Don't start that bullshit again," Tom said.

I spun on a heel and decked him. He fell backward onto the bed.

"This job isn't just orders, Tom. It's using your heart, and sometimes I think you forget to use yours."

"Not this old argument again," Tom muttered.

"Whatever happened to the young man who left the love of his life to save her?" I asked. "Where'd the man who cared for others first go? That's who should work for MI-5…not some 'follow the rules' lemming."

Tom rubbed his jaw as he sat up. "You can hit me all you want. It won't change the fact that she wanted to help and felt better for it. I mean, come on…she watched her friend turn into a werewolf in front of her. He tried to kill her, but I killed him first. You met her. Do you think there was any way I was talkin' that gal out of bein' involved?"

"They raped and beat her to death, Tommy," I blurted out. I swallowed to keep my throat from closing with emotion. Leaning down so my face was more level with his, I continued, "Then they did a piss-poor job of burying her in the desert where teenage boys found her rotting in the sun; unrecognizable. You and MI-5 better have a good reason for putting her in harm's way. A damn good reason. Because what you just told me, that's not it. That's not nearly good enough."

This time when I turned to leave, I went to the shower. I didn't want to just wash the graveyard remnants from me, but the memories of Ovida. Maybe if I didn't see her smiling face every time I closed my eyes, it would be different, but even now I could see her waving at me as I left the diner. That's when it dawned on me. Her smile was so much like Kennedy's, as was her fun energy. I'd never put that together before and the truth of it both made me smile and sad at the same time.

I pulled myself together, finished cleaning up, turned off the shower, and dried off. Wrapping the towel around my waist, I walked back into my room. Tom was sitting in the chair reading Ovida's diary. I had to admit; it surprised me he was still there.

Leaving him to it, I fetched clothes and changed into them. We were in for the night, so I dressed in a pair of gray sweatpants and a white t-shirt. I took the letter from Ovida to me out of the safe as well and sat down with it on the bed, rereading it for the umpteenth time.

I heard a feminine laugh from the hallway. It was a flirty giggle and familiar. Reaching out with my hearing, my suspicions were correct. When one door opened and closed, both voices disappearing, I grinned and sat back.

"Nothing here is definitive," Tom said.

"So, it's not just me and Brewer who think that."

"No. She has a lot of information, but it's not drilled down much."

"Except for Montoya and Sedillo, like you said. They seem very involved, but she didn't think they were calling the shots…either do I. She mentions Victor Salazar..."

"Yes. But that doesn't mean he or they killed her."

"No," he said, letting that hang in the air a second. "But I bet someone in that group ordered it. The questions are who and why."

"Agreed," I said, taking the towel to my hair again.

"So, what do you want to do about it?"

"Well hell, I say we drive up to Santa Fe and pay him a visit the first chance we get."

"I'm all for that," Tom told me.

Looking at the time I said, "Uh, where are you sleepin' tonight?"

Tom stood and grinned. "Why, in bed with you, of course."

"No way in hell," I said with a laugh.

Tom chuckled. "Kit helped me get a room down the hall from ya. I came here first since you said you'd be here. After Kit got me a room, she found the note Brewer left for her that said where you two would be. Readin' between the lines, we packed up the ammunition and came rollin' in."

"The flappin' trench coat and goggles really made it picturesque," I said with a slight grin.

"I have to admit, I like my new look," he said and handed me the diary. "Keep that safe."

"In the safe," I said and laughed.

Now he smiled big. "Yeah...and we'll talk about the trip to Santa Fe over breakfast. Eight o'clock?"

"Sounds good. I'll let Brewer know."

With a nod, Tom walked out, but before he shut the door, he leaned back in and said, "I'm sorry they killed her, Billy. I didn't think she'd get that deep in. I'm really and truly sorry."

"I know," I said. Then I admitted what sincerely burned my gut. "If it hadn't been you, it might've ended up bein' me, so...all we can do now is do right by her."

"Damn right we will. Night, Billy."

Tom left, shutting my door behind him, using a bit of his energy to lock it for me. I lay back and thought about the last woman who died because she'd thought she knew things that would help.

* * *

March 1879

What do you mean Kennedy is dead?" Tom asked as he sat by the fireplace. "Did the sun get her?"

"No. Where were you?" I said, poking him in the chest. "Why was Kennedy posing as you?"

"You think I what? Let her? Hell no!" He hit my hand away from him. "She tricked me, knocked me out, and then decided it best to bind and gag me. By the time I came to, y'all were gone. Had been for hours. There was nothin' I could do. I told Zahara, and she was mad as all hell." Tom whistled low. "Started ramblin' on about Kennedy bein' a fool. She didn't tell me anythin' else. So, we all sat down to wait."

I leaned against the wall of the cabin and sighed.

"How'd she die?" Tom asked.

"Scáthach showed up. Tried to kill who she thought was Tom Folliard. Killed Kennedy instead." There was a long silence, and I continued, "She shoved a silver stake into Kennedy's heart. Thing was, she lived long enough to tell me what to do, and because of that, I was able to separate Scáthach from Mary."

Tom all but flew at me from across the room. "What! Why didn't you say so? This is big news!"

"Bigger than Brewer almost dyin' and Kennedy givin' up her life?"

The happy pleasure drained from Tom's face. "Maybe not. But it's still a big deal. She'll have to work to find a new body. She'll be out of our hair for a good bit."

"Exactly. But I'm drained, and if I'm gonna turn myself in to Lew Wallace, I need to refill the well. I want to hunt. You in?"

"I'm always in to kill some of Scáthach's furry children."

"Hope I'm not one of them," came Edward's voice at the door.

"Is Brewer okay?" I asked automatically.

"He's resting. But he'll need a lot of rest to fully heal."

"Probably best. Will you stay here? It's safer than going to your place. Scáthach knows that location."

Edward nodded. "Yes."

"Tom and I are going to go after as many as we can find before I turn myself in to Lew Wallace to get this price off my head."

"I still think that's a dumb idea," Edward said. "But you have to do what you feel you must. I'll get word to you on how he is when you're being held for court."

"Promise?"

"I do. But that's not what I came in here for. Zahara wants to see you, Billy."

"Oh, okay." I headed out, then looked back at Tom. "Moon will come up around three in the mornin'. We'll ride by midnight. Be ready."

"All right."

"Oh, and Tom?"

"Yeah?"

"Bring all the guns."

I left Tom smiling and headed out into the orchard. Zahara stood there in her travel attire, and my heart felt heavy because of it. I knew she needed to go.

"Walk with me," she said. "There are things we must discuss."

I nodded and walked off with Zahara to be told whatever she didn't want anyone else to know.

12
50/50

May 1949

The phone in my room rang.

I reached over and fumbled to grab it, cursing as the receiver part fell between the bed and the bedside table. Finally getting it to my face, I said, "What?"

"Agent Kidwell?" the voice said.

"Who's askin'?" I grumbled.

"This is Calvin at the front desk. There is a Tommy Graham here to see you. He says it is urgent."

This woke me up. "How urgent?"

"He appears to have ants in his pants."

"Then it's seriously important…or he just has to pee. Either way, send him up."

"Yes, sir."

I hung up, threw the covers back, and swung my legs out of bed. Feet on the floor, I rubbed my eyes and grabbed a pair of clean Levi's and put them on. There was a knock at the door just as I pulled on the t-shirt I'd been wearing after last night's shower.

I opened the door and there stood Tommy, the part-owner of the mortuary. He appeared nervous and looked behind him and around.

Whispering, he said, "Can I come in?"

"Sure," I said, stepping aside, unsure if the boy had a summer cold or if he was making sure no one heard him.

"Everythin' all right?" I asked and shut the door.

"They are exhuming her body today," he whispered. "I shouldn't be here. You're not to be told. But I know you cared about her, and you'd want to be there."

I grabbed a pair of socks from the dresser and sat down on the chair to put them on. It seems the call I'd made had worked. But I couldn't tell Tommy that. Instead, I said, "How'd this happen?"

Tommy paced about my hotel room. "On the fifth, Hubert Beasley dispatched two of his men down here to look into Cricket's death and to hear our diplomatic Governor talk."

"Who's he?" I asked.

"Who? Beasley? He's the best police chief this state has ever had."

I wracked my brain to remember. "Diplomatic Governor…that would be Thomas Mabry, right?"

"That it would," Tommy said. "Anyway, Beasley insisted he wanted Cricket's body exhumed to look for skid marks or tire tracks on her body, and that same day Judge W.T. Scoggin Jr. signed a court order for disinterring Cricket's body."

"When will they exhume her?" I grabbed my boots.

"I'm to be there at noon to get her and bring her in."

I pulled on a boot as I thought. Once the second was on, I said, "Who will examine her body?"

"Dr. Leland Evans. Thing is, they've given Milo strict orders to admit no one and to release no information."

I stood. "Milo?"

"Oh, sorry…Milo Sherwood. He's an attendant at the mortuary. I was told I didn't need to be there either. But, it all feels more and more like a cover-up every day that passes. We need eyes in there, Agent Kidwell."

I glanced at my watch. It was half-past seven in the morning. "We will. If I can't get you in, I'll be in there, and I'll tell you all I see. All right?"

Tommy nodded. "You can't tell them you heard it from me."

I smiled, and it must've been a scary one because Tommy backed away from me one step. "Oh, we'll make it look like we just swung by. Just a coincidence. What's the best way to get to the room they will examine her in?"

"It's a back room. Easiest way is to slip in through the garage. I'll leave it open. Just don't tell—"

"You're safe, Tommy. I promise."

Tommy breathed out a sigh of relief, left, and I finished getting ready. Once presentable, I pulled out my guns, made sure each magazine was full, and threaded Lilly through the loops on my jeans. Buckling her up, I attached one pouch that fastened around my thigh, so I could slide a potion or two in, along with two extra magazines. Lastly, I slid my pistols into their holders at my back.

Snagging a black, short-sleeve button-up, I left it untucked to hide the guns, then placed my smaller one into my boot holster. Making sure everything was locked back up in the safe and that my badge was in my back pocket, I made a call to Duke to tell him to meet us. Placing my black cowboy hat on my head, I made my way to wake up Brewer and Folliard. By the time they were ready to go, we arrived at the diner just after nine. Thankfully Duke had beaten us there and gotten us a booth.

"You called him?" Brewer whispered.

"He knows people here, he might be helpful. Besides, we might learn about Tarack from him," I said.

We sat in a booth with Duke, and I introduced Folliard to him. "Duke, this is another agent who has come into town to assist. Tom Foley, this is Duke Touraine."

Tom shook his hand and smiled. "Nice to meet ya. Glad to have your help on all this."

Duke grinned, pumped Tom's hand twice, and let go. "Same."

Our waitress came over. "Oh no, does the new one eat like the rest of ya?" Katie said.

"No one eats like Richard," Tom said with a laugh.

"Duke does," I said.

"Well, I'm normal and just really want some coffee, darlin'. Black. Caffeinated."

"Same!" the rest of us said.

"Comin' right up," she said, and left.

We made small talk until Katie returned and took our order. Once she left to put it in, Tom talked about his trip and why he was here. Once I felt Duke was at ease, I asked the important question.

"So, were you with them last night, Duke?"

He drank some coffee and his dark brow furrowed. Setting the mug down he said, "What was last night?"

I leaned in, keeping my voice down. "Lots of wolves attacked Brewer and me at the cemetery last night. We barely got away with our lives."

Tom cleared his throat.

I sighed and rolled my eyes. "Tom and Kit saved our asses."

"Thank you," Tom said, and drank his coffee.

"I was not there," Duke said. "I didn't know they were planning to move on you. Sure, I heard Happy talking to someone in his office about a takedown, but I didn't know you were it."

My eyes narrowed. "How?"

"How what?" Duke asked.

"How did you resist her call? Scáthach called all her children in the area to her last night and so you either had to be there, or there's a reason you weren't. Talk."

"I could say the same for Richard," Duke said.

"We'll tell you a secret if you tell us yours."

"We will?" Dick asked.

I ignored him.

Duke did as well. Instead, he ran a hand down his pointy goatee and hummed as his dark eyes looked from Brewer to me. Finally, with a sigh, he said, "I was born in 1408. Got bit in battle in 1435. In the foot. Was captured and had the French amputate my leg. It didn't stop the werewolf infection, obviously. I changed at the first full moon, my leg growing back, and I ran. I was hers for a hundred years."

"Thought it was fifty," I interrupted.

He glared. "I got extra for running from her," he explained. "Once truly free, I came to this country, and I answer to no one."

I stared at him. We all did. He just drank his coffee.

"What was your name back then?" Tom asked.

Duke sighed. "John."

"I can see why you'd change it," I muttered.

"John Fitzalan, Seventh Earl of Arundel, Fourth Baron Maltravers. I was also known as the Duke of Touraine."

And there it was.

The table was so silent, every clang of silverware and clink of plates echoed in my ears.

"Here you go, gentleman," Katie said, showing up with the first plates of food.

She set them down in the silence, and Duke drank his coffee.

"Thank you, Katie," I said, and picked up a piece of bacon. Eating it, I stared at Duke. "Which country?"

"England," he said. "But I've lived all over Europe, even did ten years in Australia, so my accent can be whatever I want."

Which explained why when I met him, he sounded like he was from a bit of everywhere.

I picked up my coffee. "And how did you cover up for no body?"

"Billy!" Brewer said.

"What? I wanna know." I drank a good gulp of coffee.

Duke grinned. "I found a dying man my height and coloring, not so easy back then as men were rarely over six feet, and when he died, I amputated his leg and beat his face to a pulp. Paid a squire to return that body to England. He was handsomely rewarded; I believe they gave him fourteen-hundred marks." He waved it off when he saw we didn't know how much that was. "They placed the man in a tomb to honor my death in battle. In fact," Duke laughed and said, "In November 1857 they opened it up to find the skeleton of the man I'd given to Eyton. Few know the truth, and I'm trusting you with it."

I took a bite of the bacon in my hand. "Super cool."

Katie came by with the rest of the food, and we dug in, asking Duke questions until he tired of them. Finally, he asked what I was waiting for.

"I shared with you…" Duke's large hand splayed open, palms up, in a gesture that said we needed to tell him something.

"Scáthach has no control of my soul," Richard said before I could speak. "I was lucky enough to have a witch step in and teach a good friend how to intercede during my first change. She's never had me, and she never will."

Duke let out a low whistle. "Does she know you exist? Cause if she does, she'd hate you."

"Tell me something I don't know," Richard said with a slight grin as his right hand absentmindedly rubbed at his side where Scáthach had shot him all those years ago.

"Can't lie, I'm jealous," Duke said. "You've never had to feel the call. But I suppose you've had a target on your head for other reasons all your life."

"That I have."

There was a pause, then Duke said, "Well, you didn't call me here to learn about my past. You mentioned having more on the case. Fill me in."

* * *

March 1879

I paced about Tom's and my bedroom in Zahara's cabin, venting about the news we'd learned on our way back from killing werewolves.

"I'll say this, word sure travels fast, especially when it's that criminals have escaped," Tom said.

"Fuck!" I shouted before I collapsed onto my bed and dropped my head into my hands.

Tom shut our door the rest of the way. "You're going to wake up Richard and he needs to rest if he's gonna heal."

Even though it was three in the afternoon after our first hunt, Richard was resting to heal.

"Of course, news of escaped criminals travels fast," I said quietly. "And it wouldn't matter except for *who* those criminals are." I let out a long, disgruntled sigh. "It's one thing to turn state's evidence against Campbell and Evans while they are in prison. It's a whole other thing to do so with them free and armed."

"Don't forget Texas Jack…he escaped Fort Stanton with 'em," Tom said, crossing to add a small log into the wood-burning stove that was nestled along the wall between our beds.

I stood. "You're not helping."

Walking over to the window, I stared out at the orchard. It was strange to know Zahara wasn't here. Sure, her magic still hid this place from anyone who didn't know what to look for, and it kept the weather inside this bubble temperate, but I could feel she'd left. That was what burned my gut. I hated that she'd needed to leave, but I understood why.

"You gonna pull out of the deal with Wallace?" he asked me.

"I don't know. Maybe. Hell…"

Each room of the cabin had a door for safety. I opened the one in our room and headed over to the stable. We'd rubbed down the horses when we'd returned but I'd not checked Colonel's eyes and wanted to do that.

Tom followed me out. "Maybe wait until they are captured before you go through with this. No one would blame you."

"I would blame me," Billy said. "I'm no coward."

"No one is sayin' ya are, Billy."

I stepped into Colonel's stall and checked his eyes. They were fine. Likely the wolf he'd taken down with his hooves during our night of battles had healed his eyes to right as rain today. He only needed me to do it once every few weeks if it was a full restoration.

"What about Colonel?" Tom asked.

I pet Colonel's neck and kissed his face. "His eyes look good."

"I mean, if you let yourself get taken in, what do you want me to do with him?" Tom clarified.

"Ride him. He'll be a great help to your fightin'. Just check on his eyes every few weeks."

Tom nodded. "Okay. And what if they take me in? Then what?"

"Edward and Richard will take care of him. I've explained to them that if that is somethin' they cannot do, they should take him to see Sallie Chisum. I'll put a note in his saddle for her. Tell her he's goin' blind and to take good care of him until I can return. That way, if I'm gone longer than I'd like, they don't put him down when his sight goes."

"Good call."

I nodded, and with a last pat on Colonel, I left him to munch on the fresh hay we'd put out for him and headed out to sit on one of the benches in the orchard.

"Spring session of court will be soon," I said. "I'll testify and then be out. Free from the law and, as long as they believe me, free from Campbell, Evans, and Dolan."

"It's not even fifty-fifty odds, Billy," came Brewer's voice.

"Why are you up and about?" I asked.

"'Cause I want to be, *mom*," he sneered.

Tom snorted a laugh, and I glared at him until he stifled it.

I'd have been more upset, but if Brewer was making jokes, he was doing better than I'd have thought. "Point taken. But really…why are ya out here?"

"Heard you bitchin', wanted to see what was up and how huntin' went." He winced but sat beside me. "Besides, ya know I hate bein' cooped up for too long. Just like you're fully aware this Wallace thing is a gamble."

"I know…and I like to gamble. Besides, it is more than a fifty-fifty shot. I have the word of the governor. That said, I'll write a letter to Wilson to get further information from him with the new development."

"Which is?" Dick asked.

We told him about Evans and the gang escaping custody.

"Oh, for goodness sake, Billy, we need to leave the state and you should *not* be testifyin'."

I stepped toward him. "My freedom from the law is worth upsettin' Evans, Campbell, and Dolan."

"You're not gonna change his mind," Tom warned Brewer.

Richard just rolled his eyes to the heavens in what was likely a plea for patience, and the subject changed to the group we'd seen up in the mountains that we planned to hit when the moon rose again.

When we headed into the cabin, I took off my boots and placed them under the bench by the front door. I wanted to sleep, but I needed to write the letter and eat first. I walked across the main room to the desk. Taking a seat, I sighed.

"I'll make us some food; you write that letter," Tom said.

I thanked him and pulled out paper, ink, and a quill. By the time I finished, Tom was spooning stew over rice at the small dining table. I left the letter on the desk to dry and sat down with Tom, Edward, and Richard to eat.

"What did you write?" Tom asked.

"The truth. That I don't know what to do now that the prisoners have escaped. I asked Wilson to speak to Wallace and see what he wants me to do. Told him to send William Hudgins to the Junction at three o'clock with men he knows are all right with a note tellin' me what the governor wants. Instructed him not to send soldiers."

"Think he'll abide by all that?" Edward asked.

"Guess we'll find out," I spooned up some stew and blew on it before taking a bite and humming in appreciation.

"It's a gamble...and I don't like the odds," Richard said yet again.

"So you've said," I pointed out. "Look, I don't like 'em either. But this is in motion now...and I need to see it through."

* * *

May 1949

The chances we're gonna get let in to see Cricket's exhumed body is maybe fifty-fifty," Duke said.

"Well hey, that's pretty good," I said.

Brewer rolled his eyes. "No. No, it's not."

I tapped my pouch attached to my belt and leg. "Got somethin' special with me if that weird wolfy trance thing you two can do doesn't work."

"Only way it won't is if any of them are supernatural like us," Duke said.

I flashed what I thought of as a winning smile. "Like I said, I got your back. Come on!"

Richard parked his vehicle down a few streets, and the four of us walked to the Graham Mortuary, heading straight for the back parking lot. Looking up, I noticed the bars on the upper windows. I pointed it out to Tom. "Does that seem weird to you?"

He shrugged. "They don't want the dead walkin' out?"

"That'd probably be bad for business," I said with a wink and entered the garage that Tommy Graham had left open for me as promised.

Seeing the door to the prep room just where he told me it would be, we entered through it and made our way to the autopsy room. Only one person was in there. A gentleman with a military stance who couldn't have been over forty years old. He wore a lab coat, so I thought he might be the doctor waiting for Cricket's body to be delivered.

"Can I help you, gentlemen?" the man in the lab coat asked us when we walked in.

"Doctor Evans?" I asked.

"Yes?" he replied.

I pulled my badge out and showed it to him. "We're here with the FBI regarding the murder of Cricket Coogler and are lookin' for Mr. Graham or someone who runs the place. We'd like to speak to him."

"They should be back soon. You can wait out front if you'd like."

"No can do," Duke said, stepping up to stand in front of Dr. Evans. Once the man's eyes were on his, he continued. "We need to wait right here."

I saw Leland Evans's eyes go glassy and unfocused before he nodded and said, "Yes, it's best you should wait here."

"We'll just take a seat over there," Duke said. "You won't even notice we're here."

"Won't notice you're here. All right," Dr. Evans replied, then went back to work.

"Will he honestly not see us at all from here on out?" Tom asked.

"Only if we bump into him," Duke said. "So stay clear."

"You got it," Tom said and moved to the back wall to lean and cross his arms so his hand would be near the gun he wore in a shoulder harness under his open dress shirt.

We all waited, and it didn't take long. Soon, a few men carried in a plain casket and set it on the platform, making the top of the wooden box level with the exam table. Evans went over and signed for the body. That's when someone spotted us and headed our way. I didn't recognize him, but I'd have bet money that he was Milo Sherwood.

"Hey, you can't be in here," he said to us.

The doctor didn't pay him any mind and gave the other two men, one blonde and one brunette, gloves to wear. The doctor himself put some on as well and gave instruction to the others on how to move Cricket safely from the casket to the table.

Tom, Richard, and I all flipped out our badges to the man who came to us, and that stopped him enough for Duke to step up between us and him and catch his eye.

"Milo?" Duke said.

"Yeah?"

"I'm Duke. Happy Apodaca sent us. It's okay that we're here."

"It's okay that you're all here?" Milo said, his voice not as angry as before.

Duke nodded. "Yes. You won't even notice us."

"Won't notice you all, sure, sure," Milo said now, totally convinced.

"We mean no trouble."

"It's no trouble at all," Milo said and walked away.

The doctor and the men with the gloves opened the casket.

Dr. Evans sighed. "I was afraid of that. Oh well, place her on the table."

"What about them?" one of the two men asked.

"Who?" Dr. Evans asked but didn't look anywhere.

"Them," the blonde one clarified, pointing at us.

"They're supposed to be here," Milo said and walked back out to guard the entrance.

The two men headed toward us, but Duke and Richard stepped forward and cut them off, doing the same thing Duke had done before. They eventually shrugged and went back to the casket and helped the doctor lift a body bag of waxed canvas out and place it on the table.

"Was she embalmed?" the darker-haired of the two helpers asked.

"No," Evans said. "They poured lime into the bag to stop decomposition, cover the smell, and dry up the body."

"Lime?" I whispered. "That would slow down decomp for sure, but it would eat away any evidence."

"Maybe that was the point," Richard offered.

I pondered that. "I think it was a kill two birds with one stone situation. It would destroy evidence and it would preserve her enough to have a memorial and to bury."

"Was she X-rayed already?" Dr. Evans asked.

"Yes, before we brought her to you," the blond man said.

"Great," Evans replied. "Help me get her onto the table.

We watched in silence as they assisted Dr. Evans. Once finished, he said, "Go check on those X-rays. Bring them to me as soon as you can."

The two men agreed, rolled the platform with the casket on it away to give access to all sides of Cricket, and left the doctor to his business.

Moving toward a reel-to-reel magnetic tape recorder, Dr. Evans turned it on, hit record, and picked up the microphone.

"Dr. Leland S. Evans in the re-examination of Ovida Coogler. May seventh, nineteen hundred and forty-nine."

I tuned him out and walked to the side of the table where the casket had been. Looking down on the body of the lovely and vibrant girl who I'd fancied not a month before, my heart ached in my chest. Tears filled my eyes. I wiped them away so they'd not fall on her or the table.

Out of the corner of my eye, I saw Tom step forward to come to me, but Brewer's big hand stopped him. My partner knew I needed to stand there and deal with it on my own. While Dr. Evans spoke about what he saw, I let my eyes wander to each injury he mentioned.

There was the damage to her face and body previously mentioned to us by Tommy Graham and the boys who'd found her. Her clothes were intact as previously stated, and I looked for evidence that they had run her over. I didn't see any.

There just weren't enough bones crushed. Sure, her chest had fallen in, but that easily could have been from decomposition. Thing was, she didn't appear smashed. Even if they'd run over just the center of her, it would've split her sides open, and that hadn't happened. From what I was seeing, she didn't die from being hit or run over by a vehicle.

The blond man came back in and handed the X-rays to Dr. Evans a good while later. Evans put them up with the light behind them so he could examine each area of her body.

"We have a fracture line on the left temple," Dr. Evans said. "Appears to have a fractured cheek and jawbone as well, and a complete break in the left collarbone." He shifted, examined another X-ray, and added, "I find no evidence of a broken pelvis or leg, but the vertebra at the point where the neck meets the body is broken."

A broken neck? That's how they'd killed her? Was it intentional or accidental, that was the question now.

"COD should be changed," Dr. Evans continued as he walked back to stand over Cricket. "Instead of death from an unknown object or person, it should be death of a violent nature by an unknown cause. This was homicide, suicide, or an unfortunate accident. Be sure to have that adjusted as soon as possible."

"My money is on homicide," I muttered, again standing across the table from Evans.

"Me too," Richard said, now standing on one side of me while Tom had taken the other.

"I'm so sorry," Tom said, his voice more choked up than I'd have thought he'd be.

"You sayin' that to me or her?" I asked.

"Yes," was all Tom said before he stepped away from the table, Brewer following him, hand on his shoulder.

I knew I couldn't touch her. Instead, I said my goodbye, promised her I'd get the sons of bitches who did this, then walked toward her casket. With fingers still wet with my tears, I took out the stones she'd asked me to bury by her grave, and instead placed them inside her casket under the padding and left. The rest of my team followed me out.

I was furious and despondent in a way I'd not felt since they killed John Tunstall on my watch. I stepped into the washroom, rinsed my face off with cold water, and headed straight for Tommy Graham's office. We were about to have words...and he wasn't going to like any of them.

13
BILLY THE KID

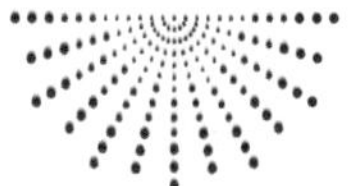

March 1879

I delivered my note to Squire Wilson, and then Tom and I were on our way to go hunting when we ran into Roy.

"Where you off to?" he asked.

We told him, and he joined. We located the party of wolves we'd seen in the mountains the day before and waited for moonrise. Once they shifted, we took them all out.

"Do we stay and bury 'em?" Tom asked. "If we don't, someone could come across them and report a mass murder."

"The silver in their bodies will be absorbed," Roy said. "Only a trained eye would see the burn inside and only a trained eye at that. But yes, we should bury them."

As we dug, I thought of something. "Roy, the silver-lead bullets that don't go through one or in one, what happens to those bullets?"

"I try to pick up as many as I find, but I don't get them all. However, they've all been spelled. They sit in the sun too long and the silver will liquify and drain into the ground. All people will find is a lead bullet."

"Why would it even matter?" Tom asked.

Roy and I looked toward him, but I spoke first. "First, we don't want anyone usin' those bullets on Richard or Edward on accident. Second… people would ask questions."

"Some already do," Roy added. "I usually catch wind of it and take care of it all."

"You really do clean up after Regulators," Tom said.

"That's my job," Roy replied, using the shovel we'd found in the group's belongings to dig the hole he was in deeper.

"I feel I should apologize then," I said.

"Oh?"

"I'm sure we all cause you a lot of work cleanin' up after us," I told him with a grin.

Roy laughed. "That you do. But that's okay."

Silence filled the air, and the only sound was a shovel in the dirt as Tom or I dragged bodies over.

"Billy?" Roy finally asked. "Are you really gonna turn evidence against Dolan and Campbell?"

I stopped what I was doing, causing a man's leg to drop to the ground. "How do you know about all that?"

"There's rumors goin' round that Wallace has an eyewitness to Chapman's murder and they're willin' to talk for immunity for other charges. Seein' as Garrett gave you an ultimatum, I figured it was you."

I shifted my weight to the other foot and stalled by looking at the horizon as the sun rose. Finally, I said, "Yeah, it's me. If Garrett wasn't threatenin' to send me to fuckin' England unless I got the law off my back, I'd not be tryin' so hard."

"Uh-huh," Roy said in a noncommittal tone as he worked. "Ya sure it's not also because you love it here and would like a fresh start?"

"Well, that too," I said. "Besides, who would want to go to England?"

Tom raised his hand. "I'd be down for some trainin' and a trip to see another country."

"Well then, go in my place," I said.

Roy smiled. "They want both of you to come. It's nice there. I think you'd like it."

"Wait, you've been there?" I asked, grabbing a man and placing him in the hole in the ground.

"Sure," Roy said, wiping his brow before handing me the shovel. "Your turn."

"That's it? Sure?" I replied before taking the shovel and digging.

Roy pulled out his canteen and took a drink. "It's where I did my trainin'. It's an estate out in the middle of nowhere, surrounded by a forest. I think you'd enjoy it there. Spendin' the 1880s in London could hold all kinds of adventures. There's a lot of excitin' things to do there, and the underground life of the supernatural world is quite active. You'd be fully entertained, I'm more than sure."

I squinted at him and shook my head. "Look at me, do I look like I'd fit in out there in London?" I burst out laughing. "No way." I went back to digging.

"We'll see," Roy said. "Who knows, maybe you and Tom could go together."

"While we're at it, Richard and Edward too," I said.

Roy choked on a sip of water. "Werewolves in the academy? That'll be the day."

I smiled. "If they want me, they will at least take Richard too. That'll be a hard line I stand on, make no mistake."

"Thought you weren't gonna go," Tom said, chiding me.

"Oh, do shut up, Folliard. You know what I mean."

"Uh-huh," Tom said and went to get another body.

Roy finally said, "I'll let 'em know."

"Yeah, you do that," I said, and got back to digging a grave.

It was a solid stance; if they wouldn't ever take Richard, then I'd never have to go.

* * *

May 1949

"That's right, sir. They should have Cricket back to her plot in the cemetery around four o'clock," I heard Tommy Graham say to someone he spoke to on the phone. "I will let you know if there's a delay. Thanks so much."

The minute I heard Tommy hang up the receiver, I walked into his office with Brewer, leaving Folliard and Edward out to guard the doors.

Shutting the main one behind us, I motioned toward the second one that led to the hallway, and Brewer went to close it and stand there.

"Tommy, Tommy, Tommy…we need to have a little chat," I said.

"Did you see her?" he asked us.

"I did. Evans is still doin' his work in there. But the lime has ruined any tissue clues you might have gotten. Why the lime, Tommy? Tryin' to hide things?"

"Embalmin' her wasn't possible. Besides, it's costly. The lime helped kill the bacteria and with it, the smell. Because of that, we could have a memorial and then let the family bury her."

"About that," I said, "If she was indigent, as you called her, how come she got a spot in the cemetery? Don't indigents get a pauper's grave?"

"Someone paid for that," Tommy said. "Why are you interrogatin' me?" He dropped his voice, finishing up with, "You'd not have even known this was happening today if I'd not come and told you."

I stepped into his face. "First there's talk of her bein' run over, but I saw no actual evidence of that. Someone broke her neck, Tommy, and I intend to find out who. If I discover you and yours have not been straight with me or with the jury, I'll expose it all. You hear me?"

"He looks properly afraid of you about now," Richard said with a grin.

"Good. 'Cause I'm not one to fuck with, Tommy." I turned around and headed for the door. Hand on the doorknob, I looked back, "I'll make whoever did this pay. They'll either spend their life in a cage, or they'll be six feet under. Those are their only choices."

I opened the door and walked out.

Brewer followed me, but he touched the brim of his hat and said, "Thanks again for the heads up, Tommy."

We left the building, and I stormed down the street to the car. I was vibrating with anger, and I knew I was barely holding it together.

"They need to pay!" I shouted.

"They will," Dick said.

"I mean with their lives. I want answers, and I want them said to my face by those assholes in Santa Fe. Tom? You still want to go up there?"

"Hell yeah!"

"Then let's pick a day and time… I want to look those bastards of the Santa Fe Ring in the face and see if they can justify the killin' of an eighteen-year-old girl."

"They can't," Tom said.

I wheeled around on him. "No, they can't, but damn it all to hell, I wanna watch 'em try. I want to see who gets uncomfortable when we ask questions, and I want to do that soon."

* * *

March 1879

Word from Wallace said that the escape of Evans and Campbell made no difference to our arrangement. On the twentieth, I wrote him back with my plan.

"I'll go with you," Tom said.

"That's not wise. Word is they arrested Scurlock in Fort Sumner. We don't want them to get any more Regulators than we have to."

"Let me read the letter," Tom said.

I handed it to him.

Finishing it, he said, "Sanger and Ballard are, or at least they *were*, friends of Campbell. Ya might want to surrender to someone ya trust, like Sheriff Kimbrell."

"Good idea," I said, taking the letter back and adding a P.S. to the bottom. "I'll go take this to Wilson."

"No, I'll take it," Edward said, already putting on his shoes. "No one knows me, so I'll draw little attention."

I looked at Richard, and he nodded, so I handed the letter to Edward. "Be sure to give this to Wilson. Don't just leave it for him."

Edward nodded, grabbed his coat, and headed out. I sat down to write a letter to Sallie Chisum and to my friend, Pete Maxwell. When I finished, I sat down with Tom and Richard to drink a little and play some cards by the fire. We were still doing that when Edward returned.

"It is all set," he told me. "Tomorrow."

"Tomorrow then," I said.

Richard and Tom shared a look I didn't understand, and I ignored it. Pouring some mulled wine into a cup, I handed it to Edward. "Wanna play a hand?"

"Sure," he said, taking the warm beverage from me. After a drink, he said, "You're sure about this, Billy? You could just not show up."

Nodding, I said, "I'm a man of my word. I'll go."

"I still think this is a bad idea," Richard said.

"You think all of my ideas are bad."

Richard grinned. "Not all...just most."

Everyone laughed, including me, and we got down to playing cards. Tomorrow would be an interesting day.

* * *

May 1949

I was filling Lilly's pockets and attaching weapons when Richard knocked twice and came into my hotel room. Shutting the door, he just stood there.

"Don't say it," I said.

Brewer leaned against the wall, and with a sly smile on his face he said, "Say what?"

I rolled my eyes. "Don't sound so innocent; I know you."

He laughed. "Do you now? What am I gonna say?"

"That this is a bad idea…that it shows our hand."

"Well then, if ya know it, why the hell are you goin' to go to Santa Fe and poke the bear?"

I stopped. "The bear? Are there were-bears now?"

Brewer burst out laughing, and I realized he wasn't being literal.

"Oh, shut up," I said and checked my guns before I slid them into their holsters at my back.

Brewer walked into the room and sat on the end of my bed. "If you go in mad as a march hare, you're gonna tip 'em off."

"Who says I'm goin' in there mad? I actually have a better idea."

"And what pray tell is that?"

I grinned and told him.

"Well now," Brewer said, sounding impressed, "maybe not all of your ideas are shit after all."

"Thank you for your confidence in me," I said, playfully smacking his arm, which felt the same as hitting a tree. I shook my hand a bit from the sting. "So, forgot to ask you yesterday. Did I hear you and Kit hangin' out the other night?"

Brewer's ruddy face went twice as red. "No."

"Liar. I knew you'd like her. She's your type. Red hair in curls…blue eyes…witchy. Take her out on a date while we're gone."

"What?" he sputtered.

"You heard me," I said as I flipped through my wallet to make sure all I needed was there before sliding it into my back pocket.

Brewer appeared horribly uncomfortable, but he smiled and said, "Maybe I'll take her out. When will you two be back?"

"I'm guessin' tomorrow. Tom wants to stop by home office while we're in Santa Fe. Says he ordered some new toy and it should be there by now."

"Toy?" Richard asked before he realized, and then he and I said, "Weapon."

"Likely a magical one so...I'm intrigued."

"Same. Be careful."

Once ready, I grabbed my leather jacket for the cool nights up in Santa Fe, and we made our way out to the car. I was about to tell Richard to contact Duke when the sound of a raven filled the air as it flew overhead. I stopped and watched. Couldn't tell if it was Gaax or not, but I got this tingling all along my skin and the smell of the apple orchard filled my nostrils.

"Zahara," I whispered.

"Hmm?" Richard said, shutting the door to the Amador Hotel behind us.

I'd been told Zahara was dead, but the air suddenly felt alive with her magic and the smell of her home. I searched the streets for her.

"What is it, Billy?" Richard asked.

"Do you not feel that? Smell the apple trees?"

Richard inhaled and shook his head. "No, why?"

Was the message for me and me alone, I wondered, then shook my head. I didn't have time for this right now. I went over to where I'd parked last night, opened the trunk, and tossed in my overnight bag as Tom stepped out of the hotel.

"Now *this* car is a dandy!" Tom said, placing his bag in the trunk before closing it and getting into the car.

I turned over the engine, and she roared to life before purring like a kitten.

"Let me drive it back?" Tom pleaded.

I put my sunglasses on. "Don't hold your breath." I looked through Tom's window at Brewer, who was leaning down to look inside. "If anything happens, call us at home office. We'll likely head back tomorrow...but still."

"But still," Brewer parroted and nodded. "Be careful."

"We will," I said.

"We never are," Tom said at the same time.

With a wicked laugh I peeled out of my spot, onto the road, and headed to the state capital.

* * *

March 1879

You don't need to follow me to my fake arrest," I told Tom.

Folliard pulled himself up into the saddle of his horse. "Yeah, I do. Someone has to watch your back."

I rolled my eyes, then looked to Brewer. "Take good care of Colonel. If his eyes start to go, Tom here can help." Stepping over to Colonel, I lay a hand on his neck and felt his sorrow. "I know, pal. I won't be gone long. Tom, Richard, and Edward will take good care of you. As soon as I can come back, I will. I promise."

Colonel lowered his head to me, and I placed my forehead on his. "Love you, too, pal. You be just the right amount of good and bad for them, okay?"

"Hey," Richard said at my wording.

"Ride him every day that you can," I said, palming Colonel some peppermint I'd stashed for today. Kissing his face, I stepped away, gave Brewer a hug, then got up into the saddle of Richard's horse, Mattie, a beautiful bay mare.

"It's time," Tom announced. "We need to go."

Taking up the reins, I said, "Then we go." I tapped the sides of Mattie, and we left, making our way to Gutierrez, one mile below San Patricio.

When we arrived, it didn't take long for Sheriff George Kimbrell to show up. He was a good man and a McSween/Tunstall sympathizer. I trusted him and true to my word, I surrendered to him when he arrived.

"Who'd have thought I'd be takin' in Billy the Kid?" Kimbrell said.

"It's William H. Bonney," I said.

"The papers like callin' you 'the Kid'," the sheriff said as he put cuffs on me.

I sighed. "Great."

Kimbrell chuckled, and then I heard something else I didn't want to. It was Tom. He was tellin' Kimbrell's men not to shoot, that he wanted to surrender too.

"What the blazin' hell are you doin'?" I asked as he sat beside me in the wagon.

"Told ya, I've come to keep an eye on ya, just wasn't clear how long or from where I planned to do it."

"I hate you," I grumbled.

Tom smiled as they put us in cuffs we could've broken out of. "I know."

I shook my head. "The horses?"

"Sent a message to Ike Ellis. He or Ben will come get them. Edward and Richard know to pick them up there."

"Wait, they knew about your stupid idea and didn't tie you down?"

Tom smiled. "It was their idea, and I agreed it'd be best if I come with ya, for now."

I rested my head in my hands. "You're an idiot." I looked up at the sky. "You're all idiots!"

"It can't always be your way, Billy," Tom said. "Sometimes you don't think things through, I'm here to make sure ya do."

Staring at the beautiful blue sky of New Mexico, which sported a cloudless afternoon and the perfect spring temperature, I hoped I'd be able to see it from where they put me while I waited. If I was lucky, they'd place me in a different room than Tom; because right now, I wanted to kick his ass.

* * *

Our first evening in town, we spent the night in the old cellar, but thankfully they transferred us to the Patrón's store just across the street the next day, March twenty-second. Once we settled into the front room on the far west side of the building, I took a seat by the window and watched the busy life of those in town as they went about their morning work.

Recognizing a friend of mine, I opened the window and shouted out to him. "Manuel!"

"Billy!" he yelled out in surprise and came to the low window. "What are you doin' here? Are you under arrest?"

"You could say that," I said with a smile. "It'll all work out fine. How's your wife and the boys?"

He took off his hat and fanned his wide, tan face. "Oh, you know they drive me crazy, but I love 'em."

"You playin' music anymore?"

"Yes, we are! We be playin' tonight at the saloon down the road. We will play loud enough that you can hear us."

"That would be wonderful," I said.

A knock came at the door to our room. I looked back. "Gotta go, give my best to your wife."

"I will, take care, Billy!" Manuel said with a big grin on his face as he left.

I shut the window and turned to face the one man I wasn't expecting to see.

"My name is Officer Smith," Roy said. "I'll be tendin' to you while you're here. Governor Wallace has informed us he plans to keep you here for a few days, until he can meet with you, and then he will move you to Fort Stanton. Do you have questions?"

"Nope," I said.

"Any chance we could get some water?" Tom asked.

Roy nodded. "Of course, I'll be right back."

When he left, I looked to Tom. "You set that up too?"

"No. He's just that resourceful. I feel better already."

That night, Roy brought us dinner. We were eating it when Manuel and his band came by the window to play for us. Opening the window, we sang with him until we all needed to call it a night. They left, and we each took a cot in the room to get some rest.

It was going to be a long wait.

* * *

May 1949

Sitting in the waiting room of Governor Thomas J. Mabry, I fidgeted. "I hate waiting. What is takin' him so long?"

"Important people doin' important things, I suppose," Tom said offhandedly as he glanced through some magazine that was out for anyone to read.

I fidgeted with my tie. I hated wearing a suit, but that's what I was in. Complete with a pair of oxfords that made my feet protest.

"Stop it," Tom said.

"How do you sit there in that thing like you are comfortable?" I asked.

Tom flipped a page in the magazine and continued to peruse. "Because for my last two assignments, I've been in one of these every day. I *am* comfortable."

I made a gagging sound.

Tom smiled. "The price to pay for workin' in New York City, I suppose."

"Not everyone in that city wears a suit," I stated.

"True. But I was undercover in a realty office."

"Excuse me, gentlemen," the secretary said, "He'll see you now."

Tom set the magazine down on the chair beside him, and we both stood.

"Just head on in," the secretary instructed us.

We did as we were told. In the office, sitting behind an old desk, was a man in his mid-sixties, but still in decent shape. His hair was silver, and his face clean-shaven, with only a little extra weight on him. He wasn't looking up at us; instead, he was on the phone.

"Billy the Kid?" he said.

I froze, and Tom and I shared a look before walking the rest of the way in, wondering what the hell was going on.

* * *

March 1879

On Sunday, the twenty-third, Lew Wallace walked into our room to talk to me. Roy escorted the governor and me to another room inside the Patrón home, and we sat down to talk. I held nothing back, telling him about the way stock was translated at Shedd's Ranch, Mimbres Spring, San Nicolas Springs, and other rustler hideouts. I provided a rundown of the careers of the Jones family as well, but Wallace, he wanted more.

"I need bigger fish, Billy. If you're going to get that pardon, I need more."

"I already told you how Dolan killed Chapman. I'll testify to that in court. You'll get your big fish."

Wallace nodded. "I better."

"You will."

He got up, but before he headed for the door, Wallace said, "I keep reading reports, and they're calling you some nickname...what was it again? Oh yes, Billy the Kid. That what you're goin' by these days?"

I chuckled. "What? No. Because I'm young lookin', I used to get called Kid Antrim, that'd be my stepfather's last name. But he was a worthless son of a bitch, so I dumped it. Seems someone is just parsing together the Billy Bonney and Kid Antrim." I shrugged. "It won't stick. You'll see."

Wallace raised an eyebrow at me. "I wouldn't bet money on that if I were you."

* * *

May 1949

Governor Mabry continued to talk to the person on the phone with him. "Let me get this straight, he claims to be *the* Billy the Kid, this man in Texas? Well, let's talk to him and see what he says. What's his name now?"

There was a pause, and he swiveled in his chair. Looking at us, he waved for us to come in as he said, "What kind of name is Brushy Bill?" He listened for a few seconds then said, "Uh-huh, well, you tell him we'll at least talk. But really, Jim, do we think it's him?"

He listened, then said, "Yeah, that's what I thought. Oh well, we can at least speak to the man. Set it up. I gotta go, keep me in the loop." He hung up the phone, and his dark eyes stared at Tom and me.

"Someone claimin' to be Billy the Kid?" I asked.

"Every so often we get nuts, but this guy seems to have details about Billy that are grabbin' the attention of some folks. So, I'm stuck seein' him. Now, how can I help two members of the FBI?"

He motioned to the chairs that faced his desk, and we sat.

"Sir," I said, "We're here to talk to you about the Cricket Coogler case."

The Governor expelled a breath of obvious frustration. "I don't know anythin' about all that. Salazar is handlin' it. In fact, I sent Beasley down to deal with it all. Have you spoken to him? He's a good man."

"Not had the honor yet, sir," Tom said. "But we'll do so when we are back in Las Cruces. Now, we understand that Joseph Montoya and Dan Sedillo were down in Doña Ana County the night she went missin'. Have you questioned them yet regardin' their whereabouts? It's been said they saw her that night."

I picked up the ball. "It's also been said that someone saw a state official's car ride away with Cricket. A car that matched a burned-out one found days later."

Mabry spread his hands wide. "I'm tellin' ya, boys, I don't know anythin' about that. You really must talk to Joe and Dan." He looked at his calendar. "But I don't think they're around right now. They went to Albuquerque for the day. Should be back tomorrow. Will you be around then?"

"We can be," Tom said.

"Great, then I'll—"

"I'd actually like to talk to you about somethin' else," I turned to Tom and leaned into his ear. "Make sure they're really not here, would you?"

"Sure, you can talk to him alone," Tom said. "Where is your restroom, Governor?"

"Uh, just out the office and down the hall to your right."

"Thanks so much," Tom said, and let himself out.

I stood up and stepped over to one window in Mabry's office. "Nice view ya got here. Tell me, Governor, what does that Brushy Bill want?"

Relaxing a bit, Mabry said, "The full pardon Wallace offered him."

I laughed. "That promise was a lie to get what he needed, then he left town. It was a trick."

"Yes, I believe it was."

I nodded, remembering my hate for Wallace. "Will you give it to him? The pardon, that is?"

"Probably not."

Lips pursed, I walked toward his desk. Putting out my hand, I said, "Well then, I suppose I'll leave you to your day."

Assuming I was done with him, Mabry put his hand out to shake mine. I let energy slip into him immediately and said, "Now we're about to have an actual conversation."

14
J. EDGAR HOOVER

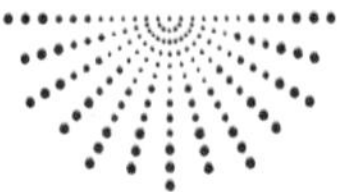

April 1879

Five days after I testified for the grand jury about Chapman's murder, Roy stepped into the room, and I sat up from the book I was reading.

"Hey, what news on the trial?" I asked.

Roy pulled up a chair and sat down. This got Tom's attention, and he sat up as well.

"It's not good," Roy said. "Wallace has left Lincoln, leavin' Ira Leonard to keep an eye on things, and it's lookin' like Rynerson isn't gonna honor anythin' Wallace promised you. I intercepted a letter from Ira Leonard to the Governor. It's not good."

"What did it say?" Tom asked.

"Leonard told Wallace that the District Attorney is not a friend to law enforcement."

"Like that's a shock. Rynerson's been in the pocket of *The House* since day one," I said.

Roy nodded. "Leonard also told Wallace that Rynerson is bent on goin' after you. He's proposed to have the evidence destroyed, as well as your influence, and push you to the wall. Explained to Wallace that Rynerson is a Dolan man and is defendin' him in every manner possible."

"Damn it," I said.

"You knew this could happen, Billy," Tom said.

"It gets worse," Roy said. "He's changed the venue of your trial to Doña Ana County. You won't stand a chance there like you would here. He's gonna go for a conviction for murder."

I stood and paced. "If found guilty, they'll hang me."

"Which you'd survive from," Tom pointed out.

"Yeah, and then it's super public that I'm not really human. This will put me on a damn boat to England. Garrett will make sure of that before he lets me hang and come back, hang and come back, and then it'll all be a mess." Pulling at my hair, I stepped to stare out the window at the town I adored. "I won't let them take me from here, Roy. I won't."

"You may reach a point where you have no choice," he pointed out.

That hung in the air for a while, and I pondered multiple plans of action.

"How is Dudley's trial going?" Tom asked.

Roy shrugged. "It only started a few days ago, so it's plodding along. You'll be called to testify there, too, Billy."

"I figured," I said, but I wasn't really listening. My mind was considering my options. I could walk out of here and disappear, or I could stick it out and see if Wallace came through. If nothing else, I needed to testify against Colonel Dudley. Once I'd done that, we'd see where we were.

I didn't have high hopes, and neither did Tom or Roy.

"I best get a letter out to Dick and Edward," I said. "Can you get me some paper and ink?"

Roy stood. "I can. I'll be back with it."

He left, and I looked at Tom.

"What are you thinkin', Billy?"

"I'll wait and testify against Dudley. Then we see how that turns out; we'll make a judgment call."

"Okay, then we wait."

"We wait."

* * *

May 1949

By the time I left Mabry's office, I was more irritated than a man covered with hives and shingles at the same time. I found Tom downstairs by the main doors sitting on a bench, reading a magazine.

I plopped down next to him. "So?"

"Oh, they're here. I couldn't get in to see them, but they're here. Was told they were in meetings all day. I showed my badge and said this trumped their meeting. Then I was told that meeting was not on the premises."

"And you think that was a lie?"

"I do."

"So, Mabry lied to give them time to prep."

"That'd be my guess," Tom said. "We could go stormin' in there and likely get a one-on-one with Montoya, but we'd be eatin' crow later as he'd call the office, and we'd have nothin' to stand on with concern to questionin' him."

I looked at the magazine in Tom's hand and saw it was the same one he'd been reading upstairs.

"Did you steal that?" I asked.

Tom looked at me and smiled. "I hadn't finished my article, so I borrowed it." He went back to reading.

"You takin' it back up there?"

"Nope."

"Then that's stealin'."

Tom grinned. "I suppose. Now that we've settled that, what did you get him to tell you?"

"He knows nothin'. Like, honestly, he doesn't know a damn thing about it all. Kept sayin' to talk to Salazar."

Tom's eyebrows furrowed. "The Revenue Commissioner?"

"Yeah."

Tom shrugged one shoulder. "Well then, let's go talk to him."

"I stopped by his office. He's not there. I pushed my way in, and honestly, he's not in today."

"Shall we go to his home?" Tom offered.

I wanted to say yes. I desperately wanted to go put pressure on him or his family, but I shook my head. "I made an appointment for tomorrow. Let's keep it from slammin' back on us. I've pissed off Director Lucas enough this year."

Tom laughed. "That you have. But hey, Dick got his job back, so it was the right thing to do. Let's go check in at the home office and talk strategy with some of the guys. They know these knuckleheads better than we do. Maybe they'll know where we need to push, and where not to, in order to get what we need."

I nodded. "All right. Anythin' to get out of this suit."

"It looks good on you," Tom said, standing up.

"I so couldn't care less."

Tom laughed, and we headed to the car.

"I swear, my hand on the Bible, that if I never have to wear one of these again, it'll be too soon."

* * *

June 1879

I testified at Dudley's Court of Inquiry on May 28, and by June seventh, Roy stopped by with information on yet another letter from Ira Leonard to Wallace. This one railed at the proceedings of the Dudley trial. It informed the governor that they, Rynerson and his ilk, meant to whitewash and excuse Dudley's glaring misconduct. That they transcended all rules of evidence to allow hearsay to come through other channels rather than direct parties.

"Ira goes on to say that he is thoroughly and completely disgusted with the way they are running the proceedings, so much so that there was a point where he almost abandoned the case and let them have their own way. He said, and I quote, 'It is a farce on judicial investigation and ought to be called and designated, The Mutual Admiration Inquiry,'" Roy said.

"Ouch," Tom said. "He's not holding anything back."

"The question is, can Wallace do anything about it?" I asked.

Roy shook his head. "I don't think so."

"Any other news?" Tom asked.

"No," he said. "But I'm going to head to Mesilla for a while on other business. I'll be back soon. When I return, you need to have decided if you are stayin' and waitin' on the governor, or if you're gonna walk away."

"All right," was all I said.

When Roy left, Tom and I turned toward one another.

"So?" he asked me.

"If I've not heard from Wallace by the time Roy comes back, we're leavin'. In no way am I goin' to trial in Mesilla. I've waited on the governor long enough."

* * *

May 1949

Driving through the big, black metal gates of the estate in Santa Fe which housed MI-5 operations, I followed the long driveway to the old, New Mexican-style mansion. Parking my vehicle in the circular drive, we got out.

Handing Tom his overnight bag, I snagged mine and shut the trunk. "Feel like I was just here."

"You were just here," Tom replied.

I rolled my eyes. "Hence the sarcasm you totally missed."

As we went up the steps to the long porch, one of the two oak doors opened, and Collin, the butler and all-around man of the manor, stood there with a cheerful smile on his face.

"Good evenin', Collin," I said.

"Masters Kidwell and Folliard," Collin said, his British accent thick and fluid. "It's good to have you both in the house. Do come in. I've had your rooms prepared for you."

Collin stepped his tall, lanky form aside, and we entered. Once he shut the door, he smirked and said, "*Sadly*, Master Whimbley is not in the house at this time."

"Yeah, that's a shame," I said flatly.

Tom snorted, catching my sarcasm this time, seeing as it was as thick as a homemade quilt.

Collin's smile widened. "Yes, I knew you'd be torn up about it. Dinner will be at six o'clock sharp. Shall I plan for you both to attend?"

"Yes, sir," I replied. "Thank you, Collin."

"Anytime, sir."

As Collin bowed and left, a well-built man who stood around my height with twice my muscle, sporting an impressive blond beard and startling blue eyes, stepped into the foyer.

An enormous grin spread across my face. "Dr. Ryan!" Dropping my bag, I went over and gave the well-built man a hug that he returned heartily. I let go and stepped back.

Dr. Ryan Roberts, who preferred to go by Dr. Ryan when he wasn't being called Agent Roberts, was a sight for sore eyes. He and I had become friends during a case we'd worked together in England, even though he was from Scotland, and I'd not seen him in quite a while.

"What are you doin' here?" I asked him.

"I could ask the same," he replied, his Scottish brogue not as thick as it once had been. He ran a hand through his short blonde hair, which was shorter on the sides than the top. Looking over at Tom, he put out his hand. "Tom! Good to see you as well! You keepin' him out of trouble?"

Tom grasped Ryan's hand and pulled him in for a hug. "What's goin' on, Hercules?" he said, using a nickname he'd given Dr. Ryan many years ago for obvious reasons. "When have I ever been able to keep him from trouble?"

"Good point," Dr. Ryan said, stepping back from Tom, his jovial blue eyes taking us both in. "It is truly good to see you. I heard you two were comin' into town earlier today. Where've you been?"

"Tom and I decided it was a wise call to stop by and see Governor Mabry," I said with a grimace on my face and roll of my eyes on the word, 'wise.'

Dr. Ryan's face mirrored mine. "Mabry, huh? Yeah, that sounds like a frustratin' trip."

"Tell me about it," I said. "I don't think that man knows what he had for breakfast unless Victor Salazar tells him. Jeez!"

Hands in his pockets, Dr. Ryan rocked back and forth in the stylish leather sandals he wore most of the time as he hated shoes that fully covered his feet. "So, you got nothin'. Not a surprise. They don't share over there."

"What about you? Here for business?" Tom asked.

"Yeah, a bit. In fact, there's a meetin' tomorrow that revolves around the situation in Las Cruces. I'm figurin' you both will be called into that too."

"I don't doubt it," I said. "Any clue what it's about?"

Dr. Ryan stepped closer and lowered his voice. "If I understood correctly, I believe that we'll be on a call with J. Edgar Hoover."

"Head of the FBI?" Tom said and whistled low.

"Yeah, it's a last-minute meetin', actually. I was here for somethin' else, then they got word you two were stoppin' by, so they set it up. Beau wanted me to come tell you."

"Director Lucas is actually in the house?" I asked. "Well, well...guess it's an important meetin'. What time?"

"After breakfast tomorrow mornin', around nine our time...eleven theirs."

"That's right, I keep forgettin' about that difference," I said. "All right. We're gonna head to our rooms and clean up for dinner. Will ya be there?"

"Was plannin' on it. I'll let you get settled and see you at the long table."

I smiled, picked up my bag, and slapped him on the shoulder. "Sounds like a plan. Good to see you, Ryan."

"Same goes."

We left the doctor in the lobby and went up the wide, oak staircase to our rooms on the third floor.

"How much do you want to make a bet they try to pull us out of Las Cruces?" I said to Tom.

"They can try, but I'm not budgin'. You?"

"Nope."

"Good, then we're on the same page. See you at dinner."

I nodded and headed into my room. Shutting the door, I placed my bag on the bed before sitting beside it. Falling back, I stared up at the ceiling. A lot had happened today, and I let my mind play over it. Mabry should've taken up most of my thoughts, but he didn't. It was that feeling I got when we'd stepped out of the Amador Hotel that played over and over in my mind.

Could Zahara be alive? I laughed and said, "With that woman, anything is possible."

I lay there for a while longer, then with a sigh, I sat up, opened my bag, and got out some more comfortable clothes than this suit. Stripping down, I grabbed the towels left neatly folded for me on the chair and headed to the bathroom for a hot shower. If I was going to be dealing with Director Lucas, I needed to be on my game.

* * *

Beau Lucas, Director of the New Mexico branch of MI-5, was a tall, sturdy man with dark hair and a goatee. The silver at his temples and woven into his facial hair made him look as distinguished and powerful as a title like his required. At this early hour of the morning, he was pacing along the windows behind the enormous desk in his office. Taking off his glasses, he cleaned them with a handkerchief.

Sarah, his short, curvy blonde secretary, cleared her throat to let the director know she had us standing there. Lucas motioned for us to take a seat. Sarah, who reminded me of Etta Candy from the Wonder Woman comic, gave us a smile, patted my arm, and headed back to her desk on high, light pink heels.

We walked into the office as Lucas held his glasses up to the light and then cleaned them again before stepping over to the window to look out. Putting his glasses on, he returned the handkerchief to his pocket. We took a seat in the silence.

"Seems you boys have stepped onto a fire ant hill down in Las Cruces," he said, his east coast accent noticeable even though he'd lived in New Mexico for many years. "I canceled your meeting with Salazar today."

"You what? Why?" I exclaimed.

"You attracted the attention of J. Edgar Hoover himself," Director Lucas said. Glaring at Tom and me, he added, "Is that a good enough reason? How do you feel about that?"

"Like our typically unlucky selves?" I offered. "And yeah, it's a good reason."

"There's a lot going on down there, and it's bigger than a missing agent, a witness on the run, or a murdered waitress," Lucas said, his Connecticut accent making his words sound staccato and important.

"Those all seem pretty big to me, sir," I said.

Tom nodded and thumbed toward me. "I'm with him on that. So, if that's just plain ol' big news, what's bigger?"

A knock came at the door, and Dr. Ryan stepped in. "Sorry, was helpin' Collin with somethin'."

"You've not missed anything, Agent Roberts. Please, take a seat." Once Ryan moved his way in and sat on the other side of me, Lucas continued. "As you all know, we originally sent William to New Mexico to look into what happened to Seymour 'Blue Jaw' Magoon and Agent Fletcher Calhoun, who was originally sent to find Blue Jaw."

Lucas took a seat at his desk. "You also are aware that Agent Calhoun is presumed dead and at the hands of the law there in Las Cruces. Before his death, he left us the clue that Scáthach was back and in that town."

"I can verify she's there. Seen her myself. Blonde this time around. It's weird," I said. "Has one of her primary three with her: Tarack. He's the first werewolf on this land."

Lucas nodded. "I read your report. But there's more going on in Las Cruces than them or the death of Miss Ovida Coogler, and yet...all three are related to it." His phone rang, and he picked it up. "Yes? Of course, Sarah, please put him through." He waited until she'd done so and said, "Good morning, Director Hoover, hold on a moment while I put our amplifier in place, this way the room can hear you, and you them."

Lucas pulled out a black box one-foot in diameter and placed the phone's receiver inside an indention on the top that was made for it. "Arthur created this for us. It's fantastic!"

There wasn't anything the twenty-year-old whiz-kid who built gadgets for MI-5 couldn't come up with, so I was rather excited to see how this worked.

Director Lucas flipped a silver switch on the side of the box. "Director, can you hear me?"

"Yes yes, quite well. You?" Director Hoover said, and the whole room could hear him from the sides of the box.

"Well, I'll be damned," I whispered.

Lucas grinned like a kid with a new toy. "Loud and clear, sir. You're on in the room with Agents Kidwell, Folliard, and Roberts."

"Good morning, gentlemen," J. Edgar Hoover said.

"Good morning, Director Hoover," we each replied.

"I know this is last minute," he said to us, "but after the reports I've been receiving from your time there in Las Cruces, we've decided it was imperative that you be brought in and told what we know."

"Any help the FBI can give us is appreciated, sir," I said.

Knowing that was a bit tongue in cheek, Lucas gave me a tiny glare. I returned it as Hoover continued.

"Unknown to the Santa Fe Ring and her affiliates there, we have been monitoring their activity in the gambling business for a while. In fact, we maintain three regular informants there, and they report directly to me. The Bureau has issued regular crime reports on southern New Mexico. In particular, those reports include the names of prominent politicians and lawmen.

"Neither the participants of these illicit affairs nor their families are aware that we know about their every move and the depth of their involvement with organized crime. We know everything from the amounts of each deposit made at the local bank to the intimate details of their sex lives."

"Damn," Tom said under his breath.

"Who is bringin' in the most dough?" I asked.

"From what we can tell, the most lucrative and prominent of the casinos belong to the Cleveland Mob. Places like the Sunland Club, Valley Country Club, and La Loma Del Rey Club. All those are in Anapra. But they have some less lucrative spots in Ruidoso and Alamogordo. But don't take the term 'less lucrative' to mean low return. Our files show that this year Judge Scoggin purchased a brand-new Oldsmobile sedan with his share of the Alamogordo payoffs."

"Just his share?" Ryan asked.

"Yes," Director Hoover said.

Tom sat up in his chair. "Is Governor Mabry in on this?"

"He looks the other way," Hoover said. "The Valley Club alone is paying twelve-hundred dollars a week to local police and politicians to keep their doors open. That includes New Mexico State Police Chief Hubert Beasley."

"That would explain why Mabry sent him to Las Cruces," I said.

"And why we've not been able to speak to him," Tom added.

"Correct again," Hoover said. "It's not just gambling that's going on; but bootlegging liquor as well. This is what your friend Miss Coogler got herself messed up in from what we can tell, and she knew too much. That's our guess, but it rings true for me."

"So, is it just the Cleveland Mob we're dealin' with?" I asked.

"Plus some boys from Murder Inc.," Hoover said.

"Which would explain why Blue Jaw was headin' out this way," I pointed out.

"Exactly," Lucas replied.

"There's more in a report I sent to Director Lucas for you boys," Hoover said, "but I wanted to talk to you. That way, you'd understand how important it is that you do not disrupt our investigation."

And there it was.

I stared at Lucas, my eyes likely as on fire as my temper, but he motioned for me to be silent. I swallowed my flaming anger and sat still, trying to calm my impulse to tell the director of the FBI to go fuck himself.

"With the investigation into Miss Coogler's death, the gambling is going to come out, and we are hoping to put things into play to bring it all crashing down. In fact, her death and the trials for it are the perfect springboards for our next step. We need you to be careful there."

"Careful how, sir?" I asked before Lucas could shut me up. "Just so we don't step on toes."

"Stop digging into the murder of Cricket Coogler," Hoover said. "We have men there who drive that narrative."

"You mean, blocking the narrative," I said before I could stop myself. "Every time I turn around in that town, someone has blocked the investigation, tampered with evidence, or not followed procedure. Has that been intentional?"

"No. That is the local law doing that to protect the politicians and the mafia. Not us."

I opened my mouth, but this time Lucas stopped me by standing up before I could say a word. He shook his head at me, so I clamped my mouth shut and counted to ten, hoping to curb my anger.

"Word has it that the Chicago syndicate went into Colorado, brought that state into the fold, and has now moved into New Mexico. Specifically, the town of Red River. It's mainly slot machines. They are threatening any tavern or café owner who refuses them in their establishment. So, needless to say…"

"They are everywhere," Tom said, his eyes following Lucas as he paced around his desk to stand beside the phone.

"Yes, and Miss Coogler's case may be what helps bring it all down, but we have to play it right. I've already sent information on this to Director Lucas, he'll be talking to you gentlemen after I go, and you'll go back to Las Cruces to help things move along the way we need them to."

I looked to Lucas with wide eyes that screamed, "You're going to let them tell us what we do now?"

Lucas made a gesture that told me just to wait, so I did.

"Please be sure to read through the files, pass them on to Agent Richard Baca when you get back to town, and we'll be in touch. I'm sorry I don't have more time, but I have another meeting I need to get to. Beau, you need anything else from me?"

"No sir, thank you for your time."

"Take care out there, gentleman. Thanks for all the work you do."

We said our goodbyes to J. Edgar Hoover, and the room went silent until the receiver was hung up and we were sure he was gone.

"Tell me we will not put our investigation on hold for the fucking FBI, Lucas. Tell me they're not calling the shots for the SIS," I raged before anyone else could say a word.

Lucas moved back to his chair. "Take a breath, William. We never have answered to the fucking FBI, and I don't plan to start now. So, sit down and listen up."

15
THE LETTER

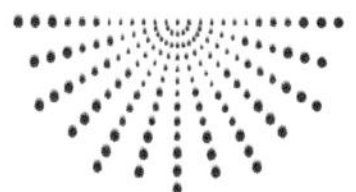

May 1949

Your job is to investigate the supernatural of that town, so you'll keep doing that," Director Lucas said. "If that leads you back into the murder of Miss Coogler, then so be it."

"Sir, we already know she was aware of our world from the letter and diary she sent to me," I said.

"But her death may have nothing to do with it," Lucas said. "Keep digging."

"If you want my opinion," Tom said, "I think it's all wound together. I think the Cleveland Mob came down here for a reason. I think they got tipped to do so by a pretty blond from the Dark Realm of the Otherworld. She wanted to come back to New Mexico and wanted to cause all the trouble she could. Best way to do that is bring the mafia in."

"I'm with Tom on this," I said. "I think the werewolves are the henchmen for the mob and that it's all intertwined."

Dr. Ryan stood up and wandered to a window. "Billy and Tom are right. With all the papers I've already read on this, it's evident that organized crime and Scáthach are one and the same. If not everywhere, in New York, Chicago, and out here for sure. My question is, why New Mexico?"

"She has unfinished business here," I said.

"Like what?" Ryan asked, turning to me.

I shared a look with Tom, and he nodded. "Three things. First, she wanted me there and knew if there were issues in New Mexico again, I'd be sent. Second, she lost there…back in 1879. I bested her, and it took her a while to find a body that worked for her. By then I was in England, and she doesn't go there if she can help it."

"And three?" Ryan asked.

"When Kennedy reappeared like that, Scáthach began to doubt Zahara was dead. Scáthach wants, no…*needs* to drive her out. She feels she can do that by comin' at me, Tom, and Richard."

"And do you?" Lucas asked.

"Do I what? Believe she's alive?" I asked.

"Yes," he replied.

How could I explain I felt her in the air? That wasn't a tangible fact but, it was all I had. "I think it's possible, sir. I've felt this…presence as of late. But I have no evidence. I just sort of feel her. I know that sounds stupid, but I think she's around, or her spirit is."

"And knowing Zahara, even her spirit might be powerful enough to help take Scáthach down," Tom said.

"Then you need more hands on deck," Lucas said. "Agent Roberts, can you head down and assist?"

Dr. Ryan Roberts nodded. "I can…but just adding me won't be enough."

"What? No, I'm enough to save the world?" Tom teased.

Dr. Ryan's hand came up to lay on his chest as true laughter took him. "You're never goin' to let me live that down, are ya?"

Tom grinned. "Hell, no."

"In my defense, I was drunk…," Dr. Ryan started to say when Director Lucas cleared his throat. With a barely suppressed smile, he finished his sentence differently. "We will need another person, sir."

"I am fully aware. I have another in mind and shall keep you posted. Now, take a folder each and a few extra for your team who aren't here. I'll be available to you for questions after lunch if you have any. For now, go read up on the work the FBI has done and start keeping better notes and reports for me." He turned to Dr. Ryan. "In fact, Agent Roberts is great with detail. He'll be your point person so that I don't have reports coming in from all of you."

"Yes, sir," Dr. Ryan said.

"Dismissed."

I stepped forward to Lucas. "If I might steal a minute of your time, sir."

Beau Lucas eyed me carefully, then said, "*One* minute."

I looked at Tom and Ryan. "I'll be out in a moment."

They nodded and left.

"What is it, William?" Director Lucas prompted.

"Sir, I'd like to talk to you about Catherine Bell and Duke Touraine."

* * *

July 1879

The tolling of the afternoon bell rang in town, and families began to close up shop for an afternoon break. It was the seventeenth if I had figured the date correctly, and I was beginning to wish I'd never put this plan in motion. We'd been in here for months now and I was close to ripping out my hair with boredom when Roy finally returned with some good news.

"Frank Coe was brought to trial in Mesilla for the murder of Buckshot Roberts," Roy said.

I laughed. "Charlie killed Buckshot, not Frank."

"That's why he was exonerated by the court," Roy explained. "Also, seeing as Widenmann has left the country, his three counts of resisting arrest were dismissed."

"Handy," I commented.

"Have you heard from Widenmann?" Tom asked.

Both Roy and I shook our heads.

"He's in England with the Tunstall family," Roy said. "But that's all I know at this point in time." Silence fell, and he asked the question I knew was coming. "So, Billy? Are you stayin' or goin'?"

"Goin'. We'll leave after sunset."

"Easy enough. Open that window, and you can walk right out."

"That was the plan," I said. "Can you get us horses?"

Roy smiled. "Sure can. I'll head that way now. I'll tap on the window when they're in place for you at the Ellis Store."

At that, Roy left with a wide grin on his face.

"He seems mighty happy we're gonna leave here," Tom said.

"Probably been bored as all hell, just like us," I said.

"Well, that's goin' to end," Tom pointed out. "Where do you plan to head?"

"Through the Capitan Gap and northeast to Fort Sumner. I can earn some money doin' some stuff for Pete Maxwell."

"Are ya sure?" Tom asked.

"About Fort Sumner or leavin'?"

"Leavin'," he clarified.

"Oh, I'm sure. I'm through with promises. Tunstall promised me a ranch, McSween promised me pay, and Wallace promised me a pardon. None of that shit has come to pass. I gave the only two things I had to give, my loyalty and my life. Put both on the line for two years and I have nothin' to show for it. So, we're goin' to start over, put together a group, and hunt down Scáthach's creatures and the bitch herself if she comes back."

"We gonna tell all those men that's what we're doin'?"

"Hell no, we'll steal horses and sell them back. It'll give us a suitable cover to roam the land and make some money while we're at it."

"But first, Fort Sumner?" Tom asked.

"Yeah, *after* we go fetch our things in the orchard. I want Colonel with me when we go check on Pete and Paulita. Pack up your stuff. Let's be ready to go when he knocks. I've had enough of this room."

"Amen!" Tom said.

It would not be easy going, but I could not stay here and be tried in Mesilla. I'd done what I could to free myself from the law legally; now it was time to do it the old-fashioned way. We would be on the run, and to be honest, that suited me right down to the ground.

* * *

Tom and I made our way back to the cabin in the orchard. We stayed there for a while since we knew no one could find us there. Edward would go out and fetch supplies and bring back information. Rumor was Big Jim French had been killed, but it wasn't confirmed.

"Bristol allowed Dolan a three-thousand-dollar bail at La Mesilla in the death of Chapman, and the DCOI for Colonel Dudley finally ended," Edward said.

"And?" I pressed, then took a sip of the mint tea we'd made that day from the herbs in the garden and sunlight in a glass jar.

Edward cleared his throat, then said, "Dudley was exonerated."

"What?!" I shouted, standing up as the glass in my hand shattered, its pieces clattering to the ground as my tea splashed all over my boots.

My cuts healed quickly, but I wasn't paying attention. "Mother fucking son of a bitch!" I hollered as I stomped across the room. "How is that possible?"

Richard stepped up behind me. Laying a hand on my shoulder, he said, "You know how. Dirty law tryin' a dirty man."

"But he violated a *federal* law!" I shouted. "He stomped all over the Posse Comitatus Act and they let him walk? Damn it all to hell!"

With that, my temper and I walked out.

* * *

May 1949

Son of a bitch," I muttered, then louder, "Son of a bitch!"

"What ya got?" Tom asked as he drove. I'd let him so I could pore over documents from the FBI.

"Get a load of this. In Doña Ana County—"

"Also known as Las Cruces," Tom interjected.

I pointed at him to signal he was correct. "One person collects the money from the casinos, then they divide it three ways. One payment goes to the Doña Ana County Sheriff."

"Happy Apodaca," Tom stated.

"Yep! Another payment goes to District Judge W.T. Scoggin, Jr., while the third finds its way to the Democratic Central Committee in Santa Fe."

"Who would handle the committee money?" Tom asked.

"You ready for this? State Corporation Commission Chairman Dan Sedillo. And gee, guess what he did with it?"

"I'm guessin' he didn't donate it to orphanages or veterans in need."

"Nope. He distributed it to the local politicians and the governor's campaign funds."

Tom whistled low. "Damn, Billy. That's…I can't think of a word worse than horrible."

"How about atrocious…or repulsive…or hey, horrendously disgusting?"

"Those all work," Tom said. "Do all the towns in New Mexico function that way?"

"Nah…looks like Hot Springs's share went directly into the street improvement fund."

"Is that the money from casinos and slot machines that are scattered all over?"

"No." I scanned for the section I'd seen on that. "Here it is. Slot machines paid forty percent to the owner of the establishment, forty percent to the owner of the machines themselves, and twenty percent to…oh, get this, to good ol' Revenue Commissioner, Victor Salazar."

"I don't like how often his name comes up."

"Me either," I said, my eyes closing as I lay my head back. I had a screaming headache, something my abilities couldn't rid me of as it wasn't a wound, and I pressed my fingers to my eyes. "I was up all night going through this shit."

"Do you think Cricket was killed because she knew too much about our world or about theirs?"

I sighed. "I don't know. We may never know which it was."

"On the bright side, Jerry Nuzum was exonerated and released while we've been here," Tom told me.

"And we get more hands on deck with Dr. Ryan," I said.

"Were you able to get him a room at the Amador Hotel?" Tom asked.

"No. They're full up with so many in town for the Cricket case. He's staying at the Campbell Hotel instead. I stayed there my first time in Las Cruces. It's nice and just a block or so away."

"Good. It'll be good to have a doctor with us…but did you need to talk about lye in caskets over dinner last night?"

"What? I wanted his take on it."

Tom shook his head and laughed. "And he was happy to talk about it at length…about dead bodies and lye and…you're lucky no one at the table was squeamish."

"If they are, they're in the wrong business."

"Point made," Tom said. "He'll be in town by tomorrow. We'll introduce him to Duke and put a new plan into action. Yes?"

"We will. Lucas said he'd be sending one more our way. Did he tell you who it would be?"

"Nope. Guess we'll just have to wait and see."

"I hate waiting," I said, and went back to reading the FBI papers as we made our way back to Doña Ana County to figure out what we were going to do next.

* * *

July 1879

My temper and I walked through the orchard until I reached the outer edge by a road which I could see but anyone traveling on it would never see me. The magic was so heavy it appeared like the wall of a mountain to passersby. I picked an apple and bit into it. I wasn't hungry, but I was hopping mad, and it was all I could do not to scream without stopping.

It didn't take long for Brewer to come join me. He said nothing, just sat on a bench I'd placed out here last year for when I needed away from the house to sit and think by myself.

"Don't say we should've known," I hissed.

"I don't need to, because you know it already."

I sighed and leaned my forehead onto a tree. "It's not fair. He violated a federal law, was the reason innocent people died, and he walks free."

"Yes," Richard said simply. "I'm sorry."

I turned to him, leaning my back against the tree. "Was there more oh-so-great news that I missed since I walked out?"

"Yeah, Dolan and Caroline Fritz got married and left on their honeymoon. He'll be gone for a couple months is my guess."

"Didn't you fancy Caroline at one point?" I asked.

"You know how I like women with curly hair," Richard said with a shy smile. "Yeah, I had an interest in her one summer, but it didn't go anywhere, and then the world turned upside down."

I sighed. "Yeah, it did." I finished the apple and tossed the core away. "What else?"

"Seems you're supposedly expected to appear in court in San Miguel County for keepin' a gamin' table."

"I totally forgot about that. When am I supposed to be there?"

"August 10."

"Guess I best plan on doin' that so they don't come lookin' for me."

"If you don't go, maybe they'll think you left New Mexico and we can leave. There's no reason to stay."

"We need to wait here for Zahara to return," I said simply. "That's why we are here."

"We can come back and check on her from time to time, but we could go anywhere we want."

I shook my head. "Scáthach is still out there, somewhere. She'll find a new body, and she'll come back. We need to be here when she does. We stay."

Brewer sighed. "Not all of us have to."

I saw the look on his face, and my heart hurt for him. "You wanna go, Dick?"

He shrugged. "I have enough potion and magic coins from Zahara for doin' things around town, but it will eventually run out. I'd like to go where no one would know my face, where I could just…live. You know?"

I came over and sat on the bench beside him. "What do you want to do with your long life?"

"I don't know," he said. Lips pressed together, he thought. Finally, he added, "I'd like to own a farm again. Live a simple life in a town where maybe I'd be a sheriff and make a difference. I feel like I can't toss my new gifts aside. I should use them somehow."

I patted his leg. "What if I could get you to London for that academy?"

Richard perked up and looked at me. "What?"

"If they want me bad enough, they have to take you too. That's my rule. Would you go with me?"

Richard thought about it for a moment. "I'd definitely get two of the three things I want out of it. Maybe the third part, too, in time. Yeah, I'd be game. But Billy, you know they're not lettin' a werewolf in there…and if they did, I'd be in so much danger of some idiot shootin' my ass with silver."

"Good thing your ass doesn't hold any vital organs then," I said with a grin.

He bumped my shoulder with his. "You know what I mean. But yeah, if two miracles were to happen, I'd go."

"Two?"

"Yeah, you decidin' to go and them lettin' me ride your coattails."

"Okay…it's a good thing to know." I spun about to look back toward the cabin. "Ya ever thought of buildin' that barn here?"

"What?" he asked.

"I mean, look at the cabin and stables."

Brewer turned around to face the cabin with me.

"The spell goes all the way past the little stream and then another good way onward. There's room to build a barn, and you could get more animals. Not cattle or anythin', but a cow and some chickens and such. You even have room for a garden." I shrugged. "Nothin' stoppin' you from makin' this place the way you want."

Richard tilted his head in thought. "You're right. Maybe. I'll think on it."

"Good," I said, and slapped his shoulder as I stood. "I'm gonna go prep for my trip to San Miguel County. I'll stop in Fort Sumner on my way back. Might stay there a bit. You gonna be okay here?"

Brewer stood. "Yeah, we'll be all right. You gonna take Tom?"

"Probably him and Gaax. Safety in numbers. I'll be sure to write you all here and check in. Send Gaax back and forth so we can stay in touch."

"Sounds good. Let's go make dinner for now and play some cards on the picnic table out back. It's a perfect night for a bonfire and a drink."

"Yeah, it is. I'll leave tomorrow."

In the morning, I attached my bag to Colonel as Tom did the same to his horse, and we rode on out of the orchard and made our way up to Las Vegas, New Mexico, so I could show up in court.

* * *

May 1949

Upon returning to Las Cruces, I headed up to my room only to find something that gave me pause. A boy, possibly eighteen, likely from one of the tribes in the area, sitting on my bed. He was dressed in black, and his long dark hair was braided in one stream down his back. I wouldn't have recognized him except for the look in his eyes.

"Gaax?" I asked.

He smiled. "Took you a minute, didn't it?"

I enveloped him in a hug. "Between the age on you and the clothes, yeah, it sure as hell did!" I laughed, taking his face between my hands in a familial gesture. "That's why your raven looks bigger. *You* are bigger."

"Yes. It's good to see and speak with you this way. It's been too long."

"It's been a good while for sure," I said, letting go of him and taking a seat in the room's chair. "I think the last time I saw you in this form was Chicago."

"Most likely, yes." Gaax sat on the bed, "Between then and now I spent a few years not changing. I had to disappear from Scáthach's radar. She got wind of a witchy woman asking questions and that Edward and I were with her. Zahara dispatched Edward first, as you know…"

"Yes, he came to the school."

Gaax nodded. "I could stay with Zahara because Scáthach has no idea what I looked like as a human. So, I learned to live on two feet, with hands, and—"

"With pants!" I said, chuckling, and motioned toward him with both hands.

He laughed. "Yes, with pants. But as you know, if I don't shift, I age. So, I grew and made a living. Turns out, I'm a very talented tailor. All that time making clothing in my village years ago paid off. In fact, I made everything I have on."

I took in the well-fitted black pants, black dress shirt and vest, with its silver accents on buttons, buckles, and the chain of the pocket watch that was neatly tucked into a spot on his vest. His shoes were black and white men's saddle shoes that brought out the white pin-stripe pattern of his vest.

"You do look rather snazzy," I admitted.

"Thank you," he said with a tiny bow of his head.

"So, why are you and your well-tailored clothes in my hotel room? *That* is the question."

"It's time to deliver this to you, and I wanted to do so in person." He handed me an envelope that looked old and worn. "It's from Zahara."

I quickly snatched it from his hand and opened it up. It wasn't signed by her, but I knew her handwriting. Reading the letter, my brow furrowed, and I had more questions than answers; a very common problem when getting orders from Zahara. "I don't understand."

"It's imperative you get that information to Scáthach. Only then can we take her down and send her back to the Dark Realm of the Otherworld where she belongs."

"But with Zahara gone, how could this even be helpful?"

"All will be explained in time, but I cannot go into that now. We cannot risk it."

"We?"

He motioned to the letter. "Zahara and me."

I nodded. "Well, I best tell Richard and—"

"No. This must stay with you. I'm sorry, I know you are like brothers, but this task is yours and yours alone."

"Tom?"

"He has already done as he was told; he came here. It's important he be here."

"So, wait, does Brewer have a job I'm not supposed to know about?"

Gaax appeared confused. "Why would I do that?"

"Gaax?"

"This was for you and you alone." He stood and pointed at the letter. "Make it happen, and soon, Cheveyo. The time is coming for you to face her."

"Will people die? Did she see if they die?"

Gaax placed a hand on my shoulder. "There cannot be victory without sacrifice."

"Bullshit," I said.

"You know it's not. I will see you again soon, and I will watch over you. All you need to do is call me, and I'll come."

"There are a ton of ravens at the cemetery where Cricket is buried," I said offhandedly.

He grinned. "I know. I've been watching."

"Of course, you have," I muttered.

"The time is soon. Find a way." He patted my shoulder and then left my room, shutting the door behind him.

I looked down at the letter. It was simple. It merely said, "Eli - We have learned that Scáthach has it backwards. She is not less powerful in her original form, but more powerful. If she were to learn this, it would hurt your mission drastically. She will choose to face off with you eventually. You must be prepared. Remember all Kennedy taught you." Then she signed it simply signed it with the letter 'Z', and a date from before I'd even met her.

Then I understood.

I slid the old and worn letter into the envelope and placed it in the safe. Locking it, I sat on the bed and thought about my task. I had an idea, but I wasn't sure it would work. Plus, it went against what I'd been told, sort of. But it was the only way I could think to do this, and to be honest, if it wasn't a gamble, what was the point? Tomorrow, I'd put the plan in motion.

* * *

August 1879

I pled guilty to the gaming table and paid a fine. Then Tom and I made our way down to Fort Sumner. Riding up to the Maxwell home, I eased down out of the saddle and brushed the dirt from my britches. "I think you and Pete will hit it off. Man, I am parched. Could use a nice tea right about now."

"I could use a drink of anythin' right about now," Tom said, dismounting from his horse. "Hope they don't mind us stoppin' in like this."

"I do it all the time. They're used to it by now. I'm sure Pete will have—"

"Billy Bonney!" came the excited shout of a young woman who now ran toward me. Her one hand lay on the top of her head to hold her wide-brimmed hat in place while her other hand was full of her long skirts, hoisting them up so she could run toward me as dust kicked up around her.

I squinted in the sun to see who this pretty, young woman was, and it shocked me to recognize the not-so-childlike face of Pete's younger sister, Paulita, running toward me with glee on her face. She was going too fast to stop, and I caught her as she leapt into my arms and hugged me with a squeal.

"What brings you out this way?" she asked, beautiful dark eyes looking at me.

It had been over a year since I'd seen her, and she was now a young woman. She was taller, more filled out, and her shiny black hair was twisted into a bun at the nape of her neck instead of flowing wildly about her as it had when she was a girl. What was she now? She had to be sixteen or damn near close.

I set her down and she collected herself as best as an excited young lady could. "I had business up in Las Vegas, and on the way back, decided we would come spend some time here in Fort Sumner for a bit," I told her. "Tom Folliard, this here is Paulita Maxwell. Paulita, this is my good friend, Tom."

She curtsied to him, and Tom removed his hat. With a slight bow, he said, "Nice to meet you, ma'am."

"Likewise," she replied, then slid her arm into mine and led me toward the house. "Pete should be around. In fact, he headed back here to clean up after helpin' Jack with buildin' a wood porch out by the saloon so that the rain wouldn't stop us from dancin'." She looked to Tom, "Mud is not an ideal dancin' floor."

Tom grinned. "No, ma'am, it is not."

"I'll fetch ya both a damp cloth to wipe down with and be back. Don't you go nowhere," she added with a wink and ran into the house.

"She's a pretty thing," Tom said.

I gave him a look. "Hands off that one."

"Because of her brother or because you want her?"

I opened my mouth to answer, but the truth stuck in my throat.

Paulita bounded out of the house with a small bucket and two small dry cloths. "Here, this water is fresh from the river. Wipe on down a bit, then we'll head in."

"William H. Bonney," came another female voice from the porch.

I looked up to see Paulita's momma. "Hello there, Mrs. Maxwell," I said with a wave.

"I thought Paulita was pullin' my leg. Then again, you always seem to know when I'm cookin' a big dinner. You plannin' to stay?"

"If you'll have me, ma'am."

"Of course. Your friend too?"

"If that'd be all right with you. This here is Tom O. Folliard." Not sure why I'd used his middle initial, but maybe because she'd used mine. She then promptly misunderstood.

"Nice to meet ya, Tom O'Folliard. You, too, are welcome for dinner," Mrs. Maxwell said, coming down the porch stairs.

Tom opened his mouth to correct her, but she continued.

"Why don't you two take a seat under that tree over there where it's cooler and I'll bring you both somethin' to drink. Ya look parched."

"You have no idea. Thank you so much, Mrs. Maxwell," Tom said, obviously deciding to let it go.

"It ain't nothin'. Paulita, go let Samuel know there's two horses to tend to."

"Yes, ma'am," she said, then looked at me. "I'll be back in a few."

I checked Colonel's front leg where he'd sustained a bit of an injury when we'd fought off some werewolves on our way to the fort. "You're lookin' right as rain, good man," I told him as I patted the side of his neck. He whinnied at me. "Sam's gonna come take you for a good rubdown and some hay, I'm sure. You be good for him."

Colonel affectionately bumped me with his nose and swished his tail in a sassy way.

I unfastened my bag from the saddle. "Yes, we'll rest here for a while." Looking up at Tom, I saw the strangest grin on him. "What? You talk to your horse too."

"That's not what I'm smilin' at. You *like* her."

"Well, of course, I like her, the woman feeds me like a champ whenever I'm here, and I'm good friends with her son."

"I don't mean *Mrs.* Maxwell."

I narrowed my eyes at Tom. "Paulita and I are friends, and she's young."

"She's what? Sixteen?" Tom said.

"If not, she almost is."

"You're frozen at nineteen. I think it's safe for you to like the girl. She is past the age of consent, Billy."

"It's weird for me," I muttered. "She's Pete's sister."

"Doesn't mean you can't like the girl."

Samuel, the Maxwell's stable hand, came jogging over. "Good to see you, Billy!"

"Same to you. This is my friend, Tom."

Samuel shook Tom's hand. "Your horses are in excellent hands with me. I'll take them on over to the stables. All you need to do is let me know when you need 'em back, and I'll get them ready for ya."

"Thanks, Samuel," I said. "It's good to see you."

"And you, sir!"

With a nod and clicking noise, Samuel took the reins of both horses and led them away.

Bags in our hands, Tom and I made our way to the shade to wipe down the dirt from the road as Mrs. Maxwell came back out onto the porch and Paulita approached.

"I've got it, Momma," she said, and took the glasses from her.

"Show them to the rooms we had fixed up recently when they're done."

"Sure thing," Paulita said with a smile, and brought us some tea that wasn't warm in the least.

"She's been keepin' the pitcher in the icebox lately. Makes drinkin' it more refreshin', don't you think?"

"That I do! Thanks, Paulita!" I said.

She gracefully eased down to sit beside me. "How long you gonna stay?"

"Not sure," I told her. "But hopefully for a little while."

Her smile spread across her face. "If you need work, I know that Mr. Johns is lookin' for some help in his field right now."

Tom and I shared a glance.

"I take it he's payin' his help?" Tom asked.

"Yes, he is. I'll go let him know y'all are interested and you two relax." She planted a quick kiss on my cheek. "It's good to see you, Billy Bonney."

She stood and headed off.

"Not a word," I told Tom. "Not a damn word."

He just laughed, and I watched the cute girl who'd turned into a pretty, young woman walk away, and I hated that Tom was right; I liked her.

16
HAPPY BIRTHDAY

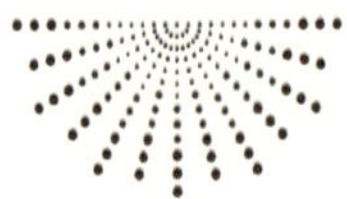

October 1879

The sun was setting, causing the sky to fade from blue above to the mixture of pinks, purples, and oranges near the horizon line that only a southwestern sky could. I sat quietly by myself, listening to the river, watching the colors of the sky spread wide, as my love for New Mexico filled me.

"Why you over here all by yourself, Billy Bonney?" Paulita said, making her way to come sit beside me on the long bench her brother and I had placed here ages ago.

I looked up into her pretty brown eyes, and they tugged at me like the sky had.

"Just thinkin'," I replied. "Sometimes I like time to myself."

"Oh, well, I can go if you want," she said, standing back up, obviously nervous that she'd stepped on my time to be away.

I stopped her from leaving by taking her hand. "No, no…you're not disturbin' me at all. Sit. I enjoy your company."

She eased down next to me and after a few moments of silence, she said, "What are you thinkin' about, if I might ask?"

"My life…what I want to do with it. If I should leave New Mexico for my safety and others'…"

"You'd leave?" she asked, obviously surprised.

This wasn't something people did often. My mother had been different in that way. She'd wanted to travel and see new land. I'd seen a lot myself and often wondered if I wanted roots here because I'd moved around before she passed away. Who knew? Not me, that's for certain.

The sad tone of her voice caused me to look at her. "Would you miss me, Paulita?"

"We'd all miss you," she said, looking down to where I still held her hand.

"But would *you*," I replied.

Her dark eyes lifted to gaze at me. "You know I would," she breathed.

The wind blew, tossing some of her dark hair across her face. Before she could reach for it, I gently brushed it out of her eyes, letting my fingers trail down her cheek, feeling the softness of her skin as the colors of the sky tinted her face.

"You're so beautiful," I said before I could stop myself.

Her head tilted, and a sly smile tugged at the corner of her mouth. "Have you just decided that, Mr. Bonney?"

I again indulged, running the back of my finger along her cheek, which flushed at my touch. "No...I suppose the beauty of the night gave me the courage to tell you. For if I'm honest, I was sittin' here thinkin' of you."

"Of me? Really? Why?"

"Because you're my friend's younger sister and—"

"I'm nearly sixteen, and I've been a woman for nearly two years. There are ladies that get married at my age, and to men older than you, so don't you go makin' me sound like a child."

I smiled at her brisk tone and laughed lightly.

"Are you laughin' at me, Billy Bonney," she asked, standing up, but this time with a slight wave of temper.

I gripped her hand tighter so she couldn't run, and said, "No...no, I'm not. There's no need to go runnin' away."

Her dark eyes bore into me with a power that pulled the truth from me before I could stop myself.

"I love your passion and your spunk...I told myself that you'd react just this way, and I was right. So, I was laughin' at myself, at the pleasure of knowin' you the way I do."

This calmed her, but she didn't sit. Instead, she stood there facing me, her left hand still in my right. I stood and took her other hand. "Please, Miss Maxwell, won't you sit with me and enjoy the setting sun?"

She turned her head away to glance at the colors. Holding in place, her eyes tracked back to me with a lifted eyebrow. "Miss Maxwell, is it now?"

A wide grin spread across my face. "I'll call ya whichever you choose if you'll just sit with me."

"I suppose," she said and sat back down.

I wove my fingers through the hand of hers I still held, and we both stared at the sky.

"Do you remember when we fell into the river here?" she said.

I laughed. "You slipped while pickin' herbs for your mother. I tried to help you, and we both slid down the mud and into the river. It was so cold!"

She giggled. "I don't think I was warm for hours! Mom gave us both a talkin' to."

"As if I'd caused it all too," I reminded her. "And you let me take that blame."

She turned to look at me. "You never told my mother the truth. Why?"

"Aw, well, really…it wasn't like it was your fault. It was an accident, and I could see she wanted to give you the business for it, and I'd not be havin' that. And besides, maybe you'd have gotten back up if I'd not bungled savin' ya."

She bumped my shoulder with hers. "Oh, I think I'd have gone down for sure, but you'd not have been there beside me to make sure I didn't float downstream."

I turned toward her now. Paulita's face glowed with happy memories and the colors of the sky, and the feelings I'd been fighting lost the battle.

"You didn't need me to save ya. Never have." I leaned in, letting my forehead rest on hers. "Strong women like you, Paulita…you undo me…"

Heat came into her eyes now, and so I took a chance and leaned in to kiss her. Hesitant at first, like a new lamb trying to walk, I let my lips brush hers. When she didn't pull away, I lay them on hers with loving intent and kissed the woman who held my heart in her hands, even if she didn't know it.

We talked, laughed, and kissed until the light burned away and the moon rose. Once it edged into the sky, I knew I needed to get her inside. With her hand still in mine, I walked her home and said goodnight with plans to see her again the next day, after I found the courage to ask her brother and mother if I could court Miss Paulita Maxwell.

I headed back to the room I was staying in and realized that not only was it the exquisite beauty of New Mexico that held me here, but the lovely young woman who made my heart sing that tied me to this place. I couldn't leave, not now, maybe not ever. How could I?

Fully wrapped up in the happy haze her kiss put me in, I returned to my room and was surprised to find Tom waiting for me.

"So, did you finally tell her?" Tom said.

"Tell her what?" I said offhandedly as I opened my bag, pulled out my nightclothes, and set them on the bed.

"Please...you've liked that girl for as long as you've known me, and I see how she looks at you. So, did ya tell her?"

"Maybe," was all I said and took off my gun belt. Setting my weapons beside the bed, I hung the belt on a hook I'd put in the wall.

Tom crossed one leg over the other. "And did she kiss you back?"

"Who says I kissed her!?" I blurted out. Then, hearing the guilt in my voice, I laughed once and sat on the bed. "Yeah, I kissed her. It was different from the other women I've met. There was..."

"Connection," Tom offered.

I stared into the fire. "Yeah...maybe that's because I've known her for a few years, but I don't know."

Tom nodded. "Now what?"

It wasn't the question that took me off guard; it was his tone of voice. It challenged more than my intentions.

Looking back at him, my brows knit together. "What do you mean?"

Tom stood and walked toward the fire. Looking down at it, he sighed. "You'll ask her brother and mother to court her, and if they say yes, you'll spend more time and energy here, with her."

"Yeah, so?"

Turning to look at me over his shoulder, he said, "You are needed elsewhere, and you know it. This is not your legacy. She is not your future. Sure, you can have some fun with her, but what could you possibly offer her?"

"Excuse me?" I said, truly shocked. Not at what he said, but that he said it.

He turned back to the fire. "I thought like you did once, Billy...and I still hurt for it."

I was an idiot. I'd forgotten his history. How he'd left the woman he'd loved behind for the cause because he'd put her in danger.

"I can protect her," I said heatedly.

"What happens when she grows old, and you don't?"

It was said with such a lightness that it took me off guard. Before answering, I thought about it and knew my reply. "I'll tell her the truth."

Now he wheeled on me. "Billy! You can't!"

I stood abruptly. "Why not?" I grabbed a log and stepping past him, threw it on the fire. "Others know the truth."

"They are fellow men in arms. You cannot tell *her*."

My gaze bore into him hot and mad. "Why, because she's a *woman*? Is that what you're gettin' at?"

"No..." He paused. "Well, yeah..."

"That's bullshit. Susan McSween —" I started.

"That's different! She was a Regulator Network Liaison. A fellow soldier."

He had a point, but I still didn't agree. "If I choose to tell her, who's gonna stop me, you? Garrett?"

"You're not irreplaceable, Billy. Remember that," he said.

This gave me pause. "What is that supposed to mean?"

Tom paced away from me. "Sure, you're good, and you'll get better, but you're not the only Spirit Warrior, and you won't be the last she makes. To protect the secrets of the Regulators, Garrett would not hesitate to remove you from this land, be it by death or to move you to another continent."

"He wouldn't dare try to kill me or force me to leave," I shouted.

"To protect us and the others who we're sworn to protect? He sure would."

"So, you're sayin' we're bound to never have love or a relationship?"

Tom sighed. "No...you just can't have one that lasts the rest of your life. You can have the 'until death do us part' if you want...just know that the death will have to be yours."

"You mean, fake my death like you did?"

"Yes, and I'm sorry to rain all over your happiness tonight. I didn't mean to. I just...I don't want you to go into this blind. You need to face the truth."

The happiness I'd floated in on bottomed out, and I sat on the bed, my heart in my throat.

"I'm not sayin' you can't court her and love each other, I'm sayin' that eventually, if you really love her, you'll have to let her go." He opened the door and looked back at me. "I'm sorry."

He walked out and quietly shut the door behind him.

"So am I," I whispered.

Sitting in the firelight, I thought of Paulita, deciding what I wanted to do. By the time I went to bed, I'd decided I would continue to be involved in her life. Tom probably would not like that very much.

* * *

May 1949

I knew Gaax told me I wasn't to involve anyone else in my plan to get the letter to "accidentally" fall into Scáthach's hands, but I saw no way to do that without it looking forced and obvious. I was going to have to involve someone people would trust, and that only left one person.

"Hey, Kit!" I said to her as I stepped into the bar/restaurant area of the Amador Hotel. She was sitting at the bar with indecision on her face. "What ya up to?"

She held out the menu to me. "They changed a few things and I'm debating what I want for lunch."

"Yeah, that's a tough decision. I have one myself, actually. I need somewhere secure to put some information."

Kit tilted her head, causing her red curls to bounce to one side. "The safe in your room?"

I gave her a lopsided grin. "You say that like I've not thought of that."

"Well, it is the obvious place."

"Not good enough. Do the banks here have lockboxes?"

"Sure but…" She looked around us like I was an idiot to talk here. Whispering so quietly I'd be the only one to hear her she said, "Walls have ears."

"I know…I'm not the most trusting soul, but I just think my room could be compromised."

Catching on, she nodded. "So, this is huge."

"Very." I looked around as if realizing where I was and dropped my voice down, making sure it was still quite audible. "It could help us defeat *her*. It's an old letter with information on how to beat you know who at her own game. She cannot get this information under any circumstances."

"Why not just burn it?"

"There's a map. I need to keep it."

"Okay, I'll ask around to find out who has the most trustworthy location," she said with a slight wink, obviously catching on to my ploy. "I'll be on break in half an hour. You'll owe me lunch."

I patted her shoulder. "Yes, I will. I'll see you in thirty minutes."

Leaving, I made my way out of the bar to the main desk area and headed up to my room to fetch the paper from Gaax. If all went as planned, Scáthach would have the information I needed her to have in the next twenty-four hours.

* * *

January 1880

I spent the fall of 1879 bouncing between Fort Sumner and Zahara's orchard, where Richard had begun building a barn and collecting animals for it. Each time I returned there was something new. Last time there'd been a cow, and Brewer had been milking her as Edward worked in a garden. It was the oddest of things, but I loved it nonetheless.

However, I missed my girl, and so by late December, I was back in Fort Sumner for the holidays with Paulita. By January, Tom and I were working for Mr. Johns again. But today I had the day off, and it was my girl's birthday.

I took Paulita on a walk by the river and gave her the brooch clip I'd bought for her the last time I'd been up in Santa Fe.

"Figured it would look good in your hair or on a scarf or somethin'. It's your favorite colors, and the minute I saw it, I knew you had to have it."

She held it lovingly. "Thank you, Billy. It's beautiful."

"Can I put it in your hair?"

She smiled and nodded.

I carefully pinned it up onto the top of her hair and the rhinestones glistened in the moonlight. "It's perfect."

She kissed me. "It's getting chilly, shall we go?"

I was hoping I'd killed enough time for the family to get over to the Convento to set up the rest of the way. "Sure, let's go."

We made our way across the fort to the building they'd built for public meetings, dances, weddings, and so on. Smoke billowed out of both chimneys, one on either end of the rectangular building, and I looked forward to getting out of the cold myself.

Stepping in, Paulita gasped.

"Happy Birthday!" everyone shouted, and the band played.

Paulita saw her family and friends, then turned to me. "This is *your* doing!"

"Guilty as charged," I said with a grin.

She grabbed me and kissed me hard enough that some people whistled. But I finally pulled back from her and offered to take her coat. Underneath, she wore a new red dress her mother had gotten her. I removed my coat as well and then twirled her out on the dance floor. We didn't stop until they played something slow.

I pulled her into my arms. "Happy birthday, Paulita."

"This is the most wonderful night. Thank you."

"Anything for you," I said, kissing her lightly.

We ate cake and danced the evening away. I walked her home, exchanged a goodnight kiss, or four, and I sent Paulita up to her room. Saying goodnight to her mother, I whistled my way around to one of the two rooms at the other side of the big house. I stepped in and shut the door. Opening my bag, I pulled out night clothes and changed into them.

I made a fire to warm the room and lit a candle, so it didn't seem odd to others that I could see in the dark like a supernatural creature. Laying down, I snagged a book and tucked in to read. It wasn't an hour later when I heard a light rapping at my door. Thinking it was Tom or Pete, I got out of bed, unlocked and opened the door, saying, "Come on in, ya rascal!"

But it wasn't Tom or Pete outside my door. It was Paulita.

"What are you doin' here?"

She motioned for me to be quiet and pushed in past me. She shut the door, locked it, then closed the indoor shutters so no one could see in if they went by.

"Your momma finds you in here, she's gonna have my hide skinned from my body and roasted as dinner for the community," I hastily whispered.

"She won't know," Paulita said, taking my hands and leading me back to the bed, where she motioned for me to sit. I got back in. "She and daddy drank tonight, and they are out cold."

She took off her coat to expose her nightgown. It was to her ankles, but it was of such a light material, with the fire on the other side of her, I could see the shape of her and the outline of her breasts through it easy enough. Then she pulled the last pin from her hair so that it cascaded down her back before sitting on the edge of my bed.

"Paulita...," I whispered, touching her beautiful hair.

"I've loved you my whole life," she said, placing her hand on my face before leaning in to kiss me.

It started slow and soft but soon became heavier as our tongues entwined. I wanted to touch her, but I didn't. Paulita placed her left hand on my right, weaving her fingers through mine, and though aroused completely, I still didn't touch her.

Lifting my hand, Paulita placed it on her breast, and I froze. "Touch me," she said softly. "I'm old enough, and I want to be with you."

I wasn't a virgin, but this was Paulita, and I hesitated, pulling my face away from hers to look her in the eye. "Are you sure?"

She smiled. "Why else would I have come down here, silly?" She leaned into me, sending me backward until my head hit the pillow. Her soft body now lay half on me and half off. "Touch me."

Instead, I merely said, "I'll love you."

She sat up and pulled her nightgown off. Laying back down on me, she smiled. "Show me."

And so I did.

* * *

Before light, Paulita made her way back to her room, and I lay there dazed. If someone had drawn a picture of me then, they'd have drawn little hearts around my head. I'd remember this night for a long time. Not just the sex, but the holding her as she slept in my arms. It was the most wonderful thing, and I worried it would show all over my face at breakfast.

Because of that, I came in late, so that there was a lot of commotion in the kitchen, and no one could pay much attention to me. As I sat at the table, my face down to stare at my plate, my eyes looked up and caught hers. Paulita was put together without a hint of our night on her face, but she winked at me once. With a smile, I focused on my eggs, bacon, and biscuits before going back out into the field to work.

The whole week, Paulita would slip out of her room and come to mine. I truly felt I was falling into a happy pattern when I got back one evening, after having my picture taken, to find a raven waiting for me.

QUARK! QUARK!

The raven held his leg at me, and I unfastened the rolled-up letter that had been attached there. Reading it, I grinned.

"Well, hot damn! Wait until Tom hears this!"

"Hears what?"

I jumped. "Damn it, you like sneakin' up on me."

Tom laughed. "Saw Gaax, figured we had news."

"Brewer is comin' to visit us. Seems he's a bit bored."

Tom grinned. "We'll have to take him out for some fun. Speakin' of, we need to go check on that pack soon. They've been movin' closer to the fort."

I nodded. "Mr. Johns talked of sending me, Charley, and Barney out that way to fetch some things from a friend of his. Wanted us to leave on the tenth. Not far, be back by dusk."

"That's tomorrow. Sounds good to me. You do that and keep an eye out for them, see where they've set up camp, and I'll stay here to keep a lookout for Brewer."

"Sounds like a plan."

* * *

May 1949

To put the rest of the plan into play, I walked with Kit to the bank.

"So, who'd you ask?" I said.

"That bartender that hangs out with Happy Apodaca all the time. He's shady as all hell. Told me he had a trustworthy friend at the bank down here on the corner."

"Depends on your definition of trustworthy," I said with a laugh.

"Dirty and in Apodaca's pocket," she offered.

"Oh, then sure. That's just the kinda trustworthy I need for this."

"I have a distinct feeling that this lockbox will be compromised."

"If we're lucky," I said with a wink.

We entered the bank and asked for the man we'd been told to speak with. Someone fetched him, and he was more than happy to help us.

By the time we left, I felt great about the chances of my belongings being reviewed or stolen, and that was exactly what I needed. Now to repay Kit.

"Lunch is on me, as promised. Come on, we'll go snag something at the diner."

"On you? Sir, I never turn down free food."

I looked at her tiny frame and wasn't sure that was totally true, but I grinned anyway. "Plus, while we're there, I'll drop more hints if there's anyone I think should hear of my newest treasure in the bank."

"I like how you think," she said.

We headed to the Deluxe Café to make sure some of the waitstaff heard my "secret." I was pretty sure one of them moved information for Apodaca. If that was the case, no matter who she was, if she'd had a hand in Cricket's death, I'd take her out with the rest of the trash.

17
JOE GRANT

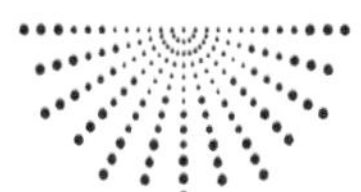

January 1880

On the tenth, Tom, Charley Thomas, Barney Mason, and I headed to get breakfast at Bob Hargrove's place. After filling our faces, Tom went to help Mr. Johns, and I headed out with the other two to scout out werewolves. Not that either Charley or Barney knew that, but that was for the best. Last thing we wanted was two of our work pals going missing like some others in town had recently.

On the way back, nearly to Fort Sumner, I saw yet another group of men camping on the land and worried it was a branch of the primary group we'd seen not five miles out. The closer we got, I realized it wasn't more than four men and a herd of cattle. Probably not werewolves, but you never knew.

"Who is campin' out here?" I muttered.

"The pack of coyotes we saw isn't far behind us," Charley Thomas said. "They can't stay out here."

They weren't coyote, but a pack of the smaller werewolves. However, I couldn't explain that. They passed for coyotes and had been causing trouble across the land lately. Tom and I had been killing them off when we could, but we'd not gotten them all.

"We should go talk to them," Barney replied.

"Huh?" I said, my head not in the right conversation.

"The men, Billy. We should warn 'em."

I looked up at the sky, and there was still a waning crescent of the moon. The moon would set around three, and then it'd be a new moon. Activity would likely be light, but it would be wise to give them the heads up. "I agree. Let's go see who we got."

The three of us trotted up to the camp and when I saw who one of them was, I hooted out a laugh. "Well, I'll be, Jim Chisum, is that you?"

James Thomas Chisum, who we'd always called Jim, stood up and squinted in my direction. His short hair was more salt than pepper now, and his mustache was fuller and winging out to the sides like his brother, John, liked to wear it. Jim was Sallie Chisum's father, and to be honest, I'd been stealing from his herd for money recently, but I didn't mean them no harm. He might not feel the same way about me, so I was a little worried, but not by much.

"Billy Bonney, is that you?" Jim said.

"Sure is." I jumped down off Colonel and reached out to shake his hand. "Good to see you. How's Sallie?"

"She's doin' well, I'll tell her you were askin' about her."

"Thank you much. Good to hear she's doin' well. I've not come out your way as of late, and I apologize."

This wasn't true. I'd come that way and taken some of their cattle, which was likely what they were taking back now. I cared little, but I didn't like the idea of them out here with that werewolf pack close on our heels.

"What are you doin' out here?" I asked.

"Takin' some of our cattle home. Found them out this way. Wouldn't know anythin' about that, would ya, Billy?"

"Nope. Care if I see the brand on 'em?"

"Don't care at all. I'll go with ya."

We moved toward the closest cow and Jim pointed out the botched branding done on the cattle to make the Chisum brand look like something else.

"Yep, it's a brand," I said, and moved further from Jim's pals, pretending to look at the cattle.

"You didn't need to see this at all, did you?" Jim said finally.

Keeping my voice down, I said, "No, I didn't. I trust their yours if you say they are."

"Then what do you need to tell me, Billy?"

"You need to keep movin'. Don't settle here for long. Trouble is comin' this way. Should be safer to move after about three o'clock in the mornin'."

"Pack trouble?" Jim asked, and my head snapped up.

"Ran across some not so normal wolves on the land," Jim continued. "Shot them with that ammunition you left for me. They shifted in death. I'd heard rumors, but that was all it took to convince me. Then a friend of yours happened by…can't remember his name, or what he looks like, now that I think on it. He was ridin' out that way to get some things for his farm, and he explained stuff to me."

Brewer. Had to be him with his potion. He'd not mentioned it, and I'd likely have to ask him why, but now wasn't the time.

I nodded. "Tom and I pissed 'em off a few days ago and they've been trackin' us. Why don't you and your men come to Fort Sumner for a bit and have a drink? Moon sets, you can keep movin' or find a place to stay for the night and then get goin'. Either way, you're in their path, and I'd rather that not be the case."

Jim gave me a once over. Lifting his hat, he ran a hand through his hair as he considered the information. Placing his hat back on, he nodded. "But you're buyin'," he said, pointing at the brand.

"Yeah, I'll be buyin'…least I can do. Come on!"

I introduced Jim and his men to Charley Thomas and Barney Mason, and we rode into Fort Sumner. Heading over to Bob Hargrove's saloon, which was housed in the old quartermaster's building in the northeast corner of the parade grounds, we stepped in. Immediately I heard a voice of great annoyance and rolled my eyes.

I didn't have time for this asshole. I just didn't.

Drunk and unruly, Joe Grant, a man from Texas who'd gotten in my face earlier that day, was shouting and wreaking havoc in the establishment.

"Not this jackass again," Barney said.

Jim raised an eyebrow at me as we approached the bar. "Who is he?"

"Ever heard of Texas Red?" I asked him.

"No."

"Not surprisin', seein' as that's the name he gave himself because he wants to have the reputation of a bad man, and that would be his 'I'm a bad man' name." I laughed and waved down the bartender. "Drinks for this man and his three traveling companions are on me."

Bob Hargrove nodded and took their orders.

"What happened earlier?" Jim asked.

"Joe was mouthin' off. What was it he said?"

Barney leaned his back against the bar. "He bet you twenty-five dollars that he'd kill someone today before you did."

Dropping my voice, I said, "My understandin' is that he is ridin' high on joinin' the pack. From how he's been talkin', he might already be infected, and it's only a matter of time until he shifts. He doesn't understand that's a death sentence."

Jim picked up his beer and drank, turning to face the rest of the room. That's when Joe Grant's eyes landed on him and me.

"Oh, shit...he's comin' this way," I said. "Charley? Barney? Be ready for this idiot, would you?"

They grunted in reply as Joe made his drunken way across the room toward us. But instead of coming to stand by me, he stopped by Chisum's pal, Jack Finan. Quick as a whip, he yanked Jack's ivory-handled revolver out of its holster and replaced it with his own.

Jack wisely didn't say anything, but just drank his beer and shared a glance with Jim. I didn't trust Joe not to use the thing, so a few minutes later I stepped over and pretended I'd not seen him take it.

"Joe, that's a mighty fine piece you have there. Mind if I admire it?"

Too drunk to know better, and in the mood to show off, he handed it to me.

I knew Jack had fired three shots at a rabbit on our way here, so I moved the cylinder about as I admired the piece. "Very nice." I handed it back to him and he slid it into his holster.

"Bad men need badass guns!" Joe shouted as he went behind the bar. He smashed bottles and shouted about how he was going to be the most kickass cowboy by the next full moon. Started bragging about all the people he'd kill. "Starting with John Chisum!" Joe pulled the ivory-handled gun and pointed it at Jim.

I tried to laugh and lighten the mood, saying, "Hold on there, Joe. You got the wrong sow by the ear. This here is Jim Chisum, Uncle John's older brother. Put that gun away."

"That's a lie! I know John Chisum when I see the bastard!"

I turned my back on him to show my disinterest. "Wrong Chisum."

Then I heard it. The click of the hammer on an empty shell. Not sure if he was trying to shoot at me or Jim, I pulled my revolver full of silver and spun about to find that pretty revolver of Jack's pointing right at me. I didn't hesitate and shot him in the head three times. Same spot.

He dropped dead behind the bar, and I leapt over it.

Staring down at Joe, I picked up the gun he'd taken, and said, "Joe, I've been there too often for you." I handed Jack his gun, holstered mine, and helped Bob carry Joe out back. When I returned, Jim simply said, "Good thing the gun misfired."

"It didn't," I said, taking up my beverage and drinking some of it. "I rolled the cylinder earlier so if he tried to kill someone, he'd hit nothin' for the first three shots."

"Well, I'll be," Jim said.

"If it hadn't been me, it would've been someone else. Or worse, he'd have made the change and lost his soul."

"Hear hear," Jim said and drank some of his beer. "Now what?"

"We get you and your cattle on the move out of the area after the moon sets, and you keep moving. If you can get inside for the night tonight, do so. If not, load the guns up with that ammunition I gave you and be on the lookout all night. Ya hear me?"

"I do," Jim said.

We all finished drinking and then rode with them for a way before parting. I wanted to get back to the fort anyway. Brewer would be here soon, and I couldn't wait to see him.

* * *

May 1949

A knock came at my hotel room door. I smelled Brewer.

"Come in!" I said.

Richard came in, worry thick on his face. "Have you seen Kit?"

"Sure, saw her for lunch this afternoon. Why?"

"I was supposed to meet her for dinner, and she hasn't shown up."

"Have you been to her place?"

"Yeah, she's not there, and the place is a mess. It smells of wolves."

"Shit. Let's get Tom and Duke, then head over there."

We went out the door and a feeling deep in my gut told me that by not playing by Gaax's rules, I'd put a friend in harm's way. I hoped I was wrong, but it didn't seem that way.

* * *

Stepping into her apartment with Richard, Duke, and Tom, we saw not a thing out of place.

I looked to Richard. "Uh…didn't you say this place had been trashed?"

Brewer spun about, looking this way and that. "I was just here, and it was a disaster. That lamp was on the floor, the rug had been tossed and bunched up, the coffee table was upended, and there was a black mark from her magic on the floor over here."

He lifted the rug that was now in place to expose the mark. "See! There it is!"

"Cleanup crew," Duke said. "They came in shortly after they took her. Richard must've just come in after they snatched her, but before those who tidy up."

"I can still smell the bastard who took her," Richard said. "Tarack."

I could smell him too. "You're not wrong. He was here."

"Now what?" Tom asked.

"We need to figure out why she was taken," Richard offered.

There was a pregnant pause as if the entire room knew it was my fault and were just waiting for me to admit it. But they didn't; it was just my guilt. Because of that, I sat on her couch, elbows on my knees, head in my hands.

"Billy?"

With a sigh, I looked up into Brewer's frantic blue eyes. "I know why and you're not gonna be happy about it."

* * *

January 1880

Stepping into my room, I found Tom and Brewer playing cards and happiness filled me.

"There he is!" I shouted.

Brewer stood up and gave me a hug. "Good to see you!" He let me go and sat back down. "Gettin' cold out there. Any excitement?"

"Not really," I said.

"Oh?" Tom replied, lifting an eyebrow.

"Damn it all to hell…word travels fast."

"Joe Grant, huh?" Tom said. "You finally killed that slimy bastard? Couldn't wait until he changed for the first time?"

"He tried to kill me first," I said, and sat down to tell them the story.

"I miss the action a bit, I can't lie," Brewer said. "Been farmin' and tendin' animals for months."

"Which is what we were discussin' when you came in," Tom said. "Was just suggestin' to Brewer we should head on out and find that pack tonight…we could take them out."

"I just took my boots off for God's sake," I complained.

"Well, put 'em back on. No moon. Now's the time."

I sighed. He was right. "Well then, let's suit up and move out. I think I know where they're at."

"Hot damn!" Tom said. "The three of us on the road again. Let's go have us some fun!"

* * *

May 1949

"Yes, he's just walked in," said the man behind the counter at the Amador Hotel, catching my attention as we started up the stairs. "Agent Kidwell?"

I turned, my gut clenching with the sixth sense coming to the forefront of my abilities. "Who is it?"

"She says you used to call her Mary and it's about Kit?"

It took every ounce of control not to move at full supernatural speed back down the stairs. Brewer controlled himself less and was next to me as I took the phone.

"This is Agent Kidwell."

"You sound so professional," she purred. "To think, when I found you, Henry Antrim, you were nothing but a street rat."

"Where is she?"

"What? You're not going to ask how I am? That's so rude."

"You want rude? I'll rephrase my question, where the fuck is she, bitch?"

The reactions of those around me, including the desk clerk, were of shock and horror at my language out in public in an upscale area. I cared not.

Scáthach just laughed deeply. "There's my street rat."

"Tell me where she is."

"On one condition."

I looked at the questions on Richard, Tom, and Duke's faces. "What is it?"

"When it comes time for us to face off, it's just you. None of your entourage."

I said nothing.

"You and I both know the day is coming soon," she said. "You alone. Your word or she dies. I'll let the pack kill her. No changing her so she has a chance…kill her true dead. You want that on your conscience?"

I heard the howling of a large pack, looked at Brewer, and thought of Tunstall. John hadn't been willing to put his friends' lives on the line, and to be honest, neither was I. "No, I don't. So, yes to your offer."

She laughed lighter this time, and yet it was more sinister than before. "Perfect. She's where the bitch you cared about was left to rot. You have fifteen minutes. You only…unless you want to bring your pretty Beta; he's always welcome. No one else."

"Leave him alone if I'm to play by your rules later."

"Done. Fifteen. Not a minute more."

She hung up, and I dropped the phone before running for the door. The rest were on my heels as I got into my sports car. Engine roaring to life, Brewer was getting into the front seat.

"She said only Brewer and me," I told Tom. "But if we're not back in thirty, get Duke and come out to get us."

"Where to?" Tom asked.

"Where they buried Cricket. Duke knows. I gotta go. She gave me a deadline, and Tarack's pack has her. Hold on, Dick!"

Looking to make sure no traffic was in my way, I pulled out and hit a hundred miles an hour in the first minute, heading south. I weaved around traffic like they were nearly stationary. Taking corners faster than a human with a normal car could, I flew down the road to where Cricket's body had been found.

"Plan?" Brewer said between gritted teeth.

"Show up and get Kit," I said plainly.

"You think she is just going to hand Kit to us and leave, the pack too?"

I thought that. I'd made her the promise she wanted. "Yes."

"Billy? What did you trade?"

"Nothin'," I lied. "We're almost there. I'll drop you off a bit early, and then I'll roll up. You shift and sneak in."

"Pants in the back?" he asked.

"What? You don't want to show Kit all the goods early?"

Brewer glared.

I make jokes when I'm under stress...they don't always land well.

"I'll take that as a no," I said with an apologetic smile. "Yes, pants in the back."

A few minutes later, Richard was out and running at werewolf speed toward where they held Kit. I stayed in the car and took the roads that the teenage boys had shown us that one day, the ones that Cricket's killer would've used.

I made my way to the body disposal spot and pulled up, the headlights of my car making Kit's red hair stand out in the dark. They'd tied her to a pole on a pile of wood. Scáthach stood there in all her glory with Tarack by her side, a torch in his hand.

Parking the car, I left it on so the headlights would illuminate the area.

"Billy!" Kit shouted, seeing me.

"What, no pretty Beta Boy?" Scáthach said with a playful pout. "I'm sad."

"I'm here and pretty enough for the both of us," I said with a charming smile. "Plus, I'm on time. Take her down, or I will."

Scáthach sauntered toward me. Curvy hips swung in a too-short, flouncy prairie skirt as ample cleavage, exposed by a low-cut red shirt, bounced in time with her wide, blonde curls. Red cowgirl boots kicked up dirt as she came close. She leaned into my ear and said, "Two nights from tonight. Come alone as you promised." She slid a paper into the front pocket of my jeans. "Coordinates. See you soon." She playfully bit my earlobe, making me cringe, and disappeared.

I turned my attention to Tarack. "Shoo...scat...follow your bitch home."

"I don't agree with the deal she made you," he said.

I laughed. "I don't give a shit." Feeling Brewer's presence approach us, I knew he was coming up behind Tarack. "You have to follow her orders, so go."

Tarack leaned the torch near the pile of wood. "The pile is soaked in kerosene. She'd be pretty in flame."

Brewer's wolf leaped out, teeth clamping down on Tarack's wrist, causing him to drop the torch. It landed inches from the wood Kit was perched on, and I was worried it would catch fire when Richard lifted a leg and peed on it, all the while keeping his eyes on Tarack.

"Well, that dowses your plan," I said with a huge grin.

The pack that surrounded Kit on three sides moved in closer, growling. Brewer leapt up to the top of the pile beside Kit and bared his teeth.

"A deal is a deal, Tarack!" I shouted. "I won't keep my promise if you don't keep hers."

Growling low, Tarack glared at Richard, then at me. "Fine. I'll be seeing you soon enough. Everyone, out!"

None of them questioned the order. The pack backed up and fled, Tarack on their heels. I went to the car, snagged the pants, and tossed them to Brewer. He headed into the shadows and shifted, and with his back turned to us, pulled his pants on as I ran up the kerosene-soaked wood. The knot was complicated, but I worked on it.

"I'm so sorry! I had no idea I was walkin' into a trap when I got a call from who I thought was my boss askin' me to pick up a new uniform."

I looked around to see tears fill her eyes. "No worry, we came, no one died."

Brewer ran up to face her.

She laughed a bit as the tears slide down her face. "Hey, at least I got another chance to see your naked ass...a girl could get—"

I looked up at the silence to find Richard had taken her face in his hands and was kissing her.

"About damn time," I muttered and finished undoing the knot.

Hands free, her fingers dove into the waves of hair he was sporting again due to all the times he was shifting and kissed him back wholeheartedly.

I walked toward my car. "When you're done, we should head back into town before Tarack changes his mind or one of her henchmen finds the strength to ignore orders and come to take on the Spirit Warrior."

Bare chested, Richard headed toward the car with Kit, her hand in his, and walked up to the passenger side.

"Where is she gonna fit, Billy? You have a sorry excuse for a back seat."

"Oh, easily taken care of." I touched a button on the side of the steering wheel and the backrest of the rear seat folded back into the trunk. "That should help."

"Slick," she said, and with Richard's help, worked herself into the back seat, and curled up on her side.

Richard put his seat back in place and got in. Doors shut, I hit the gas, and we headed back to town.

"Are you okay?" Richard asked.

"I already told you. I'm fine. In fact, I'm better than fine. I overheard them when they were holding me…when they thought I was asleep."

"What did you hear?" I asked.

"I know where Agent Fletcher Calhoun is."

18
AGENT MONTOYA

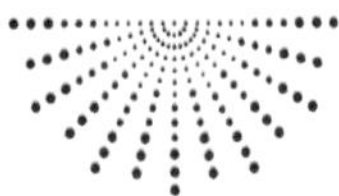

January 1880

Happy to be out on the road hunting Scáthach's beasts again, the three of us rode with purpose toward the area I'd last seen the pack.

"Is that what I think it is?" Brewer asked as he pointed in the distance.

"Looks like a huge campfire and a…party," I replied, a bit baffled.

"Out on the land so open like this?" Tom asked. "Are they just askin' for us to slaughter 'em?"

"How many did you see earlier today?" Tom asked.

"Fifteen is my guess," I said.

"Ooh, five a piece. Nice!" Tom said.

"There could be more," I reminded him. "Just because I saw fifteen doesn't mean there wasn't another fifteen somewhere else."

"So, ten a piece? Good times," Tom said.

"Bein' a little cocky, aren't ya, Tom?" Brewer said.

"It's a new moon so they can't shift, and we are more trained than they are."

Brewer and I shared a glance, and in tune, like usual, we pulled our guns with silver shot.

Tom raised an eyebrow.

"It's a trap," Richard and I said at the same time.

"Well...fuck," Tom muttered, reaching for his gun as a spell wavered in front of us and dissipated, exposing ten men on horseback and one woman at center front whose skin was darker than most women I knew. She was stunning, as always, and her long wavy black hair flowed back and away from her face with the wind. Arms outstretched, a gun in each of her hands, she pointed one at me and one at Tom. Her chocolate brown eyes stared at me specifically with disgust.

"Well, hello, Ianna," I said, my voice like ice.

"Billy Bonney and Tom O'Folliard," she sneered, her southern drawl evident.

"It's just Folliard," Tom complained.

She ignored him, her eyes landing on Brewer. "And you are?"

Dick tilted his head at her, his blue eyes going silver, "Someone who sees the darkness in you."

I looked at him and said in a voice lower than a whisper, "She's a shifter. Is that what you see?"

Dick shook his head, eyes narrowing on her. "No, being a shifter doesn't cause that kind of darkness. That's years of fear, rage, and hurt all rolled into supreme hate."

"Of who?" I asked.

"Men," she answered. "White men in particular."

That's when I noticed that the men with her were of color, all shades, and it all fell into place. She'd been a slave in Georgia, as had her family before her and before that. She had reason to hate men like me.

"I understand your anger, and you have every reason to have it," I said. "What was done to your people...hell, to all people of color, includin' the tribes, was wrong. No one should own another. But all you've done by sellin' your soul to Scáthach is trade one master for another. There may not be visible shackles and chains on you anymore, but they're there just the same."

"I'm free because of her!" Ianna shouted.

"Are you?" Dick challenged. "Do you have free will to do as you please?"

"I do what I want," she said, sounding like a petulant child.

"Really?" I asked. "Did she tell you to gather a group and monitor me?"

"I wanted to do that. *You* threaten my freedom."

"How?" Dick asked as a breeze came from behind us, tossing our scent toward her.

"Spirit Warriors kill shifters or..." She sniffed the air and knew. "Enslave them...like you."

"I'm not enslaved," Richard said.

"Really? You're his Beta, right? That's what Scáthach figured out. She shot you and yet here you are. How is that? Is it because Billy here owns a part of you? Bet you get all itchy if you're away from him for too long."

"I miss him because he's my friend," Richard explained.

She laughed. "Yeah, you keep tellin' yourself that, slave."

"Is that why you killed James?" Tom asked, not hiding the grief saying that name caused.

"What?" she said.

"James Woodland. My friend that you killed. Have you forgotten him already?"

She laughed. "That pathetic boy? His death bought me my place in her army. It showed her I could do what was needed."

Tom lifted his gun and pointed it at her. "Tell me why I shouldn't kill you where you sit."

All the men behind Ianna lifted their guns and pointed them at us.

"Because, little Spirit Warrior, you're outnumbered and surrounded... and we all have silver shot, in case you were curious."

I glanced behind us to see ten more men on foot holding rifles on us.

I rolled my eyes at my stupidity. I'd ridden us straight into a trap because I'd been too focused on Ianna and how to convince her to see the error of her ways. Because of this, I hadn't been paying close enough attention, and now here we were. "Great. Just great."

* * *

May 1949

"Come again?" I said, looking back at Kit.

"Eyes on the road, Billy," Richard said. "Pay attention to the road!"

I turned to look out the windshield. "Where is he? Where's Agent Calhoun?"

"She has him held at a horse ranch just outside of town."

"Where?" Richard pried.

I touched the pocket she'd slipped the coordinates for our meet-up into. "I bet I could figure the general area. But let's go find Duke, get a map, and make sure I'm right."

"Sleep first, Billy. She needs some rest," Richard said.

I touched Brewer so what I said next would only be heard by him. "Is that what they're calling it these days?"

"Oh, do shut up," Richard replied, but I could hear his embarrassment.

Looking at him, I saw the red creep up into his face, and I grinned. Aloud, I said, "You're right. We'll go tomorrow."

I drove up to her place and pulled over. "Richard, you stay with her tonight, keep an eye on her. Join me in the mornin'." I grinned and winked.

He didn't reply, just shut the door in my face.

"Thanks, Billy!" Kit shouted and waved at me as I left the two together.

If anyone deserved a bit of happiness, it was that man. I was hoping he didn't screw it up.

* * *

Here's the map you wanted," Duke said, tossing it onto the table at Kit's apartment.

I opened it up and found the coordinates from Scáthach on it.

Duke looked over my shoulder. "It's in the damn middle of nowhere on B005."

"Yeah, she'd want it away from everyone. Where is Loya Ranch in reference to this?"

Duke pointed to a spot on another country road out in the middle of nowhere. "No way between the two without going to the major highway unless you're on foot or horseback. Would take a bit to get there that way though."

Richard shoveled cereal into his face and munched as he looked down at the map. Swallowing, he said, "It's a trap."

"Well, no shit, Sherlock," I said. "They likely let her hear it, but we can't ignore the chance that he's alive."

"Which she's countin' on, Billy," Duke said.

"Oh, I'm fully aware, sir."

"I saw all the blood, Billy," Kit said, "If he's alive, he's not in good shape."

I sat down at the table and leaned back. Arms crossed, I sighed. "Loya is a horse ranch, right?"

"Yup," Duke said, accepting a plate of bacon, eggs, and toast from Kit. "Thank you, ma'am."

"Sure thing," Kit said. "You ready for the main course, Richard?"

Brewer finished his cereal and nodded. "Yes, please?"

She handed him a plate the same as Duke's with a wink, and I pretended not to notice. He sat at the table with his plate to my right as Duke sat to my left.

"Billy?" Kit prodded.

"Hmm?"

"Food?" she asked.

"Oh, sure. Thanks, Kit."

She nodded. "Next time you cook, by the way. I've been told you're damn good at it."

I smiled up at her. "You got it. I'll cook next time we all eat."

Kit seemed pleased with the plan and set to filling a plate for me.

"Okay," I continued, "We can't all go. If it's a trap—"

"It is," Richard said.

I rolled my eyes. "Then Duke and Kit stay behind. If we're not back in a few hours, they come in with reinforcements."

"Such as who?" Kit asked.

I'd heard two sets of boots coming up the stairs to her apartment and had timed it just right.

A knocking suddenly was heard. "Them," I said, pointing at the door just as Dr. Ryan's laughter bellowed out.

Kit set my plate in front of me and then walked off, saying, "Well, don't nobody move or anythin', I'll just do the cookin' and guest fetchin'."

"The sarcasm and sass are strong with that one," Duke said with a grin.

Richard laughed. "Wouldn't have her any other way."

I heard the voice of the man who was with Dr. Ryan, introducing himself as Agent Montoya. My heart pounded hard, and I wasn't the only one who was on their feet. Richard had stopped in mid-bite to stand up. Turning toward the living room, I saw the last person I'd been expecting MI-5 to send.

"Well, I'll be damned," I said. "Edward, how the hell are you?"

* * *

January 1880

Seven each," Tom muttered.

"All three of you will be dead if you try to do anythin', and I need you two alive, Scáthach's orders," Ianna said. "You, however,...you deserve freedom. No shifter should be a slave to anyone, no matter their color or sex."

Richard grinned. "I don't need you to—"

She fired. One shot straight into Richard's heart. He gasped and fell from his horse to the ground and lay there, unmoving.

Everything in me screamed in fear and I shouted Richard's name as all Hell broke loose. Colonel spun about, sensing my fear, which caused Richard's horse to kick out toward the men who'd come up behind us. They quickly scuttled back for fear of being trampled.

In the commotion, I lifted my gun, as did Tom, and we fired in unison on Ianna, filling her with silver shot.

She fell forward over the neck of her horse, and we kept firing at her men as their shots hit us, one after the other. But as our bullets found homes in their heads or hearts, killing them, it became a flow of healing and hurting. We'd get wounded, heal, kill another, get hit again, and so on.

More men showed up out of nowhere, and we rode off to the protection of some rocks.

"We're still outnumbered," Tom said.

"Thought you wanted big numbers," I said coldly. "Ten a piece, remember?"

"I'm sorry about Brewer, Billy."

I felt like I was reliving John Tunstall's murder. I was hidden behind rocks with my friend and horse as my other friend lay out there dead on the ground. Tears filled my eyes, and I wiped them away. Feeling the heat of them on my hand, I let the fury of John's death fill me along with Brewer's and reloaded.

"We kill them all," I said.

Tom knocked out all his empty shells from his revolver and replaced them. "Agreed."

"Is *she* dead?" I asked.

"Oh, yeah," Tom said as he put the revolver back in his holster and grabbed his shotgun. "We filled her with silver. She's done."

"Good," I said. "You ready?"

"To avenge Brewer or to die?" Tom said.

"Yes," I answered and looked at him.

He nodded. “Same.”

I touched Colonel, “If you have to leave me behind to go get help, you do it.”

Colonel whinnied and nodded his head.

Tom and I shared a glance, and then, with a guttural yell, we both rode out into the clearing firing on anything that moved, and there was a lot that did. More had joined the throng we fought, and it was now two versus twenty at least.

We gave as we got, killing as many of Ianna’s army as we could.

A man on a gigantic horse got close and swung at me with a staff. He hit me hard enough to unseat me. I landed on the ground with a curse. Coming up on my knees, I pulled my revolver and shot the man’s horse in the leg. They both dropped.

Another man came at me from behind, his arms wrapping around mine, lifting me off the ground. I kicked out and planted the heels of my boots in the chest of the man who’d fallen from the horse and risen to come at me.

Bringing my head back, I smashed the nose of whoever held me, and he let go as blood gushed from his nose all over my neck and shoulder.

Landing, I rolled and shot him with silver. He fell over, and I moved on to the next man to come at me. Pulling the trigger, it just clicked. I was officially out of ammunition.

Baring my teeth, I tossed the gun aside and ran for the closest man to take him down with my bare hands. I had him on the ground under me in seconds, but before I could hurt him, the butt of a rifle hit me in the head, and I fell over on my back.

The world spun, and I shook my head. As my vision cleared, I counted five men standing over me with guns aimed at my head. This would be my capture or my death. I prayed Tom and Colonel got away to get help, but then I heard the cry of the Apache Tribe. The sound of running horses filled the space and arrows flew. One found each of the men around me, and they fell.

By the time I got out from under the dead bodies, I found ten members of the tribe Edward had been accepted into rounding up those who’d survived and had arrows aimed at their hearts.

“Drop your guns,” Edward shouted.

They did as they were told, and I shook my head in disbelief.

Edward caught my eye and with a grin, said, “Need a hand, Cheveyo?”

“From you? Always.”

* * *

May 1949

Edward stepped into Kit's apartment, and his dark eyes twinkled, a smile spreading across his face as he stared at Richard and me. "Good to see you, Cheveyo." He looked to Brewer. "Richard," he added, that one word holding all the love of their long friendship.

I enveloped Edward, now known as Agent Montoya, in an emotional hug. "Here to lend a hand?"

"For you? Anytime."

I laughed and stepped back to allow Richard to hug his old mentor.

"What the hell are you doin' here? Did Director Lucas call you in?" Richard asked once he let go of Edward.

"Yep. Dragged me out of Montana and sent me down. Said we were all needed for this."

"He's not wrong. Come, look at the map and help us plan. It's all going to go down tonight."

"Night before the full moon?"

"Shit. Yeah. Forgot about that." That meant the night I was to face off with Scáthach alone, it would be a full moon. Figured.

"Better you go the night before than the night of," Edward stated.

"True," I said. "Okay…let's figure this out. Now that we have extra, we'll go in like we have no idea that it's a trap. Kit, you'll go with us."

Richard opened his mouth to protest.

Eyes on Brewer, Kit snapped her fingers, and the electric strings between her fingertips glowed. "Really, you think I can't handle it?"

Brewer's eyes narrowed on her. "It's not that."

"Then what?" she asked him, hands on hips.

"I suggest you take a minute to think about that reply, Dick," Duke muttered.

"It's just…," my partner started, then caught my eye. "Fuck. I lose either way here."

"You really do, pal…you really do," I said, patting his hand in solidarity.

"It's not that you can't handle yourself," Brewer finally said. "It's that they will target you first, seeing you as the weak link."

"Hurt me, hurt you," Kit said, understanding.

"Yes," he replied.

"Same could be said for you. If she goes for you, it'll hurt Billy. So, I go. Let that bitch come for me first, I've trained my entire life to deal with her. It's time we fought. I didn't spend my life away from the ones I loved learning how to use my power to just be left at home to play the dutiful woman. Fuck that!"

This caused all the men to stare at her. Not that we'd not heard women swear before, but it wasn't common.

"Any questions?" she asked.

"You gonna wear that?" Ryan asked with a smirk, popping a piece of bacon into his mouth.

Kit stared down at her robe and slippers, and with her hands still on her hips, she laughed. We all did. Ryan was good at breaking the tensions with his humor, and it had done the trick.

"I could totally fight in this, but no, I'll get dressed, and we'll solidify the plan."

She strode out of the room, and Ryan said, "Damn, I'd kinda have liked to see Scáthach have her ass handed to her by a fiery redhead in a robe. It would've made my day." He reached to steal another piece of my bacon.

I smacked his hand. "I second that, now get your own food, mooch."

Dr. Ryan's blue eyes twinkled with humor. "But stolen bacon tastes better."

Everyone laughed, and we turned our focus on the map until Kit came back out.

"Better?" she asked.

The room was silent until Ryan let out a low whistle. "I stand corrected, I'm lookin' forward to watchin' you kick ass in that a lot more."

Kit wore something I'd not seen in years. It was the traditional dress gear of a Regulator Network Liaison. Not the uniform, but the dressier attire.

"I'll be damned," Richard said, standing up to stare at her. "Where did you get that?"

"My mother. Her traditional uniform was ruined in battle. She gave me this. Does it not look okay? I am a bit more muscular than she was."

The fitted pants, made of a stretchy material, were black. As were the knee-high leather boots and corset-style top with attached skirt-like side panels that split at the center, front, and back. The buckles on everything were silver, as was the intricate design of embroidery on the shoulder piece that attached to the top of the corset, leaving an opening that showed off the top of her breasts.

"Wow," was all I could say without sounding inappropriate.

She grinned. "Thanks!" Reaching under her couch, she pulled out a flat wooden box, unlocked it with a key she'd brought out with her, and pulled out the leather hip belt that had holsters for her guns and other places to insert weapons as needed.

"Hey, that's super similar to Lilith," I said, pointing at my belt.

She grinned and put it on over her outfit. "Probably made by the same guy, since you had it made in Mexico."

Now I was stymied. "How'd you know that? Ya know what, I don't want to know. Come on over here and let's pick positions for this possible rescue mission."

Richard stepped into her path and smiled down at her. "You got the top hat that goes with this?"

She wiggled her eyebrows. "I do. I can wear it later if you want."

I bit back a comment.

"Hell, I say wear it now," Ryan said.

Richard and Kit gave him a look.

"A man can dream," Ryan said and stole my last piece of bacon before I could stop him.

19
BREWER'S WORST FEAR

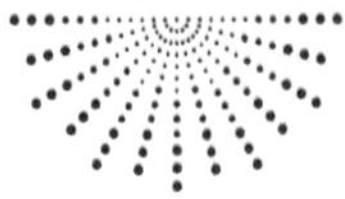

May 1949

The first wave of our group made their way to the Loya Ranch, hoping to locate Agent Fletcher Calhoun alive.

"You comin'?" Brewer asked.

I placed a rolled-up pair of pants for him in my small side bag. "Now I am. Figured if you have to shift, you'd not wanna ride back naked."

"You mean you'd appreciate it if I didn't ride naked in your new car," Richard said with a grin.

"That's also true," I said and slid the keys into my pocket.

Kit stepped up. "I'm on my way. See you inside. Good luck!" She kissed Brewer on the cheek and left.

"I didn't get a kiss for good luck," I pointed out.

Brewer beamed. "I'm not givin' you one."

I snickered and smacked his iron-hard chest with the back of my hand. "See you in a bit!"

Running off to the front of the ranch house, I knocked on the door as Richard and Kit made their way to the large warehouse out back. It was my job to make sure Calhoun wasn't in the home itself. Brewer was to take position in the warehouse at ground level while Kit was likely already up in the rafters of it.

Knocking, I waited.

An older man answered the door. "Can I help you?"

I flipped out my badge. "Hi, I'm Agent Kidwell with the FBI, and I am lookin' for one of our agents who was last seen out this way. I was wonderin' if I could come in and talk to you about him."

"Millie!" the man shouted, "We got FBI at the door!"

"We what?" came the voice of an older woman who rounded the bend into the front room. "Oh, my goodness, do let him in, Charles."

The older man stepped back and motioned me inside. "Well, you heard the woman of the house."

I took off my hat and stepped in. "Much obliged, Mr. Loya."

The white-haired man shut the door behind me and motioned me to a seat. "What's this all about?"

I sat on the sofa. "We got word from someone who said they last saw our missing federal agent here at your ranch. Just wanted to stop and see if you remember him." I took out the picture I showed anyone I questioned. "Name is Fletcher Calhoun. Seen him before?"

Mr. Loya looked carefully at the picture. "Can't say that I have."

Mrs. Loya stepped in with a pitcher of tea and glasses. Moving carefully along, she set it on the table with great effort, as if worried it would spill. "Tea?" she asked me.

"Sure, I'd love some. Thank you," I said.

She poured, and I hoped that while I kept them here that Richard and Kit were having luck out back.

Taking the drink from her, I drank some cold tea, and it was good. Tasted slightly strange, but every grandma I'd met had their own recipe for it, and this woman likely put a kick of green chile pepper into it. I mean, it was New Mexico.

"When was this young man seen out here?" she asked, pouring a glass for her husband. "We were out of town for a while, you know. Went to Texas to see our daughter and our new grandbaby."

Mr. Loya took the tea she handed him. "We only just got back two weeks ago. Was gone for a month. When was he seen out here?"

"From my understanding, it would've been early May."

"Well," she said, "We weren't here then."

I drank more of the tea to be polite. "Would you mind if I were to wander your property then? Just to see if there are any clues to if he was here when you were gone?"

"I don't mind, do you, Charles?" she said.

"Nah, don't care at all. Though I'd like to think one of our farmhands would've mentioned something upon our return if there'd been anythin' goin' on here, but ya never know." He drank some tea. "Let's go out and see, shall we?"

"Oh, you two don't need to—"

"It's no trouble at all," she said. "Now you finish your tea while I put on real shoes and we'll head out."

I did as she requested and got up when she returned. We exited through the back of the home to the stone pathway that led to the other buildings. Nothing was in the barn but animals, hay, and farming equipment, so we moved to the warehouse.

Stepping in, I followed Mr. Loya into the center of the room, and that's when I smelled it. The magic. It tickled my nose and tingled along my skin. I scanned the room but couldn't figure out what it was.

I turned about quickly, but when I did, I realized I didn't move as fast as I'd have liked. I felt weird and shook my head.

"You all right, Agent Kidwell?" the older woman asked.

"I'm fine," I lied.

"This seems odd," Mr. Loya said.

I turned my back on the old woman and stared at something in his hand. "This looks like your badge."

I stepped toward the old man and the floor below me rumbled for a second before it folded down like a trapdoor and I fell. Reaching out, my hand caught the edge at the last second, but I discovered I almost wasn't strong enough to hold on. The old woman came to stand over me and placed copper cuffs on my wrists. "If the copper in the tea wasn't enough, these should do it."

Staring at her in disbelief, I watched the magic around her shimmer. Soon, she wasn't an old woman, but Scáthach herself, in her blond bombshell body tucked into an old lady outfit. Standing beside her in old man clothing was Tarack.

"You fuckin' bitch," I said.

With a laugh, she peeled my fingers away from the edge of the trapdoor, and I fell into a dark hole.

* * *

Waking up, I felt as if I were hungover. Sitting up, I found myself in a copper cage, laying on a thin mattress set on a wooden slab along the side of the cell that had steel beams next to it to make another cage. Inside it prowled a tall man.

"Richard?" I said.

"Billy! You're awake!" Brewer said, coming toward me.

I sat up. "Yeah…where's Kit?"

"Over here!" I heard her voice.

I looked and saw she was in a small cage across from Richard.

"Well, fuck me sideways…this sucks ass," I said, rubbing my head.

"What's with the copper?" Kit asked.

"It removes his superhuman abilities," Richard told her. "Dampens them. Makes it so he's unable to use 'em."

"Shit," she said. "There's also a spell on the room. My magics won't work here either. I know because I tried."

"Dick, can you shift?"

"Yeah, but these steel bars will hold me in either form. We're good and stuck here."

I touched my collar where the magical transmitters had been placed. "Then these will have died."

"Yep," Kit said.

"Well, that's a shitty turn of events." I worked to stand and looked around.

There was a door across from me to the right and the area between Richard's cage and Kit's wasn't over five feet. They could likely reach out and touch if they wanted. Looking to my left, I saw there was another steel cage. It was empty.

"Wonder who that's for," I wondered aloud.

"Probably Duke," Richard replied. "She anticipated we'd all come, she'd have put you and Tom in that cage."

"How'd she weaken you to get you down here?" Kit asked me.

I explained about the tea.

"Didn't your mom ever teach you not to accept things from strangers?" Kit said with humor in her voice.

"Who knew you could soak pennies in water and when inside me it would do this? My guess is it was very temporary. If it wasn't, she'd not need these bars or the cuffs she'd put on me." I rubbed my wrists where the cuffs had been. "How'd you two end up down here?" I asked.

"I fought three witches at once and lost," Kit said. "Mostly because one of them could levitate."

I looked at Brewer. "You?"

"They had a gun to her head," Richard said, "So I came."

"I'm not sure if I should be touched by your sacrifice or hit you upside the head, Dick," I said.

"You wouldn't have sacrificed her either," he said to me, his tone biting.

I thought about it. "You're right. I wouldn't have." I looked up at the wooden ceiling and realized we were likely in the warehouse's basement. "Well, all we need to do now is wait." I left off the last three words, "for the cavalry," but they knew what I meant.

Richard sat on his bunk. "What's weird is they shot me with an arrow even after I told them I would surrender."

"Was it poisoned?" I asked.

"If so, I don't know what it was. I yanked it out and tossed it down, but I bled, so if there was something on it, it's in me. That's my real concern."

The door near my cage opened and in walked Tarack. His long black hair fell down his back in a perfect braid. He wore a beautifully hand-woven tribal vest in bright primary colors without a shirt under it and a pair of simple black pants. His feet were bare, and he moved like water, fluid and silent across the space.

"Speakin' of poison...," I said.

"You were not poisoned, Mr. Brewer," Tarack said. "We gave you a potion. It won't harm you."

"Then why shoot me with it?" Richard asked.

Tarack merely grinned. "Because Scáthach has need of what you can give her."

"Nothing like being cryptic," I said.

"You'd think that being trapped in there without access to your powers would make you speak more carefully," Tarack bemused.

"Nope...I'm always an asshole," I replied.

Richard nodded. "It's true."

I motioned toward Brewer. "See?"

Tarack narrowed his eyes at Brewer. "You'll know soon enough...for the moon will rise in an hour."

I'd been asleep longer than I'd thought. We all had.

"What does the moon have to do with it?" I asked.

Tarack merely sat down on the chair at the far end of the room from me, opened the book that had been sitting there, and ignored my question.

"I hate you," I muttered and lay down to brood about what Scáthach could have planned for us, wondering where the hell my backup was.

* * *

Scáthach entered the room like she was the queen of England and waved at us as she made her way down the walkway by our cages. Reaching the end, she turned to glare at the empty cage before working the catwalk back to me.

"Where's Agent Fletcher Calhoun?" I asked simply.

She laughed hard, throwing back her head. As the laugh became a cackle, she lowered her head to stare at me. "You are like a dog with a bone. Funny, that should be your Beta."

I faked a yawn in response to her attempt at humor. "Really?"

"You're no fun sometimes, Henry. Why does it even matter? He's some human male. Not your caliber of friend."

"He was a good man and a fellow Regulator Agent. He matters."

She sighed and examined her blood-red nails in feigned boredom. Lowering the same hand to her hip, she said, "Fine. He was at the hotel bar when I was. I saw that stupid tin of toothpicks...you all still do that, huh?" She waved her own question off. "I noticed his luggage with the Network Liaison initials on it."

Fletcher Calhoun had been a Regulator Network Liaison to start with. His name in that role had been Randall if I remembered correctly. Many who became agents, like Randall and Roy, had kept their baggage, literally and figuratively.

"A Regulator, in my town? I couldn't believe it! Took it as a sign though. Bought your pal a drink or two his second night in town. Mentioned your name and lo and behold, he was a friend. Someone you'd taken under your wing at one point. Who better to make disappear? I knew they'd send you...and if not, you'd come. You had to. He's one of yours and...," she tapped her temple, "I know how you think. It was my chance to play with my creations again. I couldn't pass it up."

"So, it was just bad timin'," I said. "As always, when it comes to you."

"More like perfect timing...but you say tah-may-toe, I say tah-mah-toe."

"Then he's dead because of me. Because you wanted me here."

She laughed, and it raised goosebumps on my flesh. "You always were a smart boy, Henry."

"You fuckin' bitch," Brewer said, slamming his hand at the bars of his cage.

"And look! I got two for the price of one."

Seductively, she ran her hand along the bars of my cage as she made her way to Brewer. "I couldn't have asked for a better treat. You look good, my child."

"I was *never* yours," he spat.

"True. Mores the pity, really."

"We'll have to agree to disagree there," Brewer said. "Where's Fletcher?"

Scáthach sat on the couch, sighed, and waved his question off like it wasn't important. "In the same place as that blue-jaw-whoever he was looking for. In the ground out somewhere in the desert."

"Where?" Brewer growled.

"How the hell should I know? You won't find him…unlike the idiots who killed your girl, Billy, we know how to bury our dead."

"So, you had nothin' to do with Ovida?" I prodded.

"Other than the fact that she got wrapped up with the wrong people, who are entwined with *my* people…no. Neither did I kill your blue mobster."

Realizing she meant Blue Jaw, I nodded, saying nothing. She was on a roll, and I wanted all the information she would spill.

Scáthach leaned forward. "I must say, it took some doing to find what happened to him. But I do love a good mystery. He, too, is dead out in the desert, somewhere between Santa Fe and here. But really, who cares?"

"I do," I said between clenched teeth.

Rolling her eyes, she said, "You would, wouldn't you? Fine. He stepped into the gambling ring here and got killed. No one trusted him to keep secrets after what he did in New York. Hell, they tasked Fletcher with killing him. He just got lucky and like most sinful men, met a horrible end before Fletcher got to him."

"Fletch was sent to kill him? No way," Brewer said, scratching his arm. "That makes no sense. He was gonna turn over further evidence against the mob for us."

Sitting back, Scáthach smiled at him like he was a puppy. "Oh, you big, adorable man. Still thinking the best of people and your employer too. It would be sweet if it wasn't so sad."

"A true Regulator wouldn't have killed him," Brewer stated simply.

"For your age, you have so much to learn," she said. "Not all members of your beloved company are as wholesome as you two. The mafia has men everywhere. They needed him gone, so he's gone. That's what you get when you're a murdering bad guy who blabs to the Feds…you get murdered by your bad-guy friends. Really now, it's not a difficult deduction."

"Who killed him?" I asked her, but my eyes were on Brewer as he again scratched at his skin like it was covered in chickenpox.

Her eyes cut to me, and she batted her eyelashes while wagging her finger at me. Standing, she said, "Oh, I'm not giving that up. If you live through this, you can root out your company's bad seeds yourself. That's not my job."

Turning her attention to Brewer, she stepped over to his cage. "Tell me, gorgeous, how are you feeling?"

"Like you can fuck off," he said, without even looking at her.

I glanced over to see her grin. "Why are we here?"

"Your skin starting to itch and tingle yet, pretty Beta boy? Moon is about to rise, and that potion in your system will make sure you shift for me."

This caused Brewer to react. He sat up quickly and stared at her. "What?"

"Much like in the new days of your affliction, you'll not be able to fight it."

"A forced change?" I said, standing up. "For what purpose?"

She looked at her watch. "Ten, nine, eight, seven..."

"Brewer? You can fight it!" I shouted.

"Billy? I feel the fever of it. The moon is risin', she's not lyin'."

"Three, two, one…showtime!" She shouted in glee.

The full moon rose, and Richard fought the urge to shift. He'd not felt forced to change because of the moon since the early 1900s, but with the potion in his bloodstream, he had no choice. Head thrown back, his blue eyes went blue-silver, and he wailed. His face shifted first, but he pulled the change back into himself and all you saw were the teeth. Dropping to all fours, the clothes split off his back, fur sprouting, then retracting.

"Fascinating. I've never met one of my children whose soul was this strong."

"I could fight the potion," Tarack said.

"Oh, I'm not so sure of that," Scáthach said, her finger tapping her full, red lips with a lusty expression on her face. With her other hand, she caressed Tarack's back. "I love you dearly, my first child of the moon, but there is something new here." Squatting by Richard's cage, she said, "My child...you survive this, and I'll give you almost anything to share with me why you are different."

Richard's head snapped up, and his eyes bore into hers. "I am not your child," he growled, even as his pants split at the sides and his muscles began to resemble the wolf more than the man. The fur, again, attempted to grow, but it receded almost immediately.

Scáthach's eyes were alight with the thrill of it all.

"Leave him alone!" I shouted from my copper box of a cage, banging on the bars with none of my extra strength. I might have been trying to lift a building.

"Richard," Kit said. "You can fight her. She has no hold over you!"

"Oh, darling," Scáthach said, her blond hair swinging about as she turned toward Kit. "This is all about potion magic. I have nothing to do with it."

Richard's shirt fell off, and his jeans split fully up the sides. His slender waist, also small as a wolf, didn't break the belt that held his jeans up and I, for one, was happy about that. He stood up on his bare feet, claws out on his hands as his face elongated just enough to allow for the wolf's teeth to grow to full size. Hair longer but not shaggy, he stared her down.

"I will never be yours," he said.

Scáthach hummed with pleasure. "Never say never, my beautiful man." Quick as a whip, her arm transformed to its skinny, black, spider-like form. Shooting through the bars, it wrapped around his waist and pulled him to her. "Take it now!"

Tarack rammed a container from under Richard's snout upward until his canines pierced the top. Pulling forward, he pried Richard's jaws open by force.

"Hold him," Scáthach said, and dipped something into his mouth under his tongue. Pulling it out, she looked at the amount of liquid there and a sly grin slid up half of her face. "I have enough."

Tarack released Richard, who stumbled away from the bars and coughed as best he could with an elongated face.

"Thank you for your cooperation," Scáthach said, and wandered from the room.

Tarack glared at Richard. "We'll see how important you are to your friends now."

They left, and I said, "What the hell is goin' on?"

Richard shook his head, fighting the potion. His face and nose shrank to their normal size, as did the teeth, save for the upper and lower canines that only shrunk by half. Breathing heavily, he ran at the bars, hitting them with all his might. They didn't bend at all, so he moved as far away as he could get, took a few breaths, and rammed them again. I thought I saw a small dent and stared in amazement at the strength.

Scáthach came in. "Oh, you can try that, but we reinforced your cage with a silver-steel. You're not breaking out of there." Lazily, she wandered toward my tiny box. "So, Mr. Bonney, care to beg me for your life?"

"I don't beg anyone for anythin', least of all, *you*."

"I figured you'd say that." She sighed dramatically, shifted her arm again, and grabbed my arm. Yanking it through the bars, she produced a syringe. Thinking it was a potion, I laughed at her. "Really? You're threatenin' me with what?"

Richard rammed the bars of his cage harder and shouted for her to stop. My eyes met his and suddenly I knew. My eyes grew wide, and before I could say another word, the needle pierced my flesh and injected its contents into my bloodstream.

When she finished, Scáthach laughed. "We will soon be even. You took my Beta, I will take yours…or rather, you will."

"No!" Richard shouted, and tears came to his eyes.

Pain suddenly ripped into me as what I fully understood now was Richard's saliva entered my body and filled me with the werewolf infection.

"Get him out of there," she said.

Tarack followed orders. He unlocked my copper cage and dragged my useless form out. I felt tired, sick, and sad that I couldn't even fight back. I had no choice but to allow Tarack to place me in the steel cage on the other side of Richard. He lay me on the cot that sat against the bars Brewer and I now shared, then he left.

Scáthach stepped in and set something on the floor beside me, far out of Richard's reach. "For when you're ready," she whispered, and walked out, locking the door behind her. "We'll be back, let you all talk it over for a bit," she said.

Arm in arm, she and Tarack left the room.

Richard had shifted fully back to human form and came to squat beside me. Reaching through the bars, he took my hand. "Billy…"

I looked into his eyes and saw it. His worst fear had come true, but not the way he'd thought it would. "What did she leave for you?"

With my right hand firmly held by him to steady me, I rolled to my left a bit to look at the floor on the other side of the bed. Laying there was what looked like an old-fashioned ice pick. I reached for it, grasped it with my hand after a few tries, and rolled back. "It's a silver weapon to kill you with."

"Which you will do," he said like he was my parent.

I dropped the pick on the bed by my chest and patted his hand that held mine. "No. No, I will not. I told you that back in the beginning."

"What is going on?" Kit demanded to know.

He looked toward her. "If a spirit warrior of Scáthach is infected with the werewolf virus, that werewolf must die for the warrior to live." His voice hitched as he said the last part. Clearing his throat, he continued, sounding steadier. "If someone doesn't kill me before the moon is full, then Billy will mentally disintegrate and slowly die with no hope for redemption of his soul." On the last word, Richard's head dropped. "And it doesn't count if I kill myself," he added with a humorless laugh. "Fuckin' magic."

"Why Brewer, you keep using the F-word lately," I said, and laughed. "The world truly is comin' to an end."

"Billy…," he said, that one word holding all the emotion of the seventy-plus years we'd worked together.

I swallowed my fear and pain. "I'm sorry. I should've never called you out here."

"I disagree with that," Kit said.

"You know what you need to do," Richard whispered to me.

"The hell he will!" Kit yelled at him.

Richard stared at her. "Did you not understand what I said before? If he doesn't kill me, he dies, and his soul is lost forever to wander this plane." He looked back to me. "And it's not up to me to make sure Scáthach dies, it's up to you. It has to be you who sends her back to the Otherworld."

"I'm not the last spirit warrior," I said, letting that hang in the silence. Finally, I said, "Either of us can do it."

"Either of you can do what?" the sultry voice of Scáthach said as she entered the room.

"Kill you," Kit said.

She laughed. "No, darling…no one can kill me. But just in case I need leverage to force William's hand," she said, and opened Kit's cell door. "You're coming with me."

"I'd rather die than—"

Scáthach was faster than Kit, and before anything could be done, she injected Kit with something that knocked her out immediately.

"Well, well, that was faster than I thought," Scáthach said as she caught Kit's limp body in her arms. "I do hope I didn't overdose her," she added coyly with a look back at Richard. Seeing his anguish, she laughed. "Oh, you all are so entertaining! You've truly made this century the most fun of them all."

"Pick her up and take her to the car," Scáthach told Tarack.

"With pleasure, my love," he said and stepped up to take Kit from Scáthach. Not expecting the weight of her, he tottered backward just a step, but it was far enough, and Richard was waiting.

Faster than I'd ever seen him move, he reached through the bars and grasped Tarack's head. "Get your hands off of her," he growled.

When Tarack merely laughed, Dick snapped his neck, and then, using the silver spike he'd swiped from beside me, he rammed it up through the base of Tarack's skull, killing him.

20
COLLOIDAL SILVER

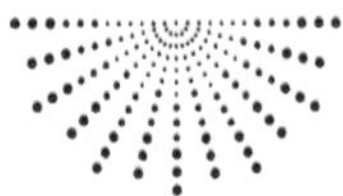

January 1880

Edward and some of his tribe had saved us from Ianna's army and had everything under control. Seeing this, I glanced toward Richard on the ground, and my chest tightened. I ran toward him. Flashes from that day at Blazer's Mill ran through my mind. Like then, I dropped beside him and checked the wound. It was a through and through. Rolling him over, I found Richard's eyes open, but not vacant.

"Richard?" I shouted at him.

He appeared to be struggling to breathe. I slapped my hand on his chest, and he gasped in air.

"Breathe, you big galoot!"

Instead, Brewer coughed out first and then inhaled deeply with a wheezing sound.

Tom dropped down on Richard's other side. "How did he survive that? Did it miss his heart?"

"No," Richard said, his voice raspy. "She's an expert marksman."

"Then how…how are you alive?" I asked.

"I may know the answer to that," Edward said.

Looking up at the tribesman, I said, "Do share."

Edward took one knee near Richard's head. "He was full of silver when he changed the first time, was he not?"

"Yes, colloidal silver," I said. "Tons in his bloodstream."

"That should've killed him when he changed," Edward said, "But you intervened. Not only did you save his soul from going to Scáthach, you both fought the silver. It can't kill him."

I stared in disbelief, then remembered all the extra pain Brewer was in leading up to the change and the battle of the first transformation itself. I'd seen others have their first change, and it wasn't half as painful. This was why. We'd not only battled Scáthach's will that night, Brewer's will and mine fought the silver curse and had won.

"Well, I'll be...Richard, you're invincible."

"No...he has something that can kill him, other than you," Edward said. "We've just not found it yet. There will be something. But for now, he's okay."

"Sore," Richard groaned.

"Yeah, it was a heart shot. That's always one of the worst," Edward told him.

"One of?" I asked.

Edward put a finger on his forehead. "Headshot is a close second."

"Agreed," Richard said.

"That was with lead," I pointed out.

"Still hurt like hell," Richard said.

"How did you know where we were?" I asked Edward.

"I got wind of Ianna's army from a member of my tribe who came to my home."

I looked at him in confusion.

"When Richard left to see you, I went back to my cabin," he clarified. "Upon arrival, I found myself in a pack of real wolves. They spoke to me of a group of smaller wolves with a woman who was also a horse. I gathered some of my tribe and we rode here immediately, fearing we would be too late, but we were right on time."

"As usual," I said.

Edward merely smiled.

"Help me up, would ya?" Richard asked.

Tom took one hand, and I took the other. We lifted the big man onto his feet, and I realized I'd never gotten the rush of power from my Beta dying. I should've known Brewer was okay, but in my anger and fear, I'd forgotten.

Thinking of these factors, I looked toward Ianna. She, unlike Brewer, was still down. I walked toward her, and the others followed me. She was truly dead.

Brewer knelt beside her and gently closed her eyes before caressing her face. "May you now be at peace and the darkness find its home somewhere else."

Most people would have hated the person who shot them, but not Richard. He was all heart all the time, no matter what. It's what made him who he was. But it never stopped surprising me.

"We'll bury her respectfully," he told us.

No one argued.

"Your capacity for compassion is unparalleled, Richard," Tom said.

Brewer didn't reply, he just lifted Ianna up and carried her off.

I knew why he said nothing. His big heart also ran the other way. He would protect what he loved and avenge them just as fiercely as he had compassion. It was both his gift and his weapon…and God help anyone who got the latter and not the former.

* * *

May 1949

The scream that expelled from Scáthach caused everyone in the basement pison to drop to the floor and cover their ears.

"No, no, no! Tarack!" she wailed. "Noooo!" She crumbled to the floor and screamed out in emotional and physical agony. He was one of her first made and her Beta. Eyes red with fury, she turned on Richard, who stood in the middle of his cage, fangs and claws out as he stared her down.

"Come on in and kill me," he said. "You know you want to!"

"But if you do," I said, "I'll be powerful enough to come through these steel bars and ruin your plans. So, it's your choice…make it."

She was torn, and I prayed she'd leave him be.

Grabbing the bars to Richard's cell, she shook them. "These have silver! How could you even touch them or that silver pick?"

He allowed the silver light to come into his eyes. "I'm not harmed by silver."

Seething, Scáthach pressed her face to the bars. "How is that possible!? Being William's Beta wouldn't grant you that gift!"

"Yeah, well…your magic doesn't take account for stupidity," I said with a laugh that was quickly followed up by a cough that wracked my body. Spitting blood through the bars onto the floor of Richard's cage, I said, "Ya see, Dick here had this brilliant idea. Instead, he almost killed himself…and ruined my favorite pair of boots."

"Really? You're still upset about that?"

I shrugged with a grin.

"Besides, it turned out to not be so stupid, seeing as it changed my genetic or magical make-up," Richard pointed out. "I'd say it was a bonus."

I opened my mouth to add something when he cut me off.

"Minus your boots, of course."

I pointed at him and smiled. "Exactly."

"So, what will it be, Scáthach? Are you gonna kill him and take me on with all that power and rage, or do you want to just walk out of here?"

She glared at us. "You think you're so smart…but you're not! I can still hurt you without doing either." She picked up Kit and with a deep, cleansing breath, she changed her tone to light and playful again. "Don't worry, boys, you won't see her alive again anyway, no matter what you decide." Wiggling red polish-tipped fingers at us she merely said, "Toodles!" and left.

Richard screamed and ran at the bars, trying to reach Scáthach, but he couldn't. Grabbing a bar in each hand, he pulled at them as he yelled out, "Kit!" And though the bars moved a bit, it wasn't enough, and he sank to the floor in defeat. "She's gone. Billy, kill me and go get her."

"I'm not so sure that's the best move. She finds out you're dead, Kit will electrocute my ass to death. So, I die anyway. But if you kill me, you'll be truly free, like Edward, and you can go save her…live your life without all the adventures I force you to take."

Richard laughed lightly. "You have never forced me to do anythin' I didn't wanna do, Billy. I thought you knew that by now."

"I remember this one time I wore a dress, and you had to pretend to be my date…"

Brewer laughed. "Okay…that was likely somethin' I was forced to do, but more by the situation, not you. Whatever happened to that picture they took of us at the party, anyway?"

"I hope it either was burned or is in someone's collection of priceless artifacts, and they think we're some famous couple."

"We are a famous couple…sort of." Laughing, I coughed up more blood and felt the room tilt. Reaching through the bars, I took his hand. "When I'm gone, you…" I couldn't finish the sentence. My tongue felt too thick in my mouth to form words, and my vision was tunneling down to a pinhole of sight…and then it was out.

* * *

I came to here and there, but not for long. Each time I found Richard in one of two places. Either he was pacing his cage or sitting by my side. One particular time I woke, I found a cool cloth on my forehead, and I felt better than before.

"Hey, there you are," Richard said.

"How long have I been out?"

"This time? About four hours."

"How long until the full moon rises?"

"An hour," he told me.

I nodded. "Is there any water to drink?"

"Yeah, I have a little left here." Richard stood up and fetched the canteen they'd left behind. He unscrewed the cap, eased it through the bars, and tilted the last few drops into my mouth.

"Thank you."

"Billy?"

"Don't," I said, simply. "Don't ask me to do it. I won't and I'm sorry. I can hope maybe, like Eli, that I've saved enough of her monsters to cross over myself. We'll see. Just promise me one thing, okay? When I'm gone, don't mope around for a century. Well, maybe half would be okay…."

Richard laughed at my lame humor, and I did as well.

"You're not dying today!" a voice said above us.

"Edward!" Richard shouted out, recognizing the voice before me.

"To the rescue as usual!" I said, swinging my arm as if I had a sword, but failing the move completely since my arms felt like noodles.

"How did you find us?" Richard shouted.

"Followed her stench. Is there a better way down to you all than this chute?"

"Only if you can find the entrance to the room that's attached to this one," Richard told him.

"Chute it is!"

Letting out a whoop, Edward came down into the room with a thud. Standing up, he rubbed his ass. "That's painful. Now, what in tarnation is wrong with you, Billy?"

Richard explained.

"Then you need to kill Richard, and we will go end this bitch."

"Wait, what?" I said my vision blurring.

"We spoke of this before."

"Too risky," I said.

Edward squatted down beside the cages. "I saw Gaax. He says you have to be alive for the next part to work. It can't be me or Richard."

"It could be Tom. Where is he?"

"He's with Duke, and he agrees, it has to be you."

"Billy," Richard said, his voice quiet. "Whatever it is, you need to do it. You need to save Kit. Please, for me. I love her. It took forever to find a woman I could be with, to not fear I'd infect…who understood me. For her to die would kill me anyway. Please, Billy, for me."

"Damn it, Brewer. I promised I'd never kill you."

Richard knelt by me. "But I'm tellin' you to. Eli made a hard decision once upon a time. Now you must. It has to be you, and deep down you know it."

Tears spilled down the sides of my face, and I reached out, placing the palm of my hand on his chest, over his heart. "I…"

"The moon rises soon, Billy. This is our only shot to send her back, and you know it. We may never have this chance again."

Anguish sliced through my heart like a knife. Taking a deep breath, I looked into Brewer's blue eyes. "I love you," I said, and I sent a shock through his heart, stopping it.

Richard's eyes lost focus, and he dropped to the floor.

Torment ripped me in two. I grasped at my chest and writhed on the cot so viciously that I fell to the ground as Richard's death restored my powers. His Beta connection flew into me like a hot ball of flame to use as a weapon, and God knew I wanted to lash out with it.

"Now, Billy! Now!" Edward shouted.

I threw the bed to the other side of the cell. "Are you sure?"

"No, but do it anyway!"

I nodded once, and then, pulling on that fiery ball of flame that was Brewer in my chest, I channeled it and reached through the bars. Pulling him closer to me with one arm, I slammed my palm down onto his chest again. With all I was, I shoved that ball of power back into his heart, shocking it, but nothing happened.

"Hit him again!" Edward said.

I shocked his heart again, but nothing. I focused again on starting his heart. But this time, I had an idea. “Edward, give me the silver spike from Tarack’s skull.”

“What? Why?”

“Trust me.”

Edward yanked it from the dead werewolf, cleaned it off, and handed it to me.

“Dear God, let this work.” I shoved the silver into his chest without piercing his heart and sent one more shock through it into him and waited.

“It could take time,” Edward said.

Suddenly there was a voice shouting from above. “We’re here!” It was Duke. He rushed into the room with Tom. “We found you!”

“No!” Tom shouted when he saw Richard dead on the ground.

Duke pulled a set of keys from his pocket and opened my door and then Brewer’s. He, along with Tom and Edward, filed into the cell and surrounded Richard.

I stepped in and took the keys from Duke. “You’re too late.”

Silence filled the air, and it was heavy with sorrow.

“Duke, where’s that map from yesterday?”

“In my truck. Parked by your car. Why?”

Solemnly, I nodded. “Then I have one thing left to do.”

Moving quickly, I exited the cage, shut the door, and locked it. I tossed the keys across the room.

Edward banged on the bars. “Billy, what are you doing!?”

“I’m going to finish this and the people I love are going to stay here, where it’s safe.” Looking at Richard’s body, I added, “I can’t take another death because of me. I can’t.”

I didn’t give them time to talk me out of it. I just ran.

* * *

December 1880

I spent the year of 1880 running from who everyone thought I needed to be. I wasn’t only some supernatural creature, I was a man. On top of that, I was a man in love and I wanted some semblance of a normal life. Because of that, I tried to mix the two halves of who I was into one. If I wasn’t with Paulita, I was hunting with Edward, Richard, and Tom. But fights became more common between Tom and me, and from what I could tell, Edward and Richard agreed that if we really wanted to stop Scáthach, we needed more training and people. Pride hurt, I pulled away from them and started riding with Dave Rudabaugh and Billy Wilson more often than not.

While that was happening, the world went on around us. Pat Garrett got married, and fights with the Apache increased, making it hard for us to maneuver on the land to hunt down Scáthach or anyone else. Susan McSween got remarried to George Barber, and Bob Ollinger, the bully and braggart that he was, killed Frank Hill. Last but not least, Jessie Evans had been captured by Texas Rangers in a running fight, or so it was said.

I wrote again to Lew Wallace on the twelfth of December, but I wasn't expecting a reply since he'd never written me back on any of my other letters. Besides, he'd had a book come out in November that everyone talked about until my ears wanted to bleed, so he wasn't thinking about me. I refused to read the book on principle.

The biggest news was Pat Garrett, secret Regulator, became Sheriff of Lincoln County. At first, I thought this would work in our favor. I was wrong, and Tom and I were fighting again.

"What do you mean you're leavin'?" I said, feeling anger flush my face as I placed the Dutch oven with the biscuits in it over the fire.

Tom finished loading his six-shooter, spun the chamber, and placed the gun in the holster on his hip. "Scáthach is on the run and has been for a year. She's lookin' for a new body that works long-term for her. If there was ever a time to get more trainin' so we can finish this once and for all, it's now."

"You've been talkin' to Garrett," I said simply.

"I have," Tom admitted.

I was so shocked by his honest answer that I didn't have a comeback. Instead, I looked to Richard and then Edward, as it was just the four of us sitting around the fire while the other rustlers huddled away from us.

"So, you're headin' to England?" Richard asked.

Tom nodded. "Yes. When we get back to Fort Sumner, Garrett will pretend to arrest me. Word will be they sent me to prison back in Texas where I'd done somethin'." He shrugged. "That way, I can return when I'm done."

I sat and scooped some of the embers of the fire and placed them on top of the lid of the Dutch oven. "There are twenty-three of us roaming the land here, killing off Scáthach's men—"

"And stealin' cattle while we're at it," Tom pointed out.

"We have to make money somehow. Not like bein' a Regulator pays anythin'."

"It would if you'd go to the academy," Tom said. "I'm tired of always bein' poor and on the run. I'm just gonna go, Billy."

"Didn't he say that academy was only a year or two long?" Edward asked.

"Yeah…but that wasn't the full truth. Any Warrior of Scáthach must do two years without their powers to level the playing field. Then they do two years with them back. Then each graduate spends four years working cases over there before moving onward to a full-time assignment somewhere."

"Eight years! That's a long time!" I said.

"Really?" Richard said dryly. "You could live forever. Hell, I could live a thousand years. Eight years is nothin' compared to spendin' your life doin' work that means somethin'. We're gettin' nowhere out here, Billy, and you know it. If he wants to go, he should go. Hell, if I could go, I would."

"With your moral compass, I'm not surprised," I muttered.

"Come on, Billy," Brewer said. "You're sayin' you wouldn't like to learn more about this world you're now a part of?"

I hesitated. I wanted to. But I had feelings for Paulita, who would be seventeen next month, and I'd promised her I'd not go anywhere when she'd overheard Garrett talking to me once. She'd not heard the full gist of things, but she made me promise, and I hated breaking those.

"Maybe, but Paulita—"

"Bring her with you!" Tom said.

I laughed. "With all the wealth her family has here, she will not leave that to live in England for eight years." It was silent, so I added, "Two years without killing werewolves and having the elevated powers means you'll age a bit, Tom."

"Two years isn't much," he replied. "Plus, I think it's important for me to feel normal again for a while…or how else am I to understand those working with me? Not everyone who works for the Regulators is supernatural.

"In fact, from what I understand, there's a lot more than just werewolves, spirit-warriors, witches, vampires, and shape-shifters. There're creatures from other folklore we would learn to fight. You've never been one to shy away from adventure, Billy. I don't get why you are now."

"Zahara," I said. "She's out lookin' for answers. What if she comes back with those or sends Gaax back to ask for help and we're not here?"

"Richard and I will be here," Edward pointed out before lifting his canteen for a sip of water.

I looked at Edward and saw the sadness behind his eyes. We both knew the last place Richard wanted to stick around was here. If he could, he'd go in my place. Which caused me to say something I'd not planned to. "If they'll let Richard attend the academy, I'll go."

"Billy…" Richard said.

"You think I don't know you want to leave this place?" I said as I sat beside him. "You always have to pretend to be someone else here. If you were there, you could maybe settle down and tend a farm like you want." Which made me think of Edward. "Hell, if they'll let Dick go, they should let you go, too, Edward."

"No," he said simply. "My people are from this land, and I'm not leaving it. But thank you," he said with a bow of his head. "Richard though, you should go if they'll let you. I can stay here and wait on Zahara. In fact, I need to. I promised Eli I would be here for her. I won't break that promise."

Richard appeared torn. He obviously didn't want to leave Edward behind, but I knew he wanted out of New Mexico. Finally, he just made this noise as he blew out a breath he'd likely been holding. "Look, they're not gonna let me, so this conversation is ridiculous."

"You ask them when you get to England," I told Tom.

"Damn, Billy. You do like to stir the pot," Tom said with a light laugh.

I grinned. "Yes…yes, I do. I go, he goes. You tell them that and see if they still want me so badly."

"Tell Garrett yourself," Tom said.

"I will if I see him before you do."

Edward looked up at the winter sky. "We need to get moving once we eat. Snow is coming. We need to get to better shelter before it arrives."

"How do you know?" I asked. "There're clouds, but they don't look like snow clouds."

Edward tapped his nose. "I can smell it…feel it. My people always know."

I checked the biscuits, and they were nearly done. "Then we best get on the road. These are about ready; I can make sandwiches with them. Maybe add some eggs and bacon to them. I'll wrap 'em up and we can eat them as we ride."

"Sounds good," Edward said. "I'll go alert the rest of the men since I'm already packed and ready to go."

I nodded, and Edward jaunted off.

"Wait, I'll come with you," Brewer shouted, and ran after Edward to help spread the word.

I stepped up to Tom. "I hate to lose you, but you should do what you feel called to do."

"Thanks," Tom said, obviously surprised by my words.

I went to pack up Colonel and said, "If you're leavin', we should go snag Bowdre and see if he wants back in for a bit. I could use him in your stead."

"You can ask him, but I think he wants to stay out of it all."

I grinned mischievously. "Well then, we'll have to convince him."

There was silence, and then Tom said, "You serious about askin' about Brewer and the academy?"

"Sure am. See what you can do, would ya?"

"It would be a great feather in their cap to have us both, so they might consider it," Tom said.

"It's the only way I'll go."

"All right then," he said.

I finished making breakfast and packaged it up to eat on the way while Tom helped prep Colonel and pack my things for the ride. We had stolen cattle to move along, and if Edward was right about the snow, and he likely was, we had little time to do it.

* * *

We sold the cattle and made our way to Yerby's Ranch at Las Cañaditas to see Charlie Bowdre. On the way, Tom ran into a nearby town and was discovered there. He outran the men chasing him, and we continued on our way.

Charlie wasn't upset to see us the way I thought he would be, but his wife, Manuela, was less than pleased…and that was putting it lightly.

"You bring trouble," she said to me. "You'll not be stayin' here long." It wasn't a question.

"No, ma'am," I said and wandered over to speak to Charlie privately. "We could use you."

"No way," he said, smoothing his full mustache.

"Tom is leavin' for a bit to take care of some business, and you are good at what we do."

"I promised Manuela I'd stay out of that life," he said.

"How are you financially? We just sold a bunch of cattle."

"Stolen cattle," Charlie said.

"Yes, but we sold them nonetheless, and I have this." I pulled out a group of bills. "This is Tom's share, minus a bit for his travel. It's yours if you join us for a bit. We'll leave it with Manuela, and once we get the next big payday, you can leave. In fact, I think one more is all I'll need to take some time off myself. What do you say?"

Charlie looked at the money. "Just one trip?"

"Just one and you get paid for two, basically."

He took the money and counted it. "Damn, Billy!"

"I know. It's a lot. Go talk to your wife. Take that with you."

He nodded. "We are thinkin' of leavin' the area after the new year. In the winter, actually. This money, plus the pay from one last run with you, would help us do that. I'll talk to her."

"Sounds fair," I said and watched him walk away.

The next morning, I was prepping Colonel for a ride when Charlie came into the stable. I didn't see the money in his hand, so I thought Manuela had it and he was coming with me to Texas to get more cattle. I wasn't wrong.

"One trip," Charlie said.

"That's the deal," I confirmed.

"All right. Where are we headed first?"

"Fort Sumner. Wanna see my girl and then we'll head out."

"All right," Charlie said, "I'll start puttin' my bag together."

"Thank you, Charlie," I said.

He slapped me on the shoulder. "Won't be long."

Within the next hour we were on the road. Not all the men we'd had on our previous trip were with us, though. We were to meet up with them after we ran a scouting mission. But we still had Dave Rudabaugh, Billy Wilson, and Tom Picket with us. The latter of which I took to calling by his last name to not confuse people when I said just Tom.

Everything seemed quiet in the area with no lawmen about, but there was word Garrett and his men had been seen close by. Because of this, we went to eat at the Wilcox-Brazil Ranch and ask around for more information.

While we were there, I received a word back about Fort Sumner in a note from José Valdéz.

"Hot damn, boys, the coast is clear. José says that Garrett and his men headed down to Roswell."

"I should still go into Fort Sumner to see if the coast is clear," Picket said.

"José wouldn't lie to me, and this is his handwritin'," I said, tapping the letter. "We'll all go down and enjoy some time in town before we head to Texas to meet up with the rest."

Picket shrugged. "Okay. If you trust him."

"We do," Tom said, answering for me.

I wanted to see Paulita, and it overjoyed me that I'd get to do just that. However, we needed to be careful, so we waited for the sun to go down. The winter storm had stopped as well. It was a clear night with a bright moon and a foot of snow on the ground.

"Beautiful night," I said.

"Cold night," Tom corrected.

I rolled my eyes. "It can be both."

We reached a crossroad, and I turned to Richard. "You and Edward go 'round the long way and meet us in town. Just in case we get in trouble, I'd like you two comin' the other way."

"Sure thing," Edward said, and they split off while the rest of us moved onward.

Tom was in the lead with me next to him, yet behind him just a bit. Dave followed Tom, and Charlie was to his left, with Picket bringing up the rear. We rode into the silence of Fort Sumner, and all hell broke loose.

21
ZAHARA

May 1949

I ran down the road at full speed until I found Duke's truck. I fetched the map and got into my car. I needed the fastest vehicle, and this was it. Laying on the passenger seat were Richard's other pants. In anger, I tossed them from the car, started it up, and headed out of town. Reaching the next road, I saw a wall of cars blocking my way just like the line of wolves had done that night to Richard, Kit, and me.

"Shit."

I threw the wheel and dropped the gear, taking a turn so fast, the tires squealed the whole way. Changing gears, I floored it and took another route that led me onto Highway 70. A glance behind me showed the cars were on my tail, but their vehicles were no match for mine.

I took the exit onto Frontage Road and hit the brakes as I threw the wheel again. Spinning about, I hit the accelerator and turned onto a back road. If I was right, this was B008 where I was to meet Scáthach. It was also out into the middle of nowhere. With this big of a posse on my ass, there was no way I was letting the fight happen in town.

I hit the accelerator and floored it. My sports car was close to outrunning them when suddenly, standing in the road, was a woman. As I got closer, I saw who it was.

"Kit!"

I swerved to miss her stumbling figure and lost control of the car. Missing her by a foot, I rolled the vehicle. When we came to a stop, my well of souls repaired my broken bones, but I still felt like hell. I crawled out the shattered window and stepped away from the vehicle as it caught fire. Home office was going to be mad as all hell.

"Fuck!"

Scáthach stepped out from the shadows to pick Kit up in her arms.

I pulled my gun and pointed it at her. "I can miss her and hit you easily. Put her down."

Scáthach just laughed and transformed. Wide triangular teeth like a shark's were visible first, then the eyes went red, and her human skin was swallowed whole by the black flesh of her real self. Seven feet tall now, her blond hair became engulfed in red flames as she cackled at me.

"You can't hurt me now!" she bragged with a smile, and with that simple declaration, I knew she'd gotten Zahara's letter that Gaax told me to make sure fell into Scáthach's hands.

I forced my face to appear furious. "That's classified information."

"I have my ways. You humans are so stupid. I had higher hopes for you, Henry."

"For fucksake, it's William…catch up with the times."

She laughed. "I'll really hate watching you die, *William*. You've been the most entertaining of my heroes."

"Yeah, 'cause that matters to me," I said flatly. "Put…her…down."

The cars that had been chasing me came to a halt in a line, having never come as far as where Scáthach stood with Kit. Their headlights were on full, lighting us up like we were on a stage.

I felt like an unprepared actor on opening night, but I pulled my second gun and stood my ground. "If I'm goin' out, I'll go with my guns in my hands," I muttered. Glancing at the wall of cars, I thought of Scáthach's other weakness. "I survive this, you let Kit live. You hear me?"

Scáthach tilted her head in consideration, but finally, she nodded. "I do like a good game of chicken. You have my word."

I turned to face her army of werewolves in cars and said quietly, "I'm a genius or an idiot. Brewer would say the latter. Let's see if I can prove him wrong." Taking a large breath, I shouted, "Come out of those vehicles and get me, assholes. You'll all not make it out of this alive, I can promise ya that!"

Doors opened, and a minimum of four exited each vehicle.

"Great," I muttered in heavy sarcasm.

They didn't waste time and with the full moon in the sky to fuel their power, they all shifted and howled.

"And here…we…go," I said.

The thunderous pounding of approaching werewolves' paws as they hit the ground filled the quiet of the New Mexico desert. Soon I could see the outline of them all in the glow from the headlights of the cars behind them as they ran for me. It was like I was watching a motion picture, and I held my ground. I was about to start firing when I heard a voice in my head.

"Run, Billy. Run!"

It was Zahara's voice.

It had to be a lie. A trick of Scáthach.

But then I heard the *QUARK* of Gaax.

"Go now!" Zahara's voice shouted in my head.

"Fuckin' hell!" I returned my guns to the holsters at my back, turned, and ran in the opposite direction of the wolves. There was no way I could outrun them all, and I was going to have to turn and face them, eventually. Without Kit, Tom, Richard, or even Duke…it was just me against Scáthach and her lost souls, and I needed to locate a spot to turn and take them on, alone.

Then I heard it. Out in the dark. The pounding of horse hooves. They were gaining on me at an unbelievable speed. I took a chance and looked behind me and did a double take. It was a black horse I'd have known anywhere. It was Colonel.

* * *

December 1880

We were quietly trotting into Fort Sumner in the snow when a voice cried out into the night, "Throw up your hands!"

It was Pat Garrett.

Before I could say a thing, Dave pulled his gun and fired toward the voice. Wilson and Picket did the same. Tom and I didn't dare shoot toward Garrett, so we made sure our aim was off a bit.

Smoke from gunfire, theirs and ours, filled the air, and we took off. Riding through the snow, the cold air whipped at my face, and anger pulsed through my veins. José Valdéz had lied to me, and he was going to pay for it.

"Billy!" Dave yelled. "My horse is done!"

I turned to see Rudabaugh's horse collapse and die. "Get up behind Tom and…"

That's when I saw that neither Tom Folliard nor his horse were with us.

"Damn it!" I shouted and rode over to Dave. "Get on behind me!"

Rudabaugh grabbed his things from his dead horse and did as I'd directed. We quickly rode to the other side of town where I spotted Edward and Richard.

"I need to go talk to them alone," I told the three with me still. "Give them some instructions. I'll be back."

Rudabaugh dismounted from Colonel and thankfully neither Picket, Wilson, nor Charlie questioned me. Happy for that, I rode over to Richard and Edward.

"Where's Folliard?" was the first thing out of Richard's mouth.

"Garrett got him."

He and Edward nodded, knowing the truth of the matter.

"How many of Zahara's potions do you have left, Dick?" I asked.

"With me? Not many. More at the cabin," he said.

"Okay. If you go back down there though, take Colonel. Extra help with the werewolf pack out there. I'm fighting humans, so he could go with you."

"You sure?" Richard asked.

"Yeah," I said.

My excuse was weak, and I hoped they didn't see through it. Simply put, if Garrett got me, I sure as hell didn't want him getting Colonel.

Edward got down off the bay mare he'd only recently started riding. "Here, take her. I'll ride Colonel since Dick here is so attached to Mattie."

"All right," I said, and got down. Placing my hands on Colonel's eyes, I gave him as much energy as I thought I could spare so it would keep his eyes healed for a while. "We'll catch up with you at our meetin' spot on the border in the next week. That'll give you time to go get more potion and get to Texas."

I took my ammunition and guns from Colonel and transferred them to the pretty bay mare as Edward did the reverse. Colonel whinnied loud and reared up a bit.

I ran over to him. "Shh…it's all right. I'll see you soon," I said with my hand on him, so he'd understand. "I need you to take care of them for me while I deal with this. Can you do that for me?"

Colonel blew air out of his lips and pawed at the ground with his front right hoof.

"I know, I just don't want Garrett to snag you if this goes sideways."

"Billy, you could just—" Richard said.

"No...Garrett is *not* forcin' me to leave here." I kissed Colonel's nose, told him how much he meant to me, then walked over to Edward's horse.

Edward mounted Colonel. "Be careful."

"Where are you headed?" Richard asked.

"Stinking Springs. Too cold to go further at this point. See you soon." With that, I pulled myself up into the saddle, rode over so Dave could mount up behind me again, and the five of us headed toward a one-room building in Stinking Springs I knew of where we could stay for the night.

* * *

May 1949

Colonel caught up, running alongside me, and whinnied as I shouted for joy. Pulling on the extra speed and grace of my gift, I grasped the reins, and with a leap, I pulled myself into the saddle. It didn't slow the boy down at all, and he kept running.

I placed my hand on his neck. "I have no idea how you're still alive, or how you got here, but it's mighty good to see you, old friend. Where are you takin' me?"

The answer I thought I got back from him didn't make any sense.

"That's not possible."

He just whinnied again and ran in a wide arc, so we were once again facing the oncoming pack of wolves head-on. Colonel only paused for a moment, and then, as if he heard an order from thin air, he charged the pack. With Colonel, I thought I might just have a chance, slim though it might be.

"Let's show 'em how it's done, boy!" I shouted, pulling my guns back out, ready for a battle.

Taking aim, I squeezed Colonel's sides tight with my legs to brace for soul overload and fired into the pack. Barreling through them, Colonel deftly avoided dead bodies as I accepted souls into the well. There were so many now that I felt dizzy, like I had when I was younger. Taking a deep breath as we came out the other side of the mass, I leaned forward onto Colonel and took a moment to find my center.

One wolf came at us from behind and as if he just didn't have time for that shit, Colonel kicked out with his back legs. His silver-infused shoes did mortal damage that flowed through him to me, rejuvenating us both. Colonel pranced to the left to dodge two more, and I shot the wolves in the head before we barreled forward toward the wolf pack and killed a few others before they pulled back to regroup. Glancing up, I saw there seemed to be more now, as if me killing one had put two more in its place.

"Where'd they come from?" I said aloud to Colonel, who merely whinnied at me. Then I saw the other line of cars facing the first set, and now our stage was lit from both sides in what felt like my final battle.

"Well, boy, if we go out like this, it will be an honor," I told Colonel, my hand on his neck.

He whinnied again, then we heard Gaax as he flew overhead, sounding out what seemed to be a battle cry. Now I understood that Colonel wanted me to wait and listen before riding into the pack. I did as I was told, and I heard them.

"Well, I'll be damned," I muttered and looked in the direction of the thundering echo of approaching horsemen; and this time, that sound wasn't fear like that day with Tunstall, but elation.

* * *

December 1880

It was cold. So much so that I kept moving my face so it wouldn't freeze. We arrived at Stinking Springs and made our way to the old forage station built by Alejandro Perea. The small building, only one room, was made of rock and had no windows. There was just the opening for a door, but no actual wooden shutter to cover it. Nor did the building have any port holes drilled into her. But it was the only place for miles and would get us all out of the open.

A long bar stuck out from the building above the door opening and we tethered our horses there before going in with our belongings and blankets to get some sleep.

"Garrett's gonna follow us," Charlie said.

"I'll tell him I forced you to come with me," I told him. "I'll say I threatened ya. If he takes us in, you have nothin' to worry about. I promise ya that."

Rudabaugh, Wilson, and Picket headed into the building, and I stepped close to Charlie. "Look, Garrett wants to send me off to England, and I don't wanna go. I have a life here."

"What the hell is in England?"

"Let's check the perimeter, and I'll explain."

We walked, and I told him all of it. Well, all except who Michael Brown really was, or that Edward was a werewolf. Other than that, though, I filled him in on what he'd missed while lying low.

"Let me get this straight," he said, "You finally got Mary free, Scáthach is on the run, and they want you to go train in England so you can finish her off?"

"In short, yeah."

"Then go. We'll all be here when you get back."

I sighed. "It's eight years away from everythin' I know." I stopped and kicked a stone. "I have a girl here, I have work…"

"You have stealin'; that's not work."

I rolled my eyes. "I'm scared, okay?"

"What?" Charlie said with a tiny laugh. "You're not scared of anythin'. Never have been."

"Look at me; do I look like a man who can blend in over there in fancy ol' London?"

"No, but so what? Don't blend! Be you and be loud and proud about it. You don't have to be some British Lord over there. It's not like you'll be hangin' out with Queen Victoria; you'll be learnin' to kick ass and kill bad guys…and beasts! They likely have men—"

"And women," I said.

"Even better!" Charlie said with a wink. "What was I sayin'? Oh yeah, they'll likely have people from all walks of life there, and you'll blend in fine. And if they don't, and you stick out like a sore thumb, who cares?"

I leaned back against the building. "I suppose *I* do."

"Sure, you're the big bad spirit warrior here and you run the show. There, you won't be runnin' nothin'. That's what bothers you the most I'm guessin'."

I poked his shoulder. "See! You know I hate havin' someone orderin' me around. Charlie, the last few years of trainin', you work *with* the law in England."

That stopped the grin on Charlie's face. "Mmm…yeah, I can see how that would give you pause. The sheriffs here, save for Garrett, are dirty as the slop we feed our swine. But there? It could be different. Ya won't know until ya try it, right?"

I kicked another rock. He had a point. "Paulita won't wanna go with me, and I can't see her waitin' eight years for my ass. No way."

"She's turnin' seventeen next month, and I'd bet all the money in my pocket that she doesn't know what she wants to do next week, let alone in the next year. However, if she loves you enough, she'll go. If she doesn't want to, then she's not the one for you, Billy."

I nodded. "It's not that you aren't makin' good points, my friend, I'm just...hesitant to trust anyone new, and over there, it would all be new, and I'm not so sure about it."

"Sleep on it," Charlie said. "You always do better when ya sleep on it."

"Truth," I said, placing a hand on his shoulder. "You're a true pal, Charlie. It's good to have ya around again, even if it is for one last run with me. Let's get some rest, and I'll do what ya said. Maybe in the mornin', I'll have a better idea of what I should do."

Charlie patted my hand that rested on his shoulder twice, and we walked back around to the door, went in, and got some rest.

* * *

It was barely light out when we heard our horses making noises. Charlie grumbled and stood up. He was still clothed and in his boots like the rest of us. He grabbed his belt, put it on, and placed his guns in their holsters. With eyes still mostly closed, he grabbed a hat and stuck it on his head before groping about in his things for his horse's nosebag.

He was making his way to the door when I stopped him. "Hey, let me do that. Better if it's me."

Charlie waved me off. "It'll be fine. It's too cold out there and too early for anyone to be upon us yet. That said, we should leave soon. Sun's comin' up, and they can follow our tracks here."

He didn't let me argue with him. Instead, he dipped out through the opening and headed to his horse. In what couldn't have been over fifteen seconds, we learned how wrong Charlie had been.

"Throw up your hands!" a voice bellowed.

I cursed, and the three other men inside with me awoke with a start.

"What's goin' on?" Dave asked.

I opened my mouth to answer as I made my way to look out the door. There were men with rifles, just twenty steps from the door. Charlie drew both of his pistols, but before he even pulled a trigger, they were firing on him. He reacted as anyone would, returning fire from both of his guns, but three shots hit Charlie in the leg. He wavered, yet didn't fall. Then two more slammed into his chest. He dropped his pistols and went reeling toward the men.

"I wish...I wish..." was all I heard Charlie say before he fell face down across one of the men.

Someone out there yelled, "Lee!" and started trying to help the man get out from under Charlie.

They rolled Charlie off the man, but I couldn't tell if he was dead or not. Chances were high he was dead. My anger was so hot it made the chilly morning air feel like a summer breeze, and hate writhed through me like spikes in my flesh.

"That you, Pat?" I shouted out, my hands shaking.

"Yes, Billy," Garrett said. "It's me."

"Why don't you come up here like a man and give us a fair fight?" I asked.

"I don't aim to," Pat replied.

Hands in fists now to hide the shaking, I yelled, "That's what I thought, you old, long-legged son of a bitch!"

I stayed hidden beside the doorway just leaning against the wall trying to compose myself. I'd convinced Charlie to come with me, and now he was likely dead.

"Billy?" Dave said.

I motioned for him to be quiet, and he shut his mouth.

Pat and his men were just as silent, and everyone waited.

"We need to get our horses in here with us," Billy Wilson said. "We'll get on, ride out shootin'. It's our only chance of gettin' outta here alive."

I could tell him no. Offer myself up to Garrett, but Rudabaugh had a price on his head, too, so there was no way they were letting him leave.

"Damn it," I muttered. "Fine, we can try."

Dave nodded and pulled out one of his knives. Reaching out carefully, he cut the ropes we'd used to tie them to the pole outside. We got two in before Garrett and his men noticed, and then they shot and killed the third one when it was halfway into the building and still in the doorway.

"Son of a bitch! We can't ride out over that." I walked over to pat Edward's bay mare, happy she got in okay.

They fired shots on the house, and I couldn't tell if it was Pat and his men or someone on the other side because the horses started stamping about, scared to death.

"They're gonna kill us," Dave shouted.

"Let 'em loose," I said.

We let them go, and the horses made their way out over the dead one and ran off.

"Now what?" Wilson asked.

"Don't know," I replied. "Give me a moment to think about it."

"They seem to be one man down," Dave said. "Must've left when we were dealin' with the horse stampede in here."

"Has Charlie moved?" I asked.

Dave shook his head.

"All right," was all I could say, and sat down in the corner away from the door to think and mourn the loss of my friend.

* * *

The man who'd left Garrett's posse returned, and soon we could smell food cooking on the fire they'd built out front.

"Damn it, Pat, are you cookin' food out there?" I shouted.

"We sure are. You can come out and get some."

I laughed. "We have food here, but we need wood."

"Like I said, you all can come on out and get some. Be a little sociable."

"Go to hell, Pat," I said, but I laughed just the same.

I heard the man from Alabama chuckle and go back to his breakfast.

"We can't stay in here forever," Billy Wilson said.

"They'll get tired and leave," Dave told him.

Rudabaugh wasn't the sharpest knife in the pile, and I rolled my eyes.

"No, they won't," Picket said. "They're gonna wait us out."

"He's right," I replied. "We can't stay here forever. We should just—"

"No!" Dave said, his face in mine. "They'll hang me."

"Then maybe ya shouldn't have killed so many people," Billy Wilson said.

Dave rounded on him, and I knew he was going to knock Wilson on his ass.

I grabbed the arm Dave pulled back to hit with and stopped him. "No fightin' in this small space with us all in here."

Dave pulled away from me and stepped to the far side. Which was fine with me, seeing as he stank all to high hell. The man just didn't understand the need to bathe regularly.

"Wilson is right. We're gonna have to surrender eventually," Picket said when he sat down beside me.

"Yeah, I know," I told him, and shivered. Looking around, I noticed my hat was missing. Then I realized it wasn't, it was just not in here. Instead, it was on Charlie's head.

Realizing this, I swore and banged my head on the wall and looked around. To be honest, I could probably pull on a bunch of soul power and break through the back wall, but there was nowhere to run to, and our horses weren't close enough to grab. I was going to have to convince Dave to give up. But I did not know how I was going to do that.

22
REGULATORS, RIDE!

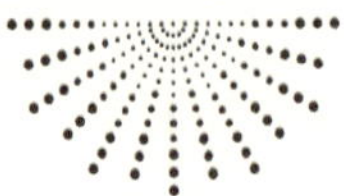

May 1949

Five men on horseback rode into the light to face me, which brought both me and the pack of wolves to a halt.

My eyes landed on my best friend first, and I felt my heart slam into my ribcage. “Richard…how…”

Edward smiled. “He came to seconds after you left us in cages.”

I cringed. “Sorry about that? How’d you get out?”

A white stallion moved out of the shadows from behind the men. Sitting upon him was a man who wore a sword across his back and carried an intricately carved Celtic axe and shield. His thick blond beard and hair shone in the light, and he was the epitome of an old warrior of the *Daoine Sith,* save for the jeans and short-sleeved black t-shirt.

Blue eyes sparkling with mischief, Dr. Ryan winked and said, “Forgot about me, didn’t ya? ’Tis not like you to leave one man free, especially when you’re bound and determined to do something stupid all by your lonesome.”

I couldn’t help but grin at the man. “I totally forgot. That’s on me.”

Dr. Ryan tsk’d at me. “How could you forget about a man like me? Really now!”

Tom snorted, and Dr. Ryan laughed heartily at him and the situation.

“I guess you thought you had to do this on your own?” Edward mused.

"That was the deal I made with her to keep Richard and Kit alive two nights ago."

Edward nodded. "I understand. Hell, we all do. But this is our fight, too, Billy. You don't own the right to be the only one to fight for humanity...and fuck your promise to that lying whore."

My eyes grew at the profanity, as Edward rarely used it, and Brewer's mouth dropped open like a fish.

I glanced back at all the wolves who were moving toward us. "I'd normally argue to keep my word, but considerin' the situation and the fact that you're right, I'll just say thank you for comin' to save my ass... again." Colonel turned us to face the mass of wolves.

Richard rode his horse to my right and placed his large hand on my shoulder. "Ride or die, remember?"

I nodded.

Edward took his place to Richard's right as Tom flanked my left, Duke and Dr. Ryan to his in that order. That's when I paid attention to Richard's attire. He was still bare-chested but thankfully had found the pants I'd thrown out of the car. Over his heart was a burn of a handprint that pulled at my emotions too hard to examine.

"Shall we end this?" I inquired.

"It's time," Richard replied.

"That it is," Tom said.

"Here they come," shouted another voice, and I turned to see the most beautiful sight.

Gaax rode up to us, riding bareback on a pinto horse, wearing an updated version of his tribal warrior gear, a bow and arrow in his hands. "It's time!"

"Let's go kick some ass then," Tom said and tossed me a rifle.

I caught it in one hand and shouted, "Regulators, ride!"

The eight of us started forward, quickly picking up speed and spreading out into the pack, picking off Scáthach's children. Seeing my friends fight was something I knew I'd never forget if I lived through this. Dr. Ryan with his axe and magical sword singing as he whooped and shouted with glee, and Gaax's arrows that never seemed to miss. Duke pulled on his powers and became a blur of motion as he took them down one by one, keeping up with Tom, Edward, Richard, and me easily. Soon there weren't many wolves left, and those who remained ran to where Scáthach stood in all her ugly glory.

"Dear God," Duke said. "No wonder she takes the bodies of beautiful women. It's her only chance."

Scáthach hissed at him.

"Kit?" Brewer said, and his horse pranced under him, feeling his rider's agitation.

"Care about this one, don't you?" Scáthach said, lifting the pretty red-headed witch above her head, the glow of the car headlights making it all look surreal.

"We made a deal!" I shouted.

"But you haven't won yet, and you're no longer alone...the game has changed."

I was about to shoot her with my rifle when there was a booming voice that filled the air as if it came from the heavens itself.

"Stop right there, Scáthach!"

A woman stepped out of the shadows wearing dog soldier attire, with long silver hair braided down her back.

"Zahara," Richard, Tom, and I said at the same time Scáthach did.

"Put her down," Zahara said. "You don't want to hurt her. She's just a witch with very little power. You want me. I'm the one who hurt you...my power will be what helps make you strong."

"What?! No!" I shouted as I attempted to urge Colonel forward, but he refused to move.

"How is this possible?" Scáthach hissed out. "You died years ago!"

Zahara laughed. "As the young kids now say, magic is cool like that." She looked toward me. "I'm sorry I had to lie to some of you..." She turned back to Scáthach, "But you? Well, you deserved it, and you know it. Now put the girl down and face me once and for all."

Scáthach didn't think twice; she tossed Kit. But before she could land, Zahara motioned toward her and stopped the brutal fall, lowering Kit to the ground carefully.

Richard leapt from his horse and ran to her. Kit raised her head and looked at Richard. Touching his face in love and adoration, she kissed him briefly, then showed him one finger as if to say, "Hold that thought, I'll be just a moment."

All long, slender, gangly limbs, Scáthach moved toward Zahara, standing between her and Kit. Towering over her first witch, Scáthach said, "You know you're no match for me."

Zahara raised her hands, closed her eyes, and said, "I am the first witch of this land; it speaks to me as it does to the people I came from and the supernatural of my kind."

Scáthach swung one of her long, skinny limbs at Zahara, but it bounced off. She wailed in anger and took a few steps back. Seeming to come to a different idea, she changed her tone, saying, "Why do we fight? Together, we will take this land! These mortals have nothing on us."

"Hey, I take offense to that. I've not been a mortal for a long time," Tom said in jest.

Seeing the nod Kit gave to Zahara, so many things fell into place, including who Kit's trainer in El Paso was. I couldn't breathe because I saw what was coming. I somehow just knew. Maybe it was my connection to Gaax and Colonel, but I suddenly understood and my heart broke.

"Zahara, no...," I whispered.

"I'm sorry, Cheveyo, but I must," she said, her eyes finding mine for an instant across the distance.

Arms now toward the sky, Zahara shouted, "From the oceans of the east that brought us here, to the water of the west that holds the power of the land, I am a part of them all."

"Because of me!" Scáthach screamed.

"From the cold of the northern land that I have walked, to the ice of the southern pole which I have tasted, I come to you now, ready for what you need of me. I am ready. From the land my people came from and to the land I will return to."

"NO!" I shouted, but my fear only fueled Scáthach, and with both spiderlike black arms, she grabbed hold of Zahara, and the world erupted in light and sound.

I recognized the crackle and looked toward Kit, whose hands were buried in the ground, sending the power of the land under the road and into Zahara. The first witch of this continent placed a hand on either side of Scáthach's face and filled her body with the power of the land.

Shielding my eyes, I felt Colonel's sadness underneath me, and I knew. He huffed out, over and over as he pounded the dirt with his hooves, and the other horses did the same. They sounded like the drums of Zahara's people, and when all suddenly went silent and Kit's magic came to a halt, I saw both Zahara and Scáthach on the ground. Unable to stop Colonel, we moved swiftly to them.

The rest of the men, save for Brewer, were behind us as we rode. Approaching the two on the ground, I leapt down from Colonel, and with a gun trained on Scáthach, I knelt beside Zahara.

"What have you done?" I asked, taking her hands, which I saw were now knotted and stiff with age and the arthritis that had plagued her joints back in 1878.

"Nothing I cannot undo," Scáthach said, her voice scratchy and weak.

"Try it, you bitch!" Kit said as the power of the earth, like wires of energy, burst from the ground and wove into a net that pinned the being from the Otherworld down to the ground.

Kit might've been covered with dirt and disheveled, but the fierceness of will on her face made her beam like a goddess.

"Jesus, you're amazing," Brewer said.

"Don't you forget it," Kit said to him with a wink.

Zahara coughed, and Edward appeared at her head, gently lifting it onto his lap as he sat on the ground. "I'm sorry, Eli," he said. "I failed my promise."

Zahara patted Edward's hand. "You did as you were told. You have become a great man and leader like you were supposed to. As I saw in the smoke. Your promise has not been broken, Nantan Lupan."

"We'll get you out of here," I said. "Dr. Ryan will help you heal. Tom, pick her up and take her somewhere safe."

"No," Zahara said quietly.

When I opened my mouth to protest, she gripped my hand as best she could. "I am the last of the four. With the loss of Eli, Kennedy, and Tarack, I am the last hold she has on this plane, but I needed to see the four corners of the world, and she had to kill me herself in her original form."

"You tricked her into believing she was more powerful that way, but it was a lie," I said simply.

"Yes," she said with a smile. "Did you hear that, Scáthach? I get the last laugh, not you," With that, Zahara did burst into laughter of the most joyous kind.

Scáthach wriggled under the web of earth energy but was too weak from Zahara's injuries to pull free. Turning her head to stare into Zahara's eyes, she said, "I made you! I gave you everything."

"You gave me nothing," Zahara spat. "Nothing but loneliness and the loss of my people. Sure, you gifted me power, but you took anything I cared about away. I feel no pity for you. May you rot in the hell you came from."

Blood leaked out of the corner of Zahara's mouth, and her eyes lost focus until they caught sight of something past Scáthach. Tom spun with his gun ready, but there was nothing there.

"You came for me?" Zahara said quietly.

"Of course, I did," a voice on the wind replied, his accent European. More specifically, it was Dutch.

Then I saw him. His transparent body walked across the desert land toward us. He had short dark hair, green eyes, and a slim build like me.

"I asked to be the one to usher you across," the man said.

Somehow, I knew who he was. Maybe it was one spirit warrior recognizing another, but it came to me, and I understood that standing before us was the soul of Elias Story, the first spirit warrior on this continent. There was a heavenly shimmer to him as he came forward to kneel across from me. He mirrored me by taking Zahara's other hand.

"Am I forgiven?" she asked. "I wasn't ready before. It was a hard road to roam."

Elias kissed her hand. "Yes, it was, but you did it anyway, and I'd not be here for you if you weren't welcome back into the arms of your people with the great Creator." He looked at me. "William H. Bonney. It's an honor to meet you. Keep up the good fight. Protect this plane and trust me to take her now."

Tears filled my eyes, and two escaped when I blinked, but I nodded. Leaning forward, I kissed Zahara's forehead. "Tell my mother I love her." With that, I squeezed Zahara's hand one last time before letting go.

Edward leaned down and placed the gentlest of kisses on her lips. "My heart to yours," he simply said.

Zahara smiled at him then me, closed her eyes, and was gone. We watched as her soul slid from her body to rise and stand hand in hand with Elias, her aged and ailing body now replaced with what she must've looked like when she was a young woman.

The ground rumbled beneath Scáthach, and I looked to Kit.

"Not me," she said, "But it's time we sent her back."

The ruler of the Dark Realm of the Otherworld's eyes opened and filled with fear. "No! You cannot!"

"Wanna make a bet," Dr. Ryan said. "My family will be waiting for you on the other side, have no fear. They'll put you where you belong."

Kit, Tom, and I took equidistant spots around the circle she was trapped in.

"Lay your hands on the netting," Kit said.

Tom and I did as she asked.

"Mother Earth, we give her to you now. Send her back to whence she came," Kit said.

The electrical net around Scáthach shimmered as she screamed and fought. Tom and I added our power to the web, and it glowed red. But something was missing.

"The power needs direction," Dr. Ryan said and touched his magical sword to webbing around Scáthach. "Take her back to the Otherworld, my home and land."

The earth shook, cracked open, and swallowed her whole, taking her home.

"Ashes to ashes…dust to dust…," Tom said.

Turning to me, Elias said, "Scáthach is now where she belongs."

"My people will not greet her with open arms," Dr. Ryan said.

"No, but at least she no longer torments this plane." Looking at me, Eli continued. "The work isn't done. She's spent the last seventy years populating the world with her demons, and not just wolves."

Brewer, Edward, and Duke grunted.

"I apologize, you three are different. Especially you, Richard. None of you are like them. You all are soul warriors who freed yourselves of Scáthach and her evil." Pausing, Elias reached and grabbed Edward's arm. "My friend, my savior, you did all I asked and more. You took care of her, so this day could arrive. I am so very excited to see what else your long life will have in store for you."

Edward nodded. Touching his heart, he then lay that hand on Elias. "Travel well; we will see you again on the other side one day."

"God willing," I said.

Elias smiled at me, and his boyish charm touched my heart. "Your mother is proud of you, William, and she'll see you when your time comes, but that time is not now. You have much work to do. Godspeed, Regulators. I will see you on the other side."

They walked away, and my heart hurt. I held my emotions in check as I stood tall, the tears held back as I knew this was how it had to be.

"Colonel? It is time," Zahara said.

Realization washed over me. "What?! No!" I shouted and turned in time to see my beautiful boy slowly lower himself to the ground. I ran to him and dropped to my knees before him. Quickly, I lay my hands on his neck. "Are you hurt? I can heal you!" I touched him everywhere, shooting energy in him that just came back to me. "No…" I sobbed. "I just got you back."

I heard him in my mind. "One last ride. It was worth the wait."

I wrapped my arms around his neck but looked at Zahara. "No, please…"

"I kept him alive with magic all this while, so he'd be here for this day. He was meant to be here to take her down. But it's time he, too, got to rest. He's earned it, Billy."

I held him tight, my tears soaking his neck. "Isn't there another way?"

Colonel shook his head, and I heard him. "It is my time."

Dr. Ryan knelt beside us and lay his hand on Colonel's neck. "May you find your way to my lands and run fast and free."

With my hand on Colonel's face, I looked into his injured eyes and nodded. "I love you. Ride fast and free."

I felt his love for me reciprocated, and with one last bump of his nose to mine, he, too, left this world. His spirit rose tall and powerful from his earthly confines, and he ran around with perfect eyes, a full tail and mane blowing in the wind. He was magnificent, and though I held his body in my arms, I watched as the spirits of Elias, Zahara, and Colonel walked away into the desert night, but not before Colonel could turn to give me one last look of affection before they all disappeared into the light.

And I wept.

* * *

December 1880

Tom had left for England, and Charlie was dead. Two of my closest companions were gone, and I fought the tears that burned not only behind my eyes, but in my soul.

Close to sunset, Garrett and his men cooked dinner out there, and I heard Rudabaugh's stomach growl from the other side of the room.

"They really aren't leavin'," Dave said.

"Nope. We'll just starve in here and get used to the smell of our own piss and shit," I pointed out.

Truth be told, I was about to go turn us all in when Dave pulled out what had at one time likely been a white handkerchief. He tied it to a stick that was in the room and stuck it out the door.

"Y'all stay in here for a minute," Dave said, taking his weapon belt off and dropping it by the door. "Let me see if I can get them to take us to Santa Fe."

"What difference does it make?" I asked.

"Trust me, we'd not survive in Las Vegas jail. We need to live long enough to escape," he said, and then he walked out the door with his hands up.

I watched as he approached the men, hands still on his head, and spoke with them. I used some of my enhanced hearing to find out what he was saying.

"Billy wants to surrender, but I wanna know where you'll be takin' us."

"Las Vegas jail," Pat said.

"No go," Dave said. "We'd rather die right here than go there where the Mexicans will mob us."

"Mob *you* maybe," I muttered lightly to myself.

"How about Santa Fe?" Pat offered.

"If you'll take us there, we'll surrender."

"Then we have a deal," Pat said.

Dave nodded and waved us to come out. Leaving our weapons inside, we all came out with our hands up and made our way over to the fire to get warm. Being civilized, we shook hands with Pat's men and sat down to have a meal with them before we packed up to leave.

"Why'd ya have to kill him, Pat?" I asked Garrett when everyone else wasn't paying us any attention.

"I didn't. He had your hat on and pulled his guns. Some men fired likely thinkin' it was you."

"Fuck you, that was mean," I said, and walked away.

I said goodbye to my friend, put his hat back on him, retrieved my own, and jumped up to ride behind Cal Polk. As we traveled the six miles, I learned that neither Polk nor Frank Stewart had aimed for the chest. That had been Lee Hall and James East. So, when we arrived at the Wilcox farm, I gifted Polk my Winchester and Stewart the Bay mare that Edward had recently been riding. He and Richard had Colonel now; he didn't need this girl.

The men loaded Charlie's body up on a wagon. Afterward, the blacksmith at the ranch made shackles for us and we all rode with him to Fort Sumner. It was Christmas Eve, and though I'd resigned myself to being arrested, I wanted to say goodbye to my woman.

"Garrett?"

"Yeah?"

"Can I say goodbye to Paulita, please? It's the least you could do, considerin'."

Garrett eyed me and nodded. "Lee and James will take you over there while the rest of us go see Mrs. Bowdre."

"I hope she knees you in the balls," I muttered.

Ignoring me, Garrett said he planned to pay for a nice suit for Charlie to be buried in. The gesture didn't land with me and sure as hell didn't quiet my anger toward him. I was too incensed and guilt-ridden to see anything he did as good, so I just nodded.

They had cuffed Dirty Dave Rudabaugh to me, and that was honestly punishment enough, so instead of getting to see Paulita privately, I'd have Dave attached. Not the romantic goodbye I'd have liked by far, but I'd get to say goodbye.

When we pulled up in front of the Maxwell home, the door opened, and framed in the light from inside was Paulita. Seeing me as I made my way toward the door, she ran out and down the stairs, pulling her shawl tight around her as a light snow fell.

"Billy…what is going on?"

"Let's go inside out of the cold, Paulita. Please?" I said, reaching up with my one free hand to caress her cheek.

She leaned into my palm and nodded. Leading us indoors, she quickly realized they had cuffed me to Dave, and her nose squinched. I couldn't blame her. He wasn't known as Dirty Dave for nothing.

Mrs. Maxwell stepped into the kitchen. "Billy, what is going on? Who are these men?"

"You know Dave, so I'm assumin' you mean these two gentlemen. They work for Sheriff Pat Garrett. They are takin' me in for the murder of Sheriff Brady."

"That's nonsense!" Mrs. Maxwell sputtered. "There's no way to know which of the Regulators that day killed the sheriff."

I nodded. "But someone has to pay for it, or so it seems."

"But Billy, Governor Wallace made you a deal," Paulita said, her voice showing her panic. She pulled me close and stared up into my eyes. "You testified in the Chapman murder trial to be free of this."

It would do no good for her to see my anger about that now. I needed her to stay calm, so she'd not be arrested with us. Holding her hand, I lay my forehead to hers. "And he didn't keep his promise. But have no fear, my love. It will all work out the way it should."

The tears fell down her face, and I kissed her like no one else was in the room. Finally, after I heard a few grunts of discomfort from those around me, I pulled away and leaned into her ear. "I'll get away. I promise. I'll be back for you."

Before she could reply, they tugged me back from her and lead me to the door. We went out onto the porch and down the stairs to the wagon. I turned to see Paulita standing alone in the doorway, tears streaming down her face with her chin held high. She nodded at me and tried to give me a slight smile.

I stepped up into the wagon, and she watched us ride away as the Christmas morning sun rose.

23
HELLO, BOB

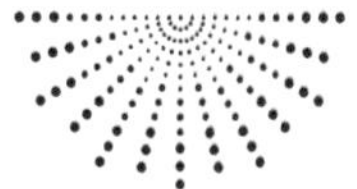

April 1881

I was barely awake when Garrett visited me in my room of a prison. I was in what had once been *The House* where Dolan and Murphy had housed their store, post office, bank, and other odds and ends. I'd been placed in the front room on the east side of the building.

"I'm headin' to White Oaks, Billy, to fetch your transportation documentation for the train to New York and the boat that'll take you from there. You're going to England whether you like it or not," Garrett said. "I told the boys I'm tax collectin' and fetchin' some wood for your hangin'. I'll be back soon. Don't do anythin' stupid while I'm gone, or you'll be in more trouble than you're in now."

"Okay, *Dad*," I said, my tone hitting its mark, making him cringe.

"This is best for you and the cause. I'm sorry you don't like it."

I got out of bed and made my way to the small table they provided me. I sat down at it, my chains and cuffs clanking as I did so. Picking up the playing cards, I shuffled. "See ya when you get back. Give my best to Susan." I knew that's who would give him my papers.

He wasn't surprised I'd figured that out.

"I will," Garrett said, giving me a look that said he didn't trust my calm demeanor.

He was smart that way, because there was no way in hell I was going to be here when he got back. Wasn't sure how I was going to pull that off, and was mulling it over when a raven landed on my windowsill and hopped in.

"Gaax," I said, "Just the bird I was wantin' to see."

* * *

The next afternoon, the spring wind kicked up from time to time, blowing the dry dirt of the town across the street in sheets and ripples as I sat at my window on the northeast corner of the building, watching the people bustle about with their day. Chickens and dogs ran free, and some of the former were being chased by the latter. Kids played or were doing their chores. A typical afternoon in Lincoln.

"Bell!" shouted Bob Olinger.

Deputy Bell, who was sitting in the room just outside mine, shouted back. "Yeah?"

"I'm takin' the other prisoners over to Wortley for lunch. You want anythin'?"

"Yeah, just bring two of whatever looks good."

"Two?" Olinger said.

"The kid needs to eat too," Bell informed the other deputy.

Olinger scoffed at that. "Fine. Whatever. Be back."

It wasn't hard to hear the big man gather the prisoners from what had been Mrs. Lloyd's room across the hall and the pounding of all those cowboy boots going down the stairs to head on over for the midday meal. Once it was quiet, I put things in motion.

"Hey, Bell!" I shouted and sat at the table.

Bell opened the door between our rooms. "Yeah, Billy?"

"You wanna play some cards to kill time?"

"Sure, we can do that."

I fidgeted and crossed my legs, letting the uncomfortable reality of my situation show on my face.

"You gotta use the outhouse?"

"I do, but it can wait. Sit."

Bell came in, sat down opposite me, and I dealt the cards. We played a hand or two and I asked the time.

"Look, I know that usually there's two of you who take me to the outhouse, but I've gotta go, and I don't just have to pee."

Bell seemed to mull it over for a moment, then set his cards down. "All right, let's go. But no funny business. I don't have patience for it today, Billy. I'm starvin'."

"I hear ya," I said, standing up. "But really, my ankles are shackled together, as are my wrists. What am I gonna do? Hop away from you at a speed so great you can't catch me? Come on, Bell. That won't happen."

He laughed a bit and nodded. "Let's go."

There was just enough chain between my ankles to allow me to go up and down the stairs. Bell sent me down in front of him and at the bottom, we entered the back room before taking the door that lead to the outhouses. Unlike when I would just need to piss, Bell stayed outside, giving me some privacy to do my business.

Once I was alone, I made the sound of dropping my pants and sighed.

Through the back window flew Gaax. I put my hands out, and he dropped a key into them.

"You're the best," I told him.

"You're welcome," Bell said, thinking I was thanking him.

Gaax chortled at me and then left the way he'd come in. Not to waste my trip out here, I took a piss and then pulled my pants back up and on. After a failed attempt to unlock one of the ankle cuffs, I tried the second. It was close, I could tell, but I needed time I didn't have to work on it. With a curse, I tried my wrists and got one of them unlocked before Bell rapped on the door.

I slid the key Gaax likely had hastily made for me into my pocket and held the unlocked cuff so it appeared closed. Opening the door, I stepped out and made my way to the two-story building again.

"Better?" Bell asked.

"Very much. Thank you."

"We'll head upstairs, and I'll bring you some water to wash up with."

I nodded and shuffled as best I could to the door. Once inside, we headed up the stairs. It was now or never, and I was not a fan of never.

We both reached the top of the stairs and turned toward the door to my room when I pulled my left hand out of the cuff and spun around. Bell was about two feet behind me, standing at the top of the stairs. That's when I made my move. With no extra power thrown in, because I didn't want to kill him, I swung with my right arm in a downward arc, causing the left cuff to slam into his head with a loud crack.

Bell fell to the floor, his head wound gushing onto the wood, and I worried I'd hit him harder than planned. But things were in motion now, and I couldn't stop.

Leaping forward, I yanked his gun from the holster and aimed it at him. "Garrett ain't gettin' his way this time. I'm ridin' out of here before he can put his plan into motion. Simple as that. I don't want to hurt you; please don't make me."

Bell stood, wavering from the head wound, and did the last thing I thought he would: he ran from me down the stairs. I moved to stand at the top of the stairs and fired a shot that would've stopped him but not been fatal. However, his dizziness benefited him, and I missed, the bullet hitting the wall. I shot again, and this time, his unsteady feet were not on his side. He stumbled again; the bullet hit him in the chest instead of the right shoulder as I'd aimed for.

"Damn it!"

Knowing everyone would have heard the shots, I turned to my left and took the first door on the right. This was the weapons room that they never locked. I pushed it open, grabbed the closest rifle to the door, and checked it. Of all the guns it could've been, it was Bob Olinger's double-barrel shotgun that he'd threatened me with over and over, and it was loaded.

"Fitting," I said and hurried as best as I could back to my room. The window was already open, and I sat on the windowsill just in time to see Olinger run across the street from the Wortley, leaving the prisoners he'd taken there standing in front. He rushed through the white picket fence gate and was now in range.

I heard Gauss shout at Olinger, "The Kid has killed Bell!"

"Hello, Bob," I said loud enough for him to hear me and look up.

"Yes, and he has killed me too," Bob said.

I gave Olinger both barrels of buckshot, thirty-six pellets slamming into his chest, side, and shoulder. He went down, and I turned my gaze to Gauss, standing below in shock. I knew him from when he was the old cook at Tunstall's ranch.

"Don't run; I wouldn't hurt you, old man. Go around front. I'll be out."

Walking away, I returned Bob's shotgun to the armory. I snagged two pistols and a Winchester then went out on the balcony at the front of the two-story building.

"I am alone," I shouted to everyone watching. "I'm now not only the master of the courthouse, but the town, for I will allow nobody to come in here." Turning to look at Gauss specifically, I added, "You, saddle one of Judge Leonard's horses, and I will clear out as soon as I can get the shackles loosened from my legs."

Gauss ran off toward the stables, and I sat down to remove a shackle from my leg. "Look," I said to everyone still watching me, "I didn't want to kill Bell. That wasn't the plan. I just didn't want him to stop me from leavin'." Turning my leg to try a better angle of working on the lock, I continued. "I do not want to kill anyone else, but if anybody interferes with me escapin' today, I'll kill you. Plain and simple."

No one argued with me on this, and I continued to work on the lock as I waited for a horse. It had been almost an hour, and I was about to give up and ride side-saddle when Sam Wortley came upstairs to help me get one of them off. Not having time to do more, I tied the loose ankle shackle to my waist, and down the stairs I went. Exiting the door that Bell had used, I found Gauss bringing a horse.

"I'm sorry I had to kill him, but I couldn't help it," I told the old man, then walked around to the front, coming up to Olinger's body. I stopped and toed him with my boot. "You aren't gonna be roundin' me up again now, are ya?"

Alexander Nunnelly, one of the Telarosa prisoners, hailed me. "Billy! Hey, Billy? That there is my rifle."

"Well hell, Alex. I'm sorry," I said as Gauss tried to settle Billy Burt's horse. "I'll take it back for ya."

I went back in and up to the armory, came back with a different gun, and another prisoner spoke up.

"Uh...Billy? That one is mine."

"For Christ's sake!" I complained, then went back inside, huffed up the stairs, got a different one, and came back down. Once out front, I held it up and said, "Is this one anybody's?"

No one said a thing.

"Great! Now maybe I can get out of here."

Another look at Gauss found him having trouble getting the saddle situated correctly on the fidgety horse.

"Alex, I trust you. Help the old man, won't you?"

"Billy, I can't be doin' that. Don't ya think, if I do, it could influence my trial next month? I'm up for murder."

"Well," I said, pointing a pistol at him, "You can tell 'em that I made you do it."

Alex nodded and helped Gauss hold the horse still long enough to secure the saddle.

"Should be good to go," Gauss said.

I saw the old man had tied two red blankets behind the saddle, and I was appreciative, for I couldn't leave here and head straight to the cabin in the orchard. I couldn't lead anyone who might follow me there. I'd need to go somewhere else.

I'd found time to fetch my two six-shooters from the armory, and it felt good to wear them again. Placing guns I'd taken, along with ammunition, into the saddlebags, I hoisted myself up into the saddle. The skittish horse danced around, and I was about to talk to them when the tie that held the extra shackle let loose, and the chain jangled and clanked, smacking the ground.

Billy Burt's little pony bucked and sent me flying off. Smacking the ground hard, I felt my collar bone break, then heal. Cursing, I shouted, "Catch him, will you, Alex!"

I retied the loose shackle up and when they caught the horse; I remounted. Quickly I lay a hand on his neck to tell him it was okay, and then, with a wave, I rode out of town toward the Capitan Gap. Once I was there, and no one could see me use my power, I used my extra strength to fully remove my wrist shackles. Now all that was left on me was the one on my ankle. I'd get rid of it later. For now, I tossed the wrist shackles onto the ground and headed for Fort Sumner.

* * *

May 1949

After we buried all of the men who had been werewolves, the group of us worked together to carry Colonel's body and place him in the bed of the biggest truck out in the desert. Richard and Kit would drive that vehicle. We gently wrapped Zahara in a blanket and set her in the back seat of a nice car I would drive while the rest of the men rode the horses back to the ranch to get their vehicles. When we got back to Las Cruces, we reported a bunch of cars sitting out in the desert and let the authorities deal with it.

"We'll be back for the trials," I told Duke. "We trust you to keep an eye on it all while we take them home."

"I will," he said and shook my hand. "By the way, I got asked the other day the names of our three FBI Agents in town. They thought one was named Tom, so I went with that and said you didn't have official names. Called you T1, T2, and T3."

I laughed. "You're a good man, Duke. We'll see you soon."

With that, Dr. Ryan headed up to Santa Fe to report to headquarters, while Richard, Kit, Gaax, Tom, and I got into vehicles and drove back to Lincoln. We stopped at the entrance to the orchard.

"Did you not visit here when you came through town?" Richard asked.

I shook my head. "I thought she was dead, along with her magic, and the wall would be closed to me. Hell, it might be now for sure."

Richard got out of the truck and said, "Only one way to find out," and stepped into what had been spelled to look like the side of a mountain and disappeared through it.

"Well, I'll be a monkey's uncle," I said.

Brewer stepped out and smiled at me. "That's a funny mental picture. Come on, let's take them in and put them to rest."

We carefully eased the vehicles in through the opening and down the path I'd taken long ago on Colonel's back when I searched for a way to save Richard's life from Scáthach. Little did I know one day I'd return here to bury the most powerful witch I'd likely ever know, and the most wonderful woman.

Driving as far as we could, the five of us carried the bodies the rest of the way in, lovingly burying them by what had been Brewer's garden. Kit used her magic to engrave a large rock she found and then pulled from the earth, causing flowers to grow in a circle around Zahara and Colonel. Words were said, tears were shed, and we all said our goodbyes.

Driving into Lincoln, the four of us gathered by the Torreon. Climbing up inside, we made our way out onto the round, flat roof, and sat there to relax.

"Brings back memories, eh, lads?" Tom said.

"That it does. I can't get over how quiet the town is now," I replied.

"Tunstall's store is a museum," Richard said. "What would he think of that?"

"It's just smashing," I said with a heavy British accent. "The bee's knees for sure."

We all laughed, and the trapdoor of the roof opened, and Gaax joined us, a six-pack of beer bottles in his hand.

"Pay up!" Tom said.

Brewer and I pulled a ten out each and gave it to Tom.

Gaax smiled. "That's what you get for betting against me."

"You still look too young to buy beer," I said. "I can't believe they let you. I may have to talk to the local law."

Gaax flipped me the finger with a smile and handed me a bottle. "I'm older than you, remember?"

I laughed. "How can I forget? You mention it all the time."

I handed my beer to Tom, pulled two from the pack, and gave two to Richard, who placed one in Kit's outstretched hand.

Gaax cleaned off a spot as best he could and sat down. Opening a beer, he took a drink and said, "I miss her."

"How long had you known she was alive?" Tom asked.

"I found out not long after she staged her second death," he admitted and caught the heated look in my eyes. "Don't be mad! The truth couldn't be told to anyone until she'd done all the things needed in order to cast that spell she did the other night. By the time we returned, we didn't know where you were, and to be honest, we had to wait for Scáthach to be back here too. It had to be here, in New Mexico, where she made you, Billy."

"Why me?" I asked and took a drink.

"Because you were only a child when she tricked you, and that goes against the code," Gaax explained.

"The Dark Realm of the Otherworld has a code?" Tom said. "I find that hard to believe."

"Yes, it does. That's what Zahara found out. She broke the rules with you and thus, it would be you who would have the power to bring the right people together to end her…but it had to be close to the location she took advantage of your youth."

"She didn't even tell *me* she was alive," Edward said.

"No," Gaax said. "She knew you'd come help her, and she'd seen your future in the smoke one night. She knew she needed to let you go."

"To the Regulator Academy," Edward said.

Gaax nodded. "Colonel and I were her only companions over the past few decades until she took Kit on as her student."

"Saw her in the smoke, too, I suppose," I said with another drink to follow.

Gaax smiled at my snark and opened his mouth to answer when Kit picked up the thread.

"Actually, I came to her in a vision, begging to use my family's power to fight against the dark that had chased my family for centuries. Zahara traveled to where I was and offered to train me when I was still a young girl, and because it was my birthright to make this decision when I was twelve—"

"Twelve?" I sputtered, nearly choking on my sip of beer.

Kit smiled. "Yes, twelve."

"Wow," Tom said.

"And of course, you were determined at twelve," I said.

"Yes, she was," Gaax replied with a huge smile.

"That's my girl," Richard said, toasting with his drink.

We all clinked bottles.

"To Kit and her journey!" I said. "The one she made, and the new one to come."

"To Kit and her journey!" they all replied and drank.

"Will you visit me in England at the Academy?" she asked Brewer.

"I've actually been asked to come teach a class," he said.

Tom and I shared a glance and smiled.

"You knew?" Richard said.

"Who do you think put you in for it?" Tom said, pointing at me.

I patted my best friend's shoulder. "I knew you'd want to be near her... and you deserve some happiness."

Brewer beamed at me. "Thanks."

"You're welcome."

"I almost didn't take it," Brewer said.

"Why?" I asked.

"I'd miss our adventures, as you like to call them."

Tom laughed. "Oh, you didn't think we were lettin' you go have all the glory at the Academy all by yourself, did you?"

Richard's mouth fell open and Gaax turned in surprise.

"Really?" Gaax said.

"Yep," Tom said, "Billy and I are also going back to teach."

"Why?" Gaax asked.

"Because I'm a glutton for punishment?" I offered.

"Because they asked us to come teach a class on triple H."

Gaax whistled low. "Yeah, that would be hard to turn down."

"It could be fun, too...ya never know," I said. "Dr. Ryan will join us as well...so it should be a hoot."

Everyone laughed and drank, a comfortable silence settling between us.

Finally, I asked one last question. "How did she know I was back in New Mexico?"

"Who, Zahara?" Gaax said.

"No, the Queen of England...yes, Zahara."

"You stepping back into New Mexico, for longer than a few days for a funeral, was part of it."

Richard smacked my arm. "I knew you came back for Garrett's funeral."

"Shut up," I said to him, but he could tell I didn't mean it. Looking at Gaax, I said, "I'm happy she had you and Colonel. I'd always hoped one day I'd see him again."

"And you did," Gaax said quietly. "It sadly was only for a short time, but you and he got to see the fight to the end. Zahara was his connection to this plane from the magic she used to keep him alive this long. When she went, he had to go too. That was a deal made a long time ago."

"So just comin' into New Mexico for longer than a day or two started it all?" I asked. "If so, why didn't Zahara show up sooner?"

"No. It's when you asked for her help. That opened the door to the spell, and she came," Gaax said. "You had to be ready to receive that help."

"When did I…?" Then I remembered. "On the steps outside Kit's apartment…I see now."

"Yes." He held his beer up high. "To Zahara and Colonel."

We all held up our bottles and clinked his, saying, "To Zahara and Colonel."

"And to you," I said to Gaax, before I drank. "You held her together for this moment too. It's your victory as much as anyone's."

"Does this mean you and Tom have earned your souls back?" Richard asked.

Silence landed upon us, heavy and hard.

"I don't know," I said. "Neither one of us truly sent her back. Zahara ended her."

"But you were a part of that," Richard said.

I shrugged and drank. "Elias said there was still work to do."

"So, we do the work," Tom said.

"Yes, we do the work," I replied.

Richard nodded. "I'm with you on that."

"Good," I said, "Not sure I could do it without you."

Richard smiled. "Or me without you."

"Aww…you two—" Tom started.

"Shut up, Tom," we both said.

Gaax smiled and downed the rest of his beer. Showing me it was empty, he said, "Isn't there somewhere around here we can get more of this?"

"I hear there's a bar called, 'No Scum Allowed Saloon' in White Oaks," Tom said.

I laughed. "Then we're not welcome, that's for sure."

"It's said that a bunch of the local werewolves hang there from time to time," Tom replied, with a taunting look in his eyes.

Everyone turned toward him.

"So, a fight to work off this sorrow? I'm in!" I said.

"Same!" Gaax said.

"Me too," Richard replied.

We all stood and jumped down the two stories to the ground, Brewer catching Kit when she jumped down after us.

"Brewer's newest vehicle is the most fun; I vote he drives," I said, slapping the back of his shoulder.

"Everyone in! We have asses to kick, people to celebrate, and beer to drink!" Richard shouted.

We all howled and squeezed into the convertible.

Driving out of town, I thought about how this wasn't the ending I'd expected, and that was okay. I considered it a new beginning. One where there was evil to hunt and destroy, classes to teach, and best friends to work with; so that was enough for me.

Sure, Scáthach was gone, but I didn't trust that she'd not find a way back. Until then, I'd work to rid the world of her creatures. But maybe, just maybe, I'd start to allow myself a life too. Stranger things had happened.

"Regulators, let's roll!" I shouted and with the top down and music on, we headed for the 'No Scum Allowed Saloon.'

24
OVER MY DEAD BODY

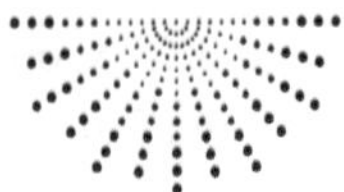

July 1881

I paced the room in the firelight as I waited for Paulita. I lit a candle and wrote her a letter, just in case. However, I never finished it, for Paulita soon rushed in to see if she'd heard correctly. I turned to see her, and she ran into my arms. First, she kissed me, then buried her face in my shoulder and wept.

"I didn't think I'd see you again. How did you get away?" she said into my neck, and I held her tight.

The feel of her, the smell of her hair, and the taste of her overwhelmed my senses. I didn't want to think about what I'd done, and I said as much.

She pulled back to look at me. "Did you kill a man?"

I nodded. "Two sheriff's deputies, one of whom was a good man. I aimed so it wouldn't be a fatal shot, but he zigged when he should've zagged, and..." Emotion clogged my throat. "Bell didn't deserve that end. Olinger, well, he had it comin'."

I held her out at arm's length so I could look at her. "I'm likely goin' to have to go on the run for a while. Garrett's gonna be gunnin' for me hard, and I don't want you wrapped up in this."

Placing her hands on my face, she said, "I'm already in this. Where will you go?"

"I'll keep on the move," I said, stepping away from her to close and lock the door.

"I'll go with you," she offered.

"Paulita," I said as affectionately as I could while I took her hand. Pulling her to sit with me on the bed, "You can't know where I'm goin'. It's not lyin' to the sheriff if you really don't know. I'll be back to visit you. I promise."

She pulled a tiny note from her pocket. It was the one I'd slipped to her on Christmas Eve. "Will you have to go to England?"

"If Garrett catches up with me, it will be my only chance to escape."

"Why England?"

Here's where I would need to lie to her, and I hated that. Choosing what I'd decided sounded the most plausible, I said, "I wrote to John Tunstall's father when I was in jail, and he wrote back. He offered to send me money and bring me to England for my safety."

"What? Why?"

"I don't know, I suppose as a thank you for all I've done to get justice for his son's death," I lied again.

"I'll go with you," she said.

I opened my mouth, but she placed her hand over it.

"I love you. I'll go with you."

"Paulita, your family…your life is here. In New Mexico, you have status, money, a home…in England you'd have nothin'."

"I'll have you."

I took her hands in mine. "Really? You'd go with me?"

She nodded. "Of course, I would."

"Your brother—"

"Billy Bonney…I'm seventeen years old and can do as I please. I have my own money from my papa and can take it out of the bank, pack a bag, and go."

Could I bring her with me? Would this country girl find love for the city? Would she believe the lies of my studying to be a cop for eight years without me telling her the truth about what I was?

"Let me write to the Tunstalls and take the offer, ask if there's room for two. When he replies, sends the money and papers for me, we'll go."

She kissed me.

"You cannot tell your brother," I said.

"I won't. I'll leave him a note when we head out of town."

I pulled her into my arms and fell backward on the bed, her laying on me, head on my chest. "It could take a while for the mail to move along, but we'll go as soon as I get his reply."

"Until then?" she asked.

"I'll have to stay on the move. I'll be back to see you as often as I can."

She looked up at me, all sultry dark eyes and smiles. "And for right now?"

"For now," I said with a grin, and playfully flipped her over so she was under me, "I'm goin' to show you how much I've missed you."

She giggled, but then her face went serious. She pulled my face down to hers and kissed me long and soft. "Not if I show you first."

* * *

Each time I found my way to Fort Sumner, Paulita asked, and I told her the truth, I'd not heard from the Tunstalls. You could say that from a certain point of view, I wasn't lying to her. But I felt bad for deceiving her.

In fact, I'd considered turning myself in so Garrett could just take her and me away. I was on the precipice of doing exactly that when I came into town early in the second week of July. I was cozily tucked up with Paulita in bed, and it was lightly rolling about in my mind when she spoke first.

"My brother knows."

"Hmm?" I said a bit lazily, still in postcoital bliss. "What does he know?" Then, before she could say anything, it got through to me, and I sat up to stare at her. "How does he know?"

"He found my bag, the note you wrote me...we had a fight."

I lay back down and rubbed my face. It didn't matter how long Pete and I'd been friends; she was his family, his blood. "What did he say?"

"That I wasn't goin' anywhere. That we had a responsibility as Maxwells on this land. He dumped the contents of my bag and took it with him." She paused, and I looked at her face. She was smiling. "But I just went out and bought a new bag and hid it here in your room. It's under that loose floorboard you showed me. He won't find it there."

"Maybe he's right," I said.

"William Henry," she scolded me. "I'm not some delicate flower. I'm a woman, and I make my own choices." Her voice softened. "And I choose you."

"Well, at least now I know what he wants to talk to me about. Tonight, he came by and said, 'We need to talk tomorrow,' and I told him sure. I figured he was going to ask me when I was goin' to make an honest woman out of you."

She laughed. "So, when are you?"

My heart leapt into my throat, and then I thought that it only made sense. If she was going with me, I'd have to marry her. "When we get to England."

"We could get married here first, tell them we're off on our honeymoon, and then just not come back from England."

This was a brilliant cover, so I agreed. "I'll talk to Pete tomorrow and tell him the news. I'll tell him we're not runnin' away to England permanently, it's just a honeymoon."

"He'll be better with that. I'm sure of it." She snuggled me again.

My stomach growled.

She laughed heartily. "How are you hungry all the time?"

"Just a curse, I guess," I said with a lopsided grin, laughing at the double entendre as I tossed back the covers and stood up. I grabbed my pants and pulled them on.

"Where are you goin'?" Paulita asked.

"I'm starvin', as you heard yourself," I said, pulling on my shirt. "I'm goin' to go get us a steak from your brother's meat house."

"You goin' in your bare feet? You know that's not a good idea."

"My feet are killin' me from today," I said, then had an idea. Grabbing my socks, I put them on. "There, that'll protect my feet better."

"Wear the boots," she said, sitting up in bed a bit with the sheet covering her breasts.

"Over my dead body," I said. "That's the only way those are goin' on tonight." Selecting a butcher knife from my small box of cutlery, I stepped to her and kissed her long and hard on the mouth. "I love you."

"I love you," she said.

"Be right back."

Without a care, riding high on the great sex, love deep enough to equal marriage, and the idea of food in my belly, I made my way across the corner of the parade ground. Feeling a breeze where I shouldn't, I noticed my pants weren't done up all the way, and I finished those buttons as I got close to Pete's home.

Approaching the stairs, I was almost on top of a man, who was partially blocked by a post as he sat near the door, before I saw him.

Pulling my six-shooter, I pointed it at him and bounded up onto the porch.

"Quien es?" I shouted into Pete's room.

With no answer, I kept my gun on the man and backed up to the doorway of Pete's room.

I asked, 'who is it,' again, *"Quien es?"*

The man on the porch stood up and came toward me. "Don't be alarmed. No one is going to hurt you."

I retreated into the Maxwell home faster, using the thick adobe wall to block my body from the man in case he fired on me. I had a lot of souls in the well, and I wasn't concerned for my safety so much as causing a commotion in a friend's home or explaining to him why my wounds heal.

I continued backing into Pete's room and saw two figures on Pete's bed.

"¿Pedro, quien sonos estos hombres afuera?" I said, asking Pete who the men outside were.

"That's him," Pete said simply.

The man sitting on the bed stood, and by the length of his legs alone I knew who it was. But before I could say a word, Pat Garrett shot me in the heart. I fired at him as well, but he'd dropped to the floor, firing off another shot that caromed off the adobe wall and hit a wooden bedstead with a crack loud enough to sound like a third shot.

I fell to the ground, my gun in one hand and the butcher knife in the other. Groaning in pain and irritation, I gasped twice, and then it all went black.

* * *

When I awoke, Garrett was standing over me in the dark, a single candle in the window of Pete's room lighting it, for the door was shut.

"There you are," Garrett said.

"You mother fuckin' son of a bitch," I began.

"Don't move," he whispered. "They all have seen I shot you in the heart. You've been pronounced dead."

"Are you kidding me?" I muttered, making sure my lips didn't move.

"No. I didn't expect to have that good of aim in the dark, but this is for the best. You are needed in England. You've not solved the problem with Scáthach and need more trainin'. Tom is already there."

I could hear the large group of people outside.

"You planned this. To force my hand."

"Yes, I did. Because you need proper trainin'. Roy will go with you."

"I'm not goin' without Brewer or Edward. They both own their souls and would be a great asset."

"No way."

"Then I'm about to rise from the dead and make the Regulators really sorry they fucked with me, Garrett. I'm goin' to let the world know of the supernatural when I walk out of here. You either give me what I want, or you're gonna have a bigger mess than you already have on your hands."

"I don't have a mess on my hands now," Pat said, his Alabama accent thick.

I narrowed my eyes at him. "Yes, you do. You've made an enemy of me."

Garrett swallowed loud enough that I heard him. "I'll send a telegram to the office and explain. If you show them you're alive, the deal is off."

I thought of Paulita, and sorrow landed on my heart. "Tell my girl I'm alive."

"I can't. You know that."

I narrowed my eyes at him. "You'll pay for this one day, I promise you that."

The door opened, and I closed my eyes, letting my face go slack.

"A lot of blood on the floor here, be careful," Garrett said. "Take him to the room behind the church."

Two men lifted me up, placed me on a stretcher of sorts, and carried me out of the Maxwell home. I wanted to open my eyes and glare at Pete with all the hate in my heart, but I knew if I was going to get Brewer a chance to stop running, I had to swallow my pride. But it hurt going down.

They eventually placed me on a wooden table. When I was left alone in the room with no windows, Garrett entered with a lantern and shut the door.

"Sit up," he whispered.

"What the hell do you want to do to me now, Pat?"

"I need to pour this blood on the table, so it looks like you continued to bleed out."

"Whose is it?"

"No one you know."

"Did you kill him?"

"No! Now sit up!"

I did as I was told, and he poured the half-full jar of blood onto the table.

"Now lay back into it."

"I hate you," I groaned.

"Stay put, act dead, and if you disappear, I'll have Brewer and your Indian friend killed. You hear me?"

"Fuck you, Garrett."

Pat picked up the lantern to leave and said, "You know, if you'd just come with me when I asked the first or second time, this wouldn't have had to happen. You forced my hand."

"And now I'll force it more. Get clearance for Dick and Edward by tomorrow or this body will disappear."

Pat grunted and left.

I lay in the dark, and my stomach rumbled.

I'd never gotten that steak, and that was one more thing I was going to hold against Pat Garrett. I'd not pay him back now, but I would someday, right when he wasn't expecting it. Wouldn't kill him. No, that would be the easy way. I'd find a better way…eventually.

* * *

The next morning, Garrett came into the room with a bucket, a small bag, and a canteen.

"I got you a bucket to piss in and a hunk of bread to eat."

"Coffee?" I asked.

He handed me the canteen. "Water."

"You just continue to be a thorn in my side," I said, but I took the food and water and was happy to have them. Biting off a chunk of bread, I chewed, drank some water, and swallowed it into my empty gullet. I could feel it travel all the way down. "Any word from England?"

"Not yet. But I sent the message last night. I should have an answer before you're buried."

I almost choked. "Buried? Oh, hell no, Garrett. I'm not goin' in the ground."

"Luckily, *you* don't have to. There was a man killed in a skirmish last night that was passin' through town. We made a show of draggin' him into a wagon and out of Fort Sumner. But he's back, and he'll be in the coffin. We just need to make the switch in the wagon that's takin' you to the cemetery. In fact, he's already in there, all wrapped up and ready to go. Now finish that, pee, and let's get movin'."

I finished the bread, glaring at him. Finally, I said, "Is she all right?"

"What do you think, Billy?" Pat said, rubbing his face.

I hung my head. "She's not. Did she kill Pete? She should."

Garrett rolled his eyes and sighed. But I got down from the table and peed into the bucket. When I finished and buttoned up my pants, I got back on the table.

"I'll be back with the casket and the men to carry you."

"Have that document ready to show me in the wagon or it's all goin' to go down a lot different than you think."

"Fine," Garrett grunted out.

"Oh, and get me my boots and some other clothes. I'm not goin' on a trip to England in this bloody outfit."

"It's already in the wagon. Now lie down."

"Fine."

Laying down, I worried about Paulita. I knew I couldn't tell her I was alive, nor was there a way to take away her pain, and that broke my heart. I'd not get to say goodbye to her. But maybe, just maybe, someday I could come back and let her know somehow. Yes, that's what I'd do. Not sure how, but it's what I focused on as I waited.

* * *

True to his word, once the covered wagon started the journey, Garrett opened the casket and let me out. We lifted the man whose name we didn't know and placed him inside before closing it up again.

Garrett handed me nails. "We can't have the top coming off as we carry this into the cemetery."

I helped nail the coffin shut and once we finished, he handed me a bag with clean clothes. I changed quickly, placed the other clothes in the bag, and gave it back to him. After pulling my second boot on, I put my hand out to him.

Garrett frowned.

"If you don't have it, I'm going to make a surprise appearance at my own funeral, Pat."

"Why are you such a bastard?" he asked me as he reached into his inside jacket pocket.

"You're just lucky, I guess."

He handed me an envelope.

I opened it, and it was a telegram in code. Thankfully, I'd had all that time waiting on Wallace to learn the Regulator code and read it. It gave full passage for Roy, Richard, Edward, and me to travel to England, and for all but Roy to attend the academy. It clearly stated that they were willing to branch out and have two soul-owning werewolves, so they'd have two spirit-warriors. They considered the trade uncomfortable but fair.

I smiled. "I can tell they're not happy, but I couldn't care less; they said yes, and that's what matters."

"Seems Tom had given them a similar ultimatum upon hearing they were bringing you in. He said he'd not stay and you two would leave if they didn't."

"I knew I kept that man around for a reason," I said in jest.

The wagon turned a tight corner, and Garrett handed me a long jacket.

"Put that on, and this wide-brimmed hat. Use the bandana around your neck to cover your nose and mouth from the dust blowin' out there, and once the service starts, you quietly drive away."

"Cause a long black coat in the summer isn't conspicuous or anythin'."

Garrett rolled his eyes.

"Where am I goin'?" I asked, putting on the items he'd handed me.

"Roy already went to fetch your friends. They will meet you in Santa Fe at the Exchange Hotel in three days' time. In the bag up front, there's ammunition, your weapons, a full canteen, and some food. Now go!"

Someone lifted the back flap of the covered wagon, and Garrett stepped out first. Men swarmed around, and I helped ease the coffin out to them, looking no one in the eye. They silently carried a man I'd never met to a spot beside Charlie, and I watched as they all left me standing at the wagon.

The crying and sorrow overwhelmed me as someone sang. I glimpsed Paulita and almost broke my promise, rushing over to tell her I was alive. But I couldn't. It would have to wait. Because I couldn't ease her pain or my own, I hurt deep in my soul.

I walked around the covered wagon to get up front, and with one last look at the woman I loved and the friends who mourned me, I snapped the reins lightly, and I rode away from Fort Sumner as my heart wept.

* * *

It was a few nights on the road, but soon I arrived at the hotel. There had been identification papers inside the bag Garrett had left for me, and his humor was not lost on me with the name he'd chosen. I thought of changing it later, but it was clever.

I presented the papers to the man behind the counter. "You have a room reserved for me."

"Yes, Mr. William Kidwell, I do." He handed me back my paper, and as I folded it up and put it away, he gave me an envelope. "This was left for you. You're in room nineteen. That is just up the stairs there and around the bend."

"Thank you, sir," I said and headed to find my room.

A proper bed sounded wonderful about now. Followed by a hot meal and a game of cards. Stepping into number nineteen though, I threw all plans out the window as a big man grabbed me and pulled me into a hug.

"Brewer…ya gotta let me go, I can't breathe."

"Oh, sorry," he said with a deep laugh. "It's just good to see you."

I glanced around the room. "Where's Roy and Edward? They have a separate room?"

Richard shook his head. "Roy saw you pull up, so he headed off to send the telegram."

It was silent, and I tossed my bag on one of the two beds in the room. "Where's Edward?"

Richard shoved his hands into his pockets. "He didn't come."

"What?" I blurted out. "I went through a lot to get him passage!"

"I know, and he sent this," Richard handed me an envelope.

I stared at it. "What does it say, the short version."

"You should read it," he said, sitting on the other bed.

"I will but tell me."

"He received word from Gaax that Zahara needed help. So, he took Colonel and left. He'll join us when he can, but we're not to wait for him."

I now sat on the bed next to my bag. "I suppose he felt that was more important. Gaax with him?"

"Yes. They know where we're headed and will get word to us."

"I hope so."

The door opened, and Roy walked in, his blonde hair a bit disheveled from the wind, but his face full of smiles.

"There he is! Good to see you, Billy." He crossed the room, and I stood to give him a hug.

"It's William Kidwell now," I said, waving my papers at him.

Roy laughed. "Yeah, Garrett came up with that. I thought it was pretty good."

"I don't hate it," I replied. "So, what's next?"

"We'll be on the train tomorrow, so tonight we get some good food in us and some sleep. We'll take the train to New York City and from there, a boat to England."

I shuddered. "I am not a fan of boats."

"Well, lucky for you it doesn't take as long as it did back when your mum came over from Ireland." He slapped me on the back. "What do you say to a good hot meal?"

"I say thank the heavens," I said and headed for the door.

Richard stopped me. "You can't actually go with us."

"What? I have new papers and everythin'."

"Someone could recognize you, and then it would all be for nothin'," Roy said. "You lay down and rest, and we'll bring you back food."

I glared at them both. "What about Brewer? He's supposed to be dead, too, why does he get to go?"

"Because he's been dead for three years, wasn't a famous outlaw with his name in the papers daily, and because I'll need his help gettin' all the food back here."

"Fine." I went to my bed and plopped down on it, wearing a frown as I huffed.

"Are you pouting?" Roy asked, his voice light and playful.

"No," I said, my voice coming out in more of a whine than I'd wished.

"Yes, he is," Richard said with a grin. "Don't worry, we'll be back soon."

"Fine," I said again, and they left, leaving me to lie down and wrestle my mental demons.

I didn't want to leave New Mexico. I loved it here. No sunrises or sunsets would ever compare to this place. I'd seen pictures of London, and it looked awful. So many buildings and streets. No open land with wide-open skies. And if John Tunstall was to be believed, and he'd lived in London, the sky wasn't as blue and the air wasn't as fresh there either.

"I'm going to hate it," I said to no one.

But then I closed my eyes, tried to relax, and something occurred to me that hadn't earlier. I didn't hate myself for the decisions I'd made. Sure, my heart hurt for losing Paulita and the pain that she was enduring with the belief that I was gone. But for once in my life, I'd made choices to help others instead of myself.

Though she was brokenhearted now, Paulita would heal and move on. She'd find someone else and be happy like Tom's wife did. Most importantly, with me gone, she'd be safer and likely get to live a long life. Not only that, but from the beginning, my decisions had forced Brewer into a life where he wasn't happy, no matter what he said to me. Now he was; you could see it in his face. His eyes were lit with the excitement of what was next in his life for the first time in years.

That was what mattered. I'd focus on that and make it enough.

I didn't know what life in England would hold, but I knew I'd made the right choice, no matter how much it hurt. Maybe I'd do well there, who knew? Stranger things had happened.

EPILOGUE

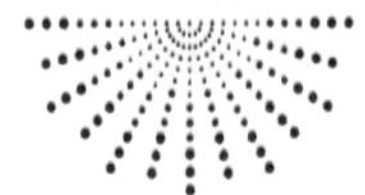

April 17, 1953

Word came down from the home office that we needed to head back to New Mexico. Richard and I came into Santa Fe for orders and then got in the car and drove south. As we did, I said, "Four years ago tomorrow we were doin' this exact same thing."

"That's right, tomorrow is the eighteenth," Brewer said.

"Yep. They buried Cricket four years ago tomorrow, and here we are about to offer help to one of those sons of bitches who let her killer get away with it."

"This could get us the answers we've wanted since that day."

I shrugged. "But at what cost?"

"I know," was all he said, and we passed the sign that welcomed us to Las Cruces as the voice of Jo Stafford sang Jambalaya on the car radio.

First thing we did was try his home, but he'd just left. After being told where he was going, we headed there ourselves. The sun had set but we spotted a Studebaker pulling away from First Baptist Church. Headlights lit the driver up enough that we identified Sandman and followed him when he turned north onto Mirada Street.

Waiting until he was a bit away, we put the light on the hood and the siren sang out as he reached Pioneer Women's Park. He quickly pulled over, and us behind him. Richard turned off the siren and placed the light back in the car, so we'd not attract attention, and with the car off, we both got out. Brewer stayed back by the front of our vehicle while I approached the driver's side of the Studebaker.

"Can I help you, officer?" Roy Sandman said through his open window.

"Hey there, Roy," I said, noticing he'd aged more than just four years. Prison time can do that to you, or so I'm told. Showing my FBI badge, I added. "Where ya headed, Mr. Sandman?"

"Just dropped my step-daughter off at church. I wasn't speedin'."

"No, you weren't. This is somethin' else. Could you please step out of the car?"

It was obvious to see he considered saying no, but he turned off the car and stepped out. Leaning against the door, he said, "This is the second time you Feds have pulled me aside today. What is goin' on?"

This caught Brewer's attention and he stepped over. "Who else pulled you over?"

"Didn't catch all their names. But the two who interviewed me earlier today were James Smith and Herbert Greathouse.

Brewer and I shared a glance.

"What did they want to talk to you about?" I asked.

"Smith and Greathouse interviewed me regarding missing money from an interstate shipment my boss thinks I stole. My guess is the others want to continue that conversation. I'm to meet them at the warehouse tonight. Is that why you two are here?"

"No, we want to talk about Cricket Coogler," Richard said.

Sandman's eyes grew just slightly but he covered it well. His face blank, he said, "I know nothin' about that."

"I think you're lyin' and that because you've kept lookin' into it, your life is in danger," I said.

Sandman's brow furrowed and I'd have bet all the money in my wallet he was considering the best choice in the matter. I decided to help him make that decision.

"You know things," I said. "And we're willing to help you and your family stay safe if you tell us what you've found."

"About what?" he baited us.

I stared him down. "You know who murdered Cricket Coogler, and we're not the only ones who think so. Sure, you claim you have no idea, but we all know that's bullshit. You know somethin' you're not sayin'."

He opened his mouth to speak, but I stopped him.

"Don't lie to my face, it'll make me mad, and I have no patience when I'm mad."

"You have little patience anyway," Brewer mumbled.

Mr. Sandman fidgeted. "But I don't know anyth—"

I stepped into his face, letting the power of the souls inside me show in my eyes, causing him to not finish his sentence. "Don't. Lie. To. Me." The words were almost a growl, and I could feel my eyes glow with the heat of soul energy rising. "We could torture you, but you'd never tell me because it would mean your family's life if you ratted him out."

"What my partner is tryin' to say, and yet not sayin' at all," Richard said, sliding an arm between Sandman and me, "Is that we understand your silence, but there are those who don't think you'll keep it. We want to help you disappear and start a new life."

"Witness protection cannot keep me safe," he whispered. "The local law is dirty."

"We know, and we'd make sure only our division knew where you went and then we'd lose the paperwork. I just need to know what you do. Can you give us anythin'?"

Roy Sandman nodded; lips pursed in consideration.

"I knew her," I said. "In fact, I'd asked her out on the day she disappeared. Wanted to take her on a date when I'd be in town again." I reached out and touched his hand, sliding a bit of soul energy into him. If he wanted to tell me, this would help him do so. "She was a lovely girl who didn't deserve what happened to her. Help me put this to rest."

He looked this way and that and said, "Let's walk and talk."

I nodded and we followed him into the park. It was a pretty spot. Big square of land with mature trees, walking paths, and an octagonal gazebo in the center.

As he walked, he started to speak. "After I got out of prison, Bob Slaughterbeck and I went out to where she was found. Got down on our hands and knees, crawlin' around for any clues we could find."

"Did you find anythin'?" I asked.

He nodded as his eyes darted about. He motioned toward the gazebo, and we continued onward. "We found Tareyton cigarette butts, two tire gauges, and dog hair."

"Okay…" I said, not sure why all that mattered.

Sandman zipped up his coat against the cold before we stepped into the gazebo. Here we were away from the lights of the park and far from the road. "There's a Las Cruces businessman I know of who smokes that type of cigarettes, carries tire gauges in his front pocket all the time, and keeps a shovel in the trunk of his car. He has two dogs and to top it off, we learned he had his car washed and bought new seat covers the day after Cricket disappeared."

"What? Why are we just hearin' about this man?" I asked.

"I've only been puttin' things together since I got out, as I said. Plus, I want to have all my facts organized, along with my research at the trucking company, before I make anything public. I've told no one this information."

"The trucking company? Why them?" Brewer asked.

"The Cleveland Mob are using it to move gamblin' equipment. I just need to prove it. I'm so close! But now there's this trumped-up charge on me…as I said, that's what the other FBI agents want to talk to me about…and I'm worried they'll make that stick. Can you help me get out of that? If so, I'll give you all my notes on Cricket."

"Yeah, we can help with that," I said, even though I could feel Brewer giving me that stare that said we don't necessarily have that power.

"Who is this business owner with the dogs and new front seat in his car?" I pried.

"W.S. Howard," Sandman said.

"*Sid* Howard?" Brewer said. "The guy who found one of the shoes?"

"One and the same," Sandman said. "He drives a blue Packard…that's the color that was on the bottom of Cricket's shoe, if you remember correctly."

My hands raked through my hair, and I pulled on it before letting go and letting my arms drop to my sides again. I walked to the half wall of the gazebo and sat to calm myself. "I don't understand…what about Apodaca and his ilk in Santa Fe? They wanted her to keep her mouth shut on what she'd learned on the gambling and such. Are you sayin' they didn't want her dead?"

Sandman stepped over and sat beside me. "No, I'm not sayin' that," he whispered, stuffing his hands into the pockets of his coat. "They wanted her gone and from my findings, it looks like Apodaca, Sedillo, and Montoya bungled her murder and someone else did it before they could."

"Wait, do *they* know that?" Brewer asked.

Sandman shook his head. "I believe they each think the other did it and are all coverin' for one another. No one has likely asked each other outright and are assuming. For example, Happy told me once that a week after Cricket disappeared, Montoya was in town. He cornered Apodaca and asked him if everythin' had been taken care of. Happy told him of course it had been.

"Thing is, Apodaca thought Montoya was makin' sure he'd gotten rid of Coogler's purse. I think Montoya wanted to know if the sheriff had gotten rid of Coogler."

Brewer stepped over to them. "Wait, Apodaca has her purse?"

Sandman shook his head. "He *had* the handbag, but he tossed it into the irrigation canal behind his house."

"Son of a bitch!" I said, standing up and walking away. When I came back, I stood beside Brewer. "What else?"

"I was there when Apodaca arrived at the crime scene. He made sure to throw a lot of sand around with his car tires. He also is the reason there were no pictures that afternoon or an autopsy later. He told the grand jury that the county couldn't afford to send her to El Paso, but I think he was coverin' for his pals, thinkin' they'd killed her."

I rubbed my face. This was all conjecture and couldn't be proved, but it was more than we'd had in years. I blew out a breath, which I could see in the air, then sat beside him. Looking him in the face, I said, "So, you're sayin' that Montoya and Sedillo thought Apodaca had taken care of her and he thought they did, and so the circus began."

"Yes," Sandman said. "Happy is also why the quicklime was put in her casket. In fact, rumor is that Montoya and Sedillo are who sent the state police from Santa Fe to Las Cruces with the quicklime. That way, if she was ever exhumed, the lime would have destroyed any possible evidence."

It wasn't like this was news to me, I'd figured this out before, but what I didn't get was how Mr. Howard fit into the story. I was going to ask, but Brewer beat me to it.

"I don't understand why or how Sid is in the picture."

"Well…umm…" Sandman said, his reply wavering.

I put my arm high on his shoulder, my finger touching his exposed neck, and again I gave some energy. "You can tell us. We can keep you safe."

He nodded in understanding and continued. "I have no proof for the rest, other than what I've already told you."

"We understand that. We just want to know what you are considering," Brewer said.

"All right then. I believe that Sedillo and Montoya thought Apodaca had picked her up after the bars closed. They'd kept tabs on her after she wandered drunkenly in the downtown area. Happy believed Sedillo was the one driving that second car the police saw that evening and that he'd been the one to pick her up.

"However, I think she saw the blue Packard, knew the owner, and ran to him for safety when she saw the other car following her. She likely asked Howard to drive her home, but he had *other ideas*."

I didn't need him to say what those ideas were, his tone of voice said it all, but he continued.

"He likely drove down Highway 80, stopped the car, and made a sexual advance. When she turned him down, he—"

I held my hand up to stop him, stood, and walked a few steps away. I could see it. A man who believed she was a whore for the Santa Fe Ring per conversation in town thought he could get a piece, too, but when she said no, he lost his temper.

"I think he thought she was dead and took her out there to bury her," Sandman continued. "He keeps a shovel in his car, so my guess is she started to come to as he dug a hole, and he beat her with it until she died. Then he buried her, smoked a few cigarettes with his dogs watchin', and left."

An idea came to me, so I turned to face him. "You found all the evidence after you got out of prison, right?"

"Yes," Sandman said.

"Then is it not also possible that Sid went out there with his dogs to see where she died, smoked a few, lost his tire gauges then, and went home...all *after* she was found, or hell, after you went to jail."

There was silence and then Sandman shook his head. "We crawled around awhile to find that stuff. It was under brush and all that. It wouldn't have been seen when we first found her."

"That's possible," I said. "It's more believable that he felt connected due to findin' her shoe and went out there later, Roy. You have nothin'."

Sandman opened his mouth to argue, and I spoke before he could. "I'm not sayin' your theory isn't a valid one to look at, but since the evidence wasn't found on the day her body was, it doesn't hold the weight you're givin' it. If it did, I'd scoop him up right now and charge him."

With head in hands, Roy just sat there looking utterly dejected. When he finally raised his head, he said, "I'm tellin' ya, my gut says it's him."

"And mine says it's the Santa Fe Ring," I said. "One of us could be right, or we could both be wrong. I don't think we'll ever know. But we'll look into Sid Howard, you have my word."

"And while we do that, we'll get you and your family somewhere far away. Between Cricket's case and what you've said about the Cleveland Mob and the trucking company, you're not safe here."

"Tell me, do you have all of this information written down somewhere that we can take to our boss?" Brewer asked.

Sandman nodded. "I do, I can give that to you if you get my family and me out of here."

"We can do that. No question," I said and again, Brewer looked at me. He knew I needed to get the word from on high before I could promise anything. But damn it all to hell, if I had to make them disappear on my own without the SIS, I would. This man didn't try to cover up her murder. He wanted answers as bad as us and for that, he deserved my help.

"I have them in a safe place. I can meet you with them."

"Okay, where and when?" I asked.

"Give me an hour. I'll go get them and meet you at the warehouse before the other FBI are meeting me."

Brewer nodded. "That works."

We walked him back to his car and watched him drive away. We were going to get his evidence and then help him disappear. It was the least we could do.

"I feel a bit bad gettin' him to tell us all that," I said as we got into the car.

"Neither of our gifts can force people to tell things they don't secretly want to say. He's probably wanted to share his findings for a while but with his family in danger, he's likely not said a single word to anyone. What do you think about the Sid Howard angle?"

I put the car in drive and headed off back the way we'd come. "That it adds one more spoke to the wheel that cannot be proved. But what he has on the Cleveland Mob will be his ticket for MI-5 to put him in witness protection. We'll see what he has, and if it's enough, we'll take him and his family tonight."

"Billy, we can't…we'll need to get orders."

"Fuck that. He needs to disappear as soon as possible if he has what I think he has."

Brewer chuckled. "Look, I know you hate following the rules, but we might have no choice."

I sighed. "I hate it when you're right."

"Must suck bein' hateful all the time," Brewer said in jest.

I laughed. "Yeah, it's a rough life bein' with you."

We fell into a comfortable silence as I drove us to get dinner while we waited for Sandman.

"He's our best shot at documents and testimony," I finally said. "MI-5 will back us. You'll see. I mean, it's not like they would go to Happy Apodaca."

"No way," Brewer said. "He'd never tell anyway, and even so, they'd never cut *him* a deal. He's too big of a scumbag."

"Yeah, and he won't talk. Even under torture, he'd cover the ass of the killer, or who he thinks is the killer, while they're alive. Turns my stomach."

"I know. But we've dealt with worse…hell, we've stood over worse."

The memory of dead girls in alleys flashed in my mind, and I shook it away. "Maybe so. But this one is personal. I want vengeance for her."

"I know, but you may never get it," he said as we came to stop at a red light. "You need to find a way to live with that."

My eyes found his. "I'm not sure I can, Dick. I'm really not sure I can."

* * *

An hour later we pulled up to Border Truckline, where Mr. Sandman was a manager. His car was out front, and the door was open so we headed in.

"Mr. Sandman, you in here?" I called out.

It was deathly silent, and I began to worry.

"Maybe he's in the back and can't hear us," Richard offered, but he didn't sound so sure.

I pulled a gun. "Possible, but I got a bad feelin'."

"Me too," he said, pulling his pistol out. "You go that way and I'll go this way," Richard said. "If he's here, we'll find him."

I nodded, and we split up.

Checking under trucks and other equipment, I made my way along one side of the warehouse. I was almost to the end when I heard Brewer curse. It was low and yet my ears picked it up.

"Billy! I found him!" Brewer shouted out, his deep voice bouncing off all the metal in the place.

I knew that tone. It wasn't good.

Running toward my partner, I found him standing over the dead body of Roy Sandman. The ex-sheriff had been shot in the back of the head and lay in a pool of his own blood, face down on the ground.

"We weren't fast enough," Richard said. "We should've tailed him to church and then here."

I wanted to say something, but words caught in my throat. Instead, I screamed out in rage. "I promised him we'd keep him safe and I failed!" Fury filled me for him and for Cricket. I punched a truck trailer and yelled out again. "Damn it, Richard!"

"We had no way of knowin' they were gonna kill him *today*," he said. "We came here because others have died who were involved. There wasn't any real data on them comin' for Sandman other than what he told us tonight about the FBI. Before that, it was just a hunch."

"Fucking hell," I said, and walked off. But before Brewer could ask, I shouted, "I'm callin' it in. Stay with him."

The cops came out to the scene, one of them being Sheriff James Flannagan. He took the report and handed us off to a young rookie before he headed out to go inform the next of kin.

"Why were you meetin' him here?" the rookie officer I'd not met before said. He was a young man, about my height and likely fresh out of the academy. His name tag said, Butterfield.

"It was about an embezzlement charge," I said, toting the company line I'd been given.

"Suicide?" I heard someone say to my left. It was Tommy Graham of Graham's Mortuary. He was looking at the paperwork he'd been handed. "Kinda hard to shoot yourself in the back of the head."

"He's got a point," I muttered, turning toward Tommy.

Brewer redirected me to focus on Butterfield. "He's not seen us and I'd like to keep it that way."

"You have a point."

Brewer spoke to Butterfield now. "We've been cooperative and need to leave to report to our own commander. If you need us, call this number." He handed the fresh-faced cop one of our cards. Staring into the young man's blue eyes, he said, "We can go now. You don't need anything more from us. In fact, you want out of here, too, and you won't look into this further."

"I get it," Butterfield said. "Go on. I'm not staying here either, as I'm not assigned to the case. Was just in the area when the call came. I'll give them your card. Thanks."

With that, the young man with a military cut of blond hair walked away.

Brewer whispered, "Drop it."

Our card slipped from Butterfield's fingers and fluttered to the ground without him noticing.

"*Now* we can leave," Richard said, picking up our card. "He'll think he lost it somewhere or claim it was in the folder. Let's go to the Amador and get a room for the night. It's late. We'll head out in the morning."

I nodded. "I just will have one more thing to do before we head to Santa Fe."

Richard nodded, for he understood.

* * *

The next day, in the cold morning air and bright sunshine, I made my way through the Masonic Cemetery and knelt on one knee, placing white roses by Cricket's grave marker.

"Hey there, Ovida. Sorry it's been a while. Last time I visited was what, after Jerry Nuzum's trial, I suppose. Glad they found him not guilty. Never thought he did it. He was just the Santa Fe Ring's fall guy."

I pulled a weed up from the ground and tossed it. "Four years ago today I knelt in this very spot and made you promises I wasn't able to keep. I'm so sorry."

My heart ached in my chest and I lay my hand on her stone. "I told your family I'd get justice for you, and I failed them too. I pray you and they can forgive me."

I stood and walked around for a moment, taking in the morning quiet. Reaching out with my gifts, I felt not only the stillness of the early hours, but of the land. New Mexico was forever changed, and she would be the better for it. It was as if I felt her sigh out in relief, and I understood something I hadn't before.

Stepping over to Ovida I dropped down again. "There's one more thing you should know. Your death wasn't for nothin'. The investigation into your murder exposed how organized crime was movin' in on New Mexico. All that illegal gamblin' has been closed, and the mafia has lost interest in the state.

"So not only did your death bring me back here, which then brought the rest of the team leadin' to us defeatin' Scáthach, but you protected this beautiful state from becomin' the gamblin' capital of the United States.

You saved it from bein' run by the mafia. Isn't that a kick in the pants?" I laughed, looked up, and saw a raven fly by.

Gaax had come to make sure I was okay. That mattered, and I smiled up at him.

Knowing he was watching made me feel at peace, and I continued. "An eighteen-year-old waitress not only helped bring about the end of Scáthach's reign on this plane but brought the crime rings of the state to their knees. They either were arrested or left for Nevada." I looked down at her name. "Your courage did that. Standin' up to them brought them down. It's important you know that. You still got them, and I hope that makes a difference."

I took a moment to breathe in the cemetery's beauty and let it calm me a little.

"I'm sorry I wasn't able to find who killed you specifically. I found out most of it. But I never got the name of who did it. Sandman was our last hope, but he didn't have the answers either. He wasn't in on it, you see, so we may never know the truth. I promise you this though, if I do know, I'll make them pay, even if they are old and near death. You have my word. But for now, it's time I moved on."

I paused and thought of all that had happened in the short time since I first came back to New Mexico. The adventure had started with a visit to one cemetery and ended in another. I wasn't sure what that said about me, but it was time I moved on to live my life. I would now start looking toward the future versus living in the past.

I kissed my fingers and placed them on her name. "Goodbye for now, sweet girl. If I'm out this way again, I'll stop by. May you truly rest in peace...oh, and remember to save me that dance for when I see you again someday."

A tear dropped from my face to the dirt below and soaked in. I stood up and turned to walk away when a breeze swam about me, giving me a chill. I turned around and no one was there. But I could've sworn I felt a kiss on my cheek and heard the words, "You got it, cowboy."

With my hands in my pockets, I left, whistling "Turkey in the Straw," making sure to wave at Pat Garrett as I walked past his grave to my car. I might've also flipped him the bird, but I'd never admit to that, even at gunpoint.

Now I had to pick up Brewer, and we needed to get back to England. Kit and Duke would graduate from the Regulator Academy soon, and we didn't want to miss that. Life moved on, and we had to make sure we enjoyed it.

With one last glance in Ovida's direction, I got into my new car and smiled. She knew now that it hadn't been all for nothing, and that mattered. She'd changed both me and New Mexico…a veritable miracle, and a journey I'd never forget. Now that old business was completed, I could head on to the next adventure, and it was all because of her. The death of John Tunstall may have given me my new life, but the murder of Cricket Coogler had set me free to live it.

The End

ACKNOWLEDGMENTS

First and foremost, I'd like to thank my support system: my parents, my best friends, my writing group, my wonderful editors, and those who live in Lincoln, NM. If it wasn't for the people in Lincoln, taking me in and helping me learn about Billy, this book never would have happened.

I'd like to lift a glass to the following people:

All the people of Lincoln for sharing their knowledge, hospitality, and affection for Billy the Kid with me. You all are the reason these books are in the world. I love you all very much!

Roy Sandman…who never stopped trying to find out who killed Cricket, until they made him stop. His son, Peter, wrote one of the books I used for research (*Murder Near the Crosses*).

Frederick Nolan…for if he'd not done so much leg work years ago, I'd not have had such a rich group of books to pull history from. So, a huge thank you to him and the other writers on my list of books listed at the back of this novel.

Lastly, I'd like to say a special thank you to the real Dr. Ryan (*that'll make more sense if you've read the book*) for his unwavering support and belief in me and my writing. You mean the world to me! Sending all my love…

ABOUT THE AUTHOR

Tamsin Silver is a Fantasy author currently based out of Albuquerque, NM. Her Urban Fantasy works include the ***Windfire*** saga, ***Mark of the Necromancer***, novellas based on her ***Skye of the Damned*** web series (*which can be seen free online*), and the ***Moon Over Manhattan*** series (*coming soon from Falstaff Books*).

She is also a writer for Faith Hunter's ***Rogue Mage Anthologies*** with *Lore Seekers Press*, the ***We Are Not This*** anthology for *Falstaff Books*, and the ***Storming Area 51*** anthology with *Bayonet Books*.

Tamsin graduated from Winthrop University in SC with a BA in Theatre and Secondary Education, along with a minor in Creative Writing and Shakespeare. She's taught middle school and high school drama in the Carolinas and run two successful theatre companies (one in NYC), where she holds awards in directing for both.

You can learn more about Tamsin by visiting www.tamsinsilver.com and www.skyeofthedamned.com.

Books Used and/or Recommended for fans of Billy the Kid

Billy the Kid - A Short and Violent Life by Robert M. Utley

Billy the Kid: The Endless Ride by Michael Wallis

Frontier Fighter by Frank Coe

High Noon in Lincoln - Violence on the Western Frontier by Robert M. Utley

Historic Lincoln NM - The Buildings and People by Rich Eastwood

History of the Lincoln County War: A Classic Account of Billy the Kid by Robert N. Mullin

Images of America - Lincoln by Ray John de Aragón

Images of America - Towns of Lincoln County by John LeMay

In the Shadow of Billy the Kid by Kathleen P. Chamberlain

Joy of the Birds by Gale Cooper

Lincoln County and Its Wars by Nora True Henn

Lincoln County, New Mexico, Tells its Stories by the Lincoln County Historical Society Publications

My Own Story - The Autobiograpy of Billy the Kid by Ralph Estes

Nuestros Antepasados (Our Ancestors) by Ernest S. Sanchez & Paul R. Sanchez

Such Men as Billy the Kid by Joel Jacobsen

The Billy the Kid Reader by Frederick Nolan

The Illustrated Life and Times of Billy the Kid by Bob Boze Bell

The Life & Death of John Henry Tunstall by Frederick Nolan

The Lincoln County War: A Documentary History (Revised History) by Frederick Nolan

The Story of Richard M. Brewer by Harry Leighton (and Elise Gomber)

The West of Billy the Kid by Frederick Nolan

These Were the Regulators (Lincoln County War) by Philip J. Rasch

They "Knew" Billy the Kid (Interviews with Old-Time Mexicans) by Robert F. Kadlec

To Hell on a Fast Horse, The Untold Story of Billy the Kid and Pat Garrett by Mark Lee Gardner

Violence in Lincoln County by William A. Keleher

Cricket in the Web by Paula Moore

Murder Near the Crosses by Peter R. Sandman

FRIENDS OF FALSTAFF

Thank You to All our Falstaff Books Patrons, who get extra digital content each month! To be featured here and see what other great rewards we offer, go to www.patreon.com/falstaffbooks.

PATRONS

Dino Hicks
John Hooks
John Kilgallon
Larissa Lichty
Travis & Casey Schilling
Staci-Leigh Santore
Sheryl R. Hayes
Scott Norris
Samuel Montgomery-Blinn
Junkle

www.ingramcontent.com/pod-product-compliance
Lightning Source LLC
Chambersburg PA
CBHW030537310726
48979CB00010B/1936/J

* 9 7 8 1 6 4 5 5 4 1 2 5 7 *